THE GRIFFIN'S
FEATHER

A MESSAGE FROM CHICKEN HOUSE

When I first started flying on a dragon's back in Cornelia Funke's amazing DRAGON RIDER, I couldn't catch my breath. Now, I'm ready to embark on new adventures: extraordinary animals and devious foes await. Luckily, I've already made some brilliant friends. Come with us – there's plenty of room on my dragon! But be sure to look carefully at the map at the front for the book, and the really useful WHO'S WHO on page 343 . . . oh, and try not to fall off!

BARRY CUNNINGHAM
Publisher
Chicken House

WRITTEN AND ILLUSTRATED BY

CORNELIA FUNKE

2 Palmer Street, Frome, Somerset BA11 1DS

Original German text © Cornelia Funke 2016
English translation by Anthea Bell © Cornelia Funke 2016

Cover illustration © Laura Ellen Anderson 2017
Map © Alexis Snell 2017
Inside illustrations © Cornelia Funke 2016

First published in Great Britain in 2017
Chicken House
2 Palmer Street,
Frome, Somerset BA11 1DS

www.chickenhousebooks.com

Cover design by Steve Wells
Typeset by Dorchester Typesetting Group Ltd
Printed and bound in by CPI Group (UK) Ltd, Croydon, CR0 4YY

The paper used in this Chicken House book is made from wood
grown in sustainable forests.

3 5 7 9 10 8 6 4 2

British Library Cataloguing in Publication data available.

ISBN 978-1-911077-88-6
eISBN 978-1-911077-89-3

*I didn't write this story for people who
want to rule the world.
Or for those who always have to show that they are
stronger, faster, and better than everyone else.
Or for those who think that human beings
are the crown of creation.*

*This story is for all who have the courage to protect
instead of dominate, to save instead of plundering,
and to preserve instead of destroying.*

Cornelia Funke

My boy, you shall be everything in the world,
animal, vegetable, mineral, protista, or virus,
for all I care – before I have done with you –
but you will have to trust my superior backsight.
The time is not yet ripe for you to be a hawk ...
so you may as well sit down for the moment
and learn to be a human being.

T.H. White,
The Once and Future King

CHAPTER ONE

A New Place and New Friends

It was a great mistake, my being born a man. I would
have been much more successful as a seagull or a fish.
Eugene O'Neill

It all looked so familiar to Firedrake. The misty woods outside
the entrance to the cave. The smell of the sea nearby in the
cold morning air. Every leaf and every flower reminded him of
the Scottish mountains where he had grown up. But Scotland
was far away, and so was the Rim of Heaven, the valley that the
last dragons in this world had called their home for two years
now.

Firedrake turned and looked at the dragon lying behind him
on a bed of moss and leaves. Slatebeard was the oldest of them
all. His wings twitched in his dreams, as if he wanted to follow
the wild geese crossing the grey sky, but he would soon be setting
out on the longest flight of all. To the Land of the Moon, as
dragons called the place to which only death opened the door.
Slatebeard was the only one who had stayed behind when the

others moved to the Rim of Heaven. Even then, the long journey had been too strenuous for him, but thanks to good friends he had found a new place to live when the ancient home of the dragons was drowned in the waters of a reservoir.

The cave where Slatebeard slept was not a natural one. A troll had built it, to the instructions of human beings who knew exactly what dragons needed. But caves for dragons were not the only accommodation to be found here in MÍMAMEIÐR. Trolls, impets, mermaids, dragons – any fabulous being could take refuge here, although some guests from the south complained of the cold Norwegian winters. MÍMAMEIÐR – Firedrake thought the name sounded as mysterious as the creatures who stayed there. They could all find suitable living quarters, and those places were all different too. Caves, nests, stables, tiny houses for impets . . . on the banks of the nearby fjord, in the surrounding forests, below the meadows that greeted the morning sunlight outside, wet with dew.

'How's Slatebeard this morning?'

The boy standing at the entrance to the cave had just celebrated his fourteenth birthday. His hair was as black as a raven's feathers. His eyes looked out at the world fearlessly and with curiosity, and Firedrake would have flown thousands of miles at any time just to see him.

Ben Greenbloom.

When they had first met in an abandoned harbour warehouse, Ben had no surname yet. He was a boy with no parents and no home. But Firedrake had made him his dragon rider, and had taken him on a journey that gave them both new homes. On the way, Ben had even found parents and a sister: Barnabas, Vita and Guinevere Greenbloom, protectors of fabulous animals, and the best family that a boy who rode dragons could wish for.

'Sleeping a lot,' replied Firedrake. 'But he's fine. He's getting ready. When I next visit you he'll be gone.'

Ben stroked Slatebeard's shimmering neck. His silver scales were getting darker every day, as if he were turning into the night, the favourite time of all dragons. A few tiny lights shone in the darkness above the gigantic sleeping body, like motes of dust dancing in the sun.

'It's beginning,' Ben whispered.

'Yes.' Firedrake laid his muzzle on the boy's shoulder. This was the first time a human being had ever been present to see a dragon peacefully leaving this life. Firedrake had had to explain it to Ben and the Greenblooms. There was nothing about it in any of their books, maybe because none of the people who had been so keen on chopping dragons' heads off in the old days had waited around to see what happened next.

Ben looked up at the roof of the cave, where more lights were gathering every day. 'When a dragon dies, he sows new stars,' Firedrake had explained. 'The more peacefully he says goodbye to life on earth, the more of them there are. But if his death is violent, there will be red stars in which his pain and anger live on. Unfortunately there are a number of those in the sky!'

Slatebeard would surely not sow any red stars. All the inhabitants of MÍMAMEIÐR would see to that. And they would all miss him, Ben in particular. He had always come to see the old dragon when his longing for Firedrake was too much for him. The Rim of Heaven was hidden in the mountains of the Himalayas, and they were terribly far from Norway.

'Firedrake! Oh, they all deserve to be barbecued! I know dragon-fire has to be used cautiously, but it would be in a good cause!'

Ben knew the voice that sounded so shrill in the cave almost as well as he knew Firedrake's.

Sorrel.

At their first meeting, Ben had taken her for a giant squirrel, much to her annoyance. By now, of course, he knew enough about fabulous creatures to see at first glance that he was looking at a Scottish brownie, and those were as essential to dragons as the moonlight that fed them.

'You should have seen the fuss they kicked up! Just for a few chanterelles!' Sorrel guiltily lowered her voice when she saw the sleeping Slatebeard. 'As if every mushroom in this darn forest belonged to them!' she whispered, putting down the basket she was carrying in her brown paws. 'And why? Because they look like walking mushrooms themselves? Whoever said we need mushrooms with arms and legs? They should be glad I don't just eat them all up!'

Slatebeard opened his golden eyes and uttered a grunt of amusement. 'Sorrel,' he murmured. 'I feel sure a brownie voice will wake me in the morning even in the Land of the Moon.'

'Too true, you can't get away from them anywhere!' The tiny manikin who made his way out of Ben's jacket pocket, rubbing his sleepy eyes, answered to the name of Twigleg. He was a homunculus, probably the last of his kind, now that a monster called Nettlebrand had eaten all his eleven brothers. The alchemist who had made Nettlebrand had also created Twigleg, and was the only kind of father he had ever known, much to his regret. It isn't easy to be an artificially-made creature, even if you are lucky enough to have such unusual beings as dragons and brownies as your friends.

'I take it you've been having trouble with the fungus-folk again?' he asked Twigleg sharply, as he climbed up Ben's arm and sat down on the boy's shoulder.

'So?' snapped the brownie. 'Fungus-folk! Mouldy midgets! Odin-dwarves! Hedgehog-men! All those little creatures would drive any brownie nuts! You ought to have a word with your parents about it,' she told Ben. 'Why not make a general rule? Something along the lines that MÍMAMEIÐR will take in only fabulous creatures who at least stand shoulder-high to a dog? And all the rest can stay where they are!'

'Oh yes? Do I conclude that you're saying *I* don't have any right to be here, either?' asked Twigleg, annoyed.

It had taken the homunculus a long time to make friends with the brownie girl, and even after knowing her for two years now, he sometimes found Sorrel's moods very aggravating. Ben used to assure Twigleg that water-sprites and leprechauns were even moodier, although his own first meeting with Sorrel had not gone smoothly. Brownies let no one and nothing come between them and their dragons, and for a long time Sorrel had been suspicious of the boy who had won Firedrake's heart so quickly.

'Okay, okay,' she muttered as she knelt down beside Slatebeard. 'As opinionated as ever. Is every homunculus like that? I suppose we'll never know, seeing that there's only one left.'

She put a paw into her basket, which was full to the brim, and brought out a milk-white, spongy fungus. 'This is a very special delicacy! I spent two hours searching for it, and I had to shake a dozen fungus-folk off my legs to pick it. Brownies eat one every day when their fur begins to turn grey, so I'm sure it will do a dragon good too! Yes, yes, I know you like moonlight best, but even Firedrake makes an exception now and then if I bring him especially tasty flowers or berries. Not that it's easy to find those in the Himalayas!' she added, with a reproachful glance at Firedrake.

Then she put the fungus down between Slatebeard's claws, like a precious sacrifice made with a heavy heart. Anyone who knows the first thing about Scottish mountain brownies can tell from that gift how fond of the old dragon Sorrel was. Brownies loved only one thing as much as the dragon that they followed: mushrooms and fungi, large or small, firm or spongy. Sorrel could spend hours describing the colour, shape and flavour of her favourite varieties.

Of course Slatebeard knew all this. In the course of his long life, he had known three brownie companions. They had all gone to the Land of the Moon ahead of him, and he missed them very much. It made him all the happier that not only Firedrake but Sorrel too had made the long journey to say goodbye to him.

'This is really extraordinarily generous of you, my dear, highly esteemed Sorrel,' he said, bowing his head to her. 'You have always been the most gifted mushroom-hunter of all the brownies I've ever known! Allow me to eat your present for supper.'

'And I'd better have a word with those fungus-folk,' said Ben. He had volunteered to come and look after all the imp-like creatures in MÍMAMEIÐR, and that surely included fungus-folk. Not a very clever idea, as it had turned out. Ben's adopted sister Guinevere had taken charge of the water creatures, and Ben now envied her. Even fossegrims, the Norwegian water-sprites who played the fiddle, couldn't compete with impets for aggression.

But when Ben left Slatebeard's cave to go over to the fungus-folk's homes, a mist-raven flew out of the trees and landed on the grass in front of him, which was wet with dew. Mist-ravens owe their names not only to their grey feathers, but also to the fact that they can make themselves invisible.

'Red alert!' croaked the raven. 'Proceed to Control Centre! Quick march!'

Mist-ravens like a military vocabulary, and expressions that sound significant and mysterious. But they are also excellent scouts, and very reliable bringers of news. This one had sounded distinctly happy, which made Ben and Twigleg exchange a glance of concern.

Only bad news makes mist-ravens as happy as that.

CHAPTER TWO

A Phone Call from Greece

*It seems to me that the natural world is the greatest
source of excitement; the greatest source of visual beauty;
the greatest source of intellectual interest; the greatest source
of so much in life that makes life worth living.*
Sir David Attenborough

Not many buildings in this world can make themselves invisible. But the main house in MÍMAMEIÐR merges so completely with the forest, the earth and the sky that most visitors don't see it until they are standing right in front of it. Ben always felt as if he were approaching a living creature made of wood, stone and glass, and it enjoyed hiding from him. And who knows, maybe the house really was alive. After all, a troll had built it.

The troll's name was Hothbrodd, and all the buildings in MÍMAMEIÐR had been built to his specifications. Usually Hothbrodd even sawed up the planks and beams himself, and he spent weeks ornamenting the façades with artistic carvings. This

morning he was up early, cleaning the carvings over the entrance of the house with a knife that looked even more fearsome than Hothbrodd himself. The carved dragon winding its way over one of the beams was a very successful portrait of Firedrake, but there were also Great Krakens, centaurs, and fossegrims playing their fiddles on the façade. Hothbrodd could carve the image of every creature on this planet.

'Drat those mist-ravens!' said the troll crossly, as Ben and Twigleg stopped beside him. 'One of these days I'll wring their grey necks if they don't stop leaving droppings all over my carvings!'

Hothbrodd towered almost a metre above even fully-grown men, but Ben was used to the troll's height by now. After all, he was best friends with a dragon. Hothbrodd's skin was as rough as the bark of an oak tree, and Ben had learned from him that, contrary to all the stories about them, trolls were not just very strong but also very clever. 'Although fjord trolls,' Hothbrodd might have added, 'are just as stupid as everyone says.' His opinion of human beings was no better. Hothbrodd preferred talking to pines, beeches and oaks (though he did make an exception for the Greenblooms), and the things that he created from the wood of those trees would make anyone believe in magic. But however you liked to explain his art, it was thanks to Hothbrodd that the buildings in MÍMAMEIÐR were as unusual as their inhabitants, and that was true above all of the main house. In many places the outer walls were made of glass, and the troll's knife had covered the beams and joists framing the large panes with such intricately twining patterns that Ben was constantly discovering new creatures among them. There was surely no house more magical anywhere in the world.

Ben remembered the house where he had been born as vaguely as he remembered his birth parents. They had both died in a car crash soon after his third birthday, and Ben spent the next seven years in a building claiming to be a 'home', although the children living there would certainly never have called it that. The word was spoken under its roof as seldom as the words *mother* and *father*. Why talk about something that you didn't have, especially when you longed for it so much that the mere idea made you feel sick? In Ben's childhood, mothers and fathers had been creatures as unreal as the dragon he met when he was eleven. At some point he had gone to live with foster parents, but they had been even worse than the home. Ben had run away from them – and from then on he hadn't let himself dream of a family any more – until he had met the Greenblooms. Maybe you have to bury your dreams to make them come true.

Ben's adopted parents, as Barnabas and Vita Greenbloom liked to call themselves, had devoted their lives to protecting the rarest beings in the world from human greed and curiosity. That didn't make them rich. When Ben moved in with the Greenblooms, they had been living in a house much too small for them in the north-west of England, where Ben shared a room with his new sister Guinevere, six snoring hobs, and a few grass fairies who had almost fallen victim to a neighbour's lawnmower. But then, one day, a cigar box containing ten flawless jewels had been left on the doorstep, the gift of several grateful stone-dwarves whose village the Greenblooms had evacuated before it was blown sky-high to make space for a new road. And Ben's adopted parents had at last been able to put their dream of a refuge for fabulous creatures into practice. They had built MÍMAMEIÐR not in England but in Norway, partly because their fabulous guests would pass unnoticed more easily in that country's remote forests – and partly because it was where Barnabas's ancestors came from.

Ben saw that Hothbrodd was not the only one up and about already when he stopped beside the troll. A dozen little nisse

children were sitting rapt at his feet, admiring his skill with his enormous knife. Hothbrodd was always surrounded by nisse and impet children – an alarming sight in view of the troll's gigantic boots – but so far none of those tiny creatures had come to any harm.

'Hi, Hothbrodd,' said Ben, while Twigleg, sitting on his shoulder, politely hid a yawn behind his hand. 'Do you know what's happened? The mist-raven who sent us here looked suspiciously happy.'

Hothbrodd frowned, and scraped raven droppings off the nose of a carved impet. 'News of some kind from Greece,' he grunted. 'And yes, I think it was indeed rather bad news.'

Ben exchanged an anxious glance with Twigleg. Greece . . . Vita and Barnabas had discovered a Pegasus couple there just under a year ago. And the other day Vita and Guinevere had set off to see how they were doing.

Ben left his muddy boots with the leprechaun who lived in the coat cupboard beside the front door, and went into the house that he loved more than any other in the world.

The portraits and photos on the walls of the entrance hall showed friends and colleagues of the Greenblooms. Some of them had creatures of legend and fable among their own ancestors, although it often wasn't obvious. Suspiciously pointed ears, a cow's tail, webbing between the toes . . . all those features were easily hidden. Even a hint of fur on the face could be explained away as an annoyingly strong growth of stubble. Accounting for the beak of Professor Buceros and Dr Eel's gills was more difficult, and so those two turned up only for meetings of the inner circle of FREEFAB (the name that Ben and Guinevere had given their parents' organisation; Vita and Barnabas preferred to describe its members as 'protectors' of fabulous species). Under

Dr Eel's photos, a family of flying Watobi pigs that a friend of the Greenblooms had rescued from poachers in the Congo were asleep in a dog's basket. The scaly tail of a photomeleon showed under the coat cupboard, and two feathered frogs were looking down at Ben from the chandelier. How could anyone fail to love MÍMAMEIÐR?

'Control Centre' – Barnabas Greenbloom disliked the term that the mist-ravens used for his library, although in many ways it deserved the name. It was the largest room in the house, and two walls were covered with books right up to the ceiling, which was exactly right for a library. The outside wall, however, was glass, so that you felt as if the books were standing among the trees outside. In winter you could look through their bare branches and see the nearby fjord, but on this rainy May morning the branches bore the fresh green leaves of springtime, and they were teeming with crow-men and tomtes who built their dwellings among the nests of buntings and leaf warblers.

The smile that Barnabas gave Ben was as warm as ever, but Ben could tell just from looking at him that something really bad must have happened.

A dozen screens hung on the fourth wall, and the films on them showed the protectors of fabulous creatures from all over the world, talking about those that they had entrusted to the care of the Greenblooms. All the screens were dark except for one, which showed Guinevere in the remote Greek valley where her parents had discovered the two Pegasi. The sound and picture were so bad that, yet again, Ben wished Barnabas would invest one of the jewels still remaining from the dwarves' gift in new cameras and computers. But Barnabas always pointed out that it was better to go carefully with the money from the jewels, in view of all the refugees that came to MÍMAMEIÐR, and he was right. All the same – 'frogspawn and bird poo!' as Hothbrodd would have cursed – the picture was so poor that Guinevere might have been standing on another planet. What she was saying, however, drove away all thoughts of better cameras, and reminded Ben that there were much worse things to worry about.

'We're assuming it was a horned viper,' she said. 'It's dreadful, Dad! Synnefo may well have trodden on its nest by mistake. The venom worked much faster than with humans. Ànemos is beside himself!'

Ben looked at Barnabas in dismay. Synnefo was the Pegasus mare, Ànemos was the stallion. The two of them were probably the last of their species, and everyone in MÍMAMEIÐR remembered the excitement when Lola Greytail, their best newsgatherer (and the only female rat aviator in the world) came back from Greece with photos of a nest and three new-laid Pegasus eggs. Hothbrodd made his way through the door and looked anxiously at the screen, which now also showed Vita. Ben didn't call Vita Greenbloom *Mother*, any more than he called Barnabas *Father*, although he loved them dearly. But they both seemed to be so much more than parents: they were his friends, teachers and protectors.

Ben had seldom seen Vita looking sadder. Her eyes, like Guinevere's, showed that she had been crying, and Vita didn't cry easily.

'We can hardly persuade Ànemos to eat, Barnabas!' she said.

'He's half-crazy with grief! And he knows, as we do, that he could lose his children as well. It won't be simple to keep the eggs warm in the Norwegian spring, but I think the only hope for the foals is for us to bring the nest and Ànemos to MÍMAMEIÐR. Guinevere agrees with me.'

Guinevere nodded vigorously. Many people were surprised to find how much the Greenblooms valued the opinions of their children. 'Remarkable, isn't it?' Barnabas had once commented. 'As if it wasn't obvious that a person's age often has little to do with their intelligence. I might even claim that in many cases, unfortunately, stupidity and pig-headedness get worse with every birthday!'

The Greenblooms set so much store by working with their children that Ben and Guinevere were taught at home. And they had wonderful teachers: Twigleg taught them history and ancient languages (a very important subject if you are dealing with beings who could easily be thousands of years old). Dr Phoebe Humboldt, who taught them about the nature of fabulous creatures, had spent four years in a sunken ship off the Ligurian coast, studying sea-nymphs and mermen. They learned geography from Gilbert Greytail, a white rat whom Barnabas had persuaded to leave the city of Hamburg with its warehouses, and move to MÍMAMEIÐR to make maps showing the original homes of all known fabulous beings. One of Ben's few human teachers, James Spotiswode, tried to teach them mathematics, biology and physics – about as easy as convincing wolves that it is a bad idea to gobble up impets – but as Professor Spotiswode rewarded Ben and Guinevere for every natural history problem that they solved successfully by giving them lessons in robotics and telepathy, he had two very enthusiastic students. In short, the pair of them were learning what they needed to know in order to devote their lives, as their parents did, to conserving all the creatures who, without their help, might be in danger of existing only in the pages of books of fairy tales.

'Keeping the stable warm won't be a problem.' Hothbrodd took a piece of wood out of his pocket and began carving a lizard from it. 'The woolspinner oaklings can pad the nest and the stable walls.'

Barnabas nodded, although he didn't look entirely convinced.

'Right,' he said. 'Hothbrodd will get the stable ready, and I'll ask Undset to be here when you arrive. I shouldn't think she's ever treated a Pegasus before, but maybe she can at least help to keep Ànemos alive.'

Holly Undset was a young veterinary surgeon from the neighbouring village of Freyahammer, and she had already given medical treatment to countless guests at MÍMAMEIÐR. It hadn't been easy to find someone who could be relied on to keep silent. Many hunters would have paid a fortune for the information that there was a hidden place in Norway where such rare prey as water-horses and dragons could be found. But Holly Undset was such a passionate opponent of wolf-hunts and bear-hunts that one day Barnabas had invited her to MÍMAMEIÐR.

When the screen on which Vita and Guinevere had given their bad news went black, there was a depressed silence in the library. Even Hothbrodd had lowered his knife. Photos of the Pegasus nest were propped against the backs of the books on one of the shelves. Ben went over and looked at the three silvery eggs. They were smaller than hens' eggs. It had seemed to Guinevere that the newly hatched foals would be tiny, until Vita explained that Pegasus eggs didn't stay so small, but began to grow larger after two months.

'We could keep the eggs warm with electric blankets,' suggested Ben. 'Or in the incubator that we used for that abandoned clutch of wild goose eggs.'

But Barnabas shook his head. 'That could be risky. Not just because, as you know, technology often fails in the presence of fabulous creatures. The eggs of certain winged species break if they come into contact with plastic or metal. That's a risk we can't possibly run. Twigleg, you were instrumental in putting this library together, and unlike the rest of us you've read every single book in it. Can you help us here?'

The homunculus obviously felt flattered. 'I think I remember that we have the facsimile of an Italian manuscript mentioning Pegasus eggs, among other things,' he said as he looked along the shelves. 'Where was it? Just a mo. Ah, yes.'

He clambered nimbly down Ben's arm and made his way over tables and the backs of chairs until he reached his own computer, which was no larger than a matchbox. Ben and Professor Spotiswode had built it for him. The manikin had learned to type on it as quickly as he picked up everything else that he was taught. He had even developed his own software, which no one else could understand.

'Yes, here we are. *Pegasus eggs, special features of, see seventeenth-century Italian alchemists' manuscript, page 27, line 16.*'

Twigleg closed the computer and climbed one of the tall bookcases as effortlessly as if he had been a fly. The homunculus loved his miniature computer. He wrote a blog on it, entering the name and species of every recent arrival in MÍMAMEIÐR, together with endless files of information about its description, origin and nutritional preferences, and he spent hours recording every new item of information about fabulous creatures and other rare beings. His great love, however, was still books. Twigleg's sharp-nosed face lit up with childish delight when he was leafing through printed pages, and the older they were the more reverently he handled paper and parchment. Ben had already found himself fearing that one of the heavy volumes the homunculus took out of the shelves would squash him some day. And once again, the volume that he found after a short search was much larger than Twigleg himself.

'Can I help you, my dear Twigleg?' Barnabas obviously shared Ben's concern. He took the book and the homunculus off the shelf, and put them down on a desk sheltering a hobgoblin who played his mouth harp, tunelessly, far too often for Ben's liking.

'Wait a moment . . . I'll soon find it . . .' Twigleg turned the parchment pages as carefully as if they might crumble to dust under his tiny fingers. '25, 26 . . . yes! Here it is. The Italian is very old-fashioned, so I'll give you a modern translation.'

He cleared his throat, as he always did when he was about to read something aloud. '"The egg of the winged horse, *Pegasus unicus*, is one of the greatest wonders of the world. Its shell, originally silver, becomes increasingly transparent as the foal grows, until it resembles the most valuable glass. Yet it is as hard as diamonds. Its most wondrous quality, however, is evident only when the foal reaches the age of six weeks, and the shell restricts its growth. At this point, the mare starts licking the shell, whereupon the egg begins to grow, while remaining as hard as ever. Although,"' Twigleg raised his head and exchanged glances of dismay with Ben and Barnabas, "'only the mother's saliva has that effect. If she comes to any harm, the egg will not grow, and the foal will stifle in the unbreakable shell.'"

Hothbrodd drove his knife so far into the desk under which the hobgoblin was sitting that its mouth harp fell from its furry fingers. Rain had begun to fall. Barnabas went over to the glass wall, where a dozen crystal snails were licking the raindrops running down, and looked out.

'Hothbrodd, can you send a mist-raven to Undset telling her what's up, and fixing it for her to be here when the Pegasus arrives?'

The troll nodded in silence, and disappeared outside, treading heavily.

The last Pegasus, here in MÍMAMEIÐR . . . Ben was glad that they could trust Undset. He dared not think what would happen if the world knew about the existence of a winged horse. In the past Barnabas had openly admitted to believing that fabulous creatures really did exist, but by now the Greenblooms were convinced that secrecy gave those beings their only chance of survival – secrecy, and a network of initiates who weren't accepted into it lightly. These days FREEFAB consisted not only of those who protected Great Krakens, sphinxes and stone-dwarves, but also many men and women who campaigned for the conservation of other threatened species – whether those were gorillas, grey seals, lynxes, sea turtles, or one of the countless other extraordinary animals that now risked extinction.

Hothbrodd returned. The troll had to stoop to fit through the doorway. When Twigleg had once asked him why, in view of the very different sizes of all the inhabitants of the house, the door frames were designed for human dimensions, the troll had only growled, 'Not human dimensions, homunculus. They're designed for Barnabas.' Guinevere suspected that Hothbrodd owed his life to her father, but neither of them could be induced to say exactly how they had met one another.

'Any idea how we can get those eggs to grow without the mare, Barnabas?' The troll often said straight out what other people were only thinking. Barnabas thought highly of that quality.

'I haven't the faintest notion, Hothbrodd,' he murmured, staring out into the rain. 'And we can consider ourselves lucky if the stallion doesn't die of grief as well. I admit it, I just don't know what to do. But then again,' he added, turning to the screens that looked down from the wall like sleeping eyes, 'what are friends for?'

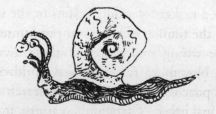

CHAPTER THREE

The Conservators

*The world is a dangerous place, not because of
the people who are evil, but because of the people
who don't do anything about it.*
Albert Einstein

A few hours later, a number of anxious faces were looking out of the screens in the library of MÍMAMEIÐR.

Among those at the gathering was Jacques Maupassant, a specialist in fantastic water creatures (of course including whales, dolphins and corals). Sir David Atticsborough, one of the most highly respected makers of wildlife films in the world, advised FREEFAB on the filming of videos to put hunters and animal traders on the wrong trail and lead them away from their intended prey. November Tan organised worldwide protection patrols against poachers, and conducted research for FREEFAB on the nutritional habits of fabulous creatures. Inua Ellams, the world-famous advocate of African birds, was FREEFAB's specialist on winged fabulous beings. Maisie Richardson had a great

reputation for her work in protecting grass fairies and fern fairies, and Jane Gridall could not only converse effortlessly with any primate, but had devised a sign language that made it possible to communicate with almost every species on the planet.

Soon a heated debate was in progress on the best way to save the foals. Maupassant suggested rubbing the eggs with dragon-spit as soon as they grew too large for their shells – all the members of FREEFAB knew that Barnabas Greenbloom had a very close relationship with dragons. November Tan wondered whether there had been any experiments with the saliva of seahorses. Maisie Richardson offered to ask the fairies in her garden to sprinkle their pollen over the eggshells in the hope that it would make them grow. Jane Gridall talked about her experience of elephant-ostrich chicks that had hatched prematurely, and Inua Ellams suggested that the song of the Healing Bird of Heaven (which he could imitate very impressively) might fortify the foals.

Barnabas nodded with interest to all these ideas, but Ben saw that the lines on his forehead were getting deeper and deeper.

'My dear friends and colleagues,' he finally said, 'I thank you very, very much, particularly on behalf of the desperate father. I assure you that we will think about all these proposals. We have a Bird of Heaven as one of our guests here, and there are even dragons available, but their saliva is so fiery that I don't advise trying it. I'm afraid it will be impossible to break the eggshells before the foals are the right age to hatch. No, we must think of something else that will make the eggs grow. But what?' Barnabas heaved a sigh that brought a dozen nisses out from among the books. 'And how can we find it in less than two weeks? One thing is certain: if we don't succeed we are going to lose the last Pegasus foals in this world, and that presumably

means the end of the species itself.'

'But that would be a disaster, Barnabas!' cried Inua Ellams.

'A loss to the planet of epic proportions!' agreed Sir David.

The cries of protest mingled until a confused chorus of voices filled the library. Then a shrill whistle abruptly halted the noise. It came from a screen that had been dark until now. The new-comer was clearly not a human member of FREEFAB. His glasses were perched on a mighty beak, and he was smoothing down the black feathers of his wings.

'Forgive my late arrival, Barnabas,' croaked Sutan Buceros, a rhinoceros bird of considerable size and legendary age who had often advised the Greenblooms on the protection of the fabu-lous beings of south-east Asia. Barnabas had estimated Sutan's

age as six hundred and twenty. The rhinoceros bird's croaking voice made that seem perfectly credible to Ben.

'My assistant,' Buceros went on, 'has told me about the problem. Has anyone yet suggested the sun-feather of a griffin to save the foals? After all, the quills of such feathers contain a substance that will make even metal and stone grow.'

The silence that followed this question from Buceros was so complete that Ben exchanged a glance of surprise with Twigleg. He saw not only disapproval on the faces looking out of the screens, but also a touch of fear. The only face that had brightened was Barnabas's.

'No, Sutan, no one has made that suggestion so far,' he said. 'Very interesting. And I feel very embarrassed for not thinking of it myself! That could indeed be the solution!'

'But Barnabas!' cried Jane Gridall. 'Griffins are hardly famous for their helpfulness – quite the opposite! They despise every other living thing! A griffin regards all life forms simply as prey. They came to terms with us humans once, just because we think in the same way, but that's more than a thousand years ago. Didn't they declare war on the entire human race after some battle or other, and hasn't all trace of them been lost since then?'

'Which, as we all know, is a very well-founded reaction to the two great obsessions of the human species,' commented Sutan Buceros.

Ben looked enquiringly at Barnabas.

'Greed and megalomania,' he whispered in reply. 'Yes, Sutan, all of us here are painfully aware of those two obsessions,' he said for all to hear. 'I think I can say that we all have evidence of them too. But we're not concerned with human beings here, we want to ensure the survival of the last winged horses!'

'I'm afraid that's the very thing that makes the problem worse,

Barnabas.' Inua Ellams always sounded as if he was singing what he said in a deep, velvety voice. 'So far as I know, griffins consider horses even more despicable and superfluous than all other life forms! Wings or no wings, it makes no difference.'

The heads on the screens nodded in agreement, visibly relieved. Ben didn't know much about griffins, but a few years ago a gigantic bird, the roc, had almost fed him to its chicks. If Ben remembered what he'd heard correctly, a griffin not only had a beak as terrifying as the roc's, but also the claws of a lion and, as if that wasn't bad enough, a venomous snake for a tail.

'I've spent more than twenty years looking for a Pegasus,' said Barnabas, 'fearing all the time that they were extinct, like so many other wonderful creatures. And am I to give up now, when there's some hope of new foals after all these centuries? Impossible! I won't stand by and watch those bringers of good luck disappear from my world and the world of my children, like so many other wonderful animals! Even if it means that I have to go to a fabulous creature that's proud of its cruelty and its skill in killing, and even ask it to help us.'

In Ben's experience, the discussion that began now could go on for hours. But a moment came when Barnabas took him aside, and asked him to let Firedrake know about the imminent arrival of the Pegasus stallion. 'But don't say a word about Sutan's idea!' he whispered, while behind him the argument went on: would the offer of gold induce a griffin to give them a sun-feather? 'Firedrake mustn't know that we may be setting off in search of a griffin! Inua is right: griffins certainly despise horses and all members of the equine family. But the only living creatures on this planet that they regard as their rivals and arch-enemies are . . .'

'Dragons,' said Ben, finishing Barnabas's sentence for him.

'Exactly! You know as well as I do that Firedrake will offer us his help if he hears of the plan, and it would put him in great danger!'

Ben nodded, although he knew how hard he would find it to lie to Firedrake. 'But what am I to tell him?' he whispered. 'If we set off before him, he'll ask where we are going!'

Barnabas frowned. 'Why don't you just say we're looking for a phoenix feather? That's not dangerous, and he'll believe we don't need his help!'

Would he? Firedrake knew Ben so well.

Twigleg would certainly have found convincing ways to tell the lie about the phoenix feather. ('Of course!' Sorrel would have remarked sharply. 'After all, he was once a traitor and a spy!') But the homunculus stayed with Barnabas, to record the discussion, as usual, in one of his notebooks. Ben missed him very much as he rehearsed his story a dozen times on the way to Slatebeard's cave. He knew, however, that Barnabas was right. Firedrake would never let them persuade him to leave them alone in their search. Griffins really did sound terrifying – and Ben had to admit that by this time he felt very curious about them.

CHAPTER FOUR

Not The Whole Truth

*I believe in fairies, the myths, dragons. It all exists, even
if it's in your mind. Who's to say that dreams and
nightmares aren't as real as the here and now?*
John Lennon

When Ben reached Slatebeard's cave, he found only a couple of Odin-dwarves there. They had made friends with Slatebeard because they were almost as old as he was. They told Ben that Firedrake had gone down to the fjord.

Even the largest fabulous creatures have an impressive talent for making themselves invisible to human eyes. Maybe that is what distinguishes them most clearly from ordinary animals. But Ben's eyes were used to spotting them even in the densest forests and darkest caves, and the shape that he was looking for was more familiar to him than any other. He found Firedrake on the bank of the fjord, at a place where it fell so steeply that the coniferous trees lining it reached far out over the water. Even now, Ben was amazed to see how the dragon could keep so still lying there – so much at one with the natural world surrounding him that most people wouldn't even guess at his existence.

The presence of Firedrake brought even more fabulous creatures to MÍMAMEIÐR than usual. He and Slatebeard attracted even those who didn't need the Greenblooms' protection. The fjord was teeming with sjöras and water-sprites, and when Ben knelt down in the grass beside Firedrake, the fiddle music of three fossegrims at once carried up to them.

'What's happened?' The dragon bent his neck until his head was level with Ben's eyes. 'You look very anxious.'

Oh yes, Firedrake knew him so well. The many months they had now spent at different ends of the earth hadn't changed that. How could he pretend to him? Well, he'd have to. Because it was to protect him. The dragon and his rider . . . There were nights when Ben's longing to be with Firedrake would hardly let him sleep. Even on those precious days that they did spend together, he could never entirely forget that the next parting was near. 'It's the price you pay for friendship with a creature so different from yourself,' Barnabas had told Ben one evening, when he found him outside the house, staring eastwards longingly. 'You will always need human beings, and Firedrake will always have to hide from them. But that makes your friendship all the more valuable.' Barnabas was right, of course, but all the same it was hard for Ben to reconcile himself to not seeing Firedrake more often – even though he had never told the dragon so. The flight from Nepal to Norway was too dangerous for him to risk it without a good reason.

'Barnabas asked me to tell you that we're soon going to have a very special visitor.'

Ben leaned against Firedrake's silvery chest. It was wonderful to feel the dragon's warmth and strength behind him.

The dragon said nothing as Ben told him the bad news from Greece.

'I'm sure Barnabas will find a solution,' he said, when Ben had finished.

'Oh yes. We're probably going to look for a phoenix feather.' Ben was glad he didn't have to look Firedrake in the eye.

'A phoenix feather? I thought they set fire to everything they touched.'

'No, not this sort. Twigleg read somewhere that they are . . . are very good for Pegasus eggs.'

Heavens above. Ben wished the earth would swallow him up. He was such a bad liar.

But fortunately Firedrake's mind was on Slatebeard slowly dissolving into stardust, and he didn't sense his dragon rider's uneasiness.

'Good,' was all he said. 'Phoenixes are helpful creatures. I'm sure they will be useful to you. And I look forward to meeting a Pegasus.'

When something rustled behind them, Firedrake put his paw protectively out to Ben, but it was only Sorrel coming through the trees.

'What's a Pegasus? Does it eat brownies?'

If it had been up to Sorrel, there would have been no one in the world but dragons and brownies. She shook her head, unable to understand why the Greenblooms were trying to save all the beings whose right to exist was disputed by the human race. But as Firedrake helped them, so did she.

She'd been mushroom-gathering again, of course. Ben was sorry to see that she had three bags full of them slung over her

furry shoulders. Sorrel was stocking up with provisions for the journey.

Firedrake gently laid his muzzle on Ben's shoulder. 'We're setting off in three days' time. Slatebeard says he wants to say goodbye before he gets even weaker. Dragons like to be alone when they look death in the face. Unlike brownies,' he added quietly. 'They can never get enough company when they're leaving this world.'

Three days. It would be full moon in three days' time. The best time for silver dragons to fly.

'It's strange to think that Slatebeard won't be here when I next come to see you,' said Firedrake. 'He's always been around, ever since I can remember. He was already a young adult dragon when my grandmother was a child. Such a long life. A time probably comes when it's been long enough. I think he can't wait to turn his back on the world.'

Ben just nodded. He felt ashamed that the tears rising to his eyes had nothing to do with Slatebeard, but with having to say goodbye to Firedrake yet again. Would he ever do it without such a heavy heart? Without this terrible feeling that he was losing a part of himself?

Of course Sorrel didn't notice any of that. Forest brownies aren't exactly sympathetic by nature. She was fully occupied spreading out her finds on the forest floor in front of them.

'Take a look at that!' she said. 'Not bad for one afternoon, is it? Three chanterelles, two hedgehog mushrooms, four forest lamb mushrooms, two saffron milk caps, a porcino and an orange birch boletus!'

'She likes MÍMAMEIÐR much better than the Rim of Heaven!' Firedrake whispered to Ben. 'She's far from impressed by the fungi of the Himalayas.'

Sorrel cast the dragon an irritated glance. 'So are you grateful for the sacrifice I'm making? No! *Sorrel, why don't you stay in MÍMAMEIÐR? Sorrel, I could manage just fine without you.* Huh!' She packed the mushrooms away in their bag as carefully as if they were fragile glass. 'Dragons need brownies. That's how it's always been, that's how it always will be, *spiss giftslørsopp!*' Sorrel had added the names of some poisonous Norwegian fungi to her rich stock of curses. 'Even if that's why I have to live on guchhi morels. I really can't think why you humans consider them such a delicacy,' she added, glancing at Ben.

Dragons need brownies . . . and dragon riders need dragons, Ben felt like saying.

He hated it when he felt so sad. But he consoled himself by thinking that at least it was much better than back in the days when there was no one he could long for.

'What do you think?' Firedrake whispered to him as Sorrel, with a cry of delight, picked a slimy yellow fungus off the bark of a pine tree. 'Why don't we see whether the Draugen are going to have one of their water-horse races?'

Ben was sitting on Firedrake's back before Sorrel had put her new treasure away. 'If Barnabas or Twigleg ask where I am,' he called to her, 'tell them we'll be back in a couple of hours' time!'

'Twigleg?' Sorrel looked up at him, frowning. 'Oh, lopsided liberty caps!' She spat, and picked a spider out of her brown fur. 'He ought to be glad I haven't wrung his scrawny neck yet. Do you know he's been showing the nisses my best mushroom-hunting spots, just because they like to feed chanterelles to their children? Nisses! Why can't they be satisfied with fly and midge grubs?'

'Sorrel,' said Firedrake sternly, 'have you forgotten that Twigleg risked his life for us?'

'After betraying us first, you mean?'

Brownies can bear a grudge for a long time. Sorrel would never forget that the homunculus had once served her dragon's worst enemy, even if Twigleg had helped them to defeat him in the end. Nettlebrand . . . anything made of gold always reminded Ben of him. The man-made monster who had killed thousands of dragons and swallowed Twigleg's eleven brothers. Griffins couldn't be half as bad . . . could they?

Firedrake made his way out of the trees and spread his wings. Ben clung to the spines on his back as the dragon rose into the air. Yes, he would even miss Sorrel. In fact he would miss her very much. The heart was a strange thing. As the dragon climbed higher, Ben felt sure, for a moment, that his own heart would break with joy. But he knew from experience that hearts are remarkably resilient in sorrow and joy alike.

CHAPTER FIVE

The Only One of his Kind

You are who you choose to be.
Ted Hughes, *The Iron Man*

When Ben returned from his flight on Firedrake's back, the others were already eating supper. As usual, Twigleg sat at a little table beside Ben's plate. Hothbrodd had made it specially for the homunculus, like the tiny chair he was sitting on (and the little house on Ben's bedside table). Barnabas was talking to Tallemaja, their Swedish cook, whose reed-green hair showed that her mother was a huldra. Ben couldn't hear what they were talking about, but he felt sure it was provisions for a journey. He knew the determined expression on Barnabas's face. They would be going in search of griffins.

Hothbrodd had given MÍMAMEIÐR's dining table the claws of a lion, but this evening Ben saw them as a griffin's hind legs. The table, like everything that Hothbrodd made, could grow or shrink to whatever size was wanted – a very important ability in MÍMAMEIÐR. At breakfast it was usually just right

for the Greenblooms and Twigleg's table (which reacted indignantly if any nisse or impet ventured to sit at it). But this evening there were several guests eating at it too: twelve of the Spanish goblins known as duendes, three woodland spirits of the Green Man type from Holstein, two trolls who were Hothbrodd's cousins, and an albatross who had brought Gilbert Greytail some information he needed for a map. More curses than usual were uttered in the kitchen, because naturally these visitors all needed very different kinds of food. It wasn't easy to put the right meals on the table in MÍMAMEIÐR, but Tallemaja had eleven nisses to help her, as well as two firemanders and a six-armed Nepalese mountain brownie.

The atmosphere, as always, was relaxed. None of the guests seemed to notice how anxious the master of the house was looking, and Ben was too deep in his own thoughts to realise that Twigleg was very quiet. This evening was the three hundred and fiftieth anniversary of the fateful day when Nettlebrand had eaten his eleven brothers, and on that anniversary Twigleg's longing for the company of someone like himself was always particularly strong.

Three hundred and fifty years, yet he couldn't stop hoping that there was still another homunculus somewhere in the world. After all, in the Middle Ages many alchemists had tried to create artificial life. But with every lonely century that passed, Twigleg's hope burned lower, like the flame of a candle.

It wasn't easy for anyone to be the only one of his kind, and it was particularly hard on a homunculus because he was an artificial being. Of course, now he had Ben and the Greenblooms, but there were some things he couldn't explain even to them. And

often he didn't even try, for fear that what he thought and felt was as strange as the way in which he had come into this world! Ben and Barnabas, to be sure, knew how he longed for another homunculus, and kept sending FREEFAB scouts in search of one, but with no luck so far.

Twigleg himself spent many nights on the Internet, looking for news of tiny men and women, but he never found anything but badly faked pictures of sprites and elves. Maybe it would be better to reconcile himself once and for all to being the only surviving homunculus.

Ben put some of his scrambled egg on the tiny plate, and Twigleg's heart melted with love. Who needed people of his own kind if he had friends like this? Think of the Pegasus eggs, Twigleg, he told himself sternly. Find out more about griffins, in case your master really does set off in search of them with Barnabas. But when one of the woodland spirits drinking forest soup told him about a video on the Internet showing a little man as small as a grasshopper, he forgot all his good resolutions. When Ben asked if he'd like to go and inspect the stable with him and Barnabas, Twigleg murmured an excuse and hurried off to his computer.

But the video didn't show a homunculus, only a human being very amateurishly reduced in size.

CHAPTER SIX

Father and Son

The heart of a father is Nature's masterpiece.
Abbé Prévost, *Manon Lescaut*

Hothbrodd had prepared a stable for the Pegasus and his unborn foals right behind the house. When Ben and Barnabas came in, several woolspinner oaklings were just pulling the last threads through the padding they had made to line the inside walls. Ben thought the oaklings were rather weird. They looked like big-bellied spiders with human heads, but Hothbrodd talked to them as happily as he did to the oak trees where they lived. The silvery down mixed with the straw on the floor had been donated by an Arctic chattergoose whom Barnabas had saved from being stuffed, and a dozen Finnish firemanders added to the comfortable warmth. Hanging over the stable door were two of the camouflage lamps developed by Ben's teacher James Spotiswode to make fabulous creatures look like domestic animals. In their light, the Pegasi would look like ordinary horses to any unexpected visitors.

'Well done, Hothbrodd!' said
Barnabas as the troll picked woolspinner oaklings off the
walls as carefully as if he were collecting butterflies. Hothbrodd
looked around and nodded, as if he could only agree with
Barnabas.

'I'll go and feed the oaklings,' he said. 'Spinning makes them
very hungry. Keep an eye on those firemanders so that they don't
set the straw alight. And chase them out before the eggs arrive.'
Then he strode away.

Barnabas crouched on the bed of down and straw, and examined the walls, which were now covered with woollen cobwebs.
'Vita says the stallion isn't eating,' he said.

'I'm sure Holly Undset will change that,' said Ben, sitting
down too. 'Remember the water horse that wouldn't eat? It was
half dead when we pulled it out of the fjord, but two visits from
Undset, and soon it got its appetite back and swam right over
the fjord with Guinevere on its back!'

Barnabas nodded. 'So it did. Thanks for reminding me. I
only wish we could tell Undset more about Pegasi! No one
disputes that they were born from the blood of a
Medusa, but even I don't know much more about them,
in spite of all the years I've been studying them. They're
still shyer and more suspicious than ordinary wild horses,
and they can be very dangerous if they think there's any
threat to them. We should be glad if Ànemos will let Undset
examine him. It's little short of miraculous that Vita managed to
persuade him to come here. Very likely he agreed only because
he's still numb from the loss of his partner.'

Behind them, a few fungus-folk were smoothing down the
straw for the Pegasus nest. Four of them looked like walking fly
agarics, the other two like button mushrooms with arms and

legs. The fungus-folk made no secret of their dislike of human beings, but they eagerly mucked out the stables of MÍMAMEIÐR because the dirty straw was very useful to them in their work of raising mushrooms. Fungus-folk, mist-ravens, hedgehog-men – many fabulous creatures from the surrounding forests worked at MÍMAMEIÐR in exchange for food, clothing, or accommodation. It made it easier for them all to survive, particularly in winter.

Ben pulled one of the silvery goose feathers out of the straw and stroked its shimmering down. 'Do you know what a griffin's sun-feather looks like?' he asked Barnabas.

'They're larger than your hand, and look as if they were made of pure gold. All the same, they're said to be as light and soft as the goose feather you're holding. Sounds like magic, don't you think?'

Yes, it did.

'Do you know,' Barnabas whispered, 'I'm beginning to quite like the idea of going in search of those creatures. Even if it's definitely not nice to think that the survival of the last Pegasi may depend on the generosity of a griffin. One of my heroes, the great Nahgib Said Nasruddin, left extensive accounts of a pride of griffins that he observed in South Anatolia over eight hundred years ago. The last entries in his records were written by Nasruddin's servant, because the leader of the pride had torn off his arm and kept him for years in a basket, like a bird. A powerful prince had ransomed him with a chest full of gold. In the account that Nasruddin dictated to his servant, he says: "Never approach a griffin without gold. The lions of the sky love only war better than their treasures.'"

It certainly didn't sound as if you could simply ask a griffin for one of its feathers as a gift.

'Do you know where we could look for them?' A firemander scuttled across Ben's hand. It felt like hot wax running over his skin. 'Didn't Jane Gridall say no trace of them has been found for hundreds of years?'

Barnabas took his glasses off his nose and began polishing the lenses with his shirt tail. By now Ben was as familiar with that process as if Barnabas Greenbloom had always been his father. That was a good feeling.

'Decades ago there was a rumour that a pride of griffins was living on an Indonesian island,' said Barnabas. 'Although I must admit that's not very precise information. After all, there are over seventeen thousand islands in the Indonesian archipelagos. And even if we do find griffins, the feather will be no use to us unless we can make it back here to MÍMAMEIÐR ten days from now at the latest. Not much time for the journey, our search, and negotiations with the griffins. But three Pegasus foals!' Barnabas perched his glasses back on his nose and put his arm around Ben's shoulders. 'Did you know that the birth of a Pegasus is said to bring seven times seven years of good luck? The world could do with that amount of luck, don't you think? We're going to save those foals! Even if I have to let a griffin tear my own arm off in return! Although please don't repeat that within earshot of Vita and Guinevere!'

The stable door opened.

Hothbrodd put his head around it, but before a word could pass his green lips, Twigleg scuttled between his legs.

'He's here, master!' he cried in his shrill voice.

Even for a homunculus more than four hundred years old, the last Pegasus is exciting.

'Can you speak Indonesian, Twigleg?' Ben whispered as he lifted the manikin up to his shoulder. He felt embarrassed to admit that he didn't know just where Indonesia was.

'It all depends, master,' replied Twigleg. 'There are over seven hundred languages spoken in Indonesia. I'm fluent only in Sundanese and Minangkabau, but I can make myself understood pretty well in ten other dialects.'

Ben could never work out how such a tiny head could hold so much knowledge. His own, by comparison, seemed to him like an empty and very dusty attic. Try as he might, he couldn't imagine how he had ever managed without Twigleg. And yes, of course it would have been good to know of a safer way to save the Pegasus foals than finding a sun-feather, yet he kept on wondering what it would be like to meet a griffin. Were griffins as terrifying as basilisks? Or as Twigleg's old master Nettlebrand, who still haunted Ben in his nightmares? Did their front legs end in birds' claws, or in lions' paws like their hind legs? The pictures he had seen didn't agree with each other.

And then Ben forgot the griffins.

Outside the stable, the night was glittering with glow-worms and the fluttering of gleaming fairies. Even the stars seemed to shine more brightly, and the wind in the trees rustled in welcome. It was as if, suddenly, the whole world was made of nothing but music and light.

The last Pegasus had come to MÍMAMEIÐR.

CHAPTER SEVEN

The Last Pegasus

O, for a horse with wings!
William Shakespeare, *Cymbeline*, Act 3, Scene 2

If you were friends with a dragon you met many wonderful beings. Every one of them had given Ben precious memories, but none had enchanted him as much as Firedrake himself – until he saw the winged stallion standing beside Guinevere in the yard. The happiness that Ben felt when he was near Firedrake was made of air and fire, of silver moonlight, of the power of flames dancing in the wind. The Pegasus made him feel a very different kind of happiness. It tasted of earth, of driving clouds and thunder, grass wet with dew, and starlight caught in feathers and fur.

Ànemos was not much larger than an ordinary horse, and certainly not white, like most of the pictures you see of winged horses. His coat and his wings were the dull red of the light of the setting sun. Only his hooves were as silver as Firedrake's scales.

So much strength and beauty. So much light. But sorrow for the loss of his companion surrounded the Pegasus like a second shadow. Vita and Guinevere followed Hothbrodd as he carried the eggs into the stable. Ànemos, however, went over to Barnabas, his hooves heavy with despair.

'Thank you, Greenbloom,' he said hoarsely. 'Sadness cripples my wings and my mind, and it is difficult for me not to give up my children for lost, like their mother. It comforts me to see that you still have hope.'

Barnabas found it terribly difficult not to tell the Pegasus about the griffin's feather, but Ànemos would want to come with them, just as Firedrake would, and griffins would be even more dangerous to him than to the dragon.

'Yes, I still have hope,' replied Barnabas. 'But first we must make sure you get your strength back. I have asked the doctor who treats the fabulous creatures entrusted to our care to come. I hope you'll let her examine you?'

'A doctor?' The Pegasus bent his head. 'She will find a broken heart, Barnabas. Can anyone live with that?'

Holly Undset didn't keep them waiting long. She was neither very tall nor very slim, she changed the colour of her hair every month, she liked Norwegian sweaters too large for her, and she almost dropped her medical bag when she saw Ànemos standing outside the stable. His red coat shone in the moonlight as if he were a copper statue woken to glorious life. Undset gave Barnabas a happy smile to thank him for all the magic that he had shown her. Then she asked the Pegasus to follow her into the stable. When she came out again, she looked both relieved and concerned.

'He's healthy, so far as I can tell,' she said. 'Of course I've never treated a Pegasus before, although their anatomy is surprisingly like a horse's. But such sadness! The foals are probably our only hope of giving him new courage to live. If he loses his children too . . .' Undset shook her head anxiously. 'You must save them, Barnabas!'

'We're working on it,' Barnabas replied. 'I only wish we had more time. '

CHAPTER EIGHT

A Long Way and Not Much Time

Living wild species are like a library of books still unread.
Our heedless destruction of them is akin to burning
the library without ever having read its books.
Congressman John D. Dingell, 'The Endangered
Species Act: Legislative Perspectives on a Living Law'

The room where Gilbert Greytail drew his maps was difficult for humans to enter, not to speak of trolls like Hothbrodd. Even for visitors of Twigleg's size, the pathways through Gilbert's mountains of books and journals were like menacingly narrow ravines. In the harbour warehouse where Ben had met the white rat for the first time, things had looked much the same. Gilbert's research material was stacked everywhere, and could easily topple over. Three days ago a nisse child had been buried under the mounds of paper, but luckily nisses were a very resilient species.

Guinevere had opened the door with the utmost caution, as

she always did, but she and Ben still sank up to the knees in what came to meet them. The avalanche didn't consist solely of books, cartons and index cards. There were press cuttings and printouts, and they were all mixed up with seashells, picture postcards, travel souvenirs and goose feathers. It was almost miraculous that in the midst of all this chaos, Gilbert could draw maps that gave the Greenblooms very accurate images of the world.

'Gilbert?'

As usual, Ben couldn't spot the rat amidst the chaos, until Guinevere pointed up to the sheet of Perspex that Hothbrodd had fitted among the shelves a few weeks ago, at Gilbert's request. A rat's tail was dangling over the edge of it, and looking through the Perspex Ben could see Gilbert sitting at a desk that was enormous for someone of his size. The rat could be heard muttering curses: cursing the ink that dried too slowly, the paint that refused to flow from his pen exactly as he had hoped, the paper that wouldn't lie flat . . . The bad language that Gilbert mixed into his curses showed that he had grown up as a ship's rat. It was better not to mention either that, or the rumour that Gilbert Greytail had become a cartographer because he was prone to sea-sickness. The rat had been convinced to draw his wonderfully comprehensive maps in Norway, instead of the city of Hamburg with its warehouses, after the Greenblooms agreed to employ all his main informants as well: an albatross, two sea-gulls, a grey goose and a dozen ship's rats. He had also demanded a new computer. But Gilbert's talents were worth all that.

'We've come about the new map, Gilbert,' Guinevere called up to him. 'The map for the journey to Indonesia. My father wants to leave soon. Is it ready?'

Barnabas had announced his decision just before midnight. Yes, they would go looking for the griffins. Vita was not

particularly happy about that, but the sight of the mourning Pegasus and the three orphaned eggs left her no choice.

'Hello, Guinevere!' The rat's tail disappeared, and Gilbert looked down at her through his gold-framed glasses. The white paws clutching the edge of the Perspex sheet were stained with ink. 'Of course the map is ready.' Gilbert's voice was as soft as the down of baby chicks – it always was when he spoke to Guinevere. Otherwise it was more like the sound of sandpaper. 'Unfortunately the information about the location of your destination was vague. So I've also put in parts of Papua New Guinea, Malaysia and the Philippines. Lyo-lyok?'

The head of a grey goose appeared beside Gilbert. Ben had been wondering who was the owner of the webbed feet that he could see through the Perspex. Lyo-lyok took the folded map in his beak and flew gracefully down to a pile of paper within reach of Guinevere.

'I assume the homunculus is going to keep a record of the journey again?' called Gilbert, as Guinevere took delivery of the map from the goose. 'Tell him to improve his handwriting, please. It took me days to decipher his account of the kraken mission!'

'I certainly will!' Ben shouted up to the rat, although he had no intention of doing any such thing. Twigleg could take great offence if anyone criticised his handwriting. He was proud of every ornate flourish.

Gilbert's maps fitted easily into any jacket pocket, but when Guinevere unfolded his latest masterpiece on the big table in the library, it took up so much space that Barnabas had to move the collection of fossilised paw prints and hoof prints away. Gilbert's maps were works of art on paper. You could unfold them again and again, and still see new details that the rat had hidden in some fold or other, even weeks later. Safe paths and places to stay, obstacles and dangers – you could even pick up information about the weather from Gilbert's maps, and Ben had often wondered whether the rat wasn't working with some kind of magic himself.

At the request of Barnabas, Gilbert had marked two routes to help them search for the griffins. Barnabas was going to take the one shown in red ink. It included a stopover in south-east Turkey. The other route, in emerald green, was the one that Firedrake would take on his return to the Rim of Heaven. The two of them intersected in India, and so Firedrake had suggested that Ben could fly to that point with him and Sorrel – an offer that Ben, of course, had happily accepted. Fortunately there were three pairs of phoenixes in south Vietnam, so the dragon had not been surprised by the planning of that route. Those few who really knew where their mission was taking them had been pledged to secrecy by Barnabas himself, so that neither Firedrake nor the Pegasus would learn of it. It was not the first secret that had to be kept in MÍMAMEIÐR.

Hothbrodd had built the aircraft in which Barnabas would travel, like the freight plane that had brought the Pegasus to MÍMAMEIÐR, almost entirely of wood. The troll could persuade almost any tree to grow exactly the branches that he needed for his work. He had made the plane that the Greenblooms used for long-haul flights like this one with the help of an oak four hundred years old; it had put out branches specially suited for the wings. The elevator, loading hatch and

propulsion drives were made of stormwood – whatever that might be. Hothbrodd was giving nothing away about that, any more than he would describe the engine itself, which would run on leaves, sand or seawater. James Spotiswode had spent many nights studying it without discovering its secret. 'I talk to it,' was all that the troll would mutter if he was asked. The plane could take between four and eight passengers (changing size according to the number). It could come down on water as easily as on land, and looked fantastic, because Hothbrodd had covered it – like all his constructions – with Viking carvings.

There had been hardly any discussion about who exactly was to go on the griffin mission. Vita and Guinevere were staying behind to look after Ànemos and, together with Undset, make sure that the eggs did not get chilled before the expedition returned, it was to be hoped with the feather they needed. Another member of Barnabas's team, as well as Ben and Twigleg, would be Lola Greytail, one of Gilbert's many cousins, who was not just the only female rat aviator but also FREEFAB's most valuable scout (among many other reasons, thanks to the fact that her plane was not much larger than a crow, and so was equally inconspicuous).

At first Hothbrodd was far from enthusiastic when Barnabas

asked him to be the fifth member of his team. Trolls are extremely reluctant to leave their native forests. But when Ben filled the screens in the library with pictures of all the trees to be found in the Indonesian jungle, the troll growled with resignation and set about packing.

Their precise destination was still uncertain, so Gilbert had drawn another map on the back of the first. It showed the many islands of Indonesia, and was anything but an encouraging sight. Where were they going to find a guide through that labyrinth of islands, someone who was both discreet and wouldn't think them crazy when they revealed what they were looking for? Barnabas had a couple of former colleagues in Indonesia, but when Vita offered to get in touch with them he shook his head. 'I doubt whether a human guide is the most promising solution on this trip. But I have another idea. Do you remember the Indian temple that the Whispering Cobra told us about?'

Vita gave him a knowing smile, but when Ben asked more about the temple, all Barnabas would say was, 'Wait and see. But I promise you, it's an interesting place!' He was rather more willing to talk about their stopover in Turkey. 'I've asked an old friend there to get me something that we can barter for the feather,' he said. 'As you've heard, griffins are very materialistic creatures. I'm afraid it would be no use even setting out if we arrive empty-handed.'

Empty-handed . . .

Vita and Guinevere tried hard not to look too worried when, in another Skype session, Inua Ellams once again warned Barnabas earnestly about the aggressive instincts of griffins. In dealing with even the most legendary of monsters, the Greenblooms themselves preferred to use not weapons, but cunning and their knowledge of those creatures' weaknesses – and generally weapons were no use against fabulous beings anyway. Years ago, Vita had discovered a plant poison that could immobilise even the most dangerous of them for a few life-saving seconds, and Ben and Twigleg had developed tiny arrows to inject the poison under any skin, however tough. They were fired off from fountain pens and ballpoints, but Ben had also used drinking straws, cigars, mobile phones and chocolate bars. As on all FREEFAB missions, those arrows would be their only weapons.

When Guinevere asked whether anyone knew what a griffin sounded like, Professor Ellams let out an impressive shriek. He added, however, that he was relying solely on very old texts that described the voice of a griffin as a cross between a lion's roar, the call of an eagle, and the hiss of a snake about to attack. Later, Ben couldn't resist the temptation of mixing all those sounds into one blood-curdling cry on his computer. When he played it back, dozens of fabulous beings assembled outside the house in alarm. He still had a playlist of the voices of fabulous beings stored on his phone – to scare them, to entice them, and just for fun. The best of his collection was the attacking roar of three different dragons, and the soft hiss that they uttered as they prepared to breathe fire. But the battery of his phone probably wouldn't last for long in the Indonesian jungle.

Twigleg had calculated that the Pegasus eggs would be too small for the foals in ten days' time. Ten days! Ben wished it wasn't such a long way to Indonesia. And suppose they didn't even find the griffins? It was an idea that kept occurring to him, however much he tried to fend it off.

He was just helping Hothbrodd and Vita with the final preparations for the journey when Barnabas asked him to come to the library. He had an expression on his face that Ben usually saw there only when Barnabas was giving him a Christmas or birthday present.

'I have a job for you to do, my dear boy,' he said. 'You can say no, of course, but I think you'd enjoy it. Vita has pointed out to me that there are no stories or other accounts of meetings between dragons and Pegasi. It's perfectly possible that the paths of those two fabulous beings have never crossed. Wouldn't it be wonderful if they did meet in MÍMAMEIÐR for the first time? Even though sad reasons have brought both Firedrake and Ànemos here. Vita and I agree that only someone very special can introduce them to each other, and no one could be better than a dragon rider. What do you think? Would you take on the job?'

Ben was speechless. 'Of . . . of course,' he finally stammered. 'If . . . if you really think I'm the right one to do it. But—'

'You're certainly right for it,' Barnabas interrupted him. 'Not even Sorrel would dispute it. I'd bet all the mushrooms in MÍMAMEIÐR on that. Right, then, I'll go and discuss the exact route with Hothbrodd and Lola.'

CHAPTER NINE

An End and a New Beginning

O Wind,
If Winter comes,
can Spring be far behind?
Percy Bysshe Shelley, 'Ode to the West Wind'

Faced with two fabulous figures who, between them, have accumulated the wisdom of life for over two thousand years, how do you introduce them to each other when you are only fourteen yourself? Ben was by no means as certain as Barnabas that he was the right person to do it. But how could he have said no? The meeting of Firedrake and Ànemos would certainly be unforgettable. On the other hand . . . wouldn't it be more polite just to introduce them to one another and then leave them alone? And would Firedrake really want a human being around when he met a creature who, like him, had inspired fairy tales and legends, even if that human being was his dragon rider?

None of those questions seemed important when Ben reached Slatebeard's cave. From the way Firedrake looked, he could tell at once that something had happened. The cavern was empty, except for a swarm of lights drifting like pollen, one by one, towards the mouth of the cave.

'He could be rather grouchy, that's for sure!' Sorrel was sitting near the cave mouth herself. She looked very small and lost. 'How can he simply have gone away? I had such good arguments with him!' Ben heard her suppress a sob. 'A few new stars in the sky. Oh, terrific. As if there weren't enough of them already! Can you argue with stars? Or touch them? Can you smell them? Hear them?'

She sobbed again. The tears had left dark tracks down her furry face. Ben went over to her and stroked her head.

'Don't you dare go and die before me!' Sorrel snapped at Firedrake. 'Do you hear? And the same goes for you, dragon rider! And even for that mildew-fungus of a homunculus!'

'I was just about to ask you all to make me the same promise,' said Firedrake, although of course he knew that dragons and brownies usually lived a good deal longer than humans. Ben found that a very comforting thought, although Firedrake certainly didn't see things the same way.

Ben followed the last lights out of the cave, and watched until they dissolved in the rays of the sun. No, it was not a bad way of saying goodbye to this life, and he was glad that he had come to know Slatebeard so well over these last two years. The old dragon had told him many things about the valley in Scotland where Firedrake grew up. He had known Firedrake's parents, and had rescued him from an eagle when he was still very young. Slatebeard could remember the days when knights went hunting dragons. He had fought some of those knights himself. Ben had often asked Twigleg to write down the stories that Slatebeard told him about his adventures. The homunculus had filled many

notebooks with those tales, and Barnabas had had them typed and bound in silvery linen covers by a bookbinder, so that Slatebeard's memories would not disappear with him to where they could still be read only in the stars.

Firedrake went over to Ben, and he too looked up at the sky.

'I can tell Ànemos that you'd rather meet him some other day,' said Ben.

But Firedrake shook his head.

'No, this is a good day. Something old leaves, something new comes. Slatebeard would have liked that. And I can't wait to meet the Pegasus.'

Ben looked back to the cave. Sorrel had not followed them out into the fresh air.

'I think she still needs a little more time,' said Firedrake. 'She loved Slatebeard very much, and not just because she had such good arguments with him. She'll probably be off soon in search of a few tasty mushrooms.'

Ben couldn't help smiling. Yes, that was exactly what Sorrel would do.

'I wish there were some way of driving my own grief away so quickly,' said Firedrake as they set off together down the path to the stables.

Dragon and Pegasus – the meadows surrounding them seemed a very ordinary place for the meeting of two such extra-ordinary creatures, but when Ben said so, Firedrake only snorted with amusement.

'You soon get tired of what's extraordinary, dragon rider. It's often the most ordinary things that bring great happiness, and I'm sure the Pegasus will value the peaceful meadows of MÍMAMEIÐR as much as I do.'

Ànemos was already waiting for them.

He stood motionless as a statue in the wild grass, with the wind blowing through his mane. Only his distended nostrils showed that he was not as calm as he made out.

Firedrake stopped when they were still ten human paces apart. The Pegasus was very much smaller than the dragon, and Firedrake lay down in the grass to compensate for the difference in size. Ànemos expressed his thanks for that gesture by going closer. Size doesn't really count, as the two of them impressively proved. In their presence, the world seemed very young and very old at the same time, and each seemed to complement the magic of the other.

'Welcome to MÍMAMEIÐR,' said Firedrake. 'To the only place in the world where you and I do not have to hide. I am very sorry that such a sad reason has brought you here, yet I am glad that you have come just now! Until today there was an old dragon keeping watch over this place, but he has left us, and I can't take his place because I am needed at the other end of the earth. For the time, therefore, there is no guardian in MÍMAMEIÐR who has our strength and can provide the protection that it deserves.'

The Pegasus bowed his head. 'I am not sure that I still have that power, firebird,' he said. 'Too much is sapping my strength.'

'I know about your sorrow, and the game of hide and seek that this world makes us all play also steals strength from you and me,' replied Firedrake. 'But as you will see, this place can give you back much of it, even if it cannot heal your heart. Enjoy the freedom of not having to hide! And of being surrounded by creatures that humans still meet only in stories. Act as MÍMAMEIÐR's guardian for a while. Its inhabitants deserve our help, and I shall be able to fly away with my mind at rest!'

Ànemos glanced back at the stable where the orphaned nest stood. Firedrake followed his glance.

'I know it's no comfort,' he said, 'but pain often makes us stronger. And you are surrounded by friends, even if we hesitate to see humans in that light. The Greenblooms saved me and my kind when there was hardly any hope left. Wait and see: they'd risk their own lives to preserve the lives of your children!'

The Pegasus looked doubtfully at the dragon. 'Tell me how they helped you.'

'It's a long story,' said Firedrake.

'All the better,' replied the Pegasus.

Ben stole away as Firedrake began his tale – even though he would have liked to hear it and be reminded of their adventures together. But there was something else he had to do. And with luck, it too would be a story worth telling some day.

CHAPTER TEN

Griffins Love Gold

Gold is a treasure, and he who possesses it does all he wishes to
in this world, and succeeds in helping souls into Paradise.
Christopher Columbus

It is often very small things that make our greatest dreams
grow. Barnabas Greenbloom's dream of meeting a Pegasus
some day began on his eighth birthday, with a present from an
aunt he didn't like: a sticker album entitled *Pictures From Greek
Mythology*. He had soon spent all his pocket money on the little
bags with the stickers to be collected, and had been disappointed
every time the pictures turned out to show gods or heroes. The
monsters had interested him much more: Scylla and Charybdis,
the Cyclops, Medusa – he had stared at them for hours on end.
But his greatest treasure was Pegasus. At night he had dreamed
of sitting between the horse's wings and flying away to the stars.

The winged horse born from the blood of a beheaded
Medusa . . . Barnabas had now met several Medusas. They had
considerably nicer natures than their reputation suggested. Of

course! How could a really horrible monster have given birth to something as wonderful as the Pegasus? He and Vita had met descendants of Scylla and great-grandchildren of Charybdis (all of whom did live up to their fearsome reputation). They had at least discovered a very well-preserved Cyclops skeleton in a Cretan cave. But they had spent twenty years searching in vain for proof of the existence of the Pegasus. They had both been almost sure that the winged horses who flew through Barnabas's childhood dreams had disappeared from this world as irrevocably as dodos and sabre-toothed tigers, or the unicorns whose existence in the past was suggested now only by a shaggy species of wild horse in Mongolia that had the maimed base of a spiral horn on its forehead. But then, in the mountains of Greece, they had finally found themselves on the trail that Barnabas had been hoping to discover for so many years: hoof prints that shone like silver, and beside them a few feathers, some white and some copper-coloured. When they finally stood face to face with the Pegasi, Barnabas had stared so ecstatically that to this day he was surprised Ànemos hadn't given a mighty kick to remove his own existence from this world.

After that, they had sent Lola Greytail to Greece regularly, to make sure that all was well, and when one day the rat brought back the photo of eggs in the nest he and Vita hadn't been able to sleep for nights. Many of the inhabitants of MÍMAMEIÐR had laid bets on whether one of the foals would be a blue Pegasus, the legendary kind that could apparently fly to the moon. But now . . . now none of them minded what colour the foals would be, so long as they just hatched safely! Barnabas would have given one of his hands to be sure of that, ten years of his life, all he possessed . . . but instead, for the foals' sake, he had to go in search of the only fabulous creature that he really had never wanted to encounter.

Barnabas Greenbloom was a peace-loving man. Even as a child, he had hated people who trod on beetles or threw stones at stray dogs. Nothing made him angrier than those humans who tormented other beings for fun or out of boredom – although by now he knew that the reason for their cruelty was often only fear of everything strange. And maybe Barnabas Greenbloom was so easy-going because he had always been very fearless and full of curiosity about all that was new to him. But what Barnabas did know about griffins made him suspect that, for all his curiosity, he would not like them in the least. They were the most warlike of fabulous beings, creatures who took cruelty for a virtue and sympathy for weakness, who lived for everything he abhorred: war, fighting, the subjugation of weaker beings . . .

Before setting out, he read every story about griffins that Twigleg had found in the library, hoping to find something that would make him like them better. By his own standards, however, even those described as good and noble were callous murderers. As for their obsession with gold and treasures – he had nothing but profound contempt for that! A voice inside him whispered: these winged monsters are never going to give you a feather, Barnabas; you're an incorrigible dreamer. But he had made Ànemos a promise. And he did want to see those foals flying over the fields of MÍMAMEIÐR . . .

When Hothbrodd announced that everything was ready for take-off, Barnabas once again went over to the stable where two geese were warming the nest they had built for the Pegasus eggs. Ànemos was standing in the doorway, as usual. It was as if he couldn't bear to look at the orphaned eggs.

'I hear that Firedrake has asked you to protect MÍMAMEIÐR while we're away,' said Barnabas. 'I'm grateful to you. Guinevere and Vita will do all they can to keep your children alive until we get back, and I give you my word of honour, we'll save them!'

By way of answer, Ànemos touched foreheads with Barnabas. 'If you succeed, Greenbloom, I will call one of the foals after you,' he said.

'Oh no, you won't!' Barnabas retorted. 'It's a strange name for a human, and certainly not suitable for a Pegasus!'

Then he went to say goodbye to Vita and Guinevere. And to Firedrake, Sorrel and Ben, all three of whom he would soon be seeing again in India.

Hothbrodd's aircraft had a nose like a dragon's, and had a cabin with seats in it behind the cockpit. Twigleg was already waiting in the cabin when Barnabas came on board. The plane spread its wings as silently as a bird when Hothbrodd started it, and the engine that took it up to the sky, which was still dark, whispered no louder than the wind. But Hothbrodd's co-pilot was Lola Greytail, so the two of them were already arguing only a few minutes after take-off. About the music to keep them awake during the long flight, about the right height for the plane, about Hothbrodd's habit of chewing wild garlic, and Lola's inability to sit still. The pair of them enjoyed these arguments, and Barnabas and Twigleg were so used to them that, in spite of the raised voices from the cockpit, they were soon fast asleep. After all, no one knew how often they

would get a chance to sleep on this expedition.

It was almost four thousand kilometres from MÍMAMEIÐR to southern Anatolia. But Hothbrodd's plane was very fast as well as quiet, and the sun was just rising behind rocks as yellow as sand when they reached the first stop on their journey.

The runway on which Hothbrodd landed (far from skilfully, in Lola's opinion) seemed as deserted as if time and humanity had forgotten it centuries ago. The woman who made sure that uninvited visitors had exactly that impression was waiting beside the abandoned runway in a dusty jeep. Bağdagül Ender and Barnabas had known each other since they were both five years old when, bored to death by the conversation of their parents, who were friends, they had gone off to watch horned salamanders together. Bağdagül had grown up in southern Anatolia, and had now made a fine reputation for herself in protecting the endangered animal species of her native land. Asian lions, rare bats – Bağdagül spoke up for them all. She was a founding member of FREEFAB, and not far from the runway, in the caves carved out in the sides of the surrounding mountains by a long-forgotten civilisation, she ran a conservation refuge similar to MÍMAMEIÐR.

Most people would probably have taken the dog beside Bağdagül for just an albino with an unusual coat pattern, but Barnabas knew that it was one of the very rare cloud-dogs she had saved from extinction.

As he walked towards Bağdagül, Barnabas could tell from her face that she didn't think much of his mission. But before she could say so with her usual forcefulness, he held a box out to her. Sounds of scraping and whispering came from it.

'Figlings,' explained Barnabas. 'Vita found them on a shelf in the supermarket.

We've kept them at MÍMAMEIÐR for a while, but Norway is simply too cold for them. Can you find room for them somewhere?'

Bağdagül peered under the lid of the box, and took it from Barnabas with a smile.

'Of course,' she said. 'Although most of our caves have too many inmates now. I'll soon have to ask your stone-dwarves to carve a few more in the rocks.'

She put the box on the passenger seat, and handed Barnabas the black casket inlaid with intarsia work that was standing on the back seat. 'I've brought what you asked me for. But I don't have to tell you what I think of this quest! I hear that Inua has warned you at length about the beings you're thinking of approaching. Are you sure there really isn't any other solution?'

'Yes, I am. Although Inua can imitate the attacking cry of a griffin most impressively,' replied Barnabas. 'We simply have no time, and the sun-feather is our only hope. Or do you have a better idea?'

Bağdagül stroked back her hair. It was grey now, but in her eyes Barnabas still saw the girl who had gone looking for salamanders with him. The only difference was that she was older and wiser these days, and knew more about the world.

'Even if you do find griffins, Barnabas,' she said, 'and I have no doubt that you will . . . they'll bite your head off just for not bowing low enough to them! They think the earth and the sky belong to them, and they certainly don't want to see a winged horse in that sky!'

'I know, I know,' replied Barnabas, sighing. 'And I really am most grateful to you for letting me have this family heirloom. It's probably worth more than all of MÍMAMEIÐR,' he added, glancing at the casket that Bağdagül had given him.

'And I'm sorry to say it's very unlikely that you will get this treasure back.'

'Who cares?' said Bağdagül, with a dismissive gesture. 'The use that's to be made of my father's old paperweight would make him very happy. Don't look so incredulous; that's what he generally did with the casket. And if the Feathered Kings, as griffins like to call themselves, will really take it in payment for the feather, and the treasure it contains saves three unborn Pegasus foals – well, what better purpose could it serve?'

Treasure. Seeing Bağdagül again made Barnabas aware again of how many treasures he had found in his life already, but his were human treasures. He opened the casket. The ends of the gold bangle inside it were shaped like two griffins confronting each other with menacingly ruffled plumage. There was a similarly fine example in the British Museum in London, but Bağdagül's bangle was older and contained more solid gold. The eyes of the griffins were tiny rubies, their wings were set with pearls.

'I can't thank you enough, my dear Bağdagül,' said Barnabas. 'You're a treasure yourself. This is truly princely payment for a feather. Inua says you mentioned something else that might make griffins look kindly on our request, if offering gold doesn't work. But he was leaving it to you to tell me about it.'

'Kindly? Griffins?' Bağdagül laughed. 'Inua is a joker. I guess he wouldn't tell you himself because he doesn't want to be the one who put the idea into your head. But I'm sure that even you, with your passion for Pegasi, wouldn't pay that price.'

Barnabas put the casket and the bangle in his backpack. 'Now you really are making me curious.'

'Or then again, there's always the possibility of throwing yourself to them as food.' Bağdagül stroked the cloud-dog's pale grey coat. Such dogs were said to be able to pick up the scent of evil. 'Inua says you could offer them a duel with your dragon. Any griffin would give you a sun-feather for that opportunity. They boast of being the only fabulous creatures that can easily defeat a dragon in single combat. But they last had the chance to prove it over six hundred years ago.'

Barnabas did not reply. It was a price that he would not pay even for three Pegasus foals. He was extremely glad that they had lied to Firedrake about the purpose of their quest.

'Who won the fight over six hundred years ago?' he asked.

'The griffin. He killed the dragon and adorned his nest with its scales. So let's hope that the griffins will accept the bangle as adequate payment. It's said that they grow sun-feathers only after doing many heroic deeds. So they're certainly not going to give one up easily.'

Barnabas had read that story himself. 'We'll do it!' he said. 'And you must come to MÍMAMEIÐR once the foals have been born!'

'That sounds like a good plan!' Bağdagül smiled, but she still looked concerned. 'Griffins can smell gold miles away, Barnabas. They'll probably just kill you instead of negotiating for the bangle.'

That seemed only too likely to Barnabas himself. But what choice did he have if he wanted flying horses to live on in this world?

'Do you know where to look for them?' Bağdagül asked. 'All I know is the rumour that a pride of griffins has settled somewhere in Indonesia. That covers hundreds of islands!'

'Seventeen thousand at the last count,' replied Barnabas. 'Although the rising sea level is said to have drowned several of them already. We have a rat pilot who is an excellent scout, and

I've thought of a way to find a guide. But you're right, it won't be easy.'

Bağdagül smiled. 'We're used to that, aren't we?' she said. 'What we do is never easy. But sometimes luck is on the side of those who mean well.'

CHAPTER ELEVEN

One Heart, Two Places

*There ain't no way you can hold onto something
that wants to go, you understand? You can
only love what you got while you got it.*
Kate DiCamillo, *Because of Winn-Dixie*

Hothbrodd's plane had already disappeared among the
clouds when Ben climbed up on Firedrake's back. The
dragon was glad to see the moon in the sky, because it made
flying easier. But Sorrel had also brought a good supply of the
flowers that could replace moonlight for silver dragons in her
backpack. Vita grew them in the hothouses of MÍMAMEIÐR
from seeds she had been given by Zubeida Ghalib, the Indian
dracologist who had discovered the flowers, and whom Ben had
met on his first journey with Firedrake. It seemed incredible that
barely two years had passed since then.

Vita and Guinevere were not the only ones who had come to
say goodbye to the dragon and his rider. Ànemos was there too.
The Pegasus looked a little more confident now that he had

talked to Firedrake. He had accompanied the mist-ravens on one of the flights that they made several times a day to patrol the boundaries of MÍMAMEIÐR, and had explored the forests bordering its land with the hedgehog-men. It was not a good idea to be inactive when you were waiting for something, and Ben was very glad that Ànemos had taken on the task entrusted to him by Firedrake for the coming weeks.

Guinevere put something else in Ben's hand before he got on the dragon's back. It was a photo of the Pegasus eggs, and showed them shining with a silvery light, like Firedrake's scales.

'To remind you all of that you want to save,' Guinevere whispered to Ben, giving him a goodbye kiss on the cheek.

It was a wonderful feeling to be travelling with Firedrake again. Even Sorrel seemed glad to have Ben with them, and the night and day that it took the dragon to reach the south-west coast of India passed much too quickly.

By now Firedrake flew so well that he rivalled the speed of the wind. It felt intoxicating to be carried around the world by so much power and beauty, and Ben lay close to the dragon's warm scales and felt sure that he was the happiest person in the world.

The hill on which they came down to land hardly twenty-four hours after their departure was many miles south of the place where the great sea serpent had put them ashore during their last adventure, and beyond the fields and huts, even without his field glasses, Ben could see the ruined temple that Barnabas had described to them as the meeting place.

The others wouldn't arrive until tomorrow morning – even Gilbert Greytail had underestimated the dragon's speed – and of course Firedrake didn't want to leave Ben alone, which gave them a few precious hours together before the dragon set off again for the Rim of Heaven, hours in which Ben, after a long time, could be nothing but a dragon rider again. Rider, friend and companion of a dragon. No word could really express what linked the boy and Firedrake.

As the sun went down beyond the Indian fields, Ben used his jacket as a supper table, spreading out some of the provisions that Tallemaja had given him on it. Sorrel wrinkled her nose when Ben offered her some of the delicacies that the cook at MÍMAMEIÐR had packed up. She was very quiet, for her. Brownies were as reluctant to leave their homes as trolls, particularly Scottish brownies, and Sorrel made no secret of the fact that she was homesick, and was going back to the Rim of Heaven with Firedrake only for love of him. She sat down with her stock of mushrooms under the nearest tree, and when she finally fell asleep, she was holding a half-eaten chanterelle in her paw, with Indian flies buzzing around it, and in her dreams was murmuring something about boletus mushroom species and wild champignons.

After his long flight, Firedrake was so exhausted that he too was silent, but Ben could tell from his expression how much he looked forward to returning to the Rim of Heaven and the other dragons. The Himalayan valley had become home for Firedrake, and Ben was sure that the dragon would never leave it again of his own accord. After a while his muzzle sank to his paws, and Ben sat there with the hot nocturnal air of India on his skin, Firedrake's peaceful breathing beside him, and wished you could carry moments like this around with you like garments – magic jackets which, when you put them on, brought back all that went to make up such times: Sorrel murmuring in her sleep, the wide expanses of the foreign landscapes where they had travelled together – and the closeness of the dragon. The dragon in particular. There was nothing that made Ben happier, nothing in the whole world.

Why was the Rim of Heaven such a terribly long way from the place that was the most wonderful home you could wish for? Over eight thousand kilometres separated MÍMAMEIÐR from the peaks of the Himalayas.

'There's something I still have to tell you.' Firedrake stretched his weary wings. 'I was really going to tell you all at MÍMAMEIÐR, but somehow it never seemed to be the right moment, first because of Slatebeard, then because of the Pegasi . . .'

Ben heard something he didn't like in Firedrake's voice. It sounded alarmingly serious.

'It's not only Pegasus foals that will be born this year. We're expecting young in the Rim of Heaven as well.'

Ben stared at the dragon, so speechless that Firedrake uttered the quiet purr that Ben called his laughter.

'Twelve young dragons if all the eggs hatch. Two of them will be Maia's children, and mine.'

Ben forgot the Pegasi and the griffins.

Young dragons!

'Oh . . . oh, I must see them!' he stammered. 'When will they hatch?'

'Our young take a little longer than Pegasus foals. In three months' time.'

Three months! Three months would pass like lightning and – he would be far away! And . . .

'And I'm afraid I won't be able to come to MÍMAMEIÐR again for some time.' Firedrake said just what Ben was thinking.

For some time? Maybe he wouldn't be able to come for years! Did dragon fathers look after their children? Firedrake surely would.

Ben didn't know where to look. Oh, this goodbye would be so much worse than all the others! Suppose he told Barnabas that he couldn't go on to Indonesia with him? Suppose he asked Firedrake to take him along, and he stayed at the Rim of Heaven until the young dragons were born? Even if the Pegasi did hatch out, they would only remind him of the young dragons whose birth he was missing.

Firedrake gently nudged his chest with his muzzle, as he always did when he wanted to cheer Ben up.

'Of course you'll see them! I'll come and fetch you. Promise! As soon as I can leave Maia alone with our little ones.'

Whenever that would be!

The last daylight was dying away, and the temple ruins where Ben was to meet Barnabas and the others disappeared into the night.

'Don't worry,' said Firedrake. 'Everything will be all right. And now we'd better go to sleep like Sorrel. We both have a long journey ahead of us.'

He stretched out beside Ben, and was soon sleeping as deeply and soundly as Sorrel. His silver scales caught the starlight, and Ben sat there wondering how you could teach your own heart to love and not pay for it with pain. Was it better, in the long run, not to need anyone and so not to miss them? That night, Ben didn't know the answer.

The possibility of not seeing Firedrake again for so long made everything he loved in MÍMAMEIÐR seem unreal. The foreign night surrounding him ate up his distant happiness, and the only thing that counted was the dragon.

When the sun rose, Ben hadn't slept a wink all night, but he had come to a decision. He would help Barnabas with the griffins, but after that he wouldn't return to MÍMAMEIÐR. Instead, he would make his way somehow or other to the Rim of Heaven. Ben couldn't say that the decision made him happy. On the contrary, he felt as if he had made a plan to cut his own heart in two down the middle and throw half of it away. But what else was he to do?

Ben made up his mind to tell Barnabas once they had the griffin's feather. Barnabas would surely understand his decision. After all, they both remembered that he had been a dragon rider first, and had only then become one of the Greenbloom family.

And what about Firedrake?

The dragon opened his eyes, as if Ben's decision had woken him.

'You look tired,' he said as he stretched his scaly limbs. 'Didn't you sleep well?'

'Not particularly,' replied Ben. He would have liked to tell Firedrake right away that he would leave with him, but he couldn't let Barnabas down. Not when he was searching for one of the most dangerous fabulous beings in the world. And then again . . . Ben had to admit that he really did want to see the griffins.

'Will I see you again before we fly on?' he asked. Barnabas had asked Firedrake to drop Ben off only somewhere near the temple, because a dragon at the temple itself would attract too much attention.

'Of course,' said Firedrake. 'I'm not starting out until this evening. I always prefer to fly by night. Send Lola to me when the rest of you are ready to take off. But now let's see whether Barnabas is waiting for you yet.'

CHAPTER TWELVE

A Temple to Garuda

When his time came, Garuda burst from the shell
of his egg, as incandescent as the sun and the fire-god
Agni. His radiance was like that of the fire which
will devour everything when this world ends.
The Mahabharata First Book: 'Adi Parva',
The Book of Beginnings

Barnabas was indeed already waiting for them. At first sight, the temple where Ben found him, in a courtyard surrounded by columns, looked deserted, as if no human being had wandered into its crumbling ruins for hundreds of years. But the god whose weathered likeness appeared everywhere on the remains of its walls probably did not think much of human worshippers. He had wings and a beak, and the ruins of his temple echoed to the voices of thousands of birds. They were sitting on the sand-brown walls everywhere, like feathered flowers: red, yellow, blue-black, emerald green or white as snow. Ben had never seen so many birds in one place before. They were

-73-

whistling, croaking, cooing, and screeching in such shrill tones that Twigleg, who was sitting on Barnabas's shoulder, put his hands over his sensitive ears.

Many of the birds were as large as him, or even larger. And all those beaks! Why hadn't he gone with Hothbrodd and Lola instead, when they went in search of a calm river where they could refuel the plane in peace? Because Barnabas needed an interpreter, and he couldn't refuse him, that was why.

'Maybe you can guess why I chose this temple as our meeting place,' Barnabas whispered to Ben. 'Do you see who it's dedicated to?' He pointed to a fresco that adorned the wall to their left.

'Garuda!' Ben whispered back. 'The creature ridden by Vishnu. Thief of immortality and god of the birds.'

'Exactly,' Barnabas replied quietly. 'Many birds come to this place from very far away to ask for divine help. Who knows, maybe one of them can help us in our quest!'

Of course. That was why he had been told to come without Firedrake. Ben looked around the ruined temple.

'Help human beings who are in league with the king of the snakes?' croaked someone between the columns.

This remark irritated Twigleg so much that he did not translate what the discordant voice said until Barnabas cast him an enquiring glance.

Everyone knew the bird who drew a shimmering train of feathers after him as he stepped out from the columns. His beauty was as famous as his unmusical voice. So far Ben had seen peacocks only in zoos and the gardens of great houses, but he thought this one would have taken it as an insult if he said so. When he fanned out his magnificent tail, all was so still among the columns that even Sorrel wished the croaking, screaming voices would start up again.

'My lord and master, the mighty Garuda,' screeched the pea-cock, as he fanned his tail again, showing colours to outdo any rainbow in splendour, 'will make you all feel the force of his wrath! How dare you bring a dragon to his shrine? That boy,' he added, with his beak swinging around to point at Ben, 'was brought here by one of those fire-breathing creatures! No less than three birds on guard here have told me so!'

'Oh, don't give yourself such airs, Magura!'

The bird calling down to the peacock so disrespectfully had a crest of red-brown feathers on his head, and was feared for his aggressive nature. He was a hoopoe, and his English was so flaw-less that he didn't need Twigleg to interpret what he said, even if he spoke with a strong Indian accent. Ben had often noticed animals communicating in human language when there was a fabulous creature present.

'A dragon is as much of a bird as a snake, O maharajah of all the vanities!' cried the hoopoe in his mocking voice. 'Furthermore, if I am correctly informed, your lord and master last showed himself in this temple over seven hundred years ago. Nor, to be perfectly accurate, was it ever just Garuda's temple. He has a single niche to himself, and it's in a rather remote spot, as you must admit. The rest of the place,' continued the hoopoe, indicating the temple building around the courtyard with his beak, 'is dedicated to Krishna. And very appropriate, if you ask me. After all, your lord and master is only the mount that Krishna rode!'

The peacock puffed himself up with indignation at such lack of respect. Every feathered eye on his tail seemed to flash fury. But the hoopoe uttered the loud cry of *huphuphup* that had earned him his Latin name of *Upupa epos*, like a challenge, whereupon the peacock, sulking, made off between the columns, tail and all. He wasn't about to play around with a hoopoe, even if the bird was considerably smaller than he was. You had only to watch one spear its prey with its long beak, or smash it with a stone.

So far Ben had kept his mouth shut. Only when the hoopoe fell silent did he hesitantly step into the middle of the temple courtyard. Hundreds of birds' eyes stared down at him from the ruined walls and towers.

'The hoopoe is right!' he cried. 'Dragons do feel related to birds and snakes. And all mammals. And the fish in the sea. A dragon is life incarnate, in all its variety. This one wouldn't hurt a single feather of any of you.'

The hoopoe uttered his cry of *huphuphup* again, and flew to a cracked column very close to Ben. In view of the bird's long beak, Twigleg had to force himself to stay put, rather than disappearing into the pocket of Barnabas's jacket.

'It's not exactly common for a human being to be friends with a dragon.' The hoopoe's crest stood up as it examined Ben

with its cool, bird's gaze. 'What kind of help are you looking for here? I'm sure you haven't come for the usual reason.'

'May I ask what the usual reason for humans to come to this temple is?' asked Barnabas, joining Ben.

'Snakebite.' The hoopoe caught a fly out of the air. 'You humans think throwing the snakes off the walls in clay pots acts as an antidote to their venom. Pretty silly, if you ask me.'

He uttered another sarcastic *huphuphup,* and many of the other birds joined in. Ben thought he sensed the gaze of those countless eyes on his skin. Round, black eyes, so different from his own. He wondered what the birds came to ask Garuda for. Were their requests the same as human beings made to their gods?

Barnabas cleared his throat. It wasn't easy to get a hearing in all the noise made by the birds. 'I have heard,' he called, 'that many of you come to this temple from very far away. Has any of you present, by any chance, ever met a griffin on your travels?'

The silence that followed his words was as complete as if the birds looking down at them had all been turned to stone.

The bird that finally flew to the hoopoe's side had almost as long a beak, but much more colourful plumage, shimmering in shades of orange, green and turquoise blue.

'A green bee-eater,' Twigleg whispered to Ben. 'We don't necessarily have to believe what it says. They have a reputation for being enthusiastic liars.'

The bee-eater didn't speak English.

'My cousin three times removed,' Twigleg translated its excited twittering, 'came upon a whole pride of griffins only a few days ago!'

'Oh, really?' said a bird ironically, spreading turquoise wings. 'And where's that supposed to have been, O master of all beaked liars?'

'That's an Indian roller,' Twigleg whispered. Ben hadn't realised that the homunculus knew so much about birds. On the other hand, what *didn't* Twigleg know about? When Ben walked in the forests around MÍMAMEIÐR with him, Twigleg could tell him the name of every beetle.

'Not far from here,' chirped the bee-eater. 'Near the temple of Mahavishnu.'

The Indian roller uttered a scornful whistle. 'By the claws of Garuda! Nothing lives there but a flock of half-starved vultures! Griffins? They're a fairy tale, that's all! Thought up by human beings who can't tell an eagle from a lion!'

The bee-eater began twittering in such agitation that Twigleg couldn't even attempt to interpret – especially as the hoopoe was looking at him with so much interest that it was really hard for him to concentrate.

'You! Spider-man!' the hoopoe croaked when the homunculus finally returned his glance, annoyed. 'I think you'd taste delicious. What are you? A descendant of Apasmara?'

Twigleg turned pale. Apasmara – even a long beak didn't excuse anyone for comparing him to a dwarf considered a byword for stupidity!

'*If* you don't mind,' he cried in such a high register that his own voice sounded to him like the shrill notes of a bird, 'I'm a homunculus – and no, we don't taste good at all,' he added in perfect Hindi, to show how educated he was. 'Far from it.

We're extremely poisonous.'

'What did you say?' Ben whispered.

'Nothing,' Twigleg replied, crossing his arms in front of his thin chest. 'I'm just tired of these idiotic birds.'

'All the same, my highly esteemed homunculus,' Barnabas said quietly, 'I'd be very grateful if you would go on interpreting. I get the feeling that there's something else the Indian roller has to say.'

If that was the case, she was taking her time so as to heighten the suspense. The roller stuck her beak in the stone on which she was perching, pulled out a struggling, protesting insect, and with relish put her prey, countless legs and all, inside her hooked beak. Then the roller swallowed, cooed with satisfaction – and gave voice to a torrent of sounds that Ben couldn't understand at all.

'She says she knows a female parrot who's met some griffins,' Twigleg translated. 'The parrot is a chattering lory who got away from a bird collector of some kind. Obviously there are many fugitives who have escaped from cages in these parts.'

'And where can we find this parrot?' asked Barnabas.

The Indian roller pointed her beak to a doorway leading into the interior of the temple. The darkness beyond competed with the feathers of two drongo birds who were as blue-black as if someone had dipped them and their extravagantly long tail feathers in ink. Twigleg was not at all happy about such darkness, but he knew from experience that gates like this one held a magical fascination for his young master.

'She's sitting above the niche where people leave gifts for Garuda. She thinks that if she doesn't eat, and just sits there day in, day out, Garuda will have pity on her some day and take her home.' You could tell from the Indian roller's voice what she thought of such hopes. She herself came here only for the tasty insects that lived in the old temple walls.

Barnabas took Ben aside. 'Do you think you could go looking for this lost parrot yourself?' he asked in a low voice. 'She might be less frightened of a boy than of a grown man. I'd really like to send Twigleg to her on his own, because he's about her size, but a parrot might only too easily . . .'

Barnabas stopped when the homunculus cast him a glance of alarm.

'Sure!' said Ben. 'I'll be happy to look for her. But if I do find her,' he added, glancing at Twigleg, 'I may need an interpreter.'

The homunculus looked anxiously at the dark gate behind which the lost parrot was said to be hiding. But he couldn't say no to anything Ben asked of him. And they had been in dark places together before.

'I'll take good care of you,' Ben promised. 'Word of honour!'

It's your own fault, Twigleg, thought the homunculus as he climbed up to Ben's shoulder. Why didn't you pick a master who was happiest among bookshelves, and found the rest of the world as disturbing as you do?

CHAPTER THIRTEEN

Very Far From Home

I will remember what I was, I am sick of rope and chains –
I will remember my old strength and all my forest affairs.
Rudyard Kipling, *The Jungle Book*

Twigleg wasn't sure what he thought of torches. Darkness stimulated the imagination so much less than the probing beam of light that Ben was shining on the interior of the old temple. Every image carved on the weathered walls seemed to waken to life as the torch picked it out from the shadows, until Twigleg was firmly convinced that Garuda himself was prowling after them, with golden claws and a beak that could break the limbs of a homunculus like matchsticks.

The sounds were almost worse than the images! All the fluttering and scurrying that came to his maddeningly sensitive ears . . . no, he really wasn't born to be an adventurer. But he had given his heart to a boy who didn't know the meaning of fear, and who was intent on looking into every nook and cranny of this world.

There!

What was that?

Twigleg clung to Ben's jacket so tightly that he almost broke his own stick-thin fingers.

Didn't it sound like a snake?

No, Twigleg, he reassured himself, this is a temple of Garuda. They throw snakes off the walls in clay pots here, didn't you hear the hoopoe say so?

Oh!

Something or other was fluttering just above their heads. But all that Ben's torch showed them was a huge bat. Not that Twigleg was sure whether it would turn down a tasty morsel of homunculus. At his size, you were on the menu of an alarmingly large number of creatures.

'There!' whispered Ben, running the beam of light over a frieze of stone birds. They surrounded a niche where dried fruits and grain lay in front of a weather-beaten statue. It was difficult to say what god it was meant to be, but Twigleg thought he saw a hint of wings.

'That could be Garuda, don't you think?' whispered Ben.

Twigleg was shaking too badly to manage a convincing nod.

'Can you say something?' Ben asked quietly. 'Something like: we come as friends. In some kind of Indonesian language? Or in South-Asian Parrot, if such a thing exists.'

'It definitely does,' Twigleg whispered back. 'I can speak twelve of the eight hundred and fifty-three known dialects of Parrot!'

'Excellent!' replied Ben, turning the torch on a very alarming ledge shaped like a snake that ran along the ceiling above them. 'Try it! Tell her we want to take her home.'

He wasn't afraid of anything! Not the faintest trace of fear

in his voice!

With his limbs trembling, Twigleg brought out a mixture of chattering, cooing, shrill screeching, and hoarse squawking that sounded to his own ears very much like parrot language.

No reaction.

Only a blue lizard showed up by way of an answer.

But when Twigleg turned instead to the dialect of *Lorius garrulus*, the chattering lory, there was a rustle above them, and a red-feathered head looked out of an opening in the weathered roof.

'There she is!' whispered Ben.

From the size of the beaked head, Twigleg worked out that the bird looking down at them with mingled panic and dislike was at least five centimetres taller than him.

'Ask her where she comes from!' hissed Ben.

The parrot replied to that question with such angry squawks that Twigleg was tempted to creep into one of Ben's pockets, but he felt too bad about his own cowardice to do so.

'What's she saying?'

Twigleg spared Ben the imaginative terms that chattering lories applied to human beings. *Thieving vermin* was the most flattering. No wonder she spoke her own language, although even the homunculus often caused ordinary animals to use human language. She had a strange name for him, too: she called Twigleg a jenglot, whatever that might be. Maybe Twigleg would have taken it as a compliment if he had known that jenglots were dwarf-like zombies who drank blood and were much feared in Indonesia.

The parrot went on squawking and screeching abuse, but Twigleg knew enough about fear to recognise it in others. The bird's black eyes were wide with fright, and Twigleg saw in them a sadness that he knew only too well. So he cleared his throat, and departed slightly from the gist of what Ben had told him to translate.

'It isn't easy to be the only one of your kind,' he said in the dialect of Parrot that she had used herself. 'Believe me, I know what it's like. But my master here has a kind heart, and you can be sure that he won't do you any harm. Far from it. He may be able to help you to get home, but if he's to do that, you must tell us where you come from!'

The parrot craned her red neck to take a closer look at Ben. Then, to the surprise of Twigleg and Ben himself, she gabbled something in English.

'Me-Rah comes from the thousand times one thousand green islands,' she croaked, 'and her heart is as sore with homesickness as the back of a donkey.' Then she let out a plaintive screech, and disappeared into her hole again.

'The thousand times one thousand islands?' whispered Ben. 'That could be Indonesia!'

He lowered the torch so that Me-Rah wouldn't feel threatened by its beam.

'Your English is very good, Me-Rah!' he called up to the parrot.

For a moment nothing moved, but then Me-Rah put her head out into the open. 'So why does that surprise you? Parrots can imitate every sound in the world,' she snapped. 'And I'm only too familiar with the primitive language you use. The man who shut me up in a cage spoke it too.'

Ben didn't explain that his mother tongue was German. He was sure that Me-Rah would consider that no less barbaric.

'Maybe we can help you to get home!' he called to her. 'Is it true that there are griffins on your islands?'

Me-Rah had crept right out of her hiding place now. She was a sad sight. Her feathers were crumpled and dull, her beak dusty and splitting, as if she had been gnawing nothing but the stones here for days.

'Griffins? What's a griffin supposed to be?' she squawked suspiciously.

'A great big bird!' Twigleg spread his arms wide – then let them sink when he realised that he could barely give any idea even of the wing-span of a sparrow. 'With a lion's body and a snake for a tail.'

Me-Rah tilted her head, looking scared. 'Are you by any chance talking about the lion-birds?' She let out a couple of whistling notes so shrill that the dark passages of the temple filled with the squeaking of alarmed bats. 'Oh, they're terrible! They can pluck a great gibbon out of the trees like a caterpillar! Even the sun bears and binturongs run for it when their shadow falls on the jungle!'

Ben exchanged a triumphant glance with Twigleg.

'Can you lead us to them?' he called up to Me-Rah. 'And of course we'd show our gratitude by taking you home!'

Me-Rah fluffed up her untidy feathers and gave a yearning coo, but then she shook her red head very firmly.

'If you fly to where the lion-birds live you'll never come back!' she squawked, as urgently as if she were repeating something she had been told as a chick. 'They'll line their nests with your feathers and adorn their treasure chambers with the horn of your beak. They'll use your bones to skewer their prey, and they'll feed your beating heart to their young!'

She turned around, and in a flash she had gone back into hiding.

A very sensible reaction, Twigleg thought. *They'll use your bones to skewer their prey?* This whole project needed more thought! Seriously, did the world really need Pegasus foals? Why did there have to be horses with wings anyway? Surely there were more than enough of the wingless sort!

But Ben had looked fascinated as he listened to Me-Rah's alarming description. Oh, Twigleg had seen that expression on his face only too often before. *Danger?* it said. *Bring it on!* And who would give up before things got started anyway?

'Me-Rah! Please!' Ben called up to the narrow gap in the wall where he knew the parrot was hiding. 'Just show us which island they live on, and then you can fly anywhere you like!'

But Me-Rah did not reappear. They could hear the rustle of feathers in her hideout, but that was all.

'I'm so sorry, master!' said Twigleg. 'I'm afraid we'll have to look for another guide.'

What a hypocrite he could be! To his shame, he had to admit

to putting up a silent prayer to Garuda, or whatever god he had to thank (there were so many of them in India that even Twigleg had lost count), for Me-Rah's refusal.

But Ben's face suddenly brightened, and Twigleg didn't have to look up to know that Me-Rah's homesickness had overcome her fear of the lion-birds.

Ben held his arm out to her invitingly.

'Let me introduce you to the leader of our expedition, Barnabas Greenbloom!' he said. 'I'm sure you'll like him. He's dead against people like the human beings who caught you and sold you.'

Even if Me-Rah hadn't understood English, there was so much of the love and respect that Ben and the Greenblooms felt for all wild creatures in his voice that she would surely have trusted him even without knowing what his words meant. And so she flew down to the boy who had won Twigleg's heart with the same ease, and dug her scaly toes into the arm of Ben's jacket.

The Pegasus rescue mission had a guide!

If Me-Rah's lion-birds really were griffins, and she hadn't just made them up as a way of getting home.

Twigleg knew that a small part of him hoped for that very thing. *They'll feed your beating heart to their young . . .* he felt sure that the heart of a homunculus was just the right size for that.

CHAPTER FOURTEEN

A Goodbye Present

Wherever you go,
Go with all your heart.
Confucius (551-479 BC)

And now it was time to say goodbye. Firedrake would be flying north, back to the Rim of Heaven, with Sorrel, while Ben went in the opposite direction with Barnabas, over southern India and Sri Lanka and then on to Indonesia.

The others were already sitting in the plane. Hothbrodd had made Me-Rah a perch in the cockpit, using a couple of branches from a mango tree. Ben thought that was very nice of him. 'Nice?' was all that Hothbrodd had growled when he said so. 'Trolls are never *nice*, dragon rider. But you clearly know just as little about parrots. They eat anything they can lay their claws on! I made the thing solely to keep our new friend from taking my aircraft apart!'

The troll was not exaggerating. Me-Rah began gnawing the mango wood as soon as she closed her sharp-clawed feet around it. Hothbrodd had put the perch right behind the co-pilot's seat, so that Me-Rah could give him and Lola flight instructions. The rat did not like that one bit.

'Flight instructions from a parrot?' she squealed in such a loud voice that Me-Rah, startled, flew down on Hothbrodd's instrument panel controls. That, of course, led to a quarrel between Lola and the troll. Hothbrodd's wooden-voiced ranting was coming out of the cockpit window, at the same volume as the rat's shrill voice, as Ben flung his arms around Firedrake's neck for the last time. He was glad that the others were already on the plane, and not just because that meant Me-Rah wouldn't give away the real purpose of their quest to Firedrake. It was bad enough to have Sorrel watching as they said goodbye: she was sitting in what was usually his own place on Firedrake's back.

'Well, then,' he murmured, trying not to look up at Sorrel too enviously. If he had, he might have noticed that Sorrel herself was avoiding the sight of Hothbrodd's plane. She was even more homesick than Firedrake and Ben had realised. Homesick for damp, green hills and pine forests, for hedgehog-men and rivers where water-sprites lurked, for the ever-cloudy sky of the north and a horizon uncluttered by snow-covered mountains. MÍMAMEIÐR came so much closer to her native Scotland than the mountains of Nepal. But brownies are considerably less sentimental than humans (or so they claim, anyway). Sorrel accepted her homesickness like a bitter mushroom that reminded her of past pleasures. And then again, she was very good at hiding it when she wanted.

Ben was just turning around – very quickly so that the dragon wouldn't see his suspiciously moist eyes – when Firedrake called him back once more.

'I have a present for you,' he said as he stretched his wings.

'And I'm telling you again, this is not a good idea!' Sorrel shouted down from his back.

The dragon ignored her.

'One of the stone-dwarves who helped us to free the petrified dragons two years ago . . .' he began.

'. . . and we all know what stupid idiots stone-dwarves are!' muttered Sorrel.

Firedrake silenced her with a stern glance.

'One of the stone-dwarves,' he began again, 'claims that in the old days all dragons gave their riders one of their scales so that they would sense when they were in danger. A dragon rider had only to close his hand around the scale, and his dragon felt what he was feeling: joy, fear . . .'

'. . . and as a result the dragons went around with great big gaps in their scales!' growled Sorrel.

By this time she was fonder of Ben than she would admit to herself, but her first concern was always for Firedrake. After all, she had spent half her life with him before the boy came on the scene. Without anyone ever talking about giving scales away or similar stupid notions. And without all that never-ending flying from one end of the earth to the other. Brownies hate change. In Sorrel's experience, however, there was nothing that human beings liked better. What made it all more of a nuisance was that her dragon had picked a human being as his best friend. Best friend after her, of course.

'Sorrel's right,' said Ben (yes, he really was one of the good humans). 'Getting rid of a scale really doesn't sound great.'

But Firedrake was already plucking it off his breast.

'It'll grow back,' he said, as Ben stared anxiously at the dark place left in his scaly coat.

'Suppose it doesn't?' snapped Sorrel.

Behind them, Hothbrodd was blowing the horn that he had designed to look like the Vikings' signal horns. It was a strange sound in the mountains of western India.

'Coming!' called Ben, as Firedrake let the scale drop into his hand.

It was almost as cool and round as a coin – and it reminded Ben of another scale: Nettlebrand's golden scale, which had helped him to defeat the enemy of all dragons.

He closed his fingers around Firedrake's gift. It might help with the longing he felt for his friend – who knew?

'Can you sense anything?' he asked the dragon.

'The sorrow of saying goodbye,' replied Firedrake. 'But we neither of us need a scale to know about each other, do we? Use it any time you need help. Promise me! Now, Hothbrodd is really getting impatient!'

The troll was standing in front of his aircraft, waving to Ben with both arms.

Ben tucked the dragon's scale into his jacket pocket, and put his arms around Firedrake's neck one last time.

'I wish I could give you something in return,' he said in a husky voice. 'But humans don't have any scales, unfortunately.'

Then he turned around and ran towards Hothbrodd.

CHAPTER FIFTEEN

Trouble in MÍMAMEIÐR

It's hard being left behind. [...]
It's hard to be the one who stays.
Audrey Niffenegger, *The Time Traveler's Wife*

Guinevere was not the kind of girl who had always dreamed of riding a horse of her own. If your friends include grass-elves and impets, and you're used to nursing mermaids injured by ships' propellers back to health in the bathtub, horses are not necessarily the most exciting living creatures in your world. Of course, Guinevere had met many fabulous members of the horse family. At the age of eight, she had ridden her first kelpie, and when she was ten she had saved three elf-horses from a swarm of wild wasps. Sea-foam horses, wind-mares, cloud-stallions – Guinevere knew them all. But none of those beings who galloped on hooves had ever enchanted her more than elves, impets or hedgehog-men. Until Ànemos came to MÍMAMEIÐR.

The task that Firedrake and Barnabas had given the Pegasus took his mind off his sorrows a little. He was to be found regularly on the banks of the fjord, settling quarrels between fossegrims and nymphs, or mustard-midgets and beavers. He met foxes, weasels and wolves on the borders of MÍMAMEIÐR, and asked them to go in search of some other hunting ground; he flew above caves, huts and houses at twilight with the mist-ravens to deter predatory birds who might have snatched an impet for a snack; and by scraping his hooves behind the stables he made water spring up from the earth that healed not only wounds, but weariness and homesickness. The new brook was soon attracting fabulous creatures both large and small. But the miracle-working water could do nothing to dispel the sadness that surrounded the Pegasus himself like a dark cloud.

Everyone in MÍMAMEIÐR knew that Ànemos almost never went into the stable where swans and geese were keeping his orphaned eggs warm. It was almost as if the Pegasus were trying to forget that they existed at all. Why set your heart on something that's as good as lost already – was that the way he was thinking? Guinevere asked herself that question when she saw Ànemos, with his head sadly bent, standing in the mead-ows behind the stable where the shining shells of his unborn children lay.

The feathered inhabitants of MÍMAMEIÐR stood in line to warm the nest. On Undset's instructions, Guinevere took the temperature of the eggs every hour, and she could soon report that (much to the annoyance of the swans) wild geese kept the nest warm best. She drew up a calendar with the days still to go

until the eggs had to grow – and regretted it as soon as she hung the calendar on the stable door. Guinevere had left space to record every observation she made of the eggs. Unfortunately that showed, only too clearly, how little time there was left. Seven dates were still empty. Seven white squares filled only with the desperate hope that Ben and her father would be back in time with the feather of a griffin, and that feather would make not just gold or stone but also Pegasus eggs grow.

Guinevere had just been feeding the two geese sitting on the nest at present when Vita took her aside, and asked if she had seen Ànemos eating.

Guinevere could only shake her head. 'The mist-ravens have tried making friends with him,' she said. 'But he keeps himself to himself, even when he's flying on their rounds with them. He hardly says anything, and he isn't eating or sleeping. I'm really worried.'

'With good reason, I'm afraid,' said her mother.

Guinevere had seldom seen Vita so depressed before. The death of the Pegasus mare had grieved her deeply; she shared the suffering of Ànemos, and hated herself for being able to offer him so little help.

'I'm going to ask the mist-ravens to find an old friend of mine,' she said. 'Maybe she can get through to Ànemos in his time of trouble. Her herd wasn't far from here when I last heard from her.'

'Herd?' asked Guinevere.

'Yes, Raskervint is a centaur,' replied Vita. 'They're more like Pegasi than people think. Though of course that doesn't mean she can help us. However, there's always hope, and often that's all we have, right?'

Yes, that was only too true. Another reason to hope was that they hadn't heard from Ben and her father for two days, because Hothbrodd, like all trolls, disrupted radio communication. They must be doing fine, she was sure of that! And they would find the feather. And get back here in time. She hoped. Guinevere only wished there was more she could have done. By now, even finding the feather of a griffin seemed easier than this helpless waiting.

'I didn't know you were friends with a centaur,' she said to her mother.

'Why does that surprise you, Guinevere Greenbloom?' retorted Vita. 'When your father and I met, we had a bet to see which of us had met more fabulous creatures. And who do you think won? Although,' she added with a smile, 'Barnabas has caught up with me now.'

CHAPTER SIXTEEN

Me-Rah Tells Her Story

*'Animals don't behave like men,' he said. 'If they have
to fight, they fight; and if they have to kill they kill.
But they don't sit down and set their wits to work
to devise ways of spoiling other creatures' lives and
hurting them. They have dignity and animality.'*
Richard Adams, *Watership Down*

This world looks rather different to all its inhabitants. To Me-Rah, it consisted of leaves, fruits, seeds and clouds, of snakes who stole eggs, apes and pine martens. She could tell Hothbrodd that it would take them six days to fly over the island that was her home from east to west, and three days to cross it from south to north, but of course she did not give animals and plants, or the four points of the compass, their human names. She spoke of where the sun is born from the sea, and where it goes to its nest in the mountains in the evening, she told them about long and short shadows, about the place where the swimming toads with horny shells bred (Twigleg translated those as turtles), or the direction in which the scentless wax flowers (orchids, Twigleg translated) turned their blossoms at noon.

Me-Rah knew a very great deal about her world.

'Because she's still at one with it,' Barnabas whispered to Ben after the homesick chattering lory had spent over an hour describing her island, with longing in her husky voice (and a slight Indonesian accent). 'It's a sense for which I deeply envy every animal. I think I'd like to be reborn as a parrot. Although not in a cage and with clipped wings.'

Me-Rah's wing feathers had grown back since her escape, but she still couldn't fly with as much certainty and stamina as before her imprisonment. Ben hoped very much that wouldn't endanger her in the wild. Hothbrodd was still watching Me-Rah with the utmost suspicion, and jumped every time she turned her beak to gnaw the tree-perch he had made for her. Lola, on the other hand, was soon talking shop with Me-Rah about upwinds and turbulence, maybe because they were both among the smaller denizens of the world.

Me-Rah assured them that there were no human settlements on her island home. The birdcatchers whose victim she herself had been came in boats, like the hunters in pursuit of monkeys, wildcats, or sun bears. But it was very unusual for any of them to reach the heart of the island.

'For fear of the lion-birds, I suppose?' commented Barnabas.

'Oh no, fully-grown Greenbloom!' replied Me-Rah. (She called Ben 'still-growing Greenbloom'.) 'The lion-birds even do business with the poachers.'

That was certainly a surprise.

'May I ask what kind of business?' asked Barnabas.

'They allow only people who pay them to hunt in their kingdom, as they call it,' squawked Me-Rah. 'They eat the others.'

Twigleg cast Ben a horrified glance, but Ben himself seemed to like Me-Rah's information.

'They eat poachers! So what?' was all he said. 'I sometimes wish all animals would do the same! Anyway, we're not poachers, so where's the problem?'

Twigleg thought that was a very optimistic attitude.

'May . . . may I ask how many lion-birds we're talking about, Me-Rah?' he asked in what he considered an admirably casual tone of voice.

Me-Rah lapsed into her dialect of Parrot.

'Enough to turn the day into night,' Twigleg translated. It sounded extremely disturbing.

Me-Rah chattered something else even faster.

'And they have many servants? What kind of servants?'

Even Ben could tell that Me-Rah was enumerating many different creatures. Twigleg didn't go to the trouble of translating the entire list. It sounded as if Me-Rah's whole island was in the service of the griffins!

'Master,' he said in a voice he had difficulty in controlling, 'I think it's about time we weighed up the ratio of risks to advantages on this expedition!'

'My dear Twigleg, we only have to let the griffins know we come with peaceful intentions!' Barnabas reassured the homunculus. 'As you've heard, they do business with poachers. So why not with us?'

Twigleg thought this line of argument as unconvincing as Ben's, but he stopped himself reminding them of the poachers who had been eaten.

'All this is extraordinarily helpful, Me-Rah!' said Barnabas. 'I'm so glad you've already said you're prepared to

help us! Could you maybe look at our map and say which of the islands drawn on it is most like the shape of your own home?'

In some confusion, the parrot looked at the patches of green that Gilbert Greytail had painted on the apparently endless surface of the sea surrounding the islands of Indonesia. Finally she pecked the largest of them.

'So there we are!' cried Barnabas, but he fell silent when Me-Rah pecked five more islands. She obviously thought that Gilbert's cartography was edible.

'Well, I suppose that would have been rather too easy!' murmured Barnabas, making a brave effort to hide his disappointment. 'Maybe there's another way to approach it. Judging by the fruits and animals that Me-Rah has described, our destination must be in the north-eastern climatic zone of Indonesia. So let's begin here.' And he put his finger on the most eastern island that Gilbert had drawn. 'And then we'll reconnoitre all the uninhabited islands within a radius of fifty miles. If that doesn't bring any results, we'll extend our search to a radius of a hundred miles, and so on and so on . . .'

He was trying hard to sound optimistic, but it wasn't difficult to see that he was worried. That morning, they had finally been in touch with Vita and Guinevere, and had heard that keeping the eggs warm presented no problems, but Ànemos still wasn't eating.

Ben looked down at the endless sea over which they had been flying for hours, and tried to think only of the Pegasi. He summoned up his memory of the despair in the eyes of Ànemos, and took the photo of the eggs that Guinevere had given him out of his pocket, but all he saw in his mind's eye was the dragon. His heart was still so heavy with longing for Firedrake that it wouldn't have surprised Ben if the weight of it had brought

Hothbrodd's plane down. What was a dragon rider without his dragon?

He sighed, sensing Twigleg's sympathetic look turned on him. As usual when they were flying, the homunculus was sitting on Ben's knee, with a belt around his stick-thin body and attached to Ben's own seat belt – not the safest of methods. In turbulence, Ben had often had to pluck Twigleg down from the air, but the homunculus preferred to be close to his master so high above the ground, although Hothbrodd had made him a seat specially for someone his own size.

'You'll soon be seeing Firedrake again, master!' he said encouragingly.

Ben could hide his troubles even from Barnabas more easily than from the homunculus. Barnabas had so many things to worry about, but Twigleg had made Ben the centre of his world, and shared every one of his feelings and anxieties. Ben would very much have liked to tell him about his decision to join the dragon when this mission was over, but it would have felt like treachery to share his plan with the homunculus and not Barnabas.

As usual, Twigleg had his notebook with him, and he had written down everything Me-Rah said about her island. It was impossible for human tongues to pronounce the name that the chattering lory gave it, but she also knew its human name: Pulau Bulu, the Feathered Island. Twigleg had noted, *No active volcano!,* adding several more exclamation marks. In the course of his research, he had found out that volcanic eruptions were as common in Indonesia as the Northern Lights in Norway.

'Right. If I've translated Me-Rah's descriptions correctly, there are orchid trees and umbrella trees on her island, teak and golden rain, elephant apples, melati, orchids, and the carnivorous

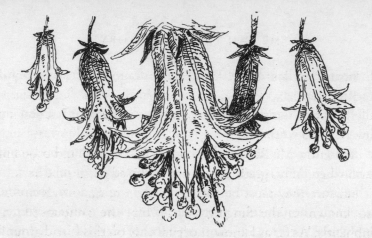

Rafflesia arnoldii, or corpse flower.' The homunculus lowered his pen. 'That means we can already rule out several groups of islands.' He looked enquiringly at the parrot. 'Can you describe any other plants that grow on Pulau Bulu? The rarer the better!'

Me-Rah cleaned her red breast feathers. She already looked less rumpled than before. Barnabas had fed her crushed oyster shells, and given her a dish of water to bathe in, even though Hothbrodd had told him disapprovingly that water was not a good idea on board an aircraft.

'Did I mention the Singing Flowers?' Me-Rah plucked a feather that always insisted on sticking out at an angle away from her wing.

Barnabas raised his head.

'The seeds are as large as nuts, and they taste as sweet as coconut flesh, but you have to get right into the cup of the flower to eat them,' the parrot went on. 'That can be difficult, because the scent of a Singing Flower can make you unconscious within seconds, and if you don't get out again quickly enough, the flower will close and digest you, feathers and bones and all.'

Shuddering, Me-Rah fluffed herself up, but Barnabas let out such a cry of delight that Hothbrodd looped the loop in alarm, and Me-Rah flew down under the seat.

'Excuse my loss of self-control, honoured and ever-helpful Me-Rah.' Barnabas knelt down between the seats and remorsefully held out the palm of his hand to the parrot. 'But singing flowers! This is fantastic!'

Hesitantly, Me-Rah climbed up on his hand – and cooed in alarm when, in his gratitude, Barnabas kissed her on the beak.

'I'm sure they must be the extremely rare *Lupina cantanda*, also known as the Singing Plant-Wolf!' he announced triumphantly. 'As far as I know, it occurs only on this island group!'

Barnabas leaned over Gilbert's map, which was lying on the seat beside Ben, and tapped a few tiny long green marks.

'Per-hi-a-san,' read Twigleg. 'That means jewellery in Indonesian!'

'A good name,' said Ben. 'The islands really do look like a pearl necklace.'

For the first time since the bad news from Greece had arrived, Barnabas was looking really happy.

'Hothbrodd! Lola!' he cried. 'Now we know where we're going!'

CHAPTER SEVENTEEN

A Thousand Times One Thousand Islands

*I just wish the world was twice as big
and half of it was still unexplored.*
Sir David Attenborough

Me-Rah's native land did indeed deserve to be described as a thousand times one thousand islands. Even for Twigleg, who had seen so much in his long life, the sight of the Indonesian archipelago turning into a mosaic of water and land below them was unforgettable. A thousand times one thousand islands, a thousand times one thousand worlds . . . some of them were so large that you could hardly call them islands at all, with cities on them that, from a height, looked like algae growing vigorously. But there were also islands with villages where the houses were built of bamboo and palm leaves, and they seemed to come from older, less turbulent times. Others rose from the blue-green water like the humps on a sea serpent's back, or had huts and tea plantations dotted about on them. Ben was as fascinated as Twigleg by what they saw. Cone-shaped volcanic peaks cast their shadows on bays such as he had dreamed of when he still wanted to be a pirate. Their beaches were covered with the tracks of turtles, and their white sand bordered jungle in which, so Twigleg told him, tigers, rhinoceroses, orang-utans and red pandas lived.

'So different from the world that we come from, isn't it?' said Barnabas. 'And yet it's on the same planet. Incredible!'

It was late afternoon when they reached the island group where Barnabas thought that Me-Rah's home must lie. Hothbrodd flew so low that the fuselage of the plane almost touched the treetops, but Me-Rah only shook her head at the first three islands and uttered a disappointed squawk. The longing glance with which she searched for her home reminded Ben of his own broken heart. What place did he love in the same way? MÍMAMEIÐR, no doubt of that, but it didn't change his yearning for Firedrake. What an infuriatingly complicated thing the heart was!

'You look sad. Is there anything you want to talk about?' Barnabas held out the box of cookies that he brought on every journey: walnut and chocolate.

'No, I'm okay.' Ben just couldn't bring himself to tell Barnabas what he had decided. He felt like a traitor, and Barnabas did not insist, as usual when he sensed that one of his children wasn't being perfectly straightforward with an answer. Vita and he left them time to work out their own thoughts. Ben couldn't have said how many times he had been grateful for that.

Lola was standing on the map, ticking off the islands they had already flown over with a pen. Gilbert would probably have bitten off one of her ears for that. Barnabas looked at the part of the map that they would not be exploring.

'What a pity,' he murmured. 'I'm afraid Me-Rah's home is on an island where there are no orang-utans! They're such an impressive species. As endangered as dragons and Pegasi, sad to say. And not half as good at hiding!'

Orang-utans, elephants, puffer fish, armadillos, tree-frogs and lemurs – to Ben, by now, every animal was a fabulous creature, and he often wished for magic he could use to protect them all. But for now he had to content himself with taking an abducted chattering lory home and rescuing a few winged horses. Better than nothing.

They flew over another island on which the Singing Flowers opened their deadly blooms, but even from a distance they could see that it was too small to match Me-Rah's description, and the parrot chattered in disappointment again. Dusk was already coming on, but Hothbrodd assured Barnabas that they could still fly to two more islands before they had to find a place to come down for the night. Me-Rah had flown from her perch to the back of his pilot's seat and kept chattering into his green ear, which annoyed the troll very much.

'Rat!' he called back, shooing Me-Rah over to Lola's empty seat. 'Come and take the controls! I can read Gilbert's map as well as you can. And I certainly know how to bring this plane down better than you! After all, it needs more space than your crow-sized aircraft!'

'Oh, really?' Lola called back. 'You don't say so! How kind of you to remind me!'

Then, giggling, she bent over Gilbert's map again. 'You wait and see!' she whispered to Barnabas. 'That troll will bite Me-Rah's head off before we've found the right island! A parrot pilot! Of all your crazy ideas this was certainly the craziest. I admit parrots are very entertaining, and they know a lot about upwinds and downwinds, but they get into such a panic! It's a wonder all that fluttering and squawking hasn't ditched us in the sea yet!'

As if to confirm it, such a penetrating whistle came from the cockpit that even Barnabas put his hands over his ears. The whistle was followed by a torrent of shrill parrot language and a very uncivilised troll curse.

'What's that dratted bird saying, Twigleg?' asked Hothbrodd crossly, as Ben and the homunculus ran to the cabin.

'She says she can see her island!' Twigleg could barely make his thin manikin-voice heard above the noise that Me-Rah was making.

'Which one is it?' roared Hothbrodd. 'Which one, bird?'

Me-Rah settled on the troll's head and went on screeching. The plane swerved alarmingly as Hothbrodd tried to take the parrot out of his hair, and in return Me-Rah dug her beak into his bark-like fingers.

'*Hvilken øy?* Which one? *Stille tie, latterlig fugl!*' he shouted as he steered the plane with one hand and held on to the screeching parrot with the other. Exhausted, Me-Rah fell silent, and took her beak out of the troll's hard skin. Then she chattered

something that sounded as if she were both insulted and very excited.

'She says it's the island to the east of us,' Twigleg quickly translated.

Hothbrodd let Me-Rah fly to her perch – after he had wiped white droppings off his instruments, with another curse – and turned the plane to the east.

Me-Rah cooed and croaked like clockwork gone wrong, and craned her neck as if she wanted to fly through the windscreen of the cockpit. Ben offered her a piece of mango. He had found that mango calmed her down.

'What's she saying now, Twigleg?' Barnabas asked. In all the excitement, Me-Rah seemed to have forgotten her English.

'She says she's quite sure,' translated Twigleg, as Me-Rah went on chattering breathlessly. 'And she suggests landing in a bay on the southern shore. Although its name doesn't sound very inviting!'

'Why? What's it called?' asked Ben.

'The Bay of Skulls.'

Hothbrodd muttered something about Odin's ravens and his own opinion of the advice of birds in general. But when the island lay beneath them, he steered towards its southern shore as Me-Rah had advised.

Pulau Bulu was considerably larger than Ben had expected. Beyond hills covered with dense jungle, the outline of high mountains stood out against the sunset sky. As Me-Rah had said, there was no sign of any human settlements.

Ben exchanged a glance with Barnabas. 'Let's just hope that Me-Rah's lion-birds really are griffins!' he whispered.

And that they didn't get eaten before they'd even had a chance to ask about the feather, Ben thought.

CHAPTER EIGHTEEN

Pulau Bulu

*The important thing about having lots of things to
remember is that you've got to go somewhere afterwards
where you can remember them, you see? You've got to stop.
You haven't really been anywhere until you've got back home.*
Terry Pratchett, *The Light Fantastic*

Even in the gathering twilight, the ripples on the surface of
the sea where Hothbrodd landed shone like dull green glass.
   Lola examined the wide bay ahead of them through her binoculars. Twigleg envied her very much for possessing those. Lola's
youngest sister, Vera Mae Greytail, had made them. Vera Mae's
optical instruments could compete with any made by human
hands, and yet fitted easily into a rat's paw (or the hand of a
homunculus). There was hardly any craft or trade that wasn't practised by one of Lola's countless relations. Barnabas thought that
was because Lola's ancestors included fabulous beings such as the
Singing Rat of Holstein, the Ship's Compass Rat and the Ratbird.

'Nothing alarming to be seen, humpelcuss,' she announced. 'Only a few crabs and turtles. Noticeably large turtles,' she added, handing Twigleg the binoculars.

What the homunculus saw through them reminded him strongly of Robert Louis Stevenson's *Treasure Island,* one of his and Ben's favourite books. (Not that Twigleg had ever felt any wish to experience the adventures described in it for himself!) The beach, which had large rocks scattered over it, was on the outskirts of a jungle so wild and impenetrable that it seemed to Twigleg the perfect hideout for a few savage cannibal tribes. Maybe Me-Rah had forgotten to mention those because she didn't consider them human beings?

At the sight of the deserted beach Ben, of course, also thought of *Treasure Island* and buried pirate treasure. Unlike Twigleg, however, he could hardly wait to set foot on the untouched sand. Even Hothbrodd, who had carved several reindeer and wolves since they set out because he missed MÍMAMEIÐR, grunted with delight when he saw the huge trees casting their shade over the beach.

Lola had already gone off on her first reconnaissance flight in her tiny propeller-driven plane (which had survived the flight from Norway intact in a baggage compartment), while Hothbrodd was still anchoring his own aircraft among the rocks. Before taking off, of course, the rat had been unable to refrain from telling Twigleg that the inhabitants of nearby Papua New Guinea were notorious headhunters.

'My dear Twigleg,' said Barnabas, as the homunculus hid behind Ben's legs in alarm, 'I don't think we need feel worried about our heads. You heard what Me-Rah said: the only hunters who venture to come to this island are after birds and monkeys. Although, of course, we should still be on our guard.'

The sun was sinking behind the mountains that Ben had already admired from the air, casting a shade of pink mother-of-pearl over the beach. The outline of the island became black, like a silhouette, against the sunset sky, and from the trees a chorus of nocturnal voices such as Ben had never heard before echoed over the beach. He couldn't have said whether the cries were those of birds, toads or mammals.

Ben had expected Me-Rah to set off at once in search of her own flock of parrots, but when he was helping Hothbrodd to unload their provisions he saw her sitting on one of the crates on the beach.

'You can fly home now, Me-Rah!' he told her. 'You've been a wonderful guide. Thank you very much.'

But Me-Rah only shook her head in astonishment, and explained that no parrot in full possession of its wits would fly in the dark. 'There are many robbers on my island, still-growing Greenbloom,' she squawked. 'And I warn you, some of them would like to eat you too. Only that wooden-skinned person is safe,' she added, glancing at Hothbrodd's bark-like skin. 'Presumably.'

'That's nice to know,' Hothbrodd grunted. He seemed to take Me-Rah's remark as a compliment.

'How about rats?' Lola landed her plane on a rock so that no sand would get into the propeller. 'I bet a lot of the inhabitants of this island would like the taste of rat. But,' she said, taking off her leather flying helmet, 'they'd all better steer clear of this one!'

Ben had never met any other creature as fond of adventures as Lola Greytail. Every patch on her well-worn flying suit bore witness to one of those adventures, and Lola did not, like Me-Rah, feel at home in only one place. There were many places that she liked, and she was really at home only in her plane.

'I'm afraid that on this island we must assume we're all on the menu of some beast of prey or another,' commented Barnabas as he dug a seashell out of the moist sand. His face cleared, and he smiled happily as he pressed the shell, with its red and white pattern, to his ear. 'My word! This actually is the shell of a balungan snail – and it really does sound as if a mermaid were singing inside it!' He put the shell in the box that he carried around with him for such purposes, and looked along the beach. 'Shall we camp here overnight? What do you say?'

'Not before I've shown you something else,' said Lola. 'Maybe Me-Rah can tell us more about what it means.'

The two of them flew ahead, side by side. It wasn't easy for Ben to follow them on foot without treading on a dozen crabs or other shellfish. He could have ridden comfortably on the giant turtle that crossed their path, but in spite of its impressive size it drew in its head and legs hastily as soon as it saw them – proof that the human beings it had encountered so far had not left it with pleasant memories.

The four poles in front of which Lola finally landed seemed, at first sight, to be man-made too. They stood like warning signals barely a step away from the trees, and they were so tall that even Hothbrodd had to look up at them. The troll didn't spare so much as a glance for the skulls lying in the fine sand in front of them, but the carvings that covered the poles made him exclaim in admiration.

'Not bad,' he growled as he looked up at the beaked heads on top of the poles. 'You need hands for that sort of thing, and as far as I know griffins have only claws and paws. Or am I missing something?'

Me-Rah examined the poles with obvious discomfort.

'The monkeys did it,' she squawked. 'The monkeys who serve the lion-birds.'

'Monkeys who can carve like this?' Ben incredulously ran his fingers over the artistically formed creepers winding their way up the poles.

'As you know, fabulous creatures often cause unusual behaviour,' said Barnabas. 'In men and animals alike.'

'Anyway, we're on the right island.' Twigleg pointed to the ears of the carved heads of birds of prey above them.

Yes. Without a shadow of doubt, Me-Rah's lion-birds were griffins.

Ben was investigating one of the skulls at his feet. 'Human skulls,' he stated.

Barnabas looked at the trees. Night was falling under them. 'Me-Rah, are you sure this bay is a good place to spend the night?'

'Oh yes,' said the parrot. 'There are poles like this in all the bays on the island. They're a warning to poachers that it's better not to go hunting here before they've paid the lion-birds.'

'Paid them with what?' asked Ben.

'Jewellery, coins, gold, precious stones,' said Me-Rah, rattling off a list. 'And shells.'

'Shells?' asked Ben, surprised.

'The calcium in shells strengthens beaks, still-growing

Greenbloom,' replied Me-Rah. 'And there is a shell in these waters that makes beaks as hard and sharp-edged as metal.'

Ben exchanged a glance with Barnabas. A crab scuttled out of the eye socket of one of the skulls at his feet.

'Well, I hope Bağdagül's bangle will be accepted as adequate payment,' said Barnabas. 'After all, we want to keep our skulls. But now let's put up the tents.'

At first sight what Barnabas threw on the beach not far from Hothbrodd's plane was a handful of apple pips. Until the pips unrolled like woodlice, and within seconds formed round tents. Only the tiny head above the entrance of each showed that they were really living creatures. On their travels, the Greenblooms kept meeting fabulous beings who proved to be very helpful members of their expeditions. Barnabas had evacuated the tent-lice to MÍMAMEIÐR when it looked as if they would fall victim to a ski run. They had quickly settled in, and were now an invaluable part of the FREEFAB team. Tent-lice are not only warm and spacious, but also very safe, because they announce the approach of any suspect creature with a shrill whistle that could easily compete with Me-Rah's squawking.

There was room for Ben and Barnabas to fit into their tents easily; only Hothbrodd was too large for one, but no one was worried about the troll's safety. Ben had already seen Hothbrodd dispose of Prickly Sludge-Eaters and a Giant Salamander. The troll simply stationed himself on the sand to sleep with one eye closed, the other open and watching his plane. Fjord trolls are of the diurnal troll genus, and spend all their nights like that, only half asleep, unlike nocturnal trolls who sleep with both eyes tightly closed so that sunlight won't turn them to stone.

Hothbrodd's snoring soon drowned out the sound of the

waves, but Ben and Barnabas sat outside their tents for some time longer, looking at the dark jungle and the mountains rising beyond it. Yes, Me-Rah's island was very much larger than they had hoped, and in six days' time at the latest they must set off on the homeward journey. There wasn't much time, even though Lola was a brilliant scout, and Barnabas had decades of experience in finding the most cleverly hidden creatures in this world.

When Ben crawled into his tent, it looked as if Twigleg was already asleep. But the homunculus was only pretending, because he knew how quickly his master could get worried if he lay awake at night. Ben knew it was often because of the memories that filled Twigleg with fear and sadness. He felt like that particularly quickly in places that were new and strange, and tonight it seemed as if the ghosts of his lost brothers lived on Me-Rah's island. Twigleg saw their faces in his mind's eye as clearly as if they were all still alive. It had been so wonderful when they had each other. Even the cruelty of their creator and the tyranny of his golden monster had been easier to bear when they were all together, and it had felt so much less peculiar to have been born in a bottle. After all, there had been eleven others who came into the world in the same way. How they used to laugh together! And weep together. It had done them so much good to have an affectionate hug when the alchemist had performed one of his experiments on them, or Nettlebrand had been in a particularly bad mood. And they had slept side by side every night, and Twigleg had heard the breathing of eleven brothers, whereas now only the sound of Ben breathing protected him from the darkness of the world.

He couldn't even remember all their names these days! Spinner, Buzzer, Dragonfly, Waterskeeter, Bumble, Flea – no, stop it, Twigleg! Even their names won't bring them back!

The homunculus listened to the nocturnal sounds coming from the strange jungle, and thought of something that Me-Rah had said in the ruined temple, and that he had not translated for Ben. 'When you are the only one of your kind, your heart withers in your breast.'

Yes, it did. Even if it was an artificial heart, made by an alchemist who had never seen his creations as anything but experimental specimens and servants without any will of their own.

Ben didn't wake when Twigleg slipped out of the tent. Hothbrodd was still standing where he had been hours ago, and the beach was covered by tiny crabs that shone more brightly than the stars in the foreign sky above Twigleg's head. Presumably the crabs were poisonous – how else could they have survived by night, lit up so clearly?

One of them stopped in front of Twigleg and scrutinised him in astonishment, with its eyes on stalks. Twigleg knew that look only too well. It asked: *What on earth are you?*

The crab scuttled on, and the homunculus surreptitiously wiped a tear that was trickling down his sharp nose. A couple of times before, he had been on the point of looking around for someone who could make him new brothers. He had pored over so many books of alchemy looking for the method that had brought him to life, but in vain! Sometimes he dreamed of going back to the castle where his creator's laboratory had once stood. But that castle was an accursed place, and Twigleg had spent so many unhappy years there that he wouldn't have ventured to set foot in it again without Ben. And how could he take his master to such a place? Quite apart from the fact that he didn't even know exactly where the castle stood! He had almost never left it.

A few months ago, he had actually felt bold enough to ask Ben's teacher, Professor Spotiswode, whether he could imagine making a homunculus some day. James Spotiswode had often asked him about his origins and his creator, and for a moment Twigleg had seen a spark of temptation behind the thick lenses of the teacher's glasses. But then he had to listen to a lecture about the dubious nature of such experiments, and Spotiswode had reminded him, in all seriousness, of the story of Frankenstein's creation. As if you could compare a homunculus to a monster stitched together from body parts!

But there the problem was again. None of them knew what he was. He hardly knew himself, after all. He couldn't even say from what creature his maker had stolen the spark of life to get him breathing!

Oh, Twigleg! He wiped another tear off the tip of his nose, and told himself off, as he so often did, for his selfishness. Who shed tears over his own fate when all his thoughts should be on the rescue of the three Pegasus foals?

A shell splintering under someone's tread made him spin around. He was expecting to see a homunculus-eating crab or a turtle with similar appetites, but it was Ben kneeling down behind him.

'How long have you been awake?' Ben stretched out on the sand beside Twigleg and propped his chin on his hand, so that they were on eye-level with each other.

He loved the boy so much – so very much! Why was he worried about his own heart? That love would protect it, even if it was sure to break sometime. Every homunculus died with the human being on whom its heart was set. Love was a dangerous thing, especially for Twigleg's kind.

Ben picked a sand flea out of his hair. 'Lola says you asked Professor Spotiswode if he fancied making a homunculus?'

That rat aviator stuck her pointy nose into everything!

'Lola Greytail!' Twigleg spat her name into the night air as if it were a medieval curse, intended to bring plague into the world. 'I just hope she'll suppress her curiosity one of these days! Or maybe someone could cut off her grey ears for eavesdropping on things that are none of her business!'

'That's exactly what makes her our best scout.' Ben let one of the glowing crabs run over his hand. Maybe they weren't poisonous after all. The tiny legs left only a shimmering trail on Ben's skin. 'Sometime we'll find another homunculus. I'm sure we will.'

Ben meant well, but Twigleg could tell from his voice that his heart wasn't really in what he said. He had something else on his mind.

'Twigleg?' Ben dug his fingers into the fine sand. 'What . . . this is a purely hypothetical question . . . what would you do if I moved to the Rim of Heaven one day?'

Hypothetical? In Twigleg's experience, that was the way human beings described things that they were seriously considering.

'What a question! I'd go with you.'

'Good!' There was no mistaking the relief in Ben's voice. 'And like I said, it's only a hypothetical question.'

'Of course, master.' Twigleg gave him a knowing smile. 'Can I say something else that's purely hypothetical? It's horrible being the only one of your kind around. *Horrible.* And there aren't any human beings at the Rim of Heaven.'

Ben rolled over on his back. One of the constellations in the sky above them was Pegasus.

'Yes, yes, I know,' he murmured. And sat up abruptly when a hoarse, long-drawn-out cry came from the forest. Ben had only once heard a similar sound: when he had mixed the voices of an eagle and a lion on his computer in

MÍMAMEIÐR.

'Did you hear that, Twigleg?' he whispered to the homunculus. 'Inua did a pretty good imitation, if you ask me! At least we know we're on the right island.'

CHAPTER NINETEEN

Raskervint

Man is a centaur, a tangle of flesh and
mind, divine inspiration and dust.
Primo Levi, *The Periodic Table*

The fifth day since the arrival of the Pegasus eggs at MÍMAMEIÐR was dawning, and Guinevere was just coming out of the house to go over to the stable when she heard hoofbeats behind her. She turned, expecting to see Ànemos, weary after another sleepless night. But the figure coming out of the trees was both horse and woman, and pale grey as the mist drifting up from the fjord. Until that morning, Guinevere had to admit, she had always imagined centaurs as male, but Tyra Raskervint changed that for ever. Her grey hair was the same colour as her horse-tail, and so long and bushy that it was like a mane. The sweater she wore over her torso was woven from grass, and around her waist, where human skin and horse's coat met, she wore an amber belt.

'Ah,' she said, in a voice that sounded like the wind blowing through tall grass. 'I think you must be Guinevere, Vita's daughter, right? Can you tell your mother that Raskervint is here?'

But Vita was already standing in the doorway. The sight of the centaur removed the anxiety of the last few days from her face. Vita and Raskervint had first met over twenty years ago, by the shore of a cold, grey sea, and they had been through many adventures together, long before Vita had met Barnabas or Guinevere had been born.

'I see you've already met my daughter!' she said after embracing Raskervint. 'How are your own children?'

Raskervint smiled, and shrugged her shoulders. 'You know us centaurs,' she replied. 'Only the wind knows. We're now here, now there, restless as the clouds, and even my great-grandchildren went their own way long ago.'

The centaur seemed as ageless as the Pegasus. There was knowledge in her eyes that no human life could understand. Raskervint looked as if she had lived for a long time already and would live on for ever, although Guinevere knew that even

fabulous beings were not immortal.

'I am very glad to meet you, Guinevere Vitasdaughter,' said the centaur. 'It's wonderful to know someone still so young. I was no longer young myself when the Vikings set out plundering from here! But I hear that you have a guest who can remember even older times?'

Ànemos was standing, as he did so often, on the bank of the fjord, where the water horses were coming up from the water to greet the day, as usual in the morning. The mist-ravens had told Vita that one of their mares reminded Ànemos of his lost companion, but when the water horses saw the centaur they went down again to the depths where they lived, and the Pegasus turned around as if awoken from a dream.

Raskervint had been speaking Norwegian to Vita and Guinevere, but when the centaur approached the Pegasus she used sounds that were more like the whinnying of a horse than human words.

Ànemos pricked up his copper-coloured ears and replied in

the same way.

'Come along!' Vita whispered to Guinevere. 'We should leave them alone. Raskervint herself lost a companion years ago. She will understand the pain that Ànemos is feeling, and maybe she can tell us how to help him better. Meanwhile you and I will go and see to the eggs.'

Two swans were keeping the nest warm that morning. They rose with some reluctance when Guinevere went over to take the temperature of the shells. By now all the inhabitants of MÍMAMEIÐR felt an almost parental responsibility for the three unhatched foals. Maybe they were also trying to make up for the way their father avoided the stable.

The eggs were as warm as if you could feel the life that they protected, and when Guinevere tucked the largest egg back under the white breast of one of the female swans, she thought for a moment that she could feel a scraping inside it, like the movement of tiny hooves. How she longed to catch a glimpse of the foals! But the shells were still like polished silver, hiding what they protected.

Vita fed the swans with water-grass and fresh grain, while Guinevere went over to the calendar on the stable door. Her heart beat a little faster as she wrote the result of the temperature she had taken in a new box, and she caught herself counting the number of days still to go, although she knew exactly how many there were.

She had heard from Ben that a parrot had guided him and Barnabas to an island where they thought that griffins lived. But the line had been so bad that she'd had to make sense of a few fragmentary words. They'll make it! Guinevere kept repeating that to herself. They'll get the feather, the eggs will grow, and soon three tiny foals will be flying over the meadows out there.

She just had to believe that firmly enough and it would come true.

The mist-ravens were making their report to her and Vita (a weasel among the Tummetott houses, an owl attacking a swamp-impet child), when Raskervint came back from the fjord. Ànemos was not with her.

'I don't know that I've been much help, Vita,' said the centaur. 'I remember the pain that he is feeling. Only my children were able to dispel the black cloud in which in which he is shrouded now. If you want to help Ànemos, you must save those foals! You're right, he dares not love them because he thinks he is going to lose them too . . . He says Barnabas has gone in search of a phoenix feather? But how will that help? I know of only one feather that will make things grow, and that's the feather of a griffin.'

Guinevere instinctively looked around in concern, but the Pegasus was nowhere to be seen.

'Barnabas is in fact looking for a griffin's feather,' said Vita, lowering her voice. 'We lied to Ànemos so that he wouldn't guess how risky the quest is and insist on going with them. I don't have to tell you what griffins think of horses!'

'No, you certainly don't!' replied Raskervint quietly. 'But it's dangerous medicine, Vita. I admire Barnabas for his courage. And I hope the griffins are not as terrible as people say. We have many songs about them, and none of them ends well.'

And none of them ends well. Raskervint's words followed Guinevere all that day, and kept her lying awake for a long time in the evening. Twigleg had once told her that he used to be able to speak to his old master even over great distances, when Nettlebrand appeared to him in the water of rivers or lakes. Guinevere wished she had as easy a way of communicating with Ben. But when she tried to get through to him after what Raskervint had said, she was answered only by a rushing noise, like the sound of the distant ocean that she had seen on Gilbert's map.

No, it really wasn't easy to be the one left waiting at home.

CHAPTER TWENTY

All We Could Wish For

*Don't walk behind me; I may not lead. Don't walk in front of me;
I may not follow. Just walk beside me and be my friend.*
Albert Camus

Dragons fly in their dreams. But for the last few nights, when Firedrake was dreaming, his wings were made of iron. They weighed him down to the ground, and hard as he tried he could not raise them.

It wasn't difficult for Firedrake to interpret this dream. He missed the boy. But he couldn't fly away to see him, because he was needed by the others. Not just Maia, for whom he was collecting moon-moss and fire-lichen in the surrounding mountains so that she would be strong enough to sit on the nest all those months, or the two young dragons now growing in their dull blue eggshells, kept warm by their mother. No, they all needed him: the dragons he had brought here from Scotland, as well as those woken from their moonless sleep by the stone-dwarves here in the valley of the Rim of Heaven. It had been possible to save them all: twenty-three dragons who had hidden away in their cave, afraid, for so long that in the end they were surrounded by a layer of stone.

By now over fifty of them were living in the Rim of Heaven – in the same caves where, if the old stories were to be believed, the first dragons of all had been born. Firedrake had never appointed himself their leader, but without a word that was what the others had made him. They came to consult him about everything: Firedrake, the brownies aren't finding enough mushrooms; Firedrake, the stone-dwarves are driving their tunnels too far into the cave walls; Firedrake, Moonscale has been arguing with Beowulf again.

No, he really didn't want to be the leader of anyone or anything. It was quite enough having to put up with Sorrel's bad temper because she couldn't find her favourite mushrooms in the Rim of Heaven. Firedrake hoped fervently that the arrival of young dragons would make her less homesick, and then this valley would be home for Sorrel too, because he had no intention of leaving it again. Firedrake had never loved any other place as much. The mountains that surrounded and protected them had a thousand tales to tell. The sky seemed so much wider, and there was no more hide and seek, no life lived only by night, like the life he had led in Scotland. Since their arrival a human being had twice wandered into this valley, but the humans who lived in these mountains were different. They bowed if they saw one of the dragons – and they went away again, just as they bowed to the mountains and were disconcerted by the foreigners who came to climb their stony sides and feel like conquerors of the peaks.

No, Firedrake really did not want to leave the Rim of Heaven. Luckily Maia felt just the same. They both wanted to teach their children to fly over the slopes where dragon-flowers grew, and see them growing up free, without the fear of the world that Firedrake had known in his youth. If only he didn't miss Ben so much . . . sometimes that made him so melancholy that even when he was awake, his wings felt like iron.

Maia raised her head from the edge of the nest.

'Did you hear that, Firedrake?'

She touched one of the eggs that she was keeping warm under her body. Yes, Firedrake did hear it! A soft tapping sound, barely audible even by dragon ears.

He looked anxiously at Maia. 'It's too soon!'

She gave the soft growl that showed something amused her very much. 'The shell is still so thick that they couldn't get out even if they tried. And how stupid do you think our children are?'

The eyes that looked mockingly at Firedrake were golden like his, but Maia's eyes were rimmed by tiny copper-coloured scales that made them look larger. And her eyelashes were dark green, like the needles of the spruce trees that grew outside the cave. Firedrake fervently hoped that their children would inherit Maia's eyes.

'You know they take almost twelve weeks to hatch,' she said. 'And Ben is only a day's flight away. You ought to take advantage of the opportunity.'

Firedrake bowed his head. He was ashamed of the nostalgia that he felt. Everything that he had ever wanted was here.

No, *more* than he had ever wanted.

'We never have all we want, Firedrake,' said Maia softly. 'I dream of flying south, on and on, to places I have never seen before. Or to the moon!'

'The moon?'

'Yes, why not? There are stories of dragons who flew there.'

'Right, then we'll do it when we first take the children out flying!'

Outside, the sun was setting. Three other pairs of dragons shared the cave where Firedrake and Maia had built their nest. By now more than twenty caves in the surrounding mountains were inhabited. The eighteen stone-dwarves who, like the thirty-four brownies who had come from Scotland with them, lived in some of those caves. Ten more dwarves from the nearby mountains had joined them in the course of time. Those dwarves had six arms each, like the local brownies, more and more of whom were moving from the Tian Shan mountains to live in the valley of the Rim of Heaven with the dragons, as they used to do. There was more than enough space and food in the valley for them all – even if the Scottish dwarves were always quarrelling with the Nepalese dwarves, because they were envious of the six arms that meant they could swing several pickaxes at once. It speeded up their search for gold and precious stones a good deal.

Yes. Firedrake came out of the cave and breathed in the cool mountain air. His place was here. Ben didn't need him; Barnabas looked after him so well.

All the same, he couldn't get Maia's words out of his head. *The boy is only a day's flight away. You ought to take advantage of the opportunity.*

No.

No, Firedrake.

He spread his wings and rose into the clear, cold evening air. The lichens that Maia needed flowered on the other side of the lake – the lake over which he had flown long ago, with Ben on his back.

Only a day's flight away . . .

CHAPTER TWENTY-ONE

In The Jungle

*'What is this,' said the leopard, 'that is so 'sclusively
dark, and yet so full of little pieces of light?'*
Rudyard Kipling, *Just So Stories*

The screech with which Me-Rah welcomed the rising sun
woke Ben from his restless sleep. He had been dreaming of
Firedrake. Of course. In his dream, he had summoned him with
the scale, and they had flown together over the thousand times
one thousand islands. The dream had felt so real that before Ben
crawled out of his tent he instinctively reached for the locket
with the scale inside it. Barnabas had given him the locket when
he showed him the scale. 'You'd better not carry that present
around in your jeans pocket,' he had said, taking the tarnished
silver locket out of his backpack. The head of a unicorn was
moulded inside the lid. 'I once bought it from a silversmith to
remind me of all that we've lost already,' Barnabas had said. 'But
it's time it had a less tragic purpose.'

The locket was just large enough to take the dragon's scale, and the clasp closed with a reassuring snap. Ben had not touched Firedrake's present itself again, for fear that it would make the dragon sense his longing to see him. Now that he and Twigleg had heard those screeches in the night, the danger that the griffins represented seemed much more real, and Ben was glad that Firedrake was far away, in safety – although he kept catching himself closing his hand around the locket.

Hothbrodd was lashing his plane down with another rope when Ben crawled out of the tent-louse. The troll had used one of the griffins' poles to help him, ramming it between the rocks.

'By Odin's ravens, I hope the griffins don't take that as a challenge!' murmured Barnabas, as he let the tent-lice scurry back into their box. 'Trolls aren't the most sensitive beings on this planet.'

'But they have very good hearing, Barnabas!' called Hothbrodd, throwing the crabs that had settled on his green skin overnight back into the sea.

Lola was refuelling her plane on the beach, and as usual the troll was winding her up by saying that her tiny aircraft consumed higher-proof fuel than his own plane. The arguments between the two of them were getting more imaginative and extensive every day, as if every insult that they exchanged consolidated the friendship that linked them.

Ben had stowed provisions and tools in their backpacks the evening before. Hothbrodd's was larger and heavier than a fridge, but the troll slung it over his shoulder as if it hardly weighed any more than Twigleg. Ben was very glad to have Hothbrodd with them, even if it was confirmed, yet again, that trolls interfered seriously with reception on mobile phones and by radio. On the other hand, the jungle waiting for them had no power sockets anyway, and it was a fact that Hothbrodd wasn't the only reason why their mobile phones hadn't been able to send messages for days now. They had sent their latest news through to MÍMAMEIÐR over the transmitter on the plane.

Lola had suggested that she could spend another day investigating the island from the air before the others set out to explore it on land. But the thought of the Pegasus eggs made Barnabas forget his usual caution. His idea was to venture on a preliminary expedition with Hothbrodd, while Ben and Twigleg stayed with the plane, trying to get in touch with Vita and Guinevere, but Ben replied only that he hadn't flown from Norway to Indonesia just to sit on a beach getting worked up over the lack of radio reception.

Twigleg ventured to interrupt them. 'There are forty-seven species of Indonesian snake whose venom can be fatal to human beings, master!' he said. 'Maybe you ought at least to sit on Hothbrodd's shoulders!'

'Heavens above, this is my first time ever on a desert island!' cried Ben. 'And I'm a dragon rider! I'm not going to have myself carried around by a troll!'

Hothbrodd wrinkled his bark-like brow as if he wasn't sure whether to take that as an insult. 'This troll will soon be nothing but a green puddle anyway!' he grumbled, with glance of disapproval at the sun, burning down fiercely even at this early hour. 'I'm surprised the parrots hereabouts don't fall from the air ready-cooked, like a shower of roast chicken.'

To Me-Rah, at least, that did sound like an insult. She announced, with a shrill squawk, that the weather on Pulau Bulu was perfect, and favoured Hothbrodd with a curse in Trollish –

very impressive evidence that chattering lories really are past masters at imitating other people's voices.

'Right, you come with us, then,' Barnabas told Ben, 'and I apologise for my paternal anxiety. One of these days you'll understand. But Twigleg ought to go with Lola in her plane. It's nice of him to worry about our safety, but I'm sure there must be over four hundred species of snake on this island that can kill people of his size.'

In any other place, the mere idea of getting into Lola's plane would have brought Twigleg's pale forehead out in a sweat of fear. The memory of his last flight with her still made his heart beat faster, although it had been over two years ago. But in this case, it really did seem the more tempting prospect – even though, as usual, he hated to be separated from Ben.

They had all been expecting Me-Rah to say a last goodbye as soon as it was light, but when Lola imperiously waved Twigleg over to her plane, the parrot settled on Ben's shoulder without any comment.

'My dear Me-Rah,' said Barnabas as their feathered guide told them, courageously keeping her voice under control, that she wanted to help them in their search for the griffins, 'my dear Me-Rah, we can't possibly accept your generous offer! You've done more than enough for us. But it would be extremely helpful if you could tell us once more exactly where you think the griffins may be nesting.'

Me-Rah could not conceal her relief. She advised Barnabas to search the mountains rising beyond the treetops to the southwest. Then, by way of farewell, she flew three times in a circle around each of them, and disappeared into the dense growth of trees along the beach. It swallowed Me-Rah up as the sea swallows up a fish, and Ben wondered whether that was just what a forest meant to a bird while he followed Barnabas in under the trees: a sea of leaves and branches in which she moved as naturally as fish move in the salty waves of the sea.

To Ben, on the other hand, it was like entering another world when, after the bright sunlight, shadows suddenly cast chequered patterns on his clothes. The hot air was humid and moist, like the hothouses in the zoo where tropical lizards dreamed of the heat in their native lands, and when he looked up he saw not one but a dozen canopies of leaves: it was a multi-storied structure of branches, creepers, flowers and foliage, and made you doubt that anything like sky existed. Guinevere would probably have been able to name any flower that added a touch of colour to the greenery. She had inherited, from her mother, a passion for everything that grew and flowered. 'Never eat anything if you don't know what it is!' she had warned Ben. 'Don't touch any leaf without gloves on, and don't trust plants that shoot their seeds into your face.'

Easier said than done. How was he to avoid touching leaves when they were all over the place? Luckily Hothbrodd trudged ahead, ploughing a path through the dense thickets that allowed them to walk on with reasonable ease. But all the same, Ben had to keep freeing himself from tendrils and thorns, or picking tiny frogs and furry caterpillars off his clothes. He had never seen

such large butterflies before, or such colourful beetles. And the monkeys! If he put his head right back, he saw them swinging from tree to tree high above him. Well, it was going rather too far to say he saw them . . . they weren't much more than shadows in the shade, a leap from one tree to the next, gone before his eyes could tell him if it was a gibbon or a macaque moving between the sky and the ground up above him.

In view of all these marvels, it was difficult to think of the dangers that came with them: the coral snake that Ben noticed only because Barnabas reached for his arm to warn him; the mottled coat of a marbled cat among the trees . . . When Ben nearly trod on a sleepy white-lipped pit viper, and Barnabas could hardly take a step without wiping spiders' webs and mosquitoes off his glasses, Hothbrodd finally put them on his shoulders after all, and Ben had to admit it was a great relief. No insects bothered Hothbrodd, maybe because his bark-like skin was too thick for any sting to get through it – or because he looked like a walking tree. Lola would certainly have added that it was on account of the fishy smell that all trolls gave off. Whatever the reason, Ben enjoyed not having to take care where he put his feet, and being able to look up undisturbed. He particularly liked the flying squirrels, and he had never seen so many fantastic birds, not even in the temple of Garuda. They made up for the sweat that drenched his clothes and the seasickness he felt because of the way Hothbrodd swayed as he walked, even if their whistling, croaking and screeching filled the hot air with deafening noise.

Hothbrodd wasn't interested in the birds, or the flying squirrels, or the monkeys. The troll had only a fleeting glance to spare for the gigantic, humming flowers of the Singing Plant-Wolf that had shown them the way to Pulau Bulu. Hothbrodd took an interest in only one species of living thing in this jungle: the trees. He kept stopping to whisper a few incomprehensible words in Trollish to them, or to stroke their bark affectionately, and he looked up at the enormously tall trunks with such delight that, in the end, Barnabas had to remind him gently of their quest.

Of course, the troll's presence attracted other fabulous beings. A fist-sized spider with a frog's head let itself down from a teak tree. A cat with fur that shone like molten gold made its way out of the thicket, and looked at the troll in amazement. Not even Barnabas knew all the fabulous creatures that Hothbrodd lured out of the jungle, and Ben could see how much his adopted father would have liked to talk to every one of them – although some were looking at their party in a far from friendly way. Once they saw a tiny figure on a branch that looked faintly reminiscent of Twigleg. But when Ben hastily asked Hothbrodd if he could take a closer look at it, the tiny being bared sharp fangs, and narrowed its red eyes with such hostility that Ben's hope of having found a companion for the homunculus died down as quickly as it had flared up. Of course, he knew how much Twigleg longed for someone like himself, but this creature would probably have eaten him.

In spite of Hothbrodd's long strides, it was not until

noon that they reached the foothills of the mountains where Me-Rah thought the griffins had their nesting places. The slopes were soon rising so steeply that Hothbrodd had to stop, more and more often, to lean against a tree, gasping for breath.

'By Surtr's flaming sword!' he cursed, raising his arms, which were dripping with sweat. 'Trolls aren't made for such weather, Barnabas!' he complained. 'This island is like an oven! Nifhel on earth! I just hope the rat has had better luck than us in finding the griffins!'

After another hour, during which a tropical rainstorm drenched their sweaty clothes yet again, they came to a clearing burned in the jungle by a flash of

lightning. Creepers had covered the charred tree stumps with fresh green, and for the first time since they set out, they could see the sky above them through the branches. Hothbrodd bent down to pick up a couple of snakes. Their teeth had as much difficulty as the insect stings in getting through his skin, and the troll was just throwing a particularly venomous viper into the surrounding trees when Ben heard a rustling above him.

At first he saw only the gibbon.

Then the two macaques.

And then he felt a sharp pain, and realised that Hothbrodd was swaying under him.

And all the green around him turned black.

CHAPTER TWENTY-TWO

A Mysterious Find

*You haven't seen a tree until you've
seen its shadow from the sky.*
Amelia Earhart

Twigleg soon felt sorry that his fear of snakes had made him
forget his fear of Lola's skill as a pilot. That crazy rat! Lola
took advantage of every upwind and strong gust to indulge her
fatal passion for looping the loop, climbing steeply and diving!
Twigleg had once asked her why she didn't appear in an aerobat-
ics show. 'Oh, you're such a dreamer, humpelclumpus!' was all
she said, pinching his cheek. 'Who wants to watch a rat aviatrix?
Anyway, why would I want to feature as a trained performing
animal when I can be wild and free?'

Yes, Lola was nothing if not wild and free. In all his long life,
Twigleg had regarded rats as his natural enemies. After all, to
someone of his size they were terrifying beasts of prey. In his
younger days, he had almost lost one arm to a rat bite, and he
couldn't count the number of times he had run away from them.

He'd have bet his life that he would never call a rat his friend, certainly not one who liked to loop the loop and always made out that she couldn't remember his name, because she had so much fun playing around with the word *homunculus*. But it was a fact that he had been friends with Lola Greytail for a long time now. Indeed, very good friends, even if she drove him demented with her taste for living dangerously.

As usual, the rat was singing out loud to herself while she steered a slalom course around the trees. Pirate songs, robber songs, drinking songs. Lola had an inexhaustible stock of them. After two minutes, Twigleg had already thrown up twice through the window, and couldn't wait for the moment when they would finally break through the leaf canopy and see the clear sky ahead, Suppose a liana disabled Lola's propeller, or one of the branches under which she zoomed at such breakneck speed skewered her plane along with the two of them inside it? But of course Lola was enjoying all this, and she was in no hurry to fly higher.

'Suppose we can't see the griffins' nests from up there?' she called to Twigleg when he cautiously reminded her of their mission. 'No, no, we ought to search down here some more first.' Whereupon they got caught in a gigantic spider's web, and couldn't break free until Lola roared the engine so that it sounded like a desperate bumblebee. And then they almost collided with a flying squirrel.

'By all my bare-tailed cousins, what was that?' cried Lola indignantly as she throttled back the engine, much to Twigleg's relief, and the plane finally climbed higher.

'A member of the *Sciuridae* genus,' replied Twigleg, pressing one hand to his queasy stomach. 'Not unusual in this climatic zone. Indonesia has thirty-seven known species of flying furry animals. Of course they don't really fly. The membrane under their arms—'

He stopped abruptly as Lola steered the plane into a tangle of wild orchids, just before it collided with a gibbon swinging from tree to tree by its long arms.

'This is impossible! How's a girl pilot supposed to manoeuvre in territory where squirrels and monkeys think they can fly?' said Lola angrily as she looked for a way out of the orchid roots. 'Spoilsports! I love to fly a slalom around trees . . . you know, like in that film with the spaceships and the talking bears on the strange planet.'

Twigleg hadn't the faintest idea what she was talking about. He and Lola had very different tastes in films.

'Whatever,' the rat murmured, putting the plane into such a steep climb that Twigleg thought his stomach had moved to just behind his forehead.

They were shooting up to the leaf canopy as if Lola was trying to fly to the moon. But suddenly Twigleg let out a loud shriek.

'Lola! Lola, there they are!' he cried – and bumped his head on the roof of the plane as Lola abruptly cut out the engine. A tree ahead of them spread mighty branches on which feathery, evergreen leaves grew. But it wasn't the leaves that had attracted Twigleg's attention, it was the fruits that the tree bore, round as melons but considerably larger.

Twigleg's heart was in his mouth as Lola made for the tree, but this time it wasn't just fear that made it beat so fast. He had found several descriptions of griffins' nests in the library at MÍMAMEIÐR. They all agreed that griffins had the caverns where they nested built for them by flocks of smaller birds, relations of *Furnarius rufus*, also known as the hornero or oven-bird.

As its name suggests, it builds oven-shaped nests out of mud. The oldest description – Twigleg had found it in a fifteenth-century Persian manuscript – claimed that griffins' nests were like the palaces of the Mesopotamian kings whose treasures the griffins had once guarded. When Lola approached the top nest, which clung to the trunk of the tree under a huge branch, Twigleg could see with his own eyes that the manuscript had been correct. The entry hole, as wide as a barn door, was framed by an artistic carving like the reliefs on the ruins of Persepolis. It was an incredible sight in the Indonesian rain forest. However, the relief looked unfinished, as if work on it had been abruptly interrupted.

'Wait! What . . . what are you doing?' cried the horrified Twigleg as Lola made for the entrance. 'Barnabas only asked us to find the nests! He didn't say anything about flying into them!'

'Take it easy, humpelcluss!' cried Lola, her voice competing with the noise of the engine as she pointed to the side of the nest. 'I don't think we're going to meet the masters of the house.'

She was right. Only now did Twigleg see that the nest had been wrecked. In many places, the mud walls looked as if gigantic claws had torn them apart. It didn't make sense. Why would the griffins destroy their own nests? The smaller nests, clinging to the branches and trunk of the tree lower down, had also been destroyed. Creatures in the service of the griffins had lived in those; in Mesopotamia, they had often been snakes, cats, or other birds of prey.

'All the same, I really don't think flying into one of these nests is a good idea!' shouted Twigleg.

But Lola's plane was already whirring through the gateway like a fly into the invitingly open mouth of a toad.

Brown twilight surrounded them.

The mud floor of the nest was so badly raked up by claws that Lola had to fly around it a couple of times before she found a place to land.

'Oh, mouse-droppings, they've gone!' she cursed as she jumped out of the cockpit. Lola's curses were not quite so imaginative as Sorrel's, but she enjoyed them just as much.

Hesitantly, Twigleg climbed out after her. The mud platform that occupied the middle of the nest was as badly damaged as the outer wall. A griffin's sleeping place. Twigleg shuddered as he saw the furrows raked by its claws at close quarters. Obviously the medieval accounts of the size of the griffins had not been over-estimating. Where was the treasure chamber? Twigleg went over to one of the holes in the floor, and retreated in a hurry when, looking through the broken mud, he saw the tree trunk descending to dizzying depths.

'It's not there,' he said. 'That's odd.'

'What?' Lola stepped over a dull brown feather lying on the floor. It was a wing feather, over thirty rats' tails long, and unfortunately not the kind of feather they were looking for. The griffins' sun-feathers were considerably shorter, for if the stories were accurate, they grew in the down around the creatures' necks.

'There's no treasure chamber!'

Twigleg looked around in search for one. 'All the texts I found say that griffins have a hatch right beside the place where they sleep, and the treasure chamber is under it.'

Lola wrinkled her nose scornfully. She took as little interest in treasure as the Greenblooms – and all other rational beings, she would have added.

'Now what?' asked Twigleg. 'What are we going to tell the others?'

He had to admit that he was slightly relieved. Who wanted to meet giant birds with the paws of lions? Lola did, of course.

'Not so fast, humpelklumpus!' she said. 'We know there are griffins on this island, and that's a start.'

She went to the gateway at the entrance and took the binoculars from her belt. Then she got so close to the brink of the abyss that Twigleg could have almost thrown up again on her behalf. But Lola just calmly whistled through her teeth.

'Homklopus!' She beckoned Twigleg closer and handed him the binoculars. 'Do you see that, down there on the broad branch?' She nudged him in the ribs so that he nearly fell head first into the depths. 'Right between the treetops.'

Horrified, Twigleg lowered the binoculars. 'A skeleton!'

Lola took the binoculars back and looked down through them again. 'Not just one. I can see three more. Monkey skeletons, if you ask me. And they didn't die of old age.'

She pulled the radio set out of her belt.

'Barnabas?' She pressed Receive, but only the voices of birds and rushing water came over the transmitter.

'Barnabas!' Lola tried another half a dozen times.

Then she turned abruptly and stalked back to her plane.

'Why do you think they're not answering?' called Twigleg, hurrying after her. 'Lola!'

The rat turned around. 'It's that troll interfering with reception! I did warn Barnabas, but he insisted on taking him on this mission. Let's hope the blockhead can make himself useful in some other way. I suggest we fly back to the beach and follow their trail from there. Who knows, maybe they'll be back already.'

The doubt in Lola's voice worried Twigleg badly. And there was another thing he didn't like. Okay, so Hothbrodd interfered with radio reception, but Barnabas and Ben hadn't even tried calling them. Usually at least their distorted voices could be heard.

Lola's route back to the beach took them over the crowns of the trees. Seen from above, the jungle of Pulau Bulu was a carpet of green – emerald, olive and dark green – peppered with thousands of flowers. But Twigleg hardly even glanced at the glorious sight. The wrecked nests and his master's radio silence were far too alarming.

It took them less than an hour to get back to the beach.

Hothbrodd's plane was drifting on the waves, but there was no sign of the troll, or of Barnabas and Ben.

CHAPTER TWENTY-THREE

A Tiny Wing

The birth of all things is weak and tender, and therefore
we should have our eyes intent on beginnings.
Michel de Montaigne, *Essays*

The two geese sitting on the nest this morning had the chequered blue plumage seen only in nightingale-geese. The song that they coaxed from their golden beaks was so beautiful that Guinevere stopped in the stable doorway for a few moments to hear it before going in. Sometimes they sang all night long, but when she knelt down beside the nest they cackled as disapprovingly as ordinary geese. Twigleg would probably have translated the cackling as, 'Oh no, here comes the girl with the cold fingers again!' Following that up with, 'Why all this taking of temperatures? Does the little human think we don't know how to keep a nest warm?'

'We're so grateful to you!' said Guinevere, as the geese reluctantly got off the eggs. 'And your singing is really beautiful.'

That mollified the two birds a little. Compared to wild geese, nightingale-geese are very vain. All the same, they watched Guinevere suspiciously as she bent over the nest. In the pale morning light that fell in through the stable windows, the eggs shone like fallen stars. The branches from which Hothbrodd had built the nest were reflected in their shells, and a pale blue goose-feather clung to one of them like a piece of the sky. Guinevere gently removed it from the eggshell – and withdrew her hand in such surprise that the nightingale-geese moved their heads in alarm. The shell had changed! It looked as if someone had polished it so thoroughly that in a few places the silver had worn off. In those places the shell looked like cloudy glass, and behind it – Guinevere almost stopped breathing! – behind it something was moving. She bent her head lower over the nest, although the two geese hissed their disapproval. There were marks like that on the other eggs as well! And Guinevere thought she could see a tiny wing behind one of them. Oh, how wonderful! She must tell Ànemos! Her heart was in her mouth as she straightened up and hurried out of the stable.

Ànemos was standing under the tree where the mist-ravens usually perched, receiving his instructions for the day. By now the ravens left it to the Pegasus to shoo any bears and wolves who failed to observe the peace of MÍMAMEIÐR back into the forest. They also trusted Ànemos to deal with the ever-hungry impet-eaters and shark-men who hid away in the fjord during the day, coming to MÍMAMEIÐR by night in search of easier prey. The Pegasus was already spreading his wings to set off when Guinevere came running towards him. The red of his shining plumage was as dark as if it were still tinged with the Medusa's blood.

'Ànemos!'

The Pegasus turned around.

'They're turning translucent!' Guinevere had been running so fast that she had hardly any breath left for talking. 'The eggs!' she managed to say. 'You can see the foals inside!'

Ànemos folded his wings again.

'Please!' Guinevere stammered. 'Come with me!'

For a moment she thought that he wouldn't follow her, but one of the mist-ravens came to her aid.

'You'd better go with her, Ànemos!' he croaked. 'She carries on like that only when it's important.'

The others nodded in agreement. Guinevere was very glad to hear that the ravens had such a good opinion of her.

In spite of their backing, Ànemos came towards her only hesitantly – and every step he took as he came closer to the stable was slower. But in the end he followed Guinevere through the narrow doorway.

The nightingale-geese thought it was a great nuisance having to get up again, even for the father of the foals.

Ànemos snorted as the eggs came into sight under the blue feathers. Then he stretched his neck until his nose was touching the silvery shells.

'Can you see it?' Guinevere was still afraid of addressing the Pegasus, whose sadness surrounded him like a warning.

At first he did not reply. But then he straightened up and looked at Guinevere.

'I think one of them is white,' he said, as the geese settled back on the nest with a soft humming sound. 'White like its mother.'

Guinevere nodded. She felt the tickling in her nose that said she was going to shed tears. Tears of happiness.

'I think the second is blue,' she said. 'I'm not sure about the third. Its coat is still damp with the egg white.'

The geese closed their eyes as if that was the only way they could concentrate on their important task.

Ànemos bowed his head to Guinevere. He bowed it very low.

'Thank you, human daughter,' he said. 'For the first time in weeks, my heart does not feel like a stone in my breast.'

Then he took a last look at the nest, and went to the stable door. Before going out, he stopped once again.

'Is there any news of your father?' he asked.

'Yes! They've found the island!' Guinevere replied. She did not add that she hadn't been able to get in touch with Ben since then.

Ànemos nodded. Guinevere could read his feelings in his face. The outline of that tiny wing brought him comfort and hope – but also the fear of losing what he loved again.

'My father has promised to save your children,' said Guinevere. 'And he's very good at keeping his promises.'

CHAPTER TWENTY-FOUR

Shrii

Everything is dangerous, my dear fellow.
If it wasn't so, life wouldn't be worth living.
Oscar Wilde, *An Ideal Husband*

Ben's head had hurt so badly only once in his life before. On the day when a Mokêle-Mbêmbe, a fabulous African animal that is a cross between a lizard and an elephant, had hit him across the temples with its jagged tail. This time the pain was further back and got worse when he opened his eyes. For a moment he saw everything in such a blur that he thought the figure bending over him was human. But when he saw it more clearly, Ben realised it was a monkey. Not just any monkey, but an Assam macaque, as Twigleg would have told him. Its amber eyes were inspecting him with a far from friendly expression. He was in the dim light of a hollow tree. Three small monkeys that Twigleg would have introduced to him as lorises perched in the air roots that hung from the roof of the hollow, and a gibbon and three more macaques were sitting on projections inside the trunk, looking down at Ben with hostility.

Barnabas and Hothbrodd were lying a few steps away from him, as thoroughly tied up with lianas as he was.

'I tell you they were bait!' Ben heard one of the macaques chattering. 'We never ought to have brought them here! The poachers that Kraa deals with don't often venture so far into the forest!'

'Patah is right, Shrii!' twittered a loris. 'Kraa sent them to find us! They're his spies!'

'Oh yes? Then Kraa is more stupid than I thought,' mocked the gibbon. 'That green giant is so heavy we had to haul him up here with lianas. Not to mention the way he stinks of fish!'

Ben suspected that he could understand the monkeys and the ape because Hothbrodd was with them. You understood the world and the creatures in it so much better if you had a couple of fabulous beings among your friends.

Ben thought he heard the rustle of feathers behind him, but he was tied up too tightly even to turn his head.

'Did you ever see a creature like this green giant, TerTaWa?'

Ben had never heard a voice that reminded him so much of Firedrake. There was the same power in it. And whoever it was talking, he was large!

Hothbrodd let out an angry roar and tried to break his bonds. The monkeys commented on his efforts with chattering that sounded both anxious and amused, and the macaque who had first bent over Ben was menacingly swinging a cudgel that looked thicker than its furry arm. Maybe that was the reason for Ben's headache.

'No, wait!' he cried. 'Hothbrodd is kind-hearted really, even if he doesn't look it! He's a fjord troll.'

The monkeys went on chattering to each other all at once.

'You might almost think he was related to the Whispering Trees,' said the voice behind Ben.

That voice didn't sound anxious, but curious. The other animals fell respectfully silent as the speaker stepped in among their prisoners on the clawed feet of a big cat.

None of the pictures that Ben had seen, none of the reliefs and statues did justice to the creature he saw above him now.

The griffin was bending over Hothbrodd with interest.

Shrii – wasn't that what the monkeys had called him?

He looked so much more fantastic than Ben had imagined a griffin. His tail was a blue-green snake with its tongue darting in and out, his muscular hindquarters and leonine body were marked like the coat of a marbled cat, but the feathers on his head and neck, like his wings, shimmered in all the shades of green in the jungle. Only his beak, ears and eyes were yellow as honey. In Ben's experience, birds' eyes were as cool as the eyes of reptiles. Even Me-Rah was no exception. But Shrii's eyes had almost the same warmth in them as Firedrake's dragon-gaze – although you could tell from looking at the griffin that he didn't live entirely on moonlight. Ben sensed the attentive stance of a beast of prey, and his readiness to go hunting was evident in every muscle.

'Whispering trees? Right you are!' Hothbrodd
was still struggling against the lianas binding him.
'If you don't let us go this minute, I'll tell them
to strike you down with their branches!
And believe you me, you cudgel-swing-
ing fur-faced kidnappers,' he shouted
up at the monkeys, 'there are lots of
trees who listen to trolls! Lots and
lots of trees!'

'Really?' Shrii was still examining
him, fascinated. 'I'm tempted to set
you free just so that you can prove it.'

He turned his feathered neck, and
looked at Ben and Barnabas. 'Hmhm.
This one is very young for a spy,' he commented. 'And the older human doesn't
really look like one of Kraa's poachers,
don't you agree, Patah?'

Barnabas was looking at the griffin, so
enraptured that for a moment he forgot
to speak.

'Poachers? Oh, no, no!' he finally
said. 'You could say we work for the
other side. My name is Barnabas
Greenbloom, and this is my son Ben.
The monkeys will tell you that they
found no weapons on us. We come in
pea—'

'Who said you could speak,
human?' Patah interrupted him
harshly. He was very

delicately built for a macaque, but he obviously made up for his lack of height by fearlessness. 'They all tell lies as soon as they open their mouths. You don't know them as I do, Shrii. Kupo is right. Of course they're spies. We ought to throw them into the sea. Or send them back to Kraa dead, like Daun, Manis and all the others whose bones are bleaching beneath the ruins of our nests!'

The other monkeys set up a howl of lamentation, but they stopped as soon as Patah raised his paw. It was brown as withered leaves, but the macaque's face was the colour of human skin, and there was thick, pale grey fur around his chin and cheeks, like a luxuriant beard.

'Yes, we ought to kill them!' he repeated. 'But first,' he said, lunging at Ben, 'first we ought to make them talk. I've found out how to do it from others of their kind! The more we know about Kraa's plans the better. He's not going to give up, Shrii! He'll never tolerate another griffin questioning his authority! I'll say it again, even if none of you want to hear it: we must leave this island!'

Shrii sat up very straight.

'No,' he said. 'The rest of you should go. Get yourselves to safety. But I am staying. This island is my home. I was born here. It coloured my feathers and my coat, and I would be sorry to hear it sighing and groaning under Kraa's rule.'

The monkeys were looking with as much concern at the gap through which the sounds of the jungle came in as if they feared that the griffin Kraa might have heard Shrii's challenge. Ben tried to imagine that other griffin, but his eyes were fixed with fascination on Shrii. Shrii made him forget that they were prisoners, and what they were looking for on this island. He even made Ben's longing for Firedrake a little less strong. The two of them would probably get on with each other very well.

'Yes, yes, all right, I know you won't leave,' muttered Patah. 'We'll all die here. A heap of dead heroes . . . that's what we'll be. And will the parrots, marbled cats, and gibbons that you defend thank you for it? No!' He crouched down beside Ben and pinched his cheek. 'Tell me, little human,' he whispered, 'what's your mission exactly? Are you meant to kill Shrii?'

The griffin growled softly, his snaky tail rearing up like an attacking cobra. 'Leave them alone, Patah! There's no evidence of their guilt yet.'

The macaque bared his teeth, but he moved away from Ben. 'Your soft heart will be the ruin of you, Shrii!' he growled. 'And the rest of us will die with you!'

Ben's heart missed a beat when he saw what was hanging around the macaque's neck. It was the locket that Barnabas had given him to keep Firedrake's scale safe. Had Patah opened it? And if so, would Firedrake sense that the scale had a new owner? Or would he take the monkey's feelings for Ben's?

'Patah is crazy, but he's right, Shrii,' chirped Kupo, the loris who had described them as spies. She jumped to Shrii's marbled shoulders and examined Ben with her round eyes. 'I suggest we make a cage and keep them in it as pets, which is the kind of thing they do to us. I can decorate the cage, the way you see cages in their markets. Although my carvings are very much better!' Kupo proudly inspected her delicate fingers – and suddenly leaned forward. 'Oh, what's that? It looks like a very good knife.'

The knife that Hothbrodd used for carving lay neatly lined up on a huge leaf, along with his other possessions. The ballpoint pens full of anaesthetic lay right beside it. Barnabas exchanged a glance of concern with Ben.

'It's very big!' twittered Kupo. 'But the blade! It looks as if wonderful things could be carved with it! Oh yes!'

She put her tiny hand out covetously – and jumped back in alarm as Hothbrodd furious fought against his bonds.

'The alligators,' said Patah, raising Barnabas's binoculars to his eyes and turning them on Kupo, 'the alligators down by the great waterfall –' he put down the binoculars and reached for one of the ballpoints – 'they eat everything. Monkeys, humans – and I'm sure they'd eat a green tree-giant like this one as well! And there are almost no leftovers! Shrii would never know what became of his spies.'

The others chattered in agreement. Except for the gibbon. His coat was almost black; only the fur around his face was reddish, like the skin of a deer. He hadn't taken his eyes off Barnabas all this time. Now he straightened up and tripped delicately over to him, using the hands at the ends of his long woolly arms as well as his feet. His name was TerTaWa, and his experience of human beings had been as bad as Patah's. He had stolen the jacket he wore from a man who took him around from village to village on a chain for years, and had trained him to be a thief. The gibbon had escaped only when, one night, he stole the key to the padlock that the man used to chain him up. Then he had hidden in the birdcatchers' boat, and so he came to Pulau Bulu. The boat had left the island again, loaded up with captured birds – for which the catchers had paid the griffins – but TerTaWa had stayed behind.

'Your name is Greenbloom?' The words came out of his lips like song. Not for nothing are gibbons known as the singing apes.

'Yes,' said Barnabas, 'and I once had the honour of calling a gibbon like you my friend. His name was E-Mas.'

TerTaWa looked up at the griffin.

'This man is not a spy, Shrii,' he said firmly. 'He is a friend. He saved the life of the Golden Gibbon!'

Ben shot Barnabas a glance of enquiry.

'A story from my younger days,' whispered Barnabas. 'I'll tell you about it if we get out of here safe and sound. Just for your information: the gibbon saved my life as much as I saved his! And Ben,' he added almost inaudibly, 'don't look at Patah too hard.'

That was a lot to ask. The macaque had lost interest in the ballpoint pen, but now he was trying to open the locket.

Give it back to me, Ben wanted to say. I'm the dragon rider, not you! But of course Barnabas was right. Patah mustn't notice how much the locket meant to him. Maybe the macaque would throw it away when he wasn't interested in it any longer. But for now his annoyance at what the gibbon had said was distracting him from the stubborn silver thing.

'Huh, *tcha tcha*, you're a hopeless dreamer, TerTaWa!' he chattered. 'You ought to know better. After all, you've lived on a humans' island! Don't trust any of them, that's the only rule that will keep you alive. Don't trust a single human! Either that, or you must be in league with them, like Kraa!'

Shrii hadn't taken his eyes off Barnabas since the gibbon had asked him his name. 'What brings you to this island if you are neither poachers nor Kraa's spies?' he asked, taking no notice of Patah's chatter of disapproval.

'We need one of your sun-feathers. Of course we are prepared to pay the proper price for it!' replied Barnabas. Shrii seemed to be an unusual griffin, but Barnabas decided not to mention the Pegasi all the same. For all he knew, the griffins' contempt for horses might be inborn, like their desire for treasure.

'We brought this,' said Ben, coming to his aid and pointing to the bag containing Bağdagül's bangle, 'as payment for the feather.'

TerTaWa reached for the bag and took out the golden bangle. Kupo smacked her lips, impressed. But Shrii's gaze became noticeably cooler.

'Gold, of course. All griffins love gold.' He fluffed up his feathers in annoyance. 'Which I suppose can also be said of human beings, am I right? Maybe that's why your species has always understood mine so extremely well. But I am not interested in your treasures, and even if I wanted your gold – only one griffin on this island has a sun-feather in his plumage, and that griffin is Kraa.'

'Hear that, Patah?' mocked one of the other macaques. 'We don't have to go to the trouble of killing them. Kraa will take their gold and bite their heads off!'

Once again the hollow tree was full of amused screeching. Only Kupo kept silent.

'A sun-feather?' she twittered, still sitting on Shrii's shoulder. 'Why would human beings need a sun-feather?'

Barnabas avoided answering. Suddenly TerTaWa put a finger to his lips in warning.

The scream that echoed through the hollow tree was the one that Ben had heard on their first night on Pulau Bulu. It sounded like death. Like hungry lions and hunting eagles.

'It's Tchraee!' screeched one of the lorises. 'Tchraee the ape-murderer!'

'I warned you, didn't I?' cried Patah. 'They were bait! Kraa's bait! How else did they find us?'

Two macaques seized Barnabas, and two more made menacingly for Ben. But they all scattered when a winged figure darkened the opening from outside.

Crowds of monkeys surged into the hollow tree. Shrii lashed out at them, defending himself with his claws and lion's paws, but even he retreated when another griffin made his way into the tree trunk. His beak and claws were black as ebony, but the centuries had bleached his coat and feathers to a dusty grey.

'Surrender, Shrii!' snarled Tchraee through the battle cries of the monkeys. 'Kraa wants me to bring you to him alive.'

Shrii shook off a dozen monkeys, and rid himself of two more who were thrusting at him with sharpened sticks.

'I'll surrender if you let the others go,' he cried.

Tchraee looked scornfully around the now empty hollow tree, while one of his monkeys threw a liana around Patah's neck. 'Is that how you see our future? A miserable hollow tree as a dwelling for the lions of the air? I'll leave your treacherous servants alive for the time being, which is more than they deserve for their rebellion. But Kraa himself will punish them – and they will certainly not die a quick death.'

He looked at the prisoners his monkeys had taken, and leaned over Kupo. His terrible beak came so close to the loris that it almost touched her fur.

'Well, well, who have we here?' he cooed. 'Kraa misses your clever fingers, Kupo! The other lorises are bunglers compared to you. How can you waste your talents on a griffin who can't even build himself a proper nest?'

Kupo was trembling so much that she couldn't say a word. But Patah bared his yellow teeth aggressively.

'We had a wonderful nest, O terrible Tchraee!' he said. 'And if I remember correctly, you destroyed it yourself. So much for Kraa's appreciation of Kupo's art! You also killed Manis, who was just as talented herself. You—'

Tchraee silenced him by raising one front claw menacingly.

'What do we do with the humans, O terrible Tchraee?' asked one of his monkeys. They were as mixed a bunch as Shrii's followers.

As Tchraee's pale yellow eyes inspected him, Ben felt he was nothing but a tasty piece of meat.

'Take them with us,' ordered the griffin. 'Maybe we can sell them as slaves. There are many mines on the surrounding islands. The humans there don't ask where workers come from. And they pay well.'

'So Kraa sells his own spies?' Shrii's beak snapped at a macaque thrusting its stick into TerTaWa's stomach. 'I thought he still had a remnant of honour left. But I suppose not even that remnant is safe from his greed for gold.'

'Spies?' Tchraee uttered a disparaging croak. 'We don't need human spies to find traitors! I've never seen these two-legged beings before. And how about that green-skinned Something? Did a tree give birth to it?'

Hothbrodd was calling the griffin a cowardly moorhen as Tchraee's monkeys dragged him outside. Five more griffins were waiting there in the branches of the nearby trees, three of them sandy brown or grey like Tchraee, two almost as colourful as Shrii. Ben had to admit that all of them together were a magnificent sight. Their wing-beats were like the wind rushing in the trees, and the jungle echoed to the sound of their triumphant cries as they took Shrii into their midst. In spite of the enormous span of their wings, they glided through the trees as easily as if the branches were respectfully making way for them. Ben wondered how long it had been since the oldest of them left the wide desert landscapes of their youth and moved to this moist jungle. How many of them had they been when they came here? Were Shrii and the other two griffins with brightly coloured feathers the only younger ones? Perhaps Tchraee's monkeys, carrying Barnabas, Hothbrodd and Ben through the treetops after their feathered masters, knew the answer as little as he did. They threw the prisoners to one another, or seemed to drop them only to catch them again high above the ground. Sometimes they acted so wildly that Ben forgot not only to think but also to breathe. They were rather more cautious with Hothbrodd. The troll was too heavy for their games, but Ben was the perfect victim, and he had never before wanted more to be on Firedrake's back.

Lola and Twigleg will find us, he thought as the furry kidnappers took them further and further into the mountains that they had seen from the beach. But how? Both Lola and Twigleg were excellent scouts when it came to following a trail, but their abductors left no trail, apart from a few broken branches.

'Griffin against griffin! Seems to me that we've arrived on this island at a very bad moment,' Barnabas whispered to Ben as the kidnappers put them down side by side in the fork of a tree in order to pick some temptingly ripe fruit. 'Maybe I should have persuaded you not to come after all!'

'You wouldn't have been able to,' Ben whispered back.

The monkeys carrying Patah and Kupo had not stopped to rest. Had they taken the locket away from Patah? Would they keep the shiny thing inside it, or throw Firedrake's scale away, not knowing what it was? Ben felt despair and relief at the same time. Despair because he had lost his only link with Firedrake, relief because he wasn't sure whether, in view of the terrible danger they were all in, he might not have called the dragon to his aid after all.

Their kidnappers blindfolded them before going on. The dirty strips of cloth came from a T-shirt. Ben tried not to wonder what had become of its owner. But at least it was a good sign that the abductors didn't want to let them see where they were being taken. Why go to that kind of trouble if their winged masters were going to eat the prisoners? Yes, thought Ben, as damp leaves brushed his face, and he felt the furry fingers of the monkeys at the back of his neck. It was a good thing that the scale was gone.

But it wasn't.

Patah had managed to open the locket. He had just taken the scale out when Tchraee's screech was heard outside the tree – and he hastily put it back in the locket. He even snapped it shut, intending to keep the treasure anyway. But when Tchraee's monkeys dragged him out of the hollow tree, he naturally tried to defend himself, and the locket slipped out of his hand. It fell and fell – down and down, through leaves and twigs, with the scale inside it, sticky with Patah's sweat of fear. A flying squirrel tried in vain to catch the shiny thing. A treasure-hunting snake almost dug its fangs into the silver, and a jenglot reached its clawed hands out so greedily that it fell head first off its branch. But the locket went on falling. Until at last it landed in the warm waters of a river that carried it past the muzzle of a sleepy crocodile, and on towards the sea.

CHAPTER TWENTY-FIVE

Linked Together

*The world is so empty if we think only of the mountains,
rivers, and cities in it; but knowing that now and then
someone agrees with us, and although distant is close to us
in spirit, is what makes this earth our inhabited garden.*
Johann Wolfgang von Goethe,
Wilhelm Meister's Apprenticeship and Travels

Firedrake was just bringing Maia some of the flowers that
were her substitute for moonlight in the cave, when he felt a
sharp pain where his scale was missing – as sharp as if a knife
were stabbing him in the breast. His heart began to race; he felt
fear, great fear. It was not Ben's fear, however, but Patah's. Maybe
that was why the feeling seemed to Firedrake so strange. As if
Ben had lost his way! And there was all the anger mingled with
the fear. Where did that come from?

'Firedrake?'

His heart was beating so loudly that he could hardly hear

Maia's voice. The pale blue eggs that she was tending were still smaller than ostrich eggs, and would stay that way. Young dragons are not much bigger than their parents' eyes when they hatch. Firedrake felt that they were spending a long time hidden away in eggshells before emerging.

'I think Ben needs help!' he said. 'I can sense fear! And anger!'

'Then off you go to find him! What are you waiting for?' said Maia.

She was so fearless. Firedrake loved her for that. Fearless and strong. She could so easily have said, 'Please stay here,' but Maia knew how fond of the boy he was. And she hadn't forgotten that without Ben he would never have found his way to the Rim of Heaven – and would never have met her.

'But who's going to look after you?' he asked anxiously.

'One of the she-dragons who aren't expecting young! Or Shimmertail can do it.'

Shimmertail was her cousin, and he either sat out in the sun with the brownies or flew races with the other dragons. But yes – he certainly wouldn't let Maia go hungry. And she had several she-dragon friends who didn't have to make themselves nests just now.

'I have only one condition,' said Maia. 'Of course I'd like best to go with you myself, but as I can't' – and she gently nudged one of the eggs with her nose – 'do me a favour and take someone else with you. You say you sense fear and anger. That doesn't sound good, and you have no idea what kind of danger Ben is in. You owe it to your children not to fly into it alone.'

Firedrake wasn't sure what he thought of that idea. Presumably it was a foretaste of what Barnabas called paternal duties.

'Alone? You know I never fly alone!' he protested. 'Sorrel will complain that we're off to another new place, but of course she's not going to miss her chance to come along.' Sorrel . . . Firedrake looked around for her, but in the valley of the Rim of Heaven she went out mushroom-hunting even more often than in her old home. She would certainly have said, 'Are you surprised, when there are so few mushrooms here? Quite apart from the fact that most of them growing in all this stony gravel don't taste good.'

'I'm not talking about Sorrel,' said Maia. 'I'm talking about another dragon.'

'But it's *my* friend in danger!' retorted Firedrake. 'I can't ask one of the others to go travelling on that account. Especially not now, when most of them are expecting young!'

The dragon who had raised his head at the word *travelling* and was now looking curiously in their direction had not come from Scotland with Firedrake. Tattoo had been born in the Rim of Heaven, and was one of the dragons awoken from their moonless sleep by the stone-dwarves. His real name was Lhag Pa, which meant Wind in the language of these mountains. But everyone just called him Tattoo, because all those years under a shell of stone had left patterns on his scales as if someone had painted artistic designs on him. The stone-dwarves thought a plant growing in the dark that often left its traces on cave walls was responsible, although they couldn't explain why only Tattoo had its patterns on his scales. Whatever the reason, the design of flowers, tendrils and leaves that covered him from his head to the tip of his tail made him look like the dragons you saw on precious Chinese porcelain. Firedrake thought that he looked fantastic, but Tattoo had to put up with a certain amount of mockery. It didn't make his life easier that he was the youngest dragon in the valley of the Rim of Heaven (if you subtracted the

years he had spent asleep under his coat of stone). Perhaps that was why he was looking forward to the arrival of dragon young even more than their parents were. Tattoo reminded Firedrake very much of himself: his restlessness, his hunger for change and adventure, his longing for what was distant and unknown, while the older dragons dreamed only of peace and safety . . .

Of course Maia had noticed which dragon he was looking at.

'Yes, Tattoo would be a good companion,' she whispered. 'He has no nest to protect, no young to feed, and he is fast and clever. I've seen him several times even defeating Ryak and Bruk in their play-fights.'

Ryak and Bruk were two of the younger dragons who had come from Scotland with Firedrake, and they were always keen to show how strong and fearless they were.

'Are those two still playing battle-games, although I banned them?' Firedrake suddenly felt very old. Maybe he had in fact grown up.

'Don't act as if that seriously surprises you. And it's a good thing for Tattoo to show the others how strong and fast he is now and then. You know how often they tease him about his scales.'

Firedrake looked over at the younger dragon. Tattoo pretended not to notice, but Firedrake saw him prick up his ears. Dragon ears could give their owners away. And yes, Maia was right: Tattoo was not just fast, he was also clever, and he had patience when necessary, which was very unusual in such a young dragon, even if Tattoo didn't yet know how important that quality was. In addition he wasn't interested in being the most popular dragon around. Or the one who talked loudest. Or the leader. And he was not cruel to weaker people – a characteristic that Firedrake prized more highly than any other.

All the same . . . if Ben was really in danger, he himself wouldn't have time to keep an eye on a young dragon.

'Please, Firedrake!' whispered Maia. 'Who knows what Barnabas has dug up this time? You say he's looking for a phoenix, but maybe he stumbled upon a less peaceful fabulous creature in the process! It wouldn't be the first time!'

No, it certainly wouldn't. Sometimes Firedrake thought that Barnabas attracted fabulous beings just as he himself did.

He glanced at Tattoo again. 'He can be thoughtless.'

Maia smiled. 'Oh, yes. You two really have a lot in common.'

Tattoo was still pretending to take not the slightest notice of what they were saying to each other. He was not a good actor! Finally he stood up and went to the mouth of the cave. Obviously he felt embarrassed about his own curiosity, and Firedrake liked that too.

He sighed.

'All right,' he said. 'So far I've always regretted it when I didn't take your advice.'

Maia let her head sink to the edge of the nest. 'Really?' she said quietly.

It would be so difficult to leave her alone. He felt terrible about his heart, torn between loving in two places.

'Right. I'll set off this evening,' said Firedrake. 'And I'll ask Tattoo if he'll come with me. I just hope this ache in my breast will be a reliable guide.'

By now the pain did indeed feel as if it were tugging at him. It was like having a fish hook in his heart.

'The stone-dwarves say that dragons used to be able to find their riders over distances of thousands of miles,' said Maia. 'The scale will be like a magnet attracting you. After all, it's a part of you.'

'Attract you? Where to?'

Sorrel had found good pickings. She sat down between Firedrake's paws and sniffed at a whitish mushroom hardly any bigger than a cherry. 'Stone,' she muttered to herself. 'They all smell of stone. We need rain!'

'And when you had rain, you said it made the mushrooms watery.' Firedrake sat up. 'Maybe you'll like the mushrooms in Vietnam better. You can soon find out.'

Barnabas was searching for the phoenix in Vietnam, wasn't he? Well, wherever he was, the scale would tell him the way.

'Vietnam? Oh no! Wait a moment!'

Of course, Sorrel came after him when he made for the mouth of the cave.

'It's the boy, isn't it?'

She jumped into his way, and pointed accusingly at the dark patch where his scale was missing. 'I knew it was a daft idea!

Daft, daft, daft! We've only just arrived back here. After flying halfway around the world twice!'

'You're welcome to stay here. Maia thought I might take Tattoo with me.'

'Tattoo?'

That deprived Sorrel of her powers of speech, something as unusual as if she had lost her appetite.

Outside the cave, the sun was very low in the sky over the mountains. It would soon be dark. The best time to start flying.

'Wait, Firedrake! You don't mean that seriously, do you?' Sorrel could talk again after all. 'He doesn't even have a brownie!' she stammered as she hurried to Firedrake's side. 'And he doesn't know anything about the world! He doesn't know a single thing! He's been inside a stone coat for ever!'

'Well, what did we know about the world before we made our way here? A misty valley and the walls of a cave! It will do him good to see a few other places.'

Tattoo was standing on a rocky ledge, looking at the distant mountains as they disappeared into the evening haze. Oh yes, he had certainly heard Maia's suggestion.

'Okay, okay, I'm coming with you!' Sorrel clung to one of

Firedrake's legs to make sure he was listening to her. 'But Tattoo stays here! He'll only get in our way. And I'm not looking after him! My paws are more than full enough being your brownie!'

'Yes, I always forget how much work I make for you,' replied Firedrake as he walked towards Tattoo. 'Don't worry. I'll explain that you're not going to search his scales or sing him lullabies.'

Tattoo turned to them.

He was trying as hard as he could to look nonchalant, but Firedrake was sure his heart was racing with expectation. He remembered the feeling so well: a wish to fly away, towards the horizon that he had stared at so often, until his eyes hurt and his wings longed to fly on and on, not just in a few circles above familiar valleys and mountains. No, he'd wanted to cross strange seas, landscapes he had never seen before, carried by winds that smelled of unknown flowers and fruits . . .

Firedrake stopped in front of the young dragon.

'I have to go in search of a friend,' he said, ignoring Sorrel's sigh of disapproval. 'I'm afraid he needs help. The others here are needed to guard the nests, but . . .'

He got no further.

'Yes,' cried Tattoo. 'Yes, of course I'll go with you. I'll go wherever you're flying.'

Sorrel heaved an even deeper sigh.

'Good. I'm setting off tonight,' said Firedrake. 'As soon as I've told the others. But I must warn you, it may be dangerous!'

'As if that would be anything new!' murmured Sorrel, but neither of the dragons took any notice of her.

'I'll go wherever you're flying,' Tattoo repeated.

Yes, Firedrake liked him a lot.

CHAPTER TWENTY-SIX

Gone!

Gone – flitted away,
Taken the stars from the night,
and the sun From the day!
Gone, and a cloud in my heart.
Alfred, Lord Tennyson, 'Gone'

They'd gone! However low Lola flew through the dense jungle – there was no sign of Barnabas, Ben or Hothbrodd. And it would be really difficult to overlook Hothbrodd.

Twigleg heard his own heart sighing and lamenting, as if the alchemist who made him had implanted a living thing in his narrow chest. He imagined his master torn apart by wildcats, or all of them snatched away by the venom of a snake. But then they'd have found them dead, wouldn't they? Oh, his mind was useless when he was worried about Ben! And in addition Lola was flying so low again that he was in constant fear of crashing into a tree trunk! They scared a lesser mouse-deer, and almost ended up between the fangs hidden in its deceptively harmless-looking mouth. A marbled cat tried to fish them out of the air with its paw. And then there was the green pit viper that almost got its venomous teeth into the wing of Lola's plane!

Twigleg would have put up with all that uncomplainingly, if only Lola's hair-raising flying manoeuvres had succeeded in finding Ben and the others. He was staring out of the plane window so hard that it wouldn't have surprised him if his eyes had popped out of his head. But all he saw was greenery! He never wanted to set eyes on anything green again!

They were gone. Gone! Swallowed up. Eaten. Digested and disappeared without trace. How he cursed the Pegasus and those eggs! Who needed flying horses? Or griffins . . . monkeys and apes . . . snakes . . . trees? His master was all he needed. He clutched his breast. Had his heart already broken? No, it was still beating. That meant the boy wasn't dead! Yes. Yes, he just had to stay alive himself, and then so would Ben. Did it work that way around?

Even Lola was looking anxious by now – or at least that was how Twigleg interpreted her twitching whiskers. And then it began to rain again! If the torrents falling on the dense layers of leaves could be called rain. The water dropped and dripped, lashed the fuselage, and ran down the panes so fast that Lola, cursing, had to keep her nose pressed to the Plexiglas if she was to see anything at all. Suddenly she let out a shrill whistle (an expression of great alarm in rat language), and wrenched the plane over to the left. Twigleg saw red feathers and felt a dull impact. The aircraft dipped forward, but Lola pulled it up before it could reach the ground. Then she steered a lurching course through some dripping wet fern fronds, and crash-landed on a cushion of moss. The plane sank into it up to its windows.

Red feathers. At first Twigleg was so dazed by the near-crash that he thought they had collided with some kind of feathered jungle traffic light! Only when a parrot landed beside them, drenched through, did it dawn on Twigleg who this was. By the test tube that had borne him – it was Me-Rah! The rain gave her plumage the deceptive camouflage colouring of a half-ripe blackberry.

'Oh, I'm so, so sorry!' she squawked, spreading her wings in agitation. 'I only wanted to stop you, but you were going so fast!'

Twigleg gave Lola a reproachful glance, but she had eyes only for her plane, which looked the worse for wear. Luckily the moss had saved it from major damage. While the rat cleaned leaves and bits of chopped liana off her propeller, Twigleg tried to understand Me-Rah's excited chattering. What she was saying didn't sound quite as terrible as the scenarios that he had been envisaging, but it was still bad enough. Me-Rah had found her flock, only to hear from the other parrots of two humans and a green giant who, apparently, had been dragged away by a gang of monkeys. Monkeys working for the lion-birds.

'Kidnapper monkeys?' said Lola in annoyance, when Me-Rah had finished her story. 'What sort of island is this? Full of traps that snap shut and rat poison? Do the monkeys around here by any chance also eat human flesh? If so, you might have mentioned it before!'

Twigleg almost swallowed his own tongue in horror. But Me-Rah energetically denied that the monkeys of Pulau Bulu showed any interest in human flesh. She added, sharply, that unfortunately the same couldn't be said of the situation the other way around.

'Well, at least that's something,' said Lola. 'So now we can only hope that they haven't already fed our friends to the lion-birds. I'm afraid those lion-birds would enjoy any kind of meat.'

The idea made Twigleg so weak at the knees that he had to hold on to the wings of Lola's plane.

When he asked Me-Rah whether she could show them where their friends had been taken, the parrot looked almost as scared as she had in the temple of Garuda. Then, resigned to her fate, she rolled her eyes and nodded.

Lola's plane spluttered and groaned as she started the engine. But it finally rose into the air and followed Me-Rah through the jungle that was still dripping wet with rain.

CHAPTER TWENTY-SEVEN

Captured

Hoping for the best, prepared for the worst,
and unsurprised by anything in between.
Maya Angelou, *I Know Why the Caged Bird Sings*

Wherever they were, it seemed that they had reached their destination. The monkeys untied Ben and threw him into something that swayed back and forth so menacingly that he felt around for something to hold on to. He got his fingers into twigs woven together, and when he took the blindfold off he saw that he was kneeling in a round cage like a basket. Beside him, Barnabas was polishing his glasses as if he wanted as clear a view of their unfortunate situation as possible, and Hothbrodd, cursing, bumped his head when he tried to sit up. As far as Ben could make out through the woven twigs that surrounded him, their basket prison was hanging from the roof of an enormous nest made of mud. He counted over twenty such baskets of various sizes. One of the monkeys who had brought them here pushed two lorises into a basket not much larger than a calabash, and then, like his companions, he swung himself up to the wide opening leading to the outside air on a liana. The basketwork of the cages consisted of twigs only loosely interwoven, even under his feet, and far below Ben saw three dog-sized creatures with scorpion bodies and the heads of jackals. They were passing the time by attacking one another with their pincers.

'Damn it all, Greenbloom! Dammit dammit dammit!' cursed Hothbrodd, looking at the twigs that imprisoned them. 'Why did I let myself be persuaded to come to this island with you? May the frost giants carry you off!' He flung himself against the interwoven twigs so angrily that the cage creaked dangerously, and Ben glanced in alarm at the scorpion creatures beneath them. 'A troll doesn't belong in a cage! Certainly not a cage hanging in the air!'

'I'm really sorry, Hothbrodd,' replied Barnabas, but he wasn't looking at the troll as he spoke, he was staring, like Ben, at the scorpions down below.

'Jackal scorpions! Fascinating! They're even larger than I imagined them. And the armoured exoskeleton and sting really are made of gold! The griffins must have brought them from Mesopotamia with them! They served the kings there as guards and hounds for hunting. These specimens may well be over two thousand years old!'

'Oh yes? And what's their favourite food? Let me guess,' growled Hothbrodd. 'Troll and human flesh?'

'I'm afraid you're right about human flesh,' said Barnabas, without taking his eyes off the scorpions. 'But I think they've probably never tasted troll. And their liking for human flesh is presumably because the Mesopotamian kings fed their enemies to the scorpions. I assume that by now these creatures will have adapted their diet to this island.'

'Unless this Kraa throws poachers who don't pay up to them,' murmured Ben. He was probably not alone in adding in his thoughts: 'Or his prisoners.' He looked at the other cages. In the twilight that filled the nest, you couldn't tell whether they were all occupied.

'I'm sure they'd like troll too,' muttered Hothbrodd. 'They remind me of the crabs that used to bite me as a child when I was gathering driftwood on the beach. Although those didn't have golden stings.' He hit the woven network of twigs so hard with his fist that the basket cage swung back and forth like a pendulum. 'What do those monkeys think I am? A dratted bird?' he bellowed. 'Maybe I ought to have a word with these twigs!'

'I don't think that's a very good idea,' said Barnabas. 'If the twigs let us go a little too suddenly, you'll probably survive the fall, but Ben and I are rather more breakable. And then there are those jackal scorpions. They love to tear their victims to pieces with their pincers. After paralysing them with their stings first.'

Ben looked down at the shining scorpions again. Barnabas was right. Even if those guards hadn't been there, escape seemed impossible. The baskets were hanging so high that they'd be sure to break their necks. Of course, with wings it would have looked different . . .

No. No! He'd forbidden himself even to think of Firedrake.

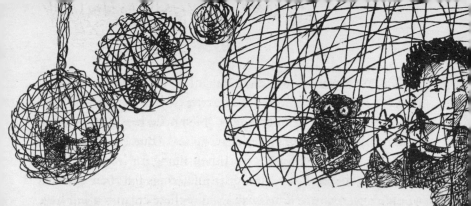

Ever since Ben had seen the griffins at close quarters, he was grateful for every mile that lay between them and the dragon. Even though he was sure that Shrii and Firedrake would have got on well with each other, in spite of all those griffin-versus-dragon stories! But where was Shrii? None of the basket cages that Ben could see was large enough for a griffin.

Barnabas came to stand beside him and looked through the twigs.

'I'm rather disappointed by this nest,' he said. 'Look at its walls. I've read that griffin nests are adorned with fantastic reliefs that can compete with the reliefs of Persepolis.'

'This is only the prison nest. Kraa's nest is covered with pictures.' The voice came from a basket hanging only a few metres away from theirs. 'They shine as if they were set with jewels, but it's only dead beetles and butterflies. The monkeys catch them.'

The boy Ben could see behind the twigs looked younger than he was. His English was very good, although he spoke it with an Indonesian accent. A tiny creature with smooth, brown fur sat on his shoulder. The face pressed to the twigs consisted almost entirely of two huge eyes, and a tail without any fur was wound around them.

'Who's your furry friend?' asked Ben.

The boy tickled the tiny creature behind the ears. 'This is Berulu. He's a kind of brownie-maki, and a very talented spy.'

Berulu twittered, sounding pleased by the flattery. His delicate, fur-less fingers clinging to the twigs that formed the bars of the cage reminded Ben of Twigleg. He hoped that Lola and the homunculus had done better than he and Barnabas. If so, they would probably be looking for them. But did they want to be found? He heard the cry of a griffin from outside. No. Tchraee wouldn't even notice if he swallowed up Lola's plane, along with everyone in it.

Berulu was staring down at the scorpions. What did the world look like, seen through such enormous eyes? His master stroked his head soothingly.

'At least we know now how my mother's parrots feel,' he said. 'If we get out of here alive I'll set them all free! That's a promise, and you're my witness!' He pressed his face to the network of twigs forming his cage. 'Are you birdcatchers?' he called to Ben. 'Monkey-dealers? Rich hunters who've lost your way and come to this island? No, wait . . . it's said that the Kucing-Burungs sometimes pluck fishermen out of their boats to feed them to their young! But you don't look like fishermen. More like the white-faced tourists who go from island to island on enormous ships.'

'Kucing-Burungs?' asked Ben. 'What's that?'

The other boy laughed. 'You're their prisoner. Did their monkeys catch you?'

'Yes – I admit the urgency of our mission made us rather careless,' said Barnabas. 'May I introduce myself? My name is Barnabas Greenbloom, and this is my son Ben. The green person you can see through the bars is our friend Hothbrodd.'

The troll turned his back to them. He was still investigating the network of twigs woven into a cage. The maki's big eyes were turned on him with interest and anxiety. The expression on his human master's face was more one of curiosity.

'What kind of monkey is that? Or is it an ape?' he asked. 'I've never seen such a large one! Even orang-utans are small by comparison!'

'Tell him I'll shrink him to the size of his furry animal if he calls me an ape again,' barked Hothbrodd.

'What are you doing with the Kucing-Burungs?' Barnabas asked the boy, trying to change the subject. 'We came here to buy one of their feathers, but we seem to have met the wrong griffin. May I ask what you did to annoy them? Excuse me, but will you tell us your name?'

'Winston.' The boy couldn't take his eyes off Hothbrodd, although he certainly couldn't see much of him. 'Winston Setiawan. I come from one of the neighbouring islands, and I'm here because I followed a fairy tale. In our village they say there's a ruined temple brim-full of treasure on this island. I wouldn't say no to a chest full of gold, but there's supposed to be something even more exciting there: one of the cast skins of Nyai Loro Kidul.'

'A famous queen of the sea,' said Barnabas, in response to Ben's enquiring glance. 'She is sometimes a fish and sometimes a snake.'

'Yes, and when you put on her skin,' Winston went on, 'you change shape. You turn into a pit viper! Imagine that. There are two boys in my village who make life hell for me. How surprised they'd be if I suddenly had black scales and venomous fangs!' He heaved a wistful sigh. 'Of course I didn't find the temple. Instead I found myself in the clearing where the Kucing-Burungs leave their prisoners for poachers and animal-catchers to pick them up. I know I never should have touched the cages, but all the same . . .'

Winston fell silent, and stared at the basket where Ben and Barnabas were imprisoned. One of the twigs was slowly coming away from the woven structure, and beginning to wind its way through the air like a dancing cobra.

'These twigs have minds of their own,' grunted Hothbrodd, 'and a very peculiar sense of humour – but they can understand me!'

Another twig pulled itself out of the basketwork. Right under Ben's feet.

'Hothbrodd!' he cried in alarm. 'Do you want us to fall to our deaths?'

The troll gave a disapproving grunt, and muttered a few incomprehensible words, whereupon the twigs, if with obvious reluctance, went back to their original places.

'He's a jungle demon!' stammered Winston. 'Of course! My mother keeps warning me against those demons, but I've always laughed at her!'

Hothbrodd would much rather be called a jungle demon than an ape. Trolls love to be thought of as monsters, although in Ben's experience very few of them lived up to their bad reputation.

'He's a fjord troll,' he called over to Winston. 'And he's really nice. If he's your friend,' he added, when Hothbrodd cast him a glance of annoyance. It was to be hoped that the griffins were prepared for prisoners of his weight. Once again the basketwork creaked alarmingly as the troll sat down on the floor of the cage.

'Nice? I hope the lion-birds will feed you all to their young!' a shrill voice was suddenly heard from a basket on their right. 'Curses on you! Shrii will die because of you, and they'll sell us or throw us to their scorpions!'

Ben thought he saw Patah's face behind the twigs.

'You're a thief, Patah!' he called to him.

'Are you talking about your locket?' Patah called back. 'But it looked so much better around my neck. That thing you were carrying about in it . . . was it some kind of human magic? Didn't do you much good, if you ask me.'

'Was.' Patah used the past tense. So he no longer had the scale.

'What have you done with it?' Ben was glad that Patah wasn't right in front of him. He would have been sorely tempted to hit the macaque. 'Have you thrown it away?'

'No. Lost it along with the locket.' Patah bared his teeth. 'When your friends dragged us off.'

Lost. Ben exchanged a glance with Barnabas. He was feeling so many emotions all at once. Anger, pain, disappointment – and relief. Ben saw the same contradictory emotions on Barnabas's face. Firedrake's gift was lost, and with it maybe their only chance of rescue. But the griffins wouldn't find a dragon's scale on them. Ben wondered whether they would have realised that the scale came from one of their oldest enemies. Beside him, Barnabas lowered his head with a sigh. You didn't very often see that. Yes, the dragons were safe, but unless some miracle happened there was no chance for the Pegasus foals.

'Kraa will clip Shrii's wings and claws!' Kupo's plaintive voice came from a basket lower down. 'And then he'll let the crocodiles have him! Or the marbled cats!'

'Nonsense. Kraa will watch as his scorpions tear him apart.' Patah made a poor pretence of hiding his despair behind mockery. 'Feather by feather, flesh and hide, and then he'll eat his heart so that Shrii's strength and youth will pass into him.'

'No!' cried another macaque. 'Never! Shrii will escape. He'll set us all free, and then found his own kingdom on this island!'

'Yes, of course, Tabuhan. Dream on.' Patah just sounded weary now, and hopeless. 'Shrii is as good as dead. We all are. Kraa won't sell us. He'll eat us, just as he'll devour Shrii. And line his nest with our skins.'

Kraa.

All was still inside the basketwork cages. His mere name seemed to echo back from the mud walls. Kraa . . .

He would certainly be more like Tchraee than Shrii. Ben, too, was worried about the young griffin. He'd have liked to see him again.

'We certainly turned up at the ideal moment,' growled Hothbrodd. 'As if those winged brutes weren't horrible enough anyway. But no, they're also going to war with each other, and where have we landed? On the loser's side, of course!'

'Since when do you give up so quickly, Hothbrodd?' said Barnabas in a low voice. 'A griffin who thinks nothing of gold and silver! What an ally Shrii could be! We must save him!'

Hothbrodd groaned.

Even Ben thought his adopted father's optimism was rather far-fetched this time.

'*We* must save Shrii?' he whispered. 'Someone will have to save us first! And the only rescuers we can hope for are a rat and a homunculus!'

'So?' Barnabas whispered back. 'Surely you're not judging the usefulness of our friends by their size? I'm disappointed in you, Ben. You didn't learn that from me.'

No. Barnabas was right there. Had he forgotten the important part played by Twigleg in the fight against his old master

Nettlebrand? And how often had Lola warned them of danger and protected them from it?

'Hey!' Winston called to them. 'How come I can understand what the monkeys are saying? Is it some kind of magic? And what do you people need a griffin's feather for?'

'It's a long story,' Ben replied.

'Good,' said Winston. 'Tell it. Or have you something better to do?'

The brownie-maki made himself comfortable on Winston's arm and looked expectantly at Ben.

Right. Where to begin? Ben was about to start with the day when he first met Firedrake, but Barnabas put his hand over his mouth.

'Don't mention the dragon,' he whispered. 'Remember: the griffins mustn't find out about him! And jackal scorpions may not be especially clever, but they have very keen hearing.'

CHAPTER TWENTY-EIGHT

Magic Time

I'm youth, I'm joy, I'm a little bird
that has broken out of the egg.
J.M. Barrie, *Peter and Wendy*

Magic time. That was what Guinevere still called it many years later: those two days when the silver eggs for which their father had flown to the other side of the world revealed their secret, and she lost her heart to three tiny winged foals. Guinevere even forgot what she was counting down as she made crosses on the calendar on the stable door. Suddenly only the entries that she wrote in the boxes mattered: *Saw a tiny face on the other side of the shell for the first time. The third foal is coppery red like its father. The white foal has a copper blaze on the forehead.*

The time when Ànemos avoided the stable was over. The Pegasus visited the nest so often that in the end Vita had a flock of indignant geese and swans standing in the living room. Only when the temperature of the eggs, as taken by Guinevere, was a little lower than usual did Ànemos overcome his longing to watch the tiny figures moving in shells that were becoming more and more translucent.

'They need names,' Guinevere told him, when they had been driven from the stable once again by two hissing swans. 'What will you call them?'

'Synnefo. Ouranos. And Chara.'

The answer came so fast that Guinevere had to smile.

'Well, Guinevere Humangirl?' Ànemos nudged her breast with his soft muzzle. 'All right, I admit it! I've been thinking about their names for a long time. Don't you like them?'

'Oh yes, I do, I do! Those are wonderful names.' And something else was wonderful: the way the Pegasus was suddenly trotting as lightly out of the stable as if he were made of pure joy.

'Well done, Vitasdaughter!' Raskervint told Guinevere. 'He didn't need a centaur. A Pegasus wants human friends! And what could warm his sad heart better than a human girl who knows all about fabulous creatures, and has inherited her parents' courage and warmth?'

Guinevere stammered her embarrassed thanks, and felt sure that she would never be paid a greater compliment in her life. She was very glad that Vita had asked Raskervint to stay until Ben, Barnabas and the others came back.

'Why, of course I'll stay,' the centaur had replied. 'You don't think I want to miss the birth of three Pegasus foals, do you?'

Yes, it was a magic time. And there were still four days white and empty on the calendar on the stable door.

'That's not long, Guinevere,' whispered a voice inside her. But she didn't want to listen to it. What was happening was simply too wonderful.

Everything would be all right.

CHAPTER TWENTY-NINE

Too Late

*Walking with a friend in the dark is
better than walking alone in the light.*
Helen Keller

One of the buttons from Ben's jacket! Trodden deeply into ground that was still damp after the rain. Twigleg wiped tears from his eyes.

'Pull yourself together, humpelkluss!' said Lola, inspecting some crushed snail shells. 'It's a button, not his dead body!'

Twigleg was very good at reading tracks, as Ben often said, but compared to Lola he felt like a child just starting school, proud of himself if he could so much as stammer out the alphabet.

'Our feathered friend is right,' she said, looking up at the trees under which the tracks left by Ben, Barnabas and Hothbrodd abruptly ended. 'It was monkeys who dragged them away, no doubt about it.'

She bent down and picked a couple of pale brown monkey hairs out of a fern. 'Macaques, I'd say.'

Me-Rah began squawking angrily in Parrot. Once again, the excitement made her forget her English.

'What's she saying?' Lola pulled a few more hairs off the tree trunk between whose roots she was standing. 'I'm always afraid she'll explode before our eyes one of these days, aren't you? How can anyone get so worked up all the time?'

Me-Rah squawked, complaining that she was afraid Lola, like all rats, was inclined to be arrogant. Twigleg didn't bother to translate that part of her remarks. But what came next was interesting. Interesting and extremely worrying.

'Me-Rah says a griffin called Shrii has rebelled against the leader of the pride here. Shrii is also known on this island as the griffin who has bathed in the rainbow. The leader's names are less poetic.' Twigleg swallowed as he went on. 'Kraa the Terrible. The Merciless. The Insatiable. The Eater of Hearts . . .'

Me-Rah enumerated a few more bloodthirsty epithets, but Twigleg spared himself and Lola those.

'But anyway,' he added, making a great effort to sound composed, 'there are rumours that this Shrii is hiding in the jungle hereabouts, which is why Me-Rah thinks his monkeys took Ben and the others away, maybe because they thought they were . . .' – and once again Twigleg's voice almost failed him – '. . . thought they were poachers!'

'Poachers? Well, thanks a million.' Lola looked enquiringly up at Me-Rah. 'What does this Shrii do to poachers?'

Baffled, Me-Rah shook her head and uttered a coo more like

a growl, which seemed to bode no good.

'Griffins on bad terms with each other.' Lola nodded thoughtfully. 'Yes, that makes sense. There's nothing like jungle gossip! It also explains the skeletons and the wrecked nests. But how do we find these kidnappers?'

She looked doubtfully up at the treetops. 'A gang of monkeys swinging from branch to branch! Even for me, following a track like that could be a challenge!'

Twigleg stroked Ben's muddy button with trembling fingers. Suppose they didn't find their friends? Suppose they never saw them again? How he hated this never-ending jungle, drenched with rain! How he hated this whole island!

'There, there, humklumpulus!' said Lola, as he wiped another tear off his pointed nose. 'We'll find them, won't we, Me-Rah?'

Me-Rah's squawk didn't sound as confident as Lola's voice, but she offered her help in following the trail, adding that parrots were more at home than rats in the treetops.

'Thank you, Me-Rah,' stammered Twigleg as he put Ben's button in his backpack.

Lola was already trudging back to her plane. 'Those rascally kidnapping monkeys haven't reckoned with an airborne rat!' she announced. 'Oh no! They're going to be very sorry they ever

tangled with friends of Lola Greytail!'

So much determination cheered Twigleg a little. But soon the light of day falling through the trees turned to green twilight, making it very difficult for Me-Rah and Lola to find the trail left in the treetops by the monkeys. Me-Rah was just saying that it was about time to look for a place to spend the night in hiding, when Lola, with a shrill cry of triumph, pointed to a tree with only a few green lianas on its bare branches, and a wide gap high up in its trunk.

'There!' shouted Lola through the engine noise. 'If that's not the gang's hideout, then my name is Gilbert from now on!'

She opened the cockpit window and raised her pointed nose to the wind. 'Yes! There's even a smell of troll still in the air! Hurrah! We'll find them now, humklupuss!'

And before Twigleg and Lola could protest, she was steering the plane to the gap in the bark of the tree.

'Lola! Let Me-Rah go ahead to find out what's waiting for us in that tree!' cried Twigleg.

The parrot favoured him with a glance that was far from enthusiastic, and Lola just shook her head scornfully.

'Nonsense!' she called back. 'Do you think Me-Rah with her bright scarlet feathers will be less conspicuous than my plane? I'm switching to silent gliding mode!'

Twigleg ducked down in his seat, while Me-Rah flew after them as quietly as a breath of air. And with a very relieved expression on her face.

Silence.

That was all that met them when Lola's plane glided through the huge opening in the bark of the tree, quiet as a falling leaf.

The hollow space inside was so high and wide that Twigleg

could hardly make out its roof and walls in the darkness. But one thing was certain: the hollow tree was empty. Me-Rah came down in the air roots of a liana with a squawk of disappointment, and Lola landed the plane in the dead leaves that lined the hollow like cushions in a nest.

'Where are they?' moaned Twigleg. 'The trail must lead on from here! Let's go and see, Lola!'

Lola climbed up on one wing and looked around the empty hollow of the tree, frowning. 'Too dark for that, humpelklumpel,' she said. 'We'd better spend the night here. We'll go on searching as soon as it gets light.'

'But it may be too late then!' cried Twigleg. His fears for his master made even the danger of the plane's crashing into a tree seem unimportant.

Lola jumped down from the wing and searched the dead leaves for tracks. 'Me-Rah, tell him about all the animals who go hunting by night here.'

Me-Rah obediently began telling him. It was a very long list.

'Ah, look at this.' Lola picked something up from the leaves. 'Yes, we're on their trail!'

Twigleg groaned when he saw Barnabas's empty backpack.

'No need to panic, humklumpus,' said Lola firmly. 'No bloodstains. If there was a fight here, it didn't last long. But there were griffins involved. These,' she added pointing to deep furrows on the ground, 'are the same marks as we found in the ruined nests. Made by paws and claws. And the creatures who left them are large. Even Firedrake doesn't have bigger paws!'

She pulled two feathers out of the leaves on the ground. They were both longer than she was tall. One was grey-brown, but the other was as green as the jungle surrounding them.

'What's this, Me-Rah?' Lola held up the green feather with an enquiring look. 'I thought griffins were the same sandy colour as the deserts that they come from?'

Rain was beginning to fall again outside. It sounded ghostly in the gathering dusk – like thousands of feet scurrying through the trees.

Me-Rah fluttered to Lola's side.

'I knew it! It comes from Shrii!' she squawked. 'The griffin who has bathed in the rainbow. Apparently he's as brightly coloured as the forest itself. He was born on Pulau Bulu! Shrii...' said Me-Rah, lowering her voice almost reverently, 'Shrii is said to want to protect the animals on this island from Kraa. That's why he turned against him! Oh, I do hope he isn't in the same difficulties as fully-grown Greenbloom and still-growing Greenbloom!'

'I'm afraid there's no doubt about that.' Lola took another green feather out of the leaves. 'What have we gone and landed ourselves in? No offence meant, Me-Rah, but I really don't fancy staying on this island for any length of time. This humid heat of yours isn't good for either my plane or me. Okay, okay, humpelklus!' she said in response to Twigleg's reproachful glance. 'No, we're not flying home without the rest of the team! What kind of rat do you take me for?'

Lola was right. Twigleg knew she would do everything she could to help the others. And he was very grateful to Me-Rah for standing by them, even though she was fluffed up like a feather pillow with fright. But the fact that a rat and a parrot were the only hope of freeing his master from the griffins' prison really wasn't particularly encouraging.

Lola went over to the opening in the tree and looked at the gathering dusk. 'Right,' she murmured. 'I think we ought to try to get some sleep. We'll set off again at first light.'

'But there are hours to go until then, Lola!' cried Twigleg. 'What if...'

Yes, what if...? He didn't like even thinking to the end of that sentence.

Lola put an arm around his slumped shoulders. 'Humklupus,' she said in an unusually gentle voice, 'I'm worried about Ben too. And Barnabas. And that dratted troll who thinks he knows more about aircraft than I do! But we won't be much use to them if we're feeding our remains to all the maggots in this jungle after crashing.'

A typical rat remark if ever there was one. But unfortunately Lola was right.

Me-Rah couldn't refrain from enumerating all the beasts of prey that were out and about in the trees, even at this height. As a result, Lola suggested sleeping in the plane, so that they could get away fast if they were attacked. To this, Me-Rah pointed out that to binturongs and masked palm civets (whatever those might be), animals about the size of Lola's plane were easy pickings, never mind rats and homunculi.

All the same Twigleg climbed into the plane, while Me-Rah perched in the roots of a liana above them. The hollow tree was full of a ghostly green light cast by the fluorescent fungi growing everywhere inside the wooden walls. It reminded Twigleg horribly of a ghost-train ride that Ben had once persuaded him to take. All those soft noises of rustling, scurrying, fluttering, scrabbling . . . and he thought he saw one of the pit vipers that Me-Rah kept on squawking about in every shadow. He was very glad when she finally tucked one leg under herself and went to sleep.

Lola had made herself comfortable in the pilot's seat. 'Don't worry, humklumpupus,' she said as she put a spanner and the signal pistol on her lap. 'I'll wake you if a masked Someone or a bintuwhatsit turns up. I can easily go for a week without sleep anyway.'

The yawn that she hid behind her grey paw made that assurance a little less credible, but as usual, Lola's confident manner finally made Twigleg close his eyes.

Night is Long in the Jungle

*Waiting is uncanny when you are
waiting for something uncanny.*
Astrid Lindgren, *The Brothers Lionheart*

It was a dreadful dream! One of the worst that Twigleg had
ever had. They were pulling his master to pieces the way
children take an insect apart! Crowds of monkeys, screeching
and baring their teeth, and he was kneeling in front of the parts
trying to put them together again, but he simply couldn't
remember what Ben had looked like. How was that possible?

Twigleg was hugely relieved when Lola shook him awake
and the dream images dissolved in green twilight. But his relief
didn't last for long.

'At last!' hissed Lola. 'Heavens, you're a sound sleeper. That
bird would wake me even if I was dead!'

Me-Rah was fluttering above them among the phosphores-
cent fungi, screeching, 'Binturong! Binturong!'

Twigleg searched his mind for a translation of the word, but

Me-Rah's panic-stricken squawking seemed to have obliterated all his knowledge. Lola told him to do up his seat belt, but his fingers were shaking as if they belonged to someone else. Something was snorting and wheezing outside the opening in the trunk of the hollow tree. A muzzle pushed its way in, followed by a stocky body with sturdy bow legs, a badger-like head, and shaggy grey-brown fur. A binturong.

Lola started the engine, but it would only spit and judder. The jungle climate really didn't suit the plane. Fly, thought Twigleg, oh, please fly! He really wouldn't have thought he'd ever want that so passionately. Luckily for them, the binturong didn't move very fast, but it was making purposefully for them, and Lola's plane wasn't much larger than its head! Its paws would scoop them out of the tiny aircraft as easily as scooping the flesh out of an avocado!

But when the attacker was only a few padding footsteps away, Lola finally got the engine to catch. The binturong stopped and looked in surprise at the humming thing rising and lurching in the air in front of it. Then it straightened up, as clumsily as a dancing bear hitting out at a moth, and raised its paw. The first blow hit the left wing. The second only just missed the fuselage of the plane. Groaning, Twigleg put his head between his knees as Lola brought the spinning aircraft up just in time, before it could crash into the wall of the hollow tree. But the hairy paws were still reaching out to it. This time they missed the propeller by a centimetre, and almost tore off one of the wheels. Next moment the world was upside down, and only Twigleg's belt kept him in his seat. Lola steered in reverse through the animal's shaggy hind legs, and so narrowly escaped another blow of its paw. The draught of that blow almost carried the plane out into the night.

'Fly higher! Higher!' cried Twigleg.

'Oh yes?' Lola shouted back. 'So that we get caught in the lianas and drop appetisingly in front of this creature's paws?'

Then binturong was obviously enjoying the hunt. It snorted and grunted like a dog chasing a ball, and Twigleg saw, in alarm, that Lola was checking the amount of fuel she had left, with a look of concern on her face. The engine began spluttering again, but just as Lola was reaching for the signal pistol in this emergency, Me-Rah came to their aid. She bravely pecked the binturong's ear and then dive-bombed its sensitive nose. Twigleg felt ashamed to see so much courage from the parrot, but the binturong soon recovered from its surprise, thrust at Me-Rah with its head and swept her out of the air.

Now it was Lola's turn to help the heroic parrot. She sent the whirring plane so boldly past the attacker's nose that Twigleg found himself wedged between the seats once more. But Me-Rah was so dazed after being head-butted by the binturong that she was still on the floor when it turned to her again.

Oh no! It was going to eat Me-Rah before their eyes!

When the piece of bark dropped from above, and hit the binturong right on the head, Twigleg thought at first it was a lucky coincidence. But a second piece of bark followed the first, and this time it hit its mark again, right between the binturong's ears. The robber howled, and rubbed its shaggy head, baffled. A

third missile struck its muzzle, and was followed by such a loud screech that the hollow tree echoed to the sound. That was too much for the nocturnal hunter. The binturong retreated with a disgruntled puffing, and scrambled hastily through the gap in the tree trunk and out into the night. Another piece of bark flew after it, followed by a chatter expressing considerable satisfaction.

Twigleg exchanged an enquiring glance with Lola, but she seemed to have no more idea than he did what to think of the help they had received. Lurching through the air, she came down beside Me-Rah, who was still sitting on the floor, stalled the engine, and threw the signal pistol into Twigleg's lap.

'Give me cover, humklupus!' she hissed, while Twigleg stared blankly at the pistol. 'I'm afraid this unexpected help just means we're going to land on a different dinner-plate!' Then she jumped out of the plane, with the spanner in her paw, and placed herself protectively in front of Me-Rah, who was wailing and plucking at her left wing.

'Hey!' called Lola into the darkness from which the chattering sound came. 'I don't know who or what you are, but one thing's for sure all over the world: rats are poisonous to eat, and this one will be particularly difficult to digest. Especially when people want to have her friends for dinner!'

The chattering that replied sounded much amused.

At this Lola lost the last of her sense of humour. 'Oh, so you think it's funny?' she shouted shrilly up to their rescuer. 'Seems to me you've let our size mislead you. You'd better be warned: there are three of us!'

And so there were. Twigleg climbed out of the plane to prove it. Why die alone as a coward, when he could do it in the company of friends? He stationed himself beside Lola and raised the pistol, though he hadn't the faintest idea how to fire it.

'A jenglot! By the hair on the head of the Golden Gibbon!' came a reply from above them. 'Why didn't you let him loose on the binturong? Although he looks very pale, and instead of pointed teeth he seems to have only a pointed nose!'

'A jeng-what? Nonsense, he's something far worse!' Lola replied, raising the spanner threateningly. 'He's a homunculus!'

So there it was! Twigleg had known all along that she got the word for him muddled up on purpose.

'Go on!' Lola whispered to him. 'Look as ferocious as you can!'

Twigleg did his best, but it took all his courage to stay put when a figure emerged from the lianas above them.

A very long-armed figure with dark body hair.

Their rescuer was a gibbon.

Wearing a man's jacket.

He landed smoothly on the withered leaves and bent down first to Me-Rah, then to Lola, and finally to Twigleg.

'Very unusual clothes for a jenglot,' he observed in an ape dialect that reminded Twigleg of the language of Madagascan lemurs.

Lola clutched the spanner even more firmly in her paw.

'What's he saying?' she whispered to Twigleg, looking darkly up at the gibbon. 'Can we trust him?'

Their rescuer didn't seem to make Me-Rah uneasy. She was paying a good deal more attention to her hurt wing, which Twigleg thought was reassuring. He was also beginning to get really curious about these jenglots.

'Ha!' said the gibbon. 'Now I know what you remind me of!'

Twigleg raised the signal pistol again as the gibbon bent over him, but he saw no ill will in the dark eyes bent on him. All that Twigleg saw there was curiosity. And a clever mind.

'I know! You look like a dwarf version of the whiteskins who come here on their big ships,' observed their rescuer. 'Do you go as red as a boiled lobster too when you've had too much sun?'

He prodded Twigleg in the chest with one finger, as if to make sure that he was real.

'Hey, watch out!' cried Lola, threatening the gibbon with the spanner again. 'He has very fragile limbs, and he really is not a toy for apes!'

Twigleg was much moved by her concern for him, not that the gibbon seemed particularly alarmed by either the spanner or the signal pistol.

'This island has had some very strange visitors recently,' he said, picking a beetle out of his white beard.

Visitors . . .

Even Me-Rah forgot her wing.

'Have you seen other strangers?' Twigleg almost swallowed his own tongue in excitement. 'Was there a boy with them, dark-haired, medium height? And a man with glasses and grey hair . . .'

'. . . and don't forget the green-skinned giant,' said the gibbon, ending his sentence for him.

That made Lola raise the spanner again at once. When she was in fighting mood, she wasn't about to make peace in a hurry.

'Oh, I see!' she said. 'You were one of the kidnappers! Where are our friends? Come on, out with it!'

The gibbon looked at her with as much interest as if he had discovered a strange clockwork toy.

'I've never seen anything like you before,' he stated. 'The rats on this island don't usually wear clothes. Or travel around in . . .' here he cast Lola's plane a mocking glance . . . 'or travel around in toy aircraft!'

Lola was about to answer him sharply, but the gibbon cut her short with a long-armed gesture.

'Your friends are in the same unfortunate situation as mine. And yes, I can take you to them. Although it looks,' he added, tapping the propeller of Lola's plane with one finger, 'it looks as if you'll need some other means of transport.'

Unfortunately the gibbon was right. The binturong had done a good deal of damage to Lola's plane. One rotor blade was cracked, and the left wing of the little aircraft had a nasty split in it. Lola looked at the plane as unhappily as if it were an old friend who had been injured, which was understandable after all the adventures they had been through together.

'Some other means of transport?' she asked sharply. 'And where are we supposed to find that?'

The gibbon mockingly bared his teeth, and pointed to his own chest. 'TerTaWa, at your service. But we'd better wait for morning.'

CHAPTER THIRTY-ONE

The Griffins' Royal Tree

There is nothing in which the birds differ more
from man than the way in which they can build
and yet leave a landscape as it was before.
Robert Lynd, *The Blue Lion and Other Essays*

Before Twigleg had met TerTaWa, he'd have bet his five fingers (and he was greatly attached to his fingers) that no kind of travel could be more uncomfortable than flying in Lola's infernal plane. He'd have lost the bet, and with it his fingers. It was a pleasant sensation when the gibbon put him on his hairy shoulder. But then TerTaWa began swinging from tree to tree – so high above the ground that in his mind's eye Twigleg saw himself smashed down there like the test tube that had given birth to him!

Aaaaahhhhhhhhhhh!

And what did that totally crazy rat do? Lola was humming happily to herself! Even though she'd had to leave her beloved plane behind in the hollow tree. It's all for my master, Twigleg reminded himself. For my master . . . Ma-ma-maaaaster!

Close your eyes, Twigleg!

Yes, that did improve things a bit.

He didn't open his eyes again until the gibbon stopped. Although it felt to him as if they had been jumping from tree to tree for days on end.

'By all the three-humped camels of Samarkand!' whispered Lola. 'Take a look at that, humklupus!'

Such an enormous tree spread its canopy in front of them that all the others seemed to retreat respectfully from it. Mud nests exactly like the ruined nests that Lola and Twigleg had found hung from its mighty trunk and its countless branches. But high above, in the crown of the tree, there was a structure, complete with battlements, beside which the other nests looked like hovels in the shade of a princely palace. Its walls shone in rich shades of red and green, as if they were set with rubies and emeralds.

'Let me make the introductions,' whispered TerTaWa. 'The Royal Tree of Kraa the Terrible! No, wait a minute. He prefers the title of Kraa of the Murderous Beak. Kraa who kills with talons, venom and claws, Kraa of the Blood-Drenched Feathers, Eater of a Thousand Hearts . . .'

The entire tree was in motion. Crowds of monkeys and apes – lorises, macaques, gibbons, sirulis – were climbing up the trunk and along the branches to a platform that had been built right below the palatial nest like a great square in the crown of the tree. There was a throne in the middle of it, with a griffin's head carved on its back, and above the throne – the sight almost made Twigleg drop Lola's binoculars – hung a dozen woven cages. Twigleg could make out the outlines of prisoners behind the twigs from which the cages were made.

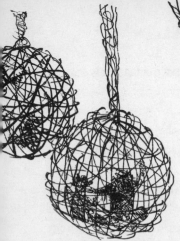

The basketwork cage hanging directly over the throne was far and away the largest, and TerTaWa uttered furious chattering when green feathers appeared, pressed against the woven side of the cage.

'Why all the excitement?' whispered Lola. 'Is this some kind of assembly?'

'No, Kraa is about to dispense justice!' TerTaWa whispered back. 'That crook-beaked monkey-murderer! He loves putting on a show!' The gibbon struck the trunk of the tree where he was sitting with his fist. 'He'll kill them!' he groaned. 'Shrii, Kupo, Patah and all the others. Or sell them to the poachers to fill his treasury!'

'How about a little more optimism?' hissed Lola. 'We must get closer to the cages. Can you do that without being recognised, TerTaWa?'

By way of an answer, the gibbon picked a fruit growing above them. He bit into it and rubbed the juice into his dark hair until it turned a reddish colour. Then he ruffled up the white whiskers on his cheeks, pulled the hair on his head over his eyes, made the tips of his ears look pointed – and bared his teeth.

'What's the plan?' he whispered.

'Plan? By my aircraft's compass and elevator,' hissed Lola, as Me-Rah stared in alarm at all the apes and monkeys still clambering up the tree, 'what kind of a plan? We'll improvise, that's what! We'll find our friends and let them know we're working to set them free? Will that do for you?'

TerTaWa glanced doubtfully at the basketwork cages – and

ducked hastily as a shadow fell on the tree where they were sitting. Rushing filled the humid, sultry air, and five griffins came gliding through the branches of the surrounding trees. They flew towards the platform, circled in the air above the throne, and finally, one by one, came down to perch on the branches above it. They dug the claws of their paws into the dark bark, they folded their wings as if clenching fingers into fists, and their eyes, the eyes of birds of prey, scanned the crowd that had assembled in the space around the throne below them.

They looked so much smaller in the pictures! That was all Twigleg could think. A ridiculous thought, for he had read often enough that griffins were the only fabulous beings that could compete with dragons in size.

As usual, of course, Lola's reaction was rather different.

'By all the storms of this world,' she whispered, in a tone of admiration, 'those creatures really *are* magnificent!'

'Magnificent?' hissed TerTaWa. 'Plagucy rapacious felines! Brood of snake-tailed robbers! See the way they're looking down at us? Roargh, Hiera, Chahska, Fierra, Greeeiiiir . . . there were more of them once, many more. But the rain and the humid heat don't agree with the older ones. And they don't often have young. There are only three females left, and Kraa claims them all for himself, so two of them flew away last year. Of course Kraa claims that Shrii persuaded them to go, but not even he knows where they are.'

Another griffin came down through the canopy of leaves.

'Tchraee!' The gibbon bared his teeth as the griffin came down to perch on a branch above the others. 'He's Kraa's adjutant, and almost as bad as Kraa himself. When Tchraee is in a bad temper he likes to eat one of the lorises that are always having to

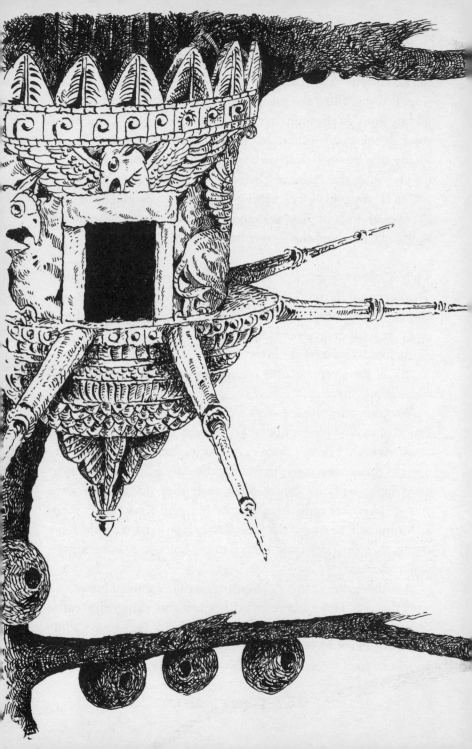

decorate Kraa's nest with new pictures. Do you see how he's staring down at the basket that holds Shrii? Tchraee has hated him ever since Shrii came out of his mother's body.'

'Out of her body?' Lola was checking the ammunition in the signal pistol. 'You mean griffin young don't hatch from eggs?'

'They'd bite your head off for that question, rat,' whispered TerTaWa. 'No, griffins have cubs in the same way as lions. Reee was Kraa's sister, and Tchraee was in love with her, but Reee didn't bother to conceal what she thought of him. Some say that Shrii's father wasn't a griffin but the god Garuda himself. The theory is that's why he's so brightly coloured! But I think his father was a Pelangi bird. They sometimes fly here from Sumatra.'

A Pelangi bird. Twigleg wished he was back in the library of MÍMAMEIÐR, with the books that told you all about the world, so that you didn't have to board a rat's plane to go and find out. Or ride on a griffin's shoulder.

'Duck down!' whispered TerTaWa. 'See those black macaques? They're the guards. If they see you, they'll feed you to the jackal scorpions without a moment's hesitation!'

Jackal scor . . .? Before Twigleg had finished thinking about this alarming name, TerTaWa was taking a great leap over to the tree with the griffins in it. Twigleg really admired the silence with which he made that leap, even if it had him feeling that his

stomach was in his mouth again. Didn't the force of gravity affect gibbons? He couldn't think of any other explanation!

And no one seemed to notice the gibbon. Twigleg nestled deep into TerTaWa's thick coat while he looked around. It wasn't difficult to distinguish between the nests of the griffins and the monkeys because of their different size. Two were surrounded by flocks of tiny birds working on the mud walls. They were all adorned with pictures, though none of the other nests could compete with the main nest in beauty. Kraa's palace would have put many castles built by human beings to shame. The reliefs on the walls showed griffins hunting, griffins at war with men and monsters – and perching triumphantly on the dead body of a dragon.

'Did lorises really create those pictures?' whispered Twigleg incredulously.

TerTaWa swung himself up on a branch growing out of the huge tree trunk right beside the throne platform. 'Yes. The most talented of them are sitting behind the throne. They can portray any of this world's creatures as accurately as if it would begin breathing next moment. Some of them have been serving the griffins for several generations.'

The six lorises crouching on the skilfully carved bench behind the throne kept their eyes down.

'We call them *The Hands*,' whispered TerTaWa. 'Don't be deceived by their bowed heads. They pride themselves a great deal on their art. But the best of them all, Kupo, followed Shrii, because she was tired of praising Kraa's cruelty in her pictures.'

'Who's the proboscis monkey beside the throne?' whispered Twigleg.

He wore a cloak of parrot feathers over his brown pelt, and held a staff in his long-fingered hand, making him look like a master of ceremonies at the court of a medieval prince.

'Nakal,' whispered TerTaWa. 'May the jackal scorpions tear him limb from limb! May the jenglots drink his blood – I'm sure it's even more poisonous than theirs! He is Kraa's personal servant. And his best spy. Anyone who crosses Nakal doesn't live long.'

Nakal gave the crowd a haughty look. His staff was made of carved bones. Twigleg looked at the platform on which the throne stood. Of course. He had been wondering if it was made of ivory, but no; it too consisted of bones, arranged in an artistic pattern by *The Hands*.

Nakal struck the platform with his staff.

Immediately there was silence. Even the parrots, sitting among the branches in their dozens, stopped squawking. Twigleg wondered what they thought about Nakal's cloak of feathers. There were some lories with red plumage among the parrots, but Twigleg had to admit that they all looked to him much the same, and he couldn't have said whether Me-Rah was among them.

TerTaWa swung himself lower until he was standing on the

platform. Of course, Lola was intent on looking around at her leisure in the crowd, and in the end Twigleg too gave way to the temptation to poke his head a little way out of TerTaWa's fur. Unfortunately, however, two of the black macaques were blocking his view of the cages. The only things that Twigleg could see – all too clearly – were the griffins perched high above them. The venomous snakes that were their tails were wound around the branches they were sitting on.

'Do you see the contempt in their eyes when they look at us?' whispered TerTaWa. 'To them, all other living things are as unimportant and worthless as the beetles and butterflies that their monkeys kill to use their wings for colouring the pictures on their nests. Only Shrii is different. He was our hope! He risked his life for us, and now he's going to lose it on our account!'

TerTaWa's eyes were fixed, full of pain, on the large basketwork cage where Shrii was held captive. But finally he made his way on through the throng of hairy bodies, and at last Twigleg had a clear view of the other cages of prisoners. When he saw the outline of a boy in one of them, Ben's name almost passed his lips. But it wasn't Ben. The boy pressing his face to the bent twigs of the cage was younger, and came from this part of the world. Where was his master? Had the griffins already eaten him and the others?

No – there! The lenses of a pair of glasses glinted inside the twigs of the cage. Lola had seen them too. Twigleg heard her suppress a curse. Barnabas! Oh, what a relief. For a moment Twigleg even forgot the cage and the griffins. Beside Barnabas, the green fingers clutching the bars of the cage unmistakably belonged to Hothbrodd. And yes, there was his master!

Ben called something to the other boy, but Twigleg couldn't

understand the words. The silence that fell when the proboscis monkey struck his staff on the platform hadn't lasted long. Kraa's followers were squawking, chattering, and growling in the crown of the gigantic tree. It was like a vast wasps' nest. Monkeys and apes were the great majority: macaques, gibbons, lorises, langurs, surilis and proboscis monkeys! In addition there were countless Indian flying squirrels, pine martens and snakes climbing or crawling on the platform or in the branches above it.

The proboscis monkey struck the platform with his staff again, but on this occasion three times, and with greater emphasis.

The huge canopy of the tree was full of anxious silence.

It was so still that you could hear the scraping of Kraa's terrible claws as he stepped out of his palace entrance. It was surrounded by flight ramps that enclosed the nest like a wreath of gilded thorns. One of them cast its shadow on the throne platform. Kraa's claws, the claws of a bird of prey, made his gait rather stiff-legged as he walked along, but his lion's body and snake-tail more than made up for that. The snake wound its way along after Kraa, like a threat traced in the sultry jungle air.

The griffin stopped at the end of the ramp and looked down at his subjects. The great beak was slightly open, as if he were drinking in the fear that rose to him, and the cruelty in his yellow eyes made Twigleg bury his face in TerTaWa's soft fur for a moment.

Then Kraa spread his wings. The rushing sound was like a gathering storm above them. Oh, he was gigantic! For a few moments Kraa's shadow made day into night. The crowd drew back even before he came down on the platform, and like all the others, TerTaWa threw himself on his knees so quickly that Twigleg almost slid off his shoulder.

'Kraaaaaa!'

Hundreds of voices murmured, growled, and squawked the name of their feathered king. Twigleg felt TerTaWa shuddering at the sound. The voices also murmured another word: *Tuanka.* Lord . . .

While Kraa strode to his throne, six creatures crawled out of his plumage. They had already troubled Twigleg when he found them beside a griffin in a book illustration. Jackal scorpions. No, oh no. He had really hoped they were just a medieval invention, like people with faces beneath their shoulders, or two-headed camels. The jackal scorpions jumped down on the platform and surrounded the throne, with the stings at the end of their tails raised to attack. With bitter satisfaction, Twigleg saw that even Lola's whiskers quivered at the sight. Curse that Pegasus! Curse the eggs as well! Curse the day when Guinevere and Vita found them!

The leap with which Kraa settled on his throne made the platform shake, and Nakal struck the floor with his staff again.

'Bow down before Kraa the Terrible, invincible and older than the world,' cried the proboscis monkey in a shrill voice, 'bow down before the Winged Tempest, the Feathered Lion of the Air, the Snake King . . .'

Kraa's viper tail bared its venomous fangs, while the griffin listened with obvious pleasure to the enumeration of his titles.

All eyes were turned on Kraa. Lola took her chance to scurry around to Twigleg from TerTaWa's other shoulder. That crazy rat!

'I'm going to climb up to Barnabas. Humpelkluss,' she whispered to Twigleg. 'You stay here.'

And before Twigleg could protest, she was already jumping down to the bone tiles of the platform, and had disappeared into the milling crowd.

Nakal was still reciting the many unpleasant titles of Kraa.

Twigleg looked up at the cage where Barnabas's glasses were glinting behind the twigs – and climbed down TerTaWa to follow Lola.

CHAPTER THIRTY-TWO

Kraa

It took the whole of Creation
To produce my foot, my each feather:
Now I hold Creation in my foot.
Or fly up, and revolve it all slowly –
I kill where I please because it is all mine.
There is no sophistry in my body:
My manners are tearing off heads –
The allotment of death.
Ted Hughes, 'Hawk Roosting'

K raa ...
  Ben looked down through the twigs enclosing him at the
enormous griffin, and didn't know whether he felt fear or amazement more strongly. Perhaps you always felt like that when you
saw a king. And Kraa was a king, there was no doubt about it.
The terrible beak, the pitiless eyes, the huge tawny lion's body
merging with dull brown plumage at the neck ... the sight of

Kraa filled the heart with horror, with the wish to escape his hungry gaze. Yet at the same time Ben couldn't see enough of the glorious griffin – for all the cruelty of his aura by comparison with the kindness that you sensed in Shrii and Firedrake. Kraa was the embodiment of everything in the world that hunted and killed. He was hunger and fury, the intoxication of the attack and of his own frenzied strength.

Was the griffin larger than Firedrake? No, they were probably about the same size. When the griffins had carried them out into the open in the basketwork cages, Ben had felt terribly small and vulnerable. Since then he had been able to imagine what Twigleg felt like most of the time a good deal better. The eagle claws of the griffins, seen at close quarters, were as unsettling a sight as their lions' paws, and the snake's tail seemed to have a life of its own. Kraa's tail looked like a Persian horned viper, and caught a bird that was careless enough to fly past his throne as the griffin was making himself comfortable on it. And in the tawny feathers at his throat, three shone as if they were made of pure gold. Those must be the sun-feathers that they had come to find! So close, and yet to Ben they seemed even further out of reach than on the day when he had first heard of them in MÍMAMEIÐR.

It was the same for Barnabas.

He looked down at Kraa, and felt as ridiculous as a mouse who had gone up to a lion to ask for a strand of his mane. And the worst of it was that he had taken his son into the lion's den with him.

Kraa preened his wings with his beak, and laid the snake-tail around his paws and claws. Then he looked up at the baskets where his prisoners were waiting for sentence to be passed on them. He inspected them all as fleetingly as a king who had already sent thousands to their death. But then his amber gaze fixed on the basket containing Shrii.

The young griffin could hardly move in his prison. His green plumage made it look as if the jungle was held captive in the basket with him.

A menacing growl came from Kraa's curved beak.

'In all my centuries of experience . . .' Kraa's voice was not loud. It was a rough, hoarse croak, but Ben thought he could feel it right to the marrow of his bones. 'In all the battles I have fought . . .' and the griffin reared up so that he could show the scars on his breast, '. . . I have never, never . . .' here the croak became a shrill scream, '. . . never seen such treachery!'

He spread his wings, like a king throwing back his cloak in anger. Except that Kraa's wings were a good deal more impressive. He held them outstretched, as if to remind everyone present of his strength and his size – and of how fast he could swoop down and bring death to every one of them with his beak and claws.

'My own sister's son!' Kraa snapped at the air as if striking Shrii with his beak. 'Did you really think you could steal this island from me in my lifetime? You and the fools who followed you. They will all pay dearly for it!'

Muted wailing rose from the cages containing Shrii's monkeys, and Ben let his eyes wander over the crowd around Kraa's throne. He saw many indignant faces, and fingers pointing accusingly at Shrii, but also monkeys looking up at the young griffin with eyes full of sadness. Maybe Shrii had more supporters than Kraa liked.

'Hothbrodd,' Barnabas whispered to the troll. 'Maybe you ought to have another word with the twigs holding this basket together. I admit I still had some slight hope of being able to negotiate with this griffin. But he's never going to believe that we're not in league with Shrii, and I'm afraid he won't forgive us for that!'

Kraa looked up at them as if he had heard what Barnabas said.

'And what kind of human beings are these that you've been mingling with?' he called up to Shrii. 'Are they as scatter-brained as the boy with the brownie-maki? My spies tell me that he's visited many islands and has often cheated our friends the poachers of their prey. I'm sure they'll pay well for him. And your furry friend will fetch a good price too!' Kraa called up to Winston. 'So far as I can see he's much the same as a rat, but I hear that makis sell in human markets for more than the largest parrots!'

Winston put a protective arm around Berulu, but Kraa was already turning to the cage with Barnabas, Ben and Hothbrodd in it.

'No, these three aren't here to rescue monkeys and parrot,' he growled. 'You were going to send them to me to buy my trust with humans' gold! Shrii the kind-hearted! Shrii the monkeys' friend! Lies, all lies! You're as hungry for blood and gold as I am! This trio were to have helped you to steal my treasures, that was the plan!'

Shrii protested, but one of the other griffins silenced him by pecking at the basketwork cage containing the monkeys who followed him.

'Nakal,' Kraa commanded the proboscis monkey, 'show my loyal servants what Shrii's spies were going to use to win the favour of Kraa the Great!'

Reaching under his cloak of feathers, Nakal held up the bangle that Bağdagül had given Barnabas.

There was excited whispering among the assembled monkeys, and the snake that was Kraa's tail writhed and bared its venom fangs.

'A bangle! Couldn't you at least have sent them to me with a chest full of gold?' Kraa shouted up to Shrii. 'And just look at your robbers! Did you want to insult me and not just steal from me? A child and a man with glass eyes! They weren't even armed! Or is that green tree-man their weapon? Well, he at least will fetch a decent price from the poachers,' he added, with a disparaging glance at Ben and Barnabas.

'I'm going to pluck your feathers out one by one, you sandy crow!' roared Hothbrodd down to him. 'I'll make myself a belt from your snake-tail and a pair of leggings from your coat!'

The troll threw himself against the basketwork of the cage so furiously that it swung back and forth like the clapper of a bell, and Ben and Barnabas thought they would end up lying in front of Kraa's paws with their necks broken. But the griffins' basket cages had already held many angry captives securely. Crocodiles and marbled cats fought for their freedom just as fiercely as a troll.

'Hmm,' purred Kraa, casting Hothbrodd a glance of amusement. 'You remind me of a demon whose flesh I tore apart and sent to all four quarters of the compass six hundred years ago. It was much the same unappetising colour as your skin.'

Hothbrodd favoured him with his entire repertory of Viking curses. But Kraa had turned to Shrii again.

'I'll tell you what, sister's son, I think I'll leave you alive until all who helped you are sold or dead!' he called to him. 'Nothing I can do to you will hurt you more. Your mother too suffered every time she swallowed a beetle by mistake in flight. Pity . . . why should we feel what others feel? The only heartbeat we have to understand is our own. No other creature is the equal of a griffin.'

'Yet you have served human kings for gold. You were nothing but their winged servant.'

Shrii's voice was so different from Kraa's. You could hear the song of gibbons in it, and the wind blowing through a thousand leaves and colourful feathers. Shrii had not been born in a desert far away. He was a child of this island.

'All your strength, wasted on nothing but enriching yourself. Yet you can't even eat gold! Every crocodile is better than you. Every beetle on the island is more useful, every fish in the ocean. You're a parasite, Kraa, and I challenge you to a duel. I challenge you on behalf of all those you have sold, although they trusted you and served you.'

A murmuring rose among the assembled monkeys, and the birds in the branches beat their wings uneasily. But Nakal struck the platform with his staff, and silenced them all with a shrill whistle.

'Ah, yes, the old rumour that you and your followers like to spread.' Kraa plucked a flying squirrel that had come too close to his beak out of the air and swallowed it whole. 'How did it go again? Kraa even sells his subjects. Kraa sells his most faithful servants. Lies. I sell only traitors and thieves. And the usual creatures born to be the prey of hunters.'

'Really?' replied Shrii. The eagle and the lion could be heard in his own voice now. 'What became of your last personal servant? Has Nakal ever asked about him? And where are the lorises who worked on your portrait in a way you didn't like? Where are the birds of paradise who were heard in the evening? Where's the albino macaque who had his nest right under your palace? Nothing and no one on this island is safe from you! All that counts to you is the glittering plunder that the poachers pay you, and the shells that sharpen your beak and the beaks of others!'

Once again, Kraa spread his wings menacingly. He beat them so strongly that the basketwork cages swayed, knocking against each other, and Hothbrodd almost crushed Barnabas and Ben with his weight. Even the monkeys and flying squirrels hanging in the branches above Kraa could hardly hold on, and something fell, with a shrill scream, and landed right in front of Kraa's throne.

Nakal picked the Something up, and held it high in the air in his fingertips.

'Twigleg!' cried Ben. 'Let go of him!'

But no one paid any attention.

Kraa was bending curiously down to the homunculus as a second figure jumped down from the branches above him, and landed beside Nakal.

'Don't you touch him, you feathered kitty-cat!' Lola's yell travelled all the way up to Barnabas. 'And as for you,' she snapped at Nakal, aiming her tiny signal pistol at the proboscis monkey, 'let go of my friend or you've drawn your last breath!'

Lola was certainly one of the bravest people Ben knew, but she didn't always stop to think. One of the jackal scorpions grabbed her with its pincers, and was obviously not impressed by the signal shot that the rat fired at its golden armour.

Ben rattled the twig bars of his cage in helpless despair. Even Barnabas had turned pale, and Hothbrodd uttered a roar that would have done credit to any griffin. The troll was very fond of the flying rat, although he would certainly have denied it to his own kind.

'Well, look at this!' Kraa scrutinised Twigleg and Lola with such interest that his beak almost touched them. 'Vermin in the form of a rodent, and a jenglot! Your choice of allies becomes more and more bizarre, Shrii!'

'I am not a jenglot!' cried Twigleg in a shaking but very determined voice. 'I'm a hom—'

'Oh yes, he is!' Lola interrupted him shrilly. 'A jenglot! That's what he is, and what a jenglot! A very dangerous one, a downright poisonous jenglot! And this rat, you avaricious desert bird . . .' her boot missed the nose of the jackal scorpion holding her only by millimetres, 'this rat is about to show you who's vermin around here!'

Ben hardly dared to breathe as Kraa raised his head and looked down thoughtfully at the two tiny prisoners, as if wondering which to eat first.

'What do you think, Nakal?' he growled. 'A rat in human clothing, and a jenglot with skin as white as ivory. Those two could fetch a good price.'

'Indeed they could, Your Majesty,' replied Nakal in a sub-servient voice. 'Every collector of rare specimens would be keen to get hold of them. The lack of size could even be an advantage. After all, they'd both fit comfortably into a birdcage!'

Lola was about to reply, but before she could say anything, Nakal removed her from the jackal scorpion's pincers and put her and Twigleg into a bag together.

'There goes our hope of rescue, I'm afraid,' Barnabas whispered to Ben. 'Still, we've often thought so before, and we're still alive and well, right?'

Ben nodded, although not with much conviction. He knew that if he had still been wearing Firedrake's scale around his neck he'd have summoned the dragon now. To save Twigleg!

With one bound, Kraa leaped off his throne, casting a last triumphant glance up at Shrii before striding to the edge of the platform. The jackal scorpions cleared the crowd out of his way by going ahead, clattering their pincers together threateningly. Then they climbed up Kraa's mighty hind legs and disappeared under his wings.

'Take the prisoners to the Beak Trees!' called Nakal, as Kraa flew up to his palace nest with a few mighty wing-beats.

The other griffins obeyed. They closed their front claws on the lianas from which the cages hung, and rose in the air with them. But when two of them raised Shrii's basket, Kraa called them back with a cry that cut the ears like a knife.

'No, no, he stays here!' he called down from the gateway of his palace. 'Didn't you hear what I said? He will be the last to die. I'll clip his claws and wings, and feed him on the gold I get for his servants until he chokes on it. And then I'll tear his heart out of his colourful breast and eat it. Although it will probably taste as soft and sweet as an over-ripe melon.'

Ben did not hear whether Shrii replied. If he did, his voice was lost in the screeching of the other griffins. Then Tchraee seized the basket in which Barnabas, Hothbrodd and Ben were imprisoned, and flew south with it ahead of the others.

CHAPTER THIRTY-THREE

Eight

There are still some blue whales. There are still some
krill in Antarctica. Half the coral reefs are in pretty good
shape, a jewelled belt around the middle of the planet.
There's still time, but not a lot, to turn things around.
Sylvia Earle

Maia had been right. The tugging in Firedrake's breast pointed the way as reliably as the needle of a compass. He and Tattoo flew all night. The younger dragon had as much stamina as Firedrake had hoped, and when the sun rose he still didn't ask to stop for a rest. There were dangers in flying by day, even though the juice of the dragon-flowers was a good substitute for moonlight. But the memory of the fear that Firedrake had felt as clearly as his own made him forget caution. The sky was almost cloudless, and speed was their only camouflage. In that Tattoo proved to be the perfect companion. The younger dragon easily kept up with Firedrake. A sailor on a Chinese freighter who looked up at the sky at the wrong moment was only mocked by his companions when he talked about seeing two dragons, because they had gone before the rest of the crew reached the ship's rail. And a child who took a photo of Tattoo on his cell-phone was very disappointed to find that it showed nothing but a shadowy blur.

Faster, Firedrake, faster. He kept reassuring himself by thinking that he supposed he would hardly feel the tugging if Ben were not alive. But was that true? The stone-dwarves' answers had been very vague when Firedrake asked them whether the scale would also make him feel fear that was past and forgotten. It was too long since a dragon had had a dragon rider. So much about the link between them was lost in oblivion, and there was no one who could have explained to Firedrake that his scale would go on calling until he found it again, like an emergency signal from a ship abandoned long ago.

The first signs of dawn were showing in the sky when one of the countless islands in the sea below them attracted Firedrake to it like a magnet. The dragons saw a couple of fishing villages on the north coast of the island, but the scale seemed to Firedrake to be directing him to a beach at its southernmost point. Sorrel jumped down from Firedrake's back into the hot sand, and looked around for Hothbrodd's plane. She could see nothing, however, but birds, crabs and turtles.

'This doesn't look very promising,' she said. 'Are you sure about it, Firedrake?'

Tattoo looked around as doubtfully as Sorrel.

Firedrake didn't know what to say. Everything in him whispered that he had reached his journey's end, but it was difficult even for him to trust that whispering voice in view of the empty beach. Farther inland, the island was densely covered with jungle. It would take days to search it all for Ben and Barnabas.

'Oh, mouldy mushrooms, how I hate beaches!' said Sorrel, annoyed, as she shook sand off her furry feet. 'The ground a brownie stands on ought to be damp and firm. Mushrooms don't grow in sand! All it produces is sand-fleas!'

The only sign of the human world was a plastic bottle, but that certainly had nothing to do with Ben or Barnabas. Plastic bottles were on MÍMAMEIÐR's black list. Guinevere had even managed to persuade the nisses to give up their passion for plastic containers.

'They must be here!' said Firedrake. 'The pull is as strong as if Ben were standing by the rocks over there!'

Sorrel knew him too well not to believe him. She trudged towards the rocks – and stopped, as if rooted to the ground. Sorrel knew the locket lying among seashells and seaweed washed up by the tide; she had seen it on Barnabas Greenbloom's study desk. But when she bent to pick it up, two red claws snapped at her fingers.

'*That,*' said a thin but very penetrating voice, 'belongs to me!'

Sorrel rubbed her fingers, which hurt, and looked incredulously at the tiny crab aggressively waving its pincers at her. It had four eyes on long, thin stalks on top of its head.

'Liar!' growled Sorrel. 'In the first place, you don't even have a neck to hang *that* around, and in the second place, this particular *that* belongs to Barnabas Greenbloom!'

Neither of these statements seemed to impress the crab.

'Flotsam and jetsam belong to the finder!' he cried, rattling his pincers. 'Unwritten law of the ocea—'

He suddenly stopped, staring over Sorrel's shoulder.

Firedrake was standing behind her. The crab, alarmed, scuttled first to the left and then to the right – he was remarkably quick on his ten thin legs. Then he closed all four eyes.

'A dragon? No. No, no, Eugene!' Firedrake and Sorrel heard him murmur. 'You've obviously eaten too many coral-grass fleas. Although . . .' Eugene opened first one eye, then the next, and finally all four of them. 'Yes. Why not? A dragon? No, two dragons. Okay. And a . . . yes, a what?' The four eyes examined Sorrel from head to foot. 'Monkey. Yes. But what species?'

Tattoo and Firedrake exchanged an amused glance. Sorrel, on the other hand, didn't think that Eugene was at all funny.

'Monkey?' she snapped at him.

Eugene inspected her again, very thoroughly. 'Hmm, no, I take that back,' he said. 'So you're a . . .?'

'Spotted Scottish brownie,' said Sorrel sharply. 'And my sort don't like anything with pincers on the ends of its arms. Especially when it steals from friends of ours!'

Eugene closed his claws even more firmly on the chain of the locket, and planted two legs on its silver lid. 'Right. Prove that it belongs to this so-called friend of yours. What's inside it?'

'One of my scales,' said Firedrake. 'Or so I assume.'

Eugene looked very disappointed. With all four eyes.

'Ah. I see,' he murmured, and lowered his pincers. 'A dragon's scale. I'd been wondering why someone would keep such an insignificant metal thingy in a beautiful silver case like this. But any reasonable crab must admit that it looks very much like your other scales.'

Eugene sighed, and his four eyes went to Firedrake's breast, with the dark patch showing where the missing scale had been.

'Was the locket lying exactly here when you found it?' asked Firedrake. 'I gave the scale to a friend, and I'm afraid he is in danger.'

Eugene guiltily avoided the dragon's glance.

'Er, no,' he murmured, while two of the eyes taking evasive action looked at the sky and another two looked at the sand. 'To tell you the truth, I didn't really find it. I took the silver thing away from a lanternfish. Out there,' he said, waving one pincer at the sea. 'Where the shipwrecks lie and the coral nixies live.'

Sorrel tried very hard not to look too worried, but she could sense how heavy-hearted Firedrake was. Brownies don't need any dragon scale to know what their own dragon is feeling.

'Where the shipwrecks lie?' repeated Firedrake. 'When you were there –' he hardly dared to ask – 'did you see the wreck of an airplane among them? A flying machine made of wood?'

Eugene looked at him with obvious sympathy (it gave the crab a slight violet tinge). 'A flying machine? No. But Eight swears he saw something of that kind. A machine made of wood, with wings. I thought it was just one of his stories. He simply has too much imagination!'

'Where?' asked Tattoo. 'Where did he see it?'

Yes, he was a rather impatient young dragon.

'On the beach of Pulau Bulu,' replied Eugene. 'You know: the island of the lion-birds.'

'Lion-birds?' Tattoo exchanged a quick glance with Firedrake and Sorrel.

'Yes. There are all kinds of strange creatures around the place on Pulau Bulu,' commented Eugene, with a dismissive wave of his pincers. 'Though, mind you, Eight also says a green man climbed out of the flying thing. Oh no, I said to myself when he came out with that, he's gone and found a barrel of rum among the wrecks again! When he does that he always talks sheer nonsense for days on end, and he ties knots in his own arms!'

'Eight?' Firedrake was trying hard not to lose patience with Eugene. After all, the crab could be their only hope of finding Ben in spite of everything. Lion-birds. That didn't sound much like a phoenix!

'Do you think your friend Eight could take us to this island?'

'Sure! I don't know exactly where he is at the moment, but I can call him,' offered Eugene. 'He's probably painting a ship's hull again. He doesn't even leave the drilling rigs alone. "Eight," I always tell him, "human beings don't know how to appreciate your works of art!" And believe you me, his ink lasts a long time, even under water. One of these days they'll make him into octopus salad, but he doesn't even know what that is. My friend Eight is such a little innocent!'

Eugene looked at his reflection in the silver of the locket. Then he picked it up by the chain – and dropped it in front of Sorrel's paws.

'I once heard that dragons bring out the best in every living being,' he sighed. 'But I'd never have thought, not in a hundred years, that it also applied to four-eyed crabs. What a nuisance.'

Eugene tripped towards the surf breaking over the beach in shallow waves, and began rattling his pincers faster than a flamenco dancer rattling her castanets.

At first it almost looked as if the entire Pacific Ocean was answering Eugene.

Out in the open sea, a wave began to swell. It towered up and up, until Sorrel took shelter behind Firedrake's legs. Then arms densely covered with suckers reached up out of the wave, and a gigantic head with eyes so large that Sorrel could have fitted comfortably into them.

Eight. A good name for a Great Kraken.

The long arms winding their way over the beach were in all the colours of the rainbow, while Eight's body – or what could be seen of it – was dark green, like the uttermost depths of the ocean.

'You see?' Firedrake whispered to Sorrel. 'It's sensible to be polite even to tiny four-eyed crabs. You never know, they may have powerful friends.'

One inky blue kraken arm wound over the sand to Eugene, while the others, to Sorrel's relief, stayed in the water. The crab climbed up on the kraken's arm, and pointed one of his claws at Firedrake and Tattoo.

'Look at that, Eight!' he called. 'They really are dragons. Would you have thought there were still any around? No! So why wouldn't there also be another nice Great Kraken somewhere or other?'

'Oh, there definitely is,' said Sorrel, who had quickly overcome her alarm at Eight's size. 'In fact, I've met him myself. Although I'm not so sure about the "nice" bit. Most of the time he acts . . .'

Firedrake cast her a warning glance.

'The friend I'm looking for knows the kraken she mentions very well!' he called to Eight. 'And I'm sure he will help you to find him.'

The kraken's huge eyes widened as if to take in the whole world. Eight raised two more arms out of the water, and passed them through the air as if he were writing invisible letters there.

'Eight would like to know what ocean this kraken calls his home,' Eugene translated. 'The only one we know is a very bad-tempered one off the coast of New Zealand.'

'This one lives off the north coast of Norway,' replied Firedrake. 'And the friend I'm looking for can certainly tell you more about his temper.'

That was putting it very diplomatically, and Sorrel bit back the comment that Hafgufa, the name of the Norwegian kraken, certainly had a temper every bit as bad as the one from New Zealand.

Eight's arms wrote in the air again.

'He will take you to the beach where he saw the wooden machine and the green man,' Eugene translated. 'But first Eight would like to know who painted your scales,' he said, pointing to Tattoo. 'He likes the pattern very much.'

CHAPTER THIRTY-FOUR

Synnefo, Chara, Ouranos

It takes a very long time to become young.
Pablo Picasso

Synnefo really was as white as her mother. Chara had his father's copper-coloured coat, and Ouranos – yes, Ouranos was blue! Guinevere couldn't have said which she liked best. All three were so beautiful! She and Vita spent every free minute in the stable, to catch a glimpse of the foals as often as they could, and Ànemos came too, to kneel beside the nest for hours, although his children's feathered nursemaids were still very strict about visiting times.

Even in the moments, only too short, when the eggs were not hidden under the feathers that kept them warm, the foals were already giving away a good deal about their characters. Synnefo was the calmest of the three. She drifted inside her egg as dreamily as if she were hardly aware of the outside world. Chara, on the other hand, often pressed his nose against his eggshell, which was clear as glass now, and always seemed glad if he could see more than just feathers! And Ouranos – he was always moving, beating his tiny wings, kicking his legs as if his hooves were already trying to find solid ground, or throwing his little head back and blowing miniature bubbles as he whinnied.

No, you could never tire of looking at them. Guinevere only wished they wouldn't grow so fast.

When she caught Ànemos looking at the remaining blank spaces on the calendar, she took it off the stable door and hid it in her room.

Please, she thought as she hung the calendar over her bed. Ben! Dad! Hothbrodd! Twigleg! Lola! Tell us that you have the feather! Get in touch! But suppose they had bad news? Suppose they hadn't found the griffins. Or suppose they'd found them, and . . . no! Guinevere wouldn't think out that question to the end, even though she thought she saw it on every face in MÍMAMEIÐR.

Synnefo.

Chara.

Ouranos.

Their tiny mouths drank the shimmering liquid in which they swam. But it would soon be finished if the eggs didn't grow.

Guinevere looked at the sky as she went back to the stable. She caught herself staring intently at the clouds more and more often, as if that would bring Hothbrodd's plane back.

But the sky over MÍMAMEIÐR was still empty.

They would get back in time. And the feather would help.

It must!

Synnefo . . . Chara . . . Ouranos.

CHAPTER THIRTY-FIVE

Sold

*The sun, the moon and the stars would have
disappeared long ago . . . had they happened to be
within the reach of predatory human hands.*
Havelock Ellis, *The Dance of Life*

Looking through bars for too long is bad for the heart. Even if those bars are only made of twigs. Ben realised he was forgetting what it felt like to be free. No, it was even worse – he began to think that he would never be free again. The griffins had put the cages down in a dark clearing where the shadows of the trees reached out, like black fingers, for everything that grew under them. In the middle of the clearing stood a huge statue of a griffin, carved from such precious tropical wood that, in spite of their unhappy situation, it drew a sigh of longing from Hothbrodd. The dish in its claws reminded Ben of the sacrificial vessels in which bloody gifts to the gods had once been left in ancient temples. Not a very reassuring sight. Nor were the beaked faces of griffins that looked down on them from the surrounding trees. They were high up on the trunks, with golden feathers, eyes made of red jewels, and beaks of shimmering mother-of-pearl. Hothbrodd scrutinised them as thoroughly as if his life depended on working out what tool *The Hands* had used to erect such an impressive monument to their masters. But it was good to see the troll showing an interest in something. Hothbrodd took captivity even worse than Ben. No wonder, when he could hardly move in the cramped space of the cage – and when he made a second attempt to persuade the twigs to let them go, the prisoners were first almost skewered, and then nearly suffocated. Since then, the troll had just looked darkly ahead in silence. Barnabas was the only one who still seemed unbroken. Even now, he was looking around with as much interest as if he were actually in a cage in the middle of the Indonesian jungle of his own free will.

'Fascinating!' he whispered, while Hothbrodd gazed grimly at the black macaques guarding them. 'Those lorises are extraordinarily talented. I wonder if they were carving images of other creatures before the griffins arrived. I don't know of any monkeys who do that, but maybe these are a different species. What do you think, Hothbrodd?'

The troll uttered a morose grunt. 'Yes, they're not bad,' he murmured. 'But if I'd made that statue it would beat its wings!'

Ben was sure it would. But Barnabas was already thinking of something else. He looked at the sacrificial vessels.

'I'm surprised that Kraa's flourishing trade with the poachers hasn't yet brought anyone here to try catching him and the other griffins,' he murmured. 'On the other hand, maybe those skulls on the beach are all that's left of those who did try!'

'Probably,' murmured Ben.

He couldn't think any more. The world was striped as long as he saw it through bars. And what would Vita and Guinevere be thinking by now? Would they think the griffins had eaten them? He took the photo of the eggs out of his pocket. It was crumpled and dirty, and soon, presumably, it would be the only remaining evidence of the last Pegasi. They'd never be able to keep the promise they had made to Ànemos, that was for sure. Even if, sometime or other, they could free themselves. Four days! That was all they had left. And they'd need two of those days just for the flight home!

'I'm so sorry!' Barnabas put an arm around his shoulders. 'I feel wretched for getting you and the others into this situation. There's almost nothing more humiliating than being a prisoner. I hate to remember the four endless months I spent in the cave of a nocturnal troll. But for Hothbrodd's help I'd probably still be there.'

'No, he'd have eaten you by this time,' growled the troll. 'And I haven't the faintest idea, *skitten svinge av skjebene,* how you didn't go out of your mind in those four months!'

'Master!' called a little voice. Twigleg's tiny cage hardly gave him room to stand up straight. 'How are you and Professor Greenbloom? I'm terribly sorry! We didn't do very well as rescuers!'

'Nonsense! It was very brave of you and Lola to have a go!' Ben called back. It went to his heart to see the homunculus imprisoned like that. Lola's cage was just as small, but Ben wasn't worried about her. He couldn't imagine any cage that would hold Lola for long.

'We had bad luck, humklupus, that's all,' said the rat

as she forced her paws through the twigs to extract a few tasty-looking seeds from a plant. 'It was a pretty hopeless mission, as I am sure all present will admit!'

Berulu whispered something into Winston's ear, and clung to him desperately. Winston could still hardly believe that he really could understand what the maki was saying. He would miss it when there was no fabulous creature still near him to decipher Berulu's twittering by its mere presence. On the other hand, the way things looked just now there soon wouldn't be any Berulu near him either. It was a heartbreaking thought.

'Berulu says that makis don't make good pets,' he told the others. 'And he needs the night and the forest and would be very unhappy in a house.' He hugged Berulu. 'I'll protect you!' he promised. 'We won't let them separate us!'

Winston cast Ben a helpless glance. He knew he was promising more than he could perform.

'There must be something we can do!' Ben struck the twigs of his cage. 'Something or other!'

One of the black macaques bared his teeth and hit out at Ben's hands with a stick. The leader of the macaques, who was sitting on the head of the griffin statue, brusquely called him off. His dark pelt was grey in many places, and he was blind in one eye. Awan Petir, as he called himself, had been serving the griffins for a very long time.

'That's Kraa's property you're damaging, Kachang!' he snarled hoarsely. 'Do you want me telling him that the boy fetched a lower price because of you?'

The macaque who had been told off retreated, looking as intimidated as if Kraa himself had spoken to him harshly. Ben wondered whether there was anyone living on Pulau Bulu who wasn't afraid of the king griffin. He was coming to admire Shrii's

courage in standing up to Kraa more and more. And not only his courage. It was so much easier simply to do what everyone else did without asking questions, instead of looking for new and better ways to act. Barnabas had a tale to tell about that himself. But the world would be so much darker and poorer without Shrii and without Barnabas Greenbloom. No one would say the same of Kraa. It was really difficult to go on believing that some miracle might yet save them. Yet nothing was more dangerous than losing hope. If your hope dies, Barnabas had once said to him, then you've given up the fight and there's no going back.

Ben looked at Winston. Had he given up hope? His face was buried in Berulu's fur.

'When do you think they'll kill Shrii?' Ben whispered.

Winston raised his head. 'As soon as Kraa gets the gold the poachers are paying for us,' he whispered back. 'He can't wait to eat Shrii's heart. Griffins think that their enemies' strength passes to them like that. Our hearts are probably too small for Kraa. Or too frightened.'

He tried a smile, but it wasn't a great success.

'I'm terribly worried about Berulu,' he whispered, putting his hands over the tarsier's ears. 'They die in captivity! Suppose they put him on one of those ships that take half the ani—' Winston interrupted himself. He was listening.

They all heard it. Footsteps, voices, machetes cutting a way through the jungle.

Barnabas put his arm around Ben's shoulders, and Berulu hid under Winston's T-shirt. Sorrel liked to say, 'Humans make more noise than wild boar,' and it was certainly true of these ones. English and Indonesian words came through the forest to their ears.

'Will they really sell us as slaves?' Ben whispered to Winston. Only Berulu's tail was still in sight. 'That's ridiculous! I mean, this is the twenty-first century!'

'So?' Winston retorted. 'Didn't you hear Kraa? There are a great many mines on the nearby islands. They always need cheap labour there. And what comes cheaper than slaves?'

Shrii's monkeys set up a plaintive chattering.

'Stop that!' cried Patah. 'Or do you want Kraa's henchmen to tell him we were scared?'

TerTaWa began singing softly. They had caught the gibbon as he was trying to reach Shrii's cage. If only one of them at least had escaped!

Awan Petir smoothed down his greying coat with his hands, as if smartening himself up for the coming negotiations. Then, from the head of the griffin statue, he directed the other macaques to crouch beside the basketwork cages.

Seven men emerged from the trees. They did not all come from this part of the world. Two were in such ragged clothes that Ben remembered what Barnabas had once said about the poachers of Africa. 'Often they only want to feed their families, Ben. Hunger and poverty seldom teach people to feel compassion.' The third poacher was almost as large as Hothbrodd, and looked even grimmer than the troll. The fourth had so many tattoos on his brown skin that you could probably have read his entire life history from them. The remaining three were the kind of hunters and trophy-collectors that Ben had met only too often by now: men who knew only one way of approaching other creatures; by showing them that they themselves were stronger. Men who felt considerably better in the presence of dead animals rather than those still living.

The leader nodded to Awan Petir like an old acquaintance. He called himself Catcher, and had already done many deals with Kraa's black macaques. Awan Petir nodded back as he stared down, with an expressionless face, at the troop of men. He wouldn't have been able to say how many animals had already lost their lives and their freedom because of him. Awan Petir was interested solely in his own freedom, and he liked bargaining with Catcher, even if the latter always stank of sweat and onions, and made even crocodiles seem warm-hearted. But Catcher paid well, and had never tried to hunt in the mountains, which Kraa had declared his own preserve. Not all humans were as clever as that. Awan Petir used to take their skulls down to the beach in person.

'No marbled cats today?' Catcher was strolling past the cages as if inspecting the display in a supermarket. The skin of his fat face was peeling in the sunlight, and Ben could see neither hunger nor the thrill of the chase on it. Catcher was a salesman. Ben had learned that you had to fear those more than anyone else, and Winston could have confirmed it. He knew Catcher only too well.

'My word, who do we have here? Winston Setiawan. I thought this island, at least, would be safe from you.' Catcher spoke English with an Australian accent, but he didn't say exactly where he came from. 'Kamaharan! How many of our monkeys has this little imp of Satan already freed?'

Not for nothing did the man whom Catcher beckoned over to his side bear the name of Kamaharan; it means 'storm' in Indonesian.

'Thirty-seven.' Winston got in first with the answer. His voice was shaking slightly, but you could hear how proud he was of the number.

'And over a hundred birds. Let's see if you can open the locks of cages so easily from the inside, sonny!' Kamaharan kicked Winston's basket so hard that he fell back against the bars, and Berulu's horrified screech emerged from his T-shirt. 'Very stupid of you to come to this island. Didn't you know that the lion-birds allow only visitors who pay to come here, and are well-disposed to poachers? And how about the others – since when did you go around with humans? I thought all your friends were lousy monkeys and tarsiers.'

He stepped back, with a curse, when Hothbrodd, in the next basket, pressed his face to the twigs with a threatening expression, and called them all *follet feiltakelse fra Odin*.

The tattooed man went over to Kamaharan and stared incredulously at the troll.

'Maybe we'd better let this one go,' he murmured in awe. 'Looks like a forest demon!'

'Nonsense.' Catcher examined Hothbrodd as if he was already counting the money he'd get for the troll. 'Why, we could even offer him to a TV network. Or one of those crazy billionaires who'll pay a fortune for a horror like this.'

Hothbrodd spat in his sunburned face when Catcher thoughtlessly came close to his basket. Troll saliva is not at all appetising, and Catcher got so much of it that he looked as if he had been washing in stomach fluids stinking of fish. Barnabas hastily got in front of Hothbrodd when Kamaharan raised his shotgun, but Catcher reached for the barrel and pulled it roughly out of Kamaharan's hands.

'What's the idea?' he snapped at him, wiping the slimy saliva off his face with his sleeve. 'D'you think he'll make as much money dead and stuffed?'

'Some time or other,' growled Hothbrodd, ignoring Barnabas's warning glance, 'you'll have to let us out of this basket, and then I'll skin you all and make a fine big sail out of you. I'd think– ' he added, pointing to the tattooed man – 'your skin in particular will look just fabulous!'

Kamaharan liked to boast of strangling crocodiles with his bare hands, but even he took a step back on hearing Hothbrodd's grisly threat.

'How about this one?' asked another of the men, pointing to Barnabas. 'I guess they'll never take him off our hands for the mines. Looks like some kind of professor who's lost his way in the jungle!'

The others laughed, although they still kept a respectful

distance away from Hothbrodd.

'Some kind of professor?' cried Winston.

Ben gave him a warning look, but unfortunately Winston was so indignant that he didn't notice.

'You'd better let him go free if you value your lives. That's Barnabas Greenbloom! He and his son are friends with sea serpents and dragons. And Great Krakens and centaurs!'

With a sigh, Barnabas closed his eyes, and Winston realised his mistake when Catcher gave his men as triumphant a glance as if he had just caught the last white tiger.

'Sea serpents, dragons, Great Krakens and centaurs,' he repeated. 'I've heard rumours that all those creatures still exist. And that there's a conspiracy of crazy conservationists keeping the world in the dark about it. The name Greenbloom was mentioned more than once in that connection, if I remember correctly. Not a name you'd forget in a hurry. And now that green giant makes sense too . . .'

'Dragons?' growled Kamaharan doubtfully. 'Great Krakens? Sounds to me like the kind of old wives' tales that peasants tell!'

'All the better. Then I won't have to cut you idiots in on the price I get for these fairy-tale beings.' Catcher hit out at a butterfly that had settled on his fat neck. 'What do you think, Professor?' he asked, giving Barnabas an unpleasant smile. 'Will you introduce your fabulous friends to us if I spare you working in the mines in return?'

'Sorry, I'm afraid that's out of the question,' replied Barnabas casually. 'My friend Winston is wrong, unfortunately, if he thinks I know such illustrious beings. I agree with your poacher colleagues. They exist only in fairy tales, sorry as I am to say so.'

Catcher was about to answer back, but suddenly he was inter-rupted by one of the other poachers who had been inspecting the rest of the cages.

'They caught a jenglot!' he stammered, and to Ben's horror he held up Twigleg's cage.

The poachers stepped back even faster than when Hothbrodd had lost his temper. Only Catcher scrutinised the homunculus and shook his sweaty head.

'If that's a jenglot, I'm an orang-utan!' he said sarcastically. 'What is it, Professor? Out with it! Some kind of hob or impet? This gets better and better!' he whispered to Kamaharan. 'A midget like this will bring in more than thirty monkeys, although,' he added with a glance at the black macaques, 'we'd better not say so to our trading partners.'

'A hob?' cried Twigleg. 'Or an impet? Allow me to tell you that I'm a . . .'

He stopped abruptly when Catcher gave Barnabas a triumphant look.

'Yes, a what?' asked Catcher. 'Something else that lives only in fairy tales, Professor? No more lies. Kamaharan here is a master of persuasion, but maybe we won't need his arts.' He favoured Barnabas with a totally heartless smile. 'If I understand correctly, this –' he pointed to Ben – 'is Greenbloom junior. And what kind of loving father condemns his son to a life of slavery in the mines just on account of a few animals?'

Barnabas turned pale, and for the first time Ben saw something like fear on his adopted father's usually fearless face. The sight of that was worse than his own fear.

'I wouldn't have thanked him for leaving me at home!' he told the poachers. 'He's the best of all fathers! And you won't learn anything from us! Not a single word!'

Catcher seemed greatly amused by his angry outburst. 'I very much doubt that,' he said. 'But we'll carry on with this conversation someplace else. This island makes me sick to my stomach after dark. Take the cages down to the boats!' he ordered the others.

When they picked up the first basket, however, Awan Petir, who hadn't taken his eyes off the poachers, pointed to the dish in the statue's claws with a warning cry.

'Okay, okay!' called Catcher to the macaque. 'Have I ever wriggled out of paying? And I'll pay well too, as is only right for such good wares.'

Kamaharan, the tattooed man, and the grim giant dragged two full sacks over to the dish. They tipped coins, jewellery and freshly mined nuggets of gold out of the first, and pale yellow seashells out of the second.

'Oh, of course!' Barnabas whispered to Ben. 'Those are the shells that Shrii mentioned. Yes, indeed, a very rare species, and found only so deep in the sea that the griffins can't get at them.'

The black macaques were beginning to put the contents of the dish into bags that they could carry easily through the tree-tops, when their leader suddenly raised his head in annoyance. A red parrot flew over Awan Petir's greying head, and then circled around the statue.

Ben's heart leaped up. Me-Rah! She'd had a bad time after Twigleg and Lola were caught, but the parrot hadn't left her new friends in the lurch. She had watched despairingly as the black macaques sold her rescuers to the poachers, and then ... then she had heard a rushing in the air above her, and had watched two shadows of a kind that she had never before seen falling on the treetops of Pulau Bulu.

'To think that I have lived to see this day!' squawked Me-Rah, as she deposited a large blob of parrot-droppings on the beak of the griffin statue. 'In a hundred times a hundred years, they'll still be celebrating it on Pulau Bulu! The day when justice came to this island. And as for you,' she screeched down to the poachers, 'at last you'll all get what you deserve!'

Kamaharan took the shotgun from his shoulder and aimed at the parrot, but he lowered it when a roar such as had never before been heard on Pulau Bulu came from the sky.

'Yeeeees!' squawked Me-Rah. 'Yeeeees! They're coming!'

The poachers staggered back. But Ben closed his fingers so tightly on the basketwork of his cage that the marks still showed days later. Barnabas's face showed the same incredulous joy that he was feeling himself – and the same alarm.

'What's that?' cried Winston, while the poachers threw their guns away and Catcher looked up in astonishment.

'What do you think it is?' cried Hothbrodd, laughing. 'By Thor, Loki and Odin. It's a dragon!'

And then the jungle was full of silver scales.

CHAPTER THIRTY-SIX

The Anger of Dragons

*The insufferable arrogance of human beings to think
that Nature was made solely for their benefit, as if it
was conceivable that the sun had been set afire merely
to ripen men's apples and head their cabbages.*
Savinien de Cyrano de Bergerac,
*The Comical History of the States and Empires
of the Worlds of the Moon and Sun*

It was a very long time since Firedrake had felt such anger.
Ben and Barnabas in a cage!

Picking up the scent of the men standing beside the basket-work cages, Tattoo could tell as clearly as Firedrake what they were like. Such men smelled the same everywhere, as if cruelty grew from their skin like a poisonous fungus. But the worst of it was that they aroused that cruelty even in the heart of a silver dragon. Oh, the wish to simply burn all human darkness away! Sorrel felt it like a fit of shivering in Firedrake's body as the dragon swooped down on the poachers. She called his name soothingly, to keep him from losing himself in his anger, and was relieved to see the poachers running under the trees for shelter, leaving their prisoners behind without a fight. Firedrake had never yet killed, and there were terrible stories about what killing did to a silver dragon.

Tattoo had no brownie on his back to warn him of the anger in his heart. Sorrel tried to call him back, but the thrill of aggression flaring up in him made the blood rush in his ears and deafened him to her voice. Tattoo followed the poachers down to the beach, and Catcher and his men escaped only because they knew their way, and the trees were obstacles to the dragon in his flight. Their boat was already moving out to sea when Tattoo, snorting, broke out of the forest. Presumably that saved their lives. He breathed fire after them, and when the blue flames reached the boat's hull it sank into the waves with the poachers, as suddenly as if dragon-fire had made it forget to float. In all the excitement neither Tattoo nor Catcher and Kamaharan felt surprised. Those two were the only ones to save themselves by jumping over the rail. Catcher was such a poor swimmer that he clung to Kamaharan, and that was all that prevented him from going under.

Tattoo saw the two of them swim away, but he didn't breathe any more fire. He stood on the beach and felt his own anger like lava in his veins, so hot and burning that he thought he would be singed by his own flames. The young dragon had never known anything like it before, and he didn't like what he was feeling. That wish for destruction, taking pleasure in the fear of others . . . yes, it was pleasure that he felt! In spite of his youth, Tattoo knew himself too well to deny it. It made him shudder, and he was a stranger to himself for the first time in his life. When he finally turned around to rejoin the others, it was with a longing in his heart to have a brownie, the way Firedrake had Sorrel. Or a boy like the one for whom Firedrake had flown all this way, and about whom he talked to Tattoo with so much love.

While Tattoo was breathing fire after the poachers, Firedrake had already landed among the griffins' trees, and Sorrel had started opening the basketwork cages. Ben didn't want to let go of her again when she set him free, and Barnabas shook her paw so vigorously that she worried about her furry fingers, but worst of all was the troll. Hothbrodd tossed Sorrel so high into the air that she was almost bitten by a pit viper! Only Twigleg said thank you in his own very civilised way with a deep bow, first to Sorrel and then to Firedrake. She had to admit that she was almost as relieved to see the homunculus intact as to find Ben and Barnabas safe and well. Brownies don't forgive easily, and Sorrel still held it against Twigleg that he had once served one of Firedrake's worst enemies. But it's his size, Sorrel, she told herself as the homunculus thanked her with another bow. That's what it is, yes. These tiny little creatures just steal into your heart!

That, however, didn't apply to rats. Sorrel left it to Twigleg to set Lola free. It's better for rats and brownies to watch one another from a safe difference. How about monkeys? No. Definitely not. Sorrel didn't notice the second human boy until Winston was enthusiastically shaking Twigleg's tiny hand, and of course he was staring at her and Firedrake with as much astonishment as Ben had done at their first meeting! Thanks a million. As if one human boy in a brownie's life wasn't enough! When Tattoo came back it was to be feared that Winston's brown eyes would pop out of his head with awe.

As soon as the monkeys were out of the baskets, they disappeared up the trees.

'Hey, how about a polite thank you?' Sorrel called after them. 'And where does that crazy rat think she's going?' she asked Ben when she spotted Lola on Patah's shoulder.

'Oh no, Lola is far from crazy,' said Barnabas, stretching his legs, which were stiff from his imprisonment. 'She and Shrii's monkeys are following the macaques who supervised trade with the poachers. Let's hope they catch up with them before news of the dragons who set us free gets around this island!'

'Monkeys trading with poachers?' Sorrel went over to the dish full of treasure, with the statue of the griffin watching over it. 'What do they want with gold and seashells?'

'Oh,' said Barnabas evasively, 'that's a peculiarity of the monkeys on this island.' He glanced at Ben, who was standing between Firedrake and Tattoo, with Twigleg on his shoulder. All the anxiety had left his face, and he looked as happy as he did only when the dragon was near him.

'But how did you find your way here?' Barnabas heard him ask, while he stroked Firedrake's silver scales, as if he couldn't believe that the dragon had really come to his rescue. Winston was standing at the respectful distance of a few paces away from him, looking at the dragons as if all the dreams he'd ever had were coming true.

'Tattoo?' said Ben. 'That's not really a dragon name, is it?'

'His real name is Lhag Pa,' said Firedrake, while Tattoo responded to Winston's gaze. The younger dragon seemed to be visibly enjoying the boy's admiration. Well, he deserved it. He was a magnificent sight.

Barnabas sighed.

'What's the matter, Greenbloom?' Sorrel asked, pushing him in the chest with her paw. 'You don't look like a man who's just been saved from a gang of animal-catchers and poachers. More like someone who – what is it you humans say? – who's jumped out of the frying pan into the fire.'

By way of answering her, Barnabas heaved another deep sigh. A deep and extremely worried sigh.

'Sorrel,' he whispered to the brownie girl. 'I need your help. The two dragons must leave this island again as quickly as possible!'

Sorrel never got around to asking why.

'Leave it?' Firedrake laid his head on her shoulder. 'What's the hurry, Barnabas?'

Dragons have very keen hearing. Barnabas cursed himself for being such a fool as to forget it.

'If you're thinking of setting off, then you must have the phoenix feather already?' Firedrake looked from Barnabas to Ben. 'I can't forget how desperate Ànemos was. I'm sure you'd never leave the island without the feather, would you?'

Ben avoided the dragon's glance. He thought he saw irony in Firedrake's eyes. And even worse, disappointment.

'It does seem to be a dangerous island,' Firedrake continued. 'A kraken told us about the lion-birds. I assume they regard this island,' and here he looked at the statue of the griffin, 'as their property? What a good thing it isn't their feathers that you need. Those griffins sound very unpleasant.'

'Ah, yes, the phoenix feather! Of course. Yes! Yes, we have it.' Barnabas did his best, but he was only making matters worse. He was hopelessly bad at telling lies. His voice died away as Firedrake gave him a stern and far from friendly look.

Then Firedrake looked at his dragon rider. Ben felt like sinking into the ground, where he would be invisible.

'How about the truth, Ben?' asked the dragon. 'Does a dragon rider lie to his dragon? And what's the matter with the rest of you? Barnabas! Hothbrodd! Twigleg!' He scrutinised them one by one.

'Dammit all!' growled the troll. 'That's enough bad acting! Yes, there are griffins here, and we need one of their sun-feathers for the Pegasus eggs. That's why Barnabas is in such a hurry for you two to leave the island, and fast! Dragons and griffins . . . you know about that . . .'

Firedrake stood up very straight. His whole body was taut. Tattoo looked at him anxiously.

'So you all lied to me?' Firedrake sounded so hurt that Ben would have liked to crawl back into his basketwork cage. 'What were you planning to do? Let the Pegasus foals die rather than ask me for help? And you, dragon rider? Wouldn't you have given me a chance of protecting you, even though I gave you my scale?'

Ben had never seen Firedrake in such an aggressive mood before, but the dragon was still feeling the darkness that the poachers had aroused in him, and the lies told by Ben and Barnabas did nothing to cast any light into it.

'The monkeys stole the scale from me!' cried Ben. 'But even

if I'd still had it – how could I want you to come here? We all wanted to protect you. Believe me! You haven't seen the griffins! They're terrible. Except for one of them . . .'

One whom they wouldn't be able to save without the help of the dragons. But much as Ben liked Shrii, even for him he couldn't allow Firedrake to put himself in danger. Not to save Shrii, or the Pegasus foals, not even for himself! He loved the dragon too much for that.

Ben felt tears coming to his eyes. And knew that Firedrake saw them.

'It's all my fault,' said Barnabas. 'I persuaded Ben to lie to you. There's almost no deeper enmity between fabulous creatures that the hostility of griffins and dragons!'

'But they'll defeat them!' Winston went to stand between Firedrake and Tattoo, and looked admiringly from one to the other. 'Just look at them! They'll defeat Kraa and set Shrii free! How can you doubt it?'

'Thank you!' Tattoo bowed his head to Winston. 'Spoken like a dragon rider.'

'But it's not just Kraa!' cried Ben. 'There are seven griffins, Firedrake, and only two of you. And then there are all the monkeys who serve Kraa and his jackal scorpions!'

Winston swallowed.

'Yes, that's true,' he murmured. 'Forget what I said! I was only thinking of Shrii! And you chased Catcher and his men away so easily . . .' He fell silent, and cast Ben a remorseful glance, while Berulu stared at the dragons with his big, round eyes. 'I'm sorry,' muttered Winston. 'They're right. You must go.'

The two dragons exchanged a glance.

Neither Ben nor Barnabas liked it.

'I entirely agree with you,' Tattoo told Firedrake. 'All this sounds as if they'd be lost without our help.'

'Exactly. Entirely lost. And I'm sure you'd be very disappointed if you had to set off for home right away, wouldn't you?' added Firedrake, ignoring the dismayed glances of his friends.

Tattoo nodded firmly.

'Just a moment!' cried Sorrel. 'Look at their beaks!' She indicated the griffin heads in the trees. 'And their claws!' She pointed to the griffin statue. 'Claws and paws! As if just one of those wasn't enough for them!'

'And don't forget the snaky tails,' Twigleg said, from Ben's shoulder. 'And those jackal scorpions are really horrible! Lola will say the same!'

'That's true! It's noble of you both to offer us your help. But you – can't – stay – here!' said Barnabas firmly. 'And Ben and Winston shouldn't really be here either, Firedrake! If you don't want to leave because of the griffins, then at least do it to get the two boys to safety.'

But now it was Ben and Winston who took offence. Ben went to Firedrake's side, and Winston instinctively went over to Tattoo.

'If Firedrake wants to stay,' said Ben, 'then his dragon rider stays too, of course. And he's right. We can't simply give up on the Pegasus foals. Or Shrii, either!'

'Exactly,' said Winston, although Berulu looked far less convinced. When Tattoo gently laid his nose on Winston's shoulder, the boy looked up in delight.

'I could do with a dragon rider myself!' Tattoo whispered. 'My attacking instincts run away with me very easily. I think a dragon rider is the only thing to be done about that.'

Winston was so happy that his knees almost gave way. 'Of course,' he stammered. 'Of course. I'd love to try. I'm sure Ben can give me some useful tips.'

Firedrake looked at Barnabas with amusement in his eyes.

'Okay,' growled Hothbrodd. 'Then that's all settled. Can we get away from this clearing now? I'm tired,' he said, pointing to the griffin faces on the trees, 'of having those things staring down at me. Or do the rest of you want to hang about until the living models turn up?'

No, none of them wanted that, although Barnabas was still looking very concerned.

'The tree-man is right, fully-grown Greenbloom,' squawked Me-Rah. 'You must leave this place. I can take you to a tree that will protect you. No monkey on this island dares to approach its branches!'

'Liberty cap mushrooms!' Sorrel whispered to Hothbrodd. 'Is that the lost parrot from the birds' temple?'

'It's a long story,' grunted Hothbrodd. 'But a tree to protect us sounds good. And I've lost the knife I use for carving. I don't plan on going home until I get that knife back.'

CHAPTER THIRTY-SEVEN

The Whispering Tree

*Trees have long thoughts, long-breathing and restful,
just as they have longer lives than ours. They are wiser
than we are, as long as we do not listen to them. But when
we have learned how to listen to trees, then the brevity and the
quickness and the childlike hastiness of our thoughts achieve
an incomparable joy. Whoever has learned how to listen to
trees no longer wants to be a tree. He wants to be nothing
except what he is. That is home. That is happiness.*
Hermann Hesse, *Trees*

The tree known on Pulau Bulu as the Whispering Tree grew on the banks of a broad river flowing through jungle so dense that many of its inhabitants had never seen the sky. That didn't bother a parrot like Me-Rah in the slightest, of course, but soon even Hothbrodd could hardly make his way through the thickets, and in the end Firedrake and Tattoo were carrying the whole party on their backs, with Me-Rah following. The two dragons were gliding so low over the sluggishly flowing water that crocodiles snapped at their shadows, and flocks of birds scattered like spray. The trees on the bank, often leaning so far out over the grey-green water that their leaves drifted on the ripples like green hair, seemed to raise their trunks to let Firedrake and Tattoo pass. Butterflies settled on their shimmering scales, adorning them with even brighter colours than Kraa's palace nest. Innumerable birds filled the humid, sultry air with their twittering, and snakes and lizards darted out their forked tongues from the branches in welcome.

'Whatever the griffins think of dragons,' Barnabas whispered to Ben as he clung to the spines on Firedrake's back, 'the inhabitants of this island give them a very warm welcome!'

They all knew they had reached their destination even before Me-Rah came down in the mighty tree that covered the water of the river before them with a carpet of blossom. The trumpet-shaped flowers hanging from the spreading branches were so pale a green that they could hardly be told from the hand-sized leaves. Inside, however, the calyxes were bright orange, and flocks of humming birds and sun-birds hovered around them to taste the pollen. It clung to their beaks like gold dust, and even the crocodiles drifting in the river below the tree had pollen on their backs.

The dragons landed only a few metres away from them, but even the huge reptiles retreated from Firedrake and Tattoo with as much respect as all the other creatures they had met.

'Twigleg, can you explain why the inhabitants of Pulau Bulu are so respectful to the dragons?' Barnabas asked as they climbed off Firedrake's back. 'I admit that I'm surprised.'

'It's not only humans who tell tales about dragons, Greenbloom!' called a voice from a fig tree, before Twigleg could answer. TerTaWa was sitting in the branches with Kupo, Patah, and Shrii's other macaques. 'Many of us have dreamed that one of them might find the way to our island. And now here are two at the same time!'

'What about the black macaques?' called Winston. 'Did they get away?'

'Get away? Huh!' Lola was swinging from a liana as naturally as if she had been born on Pulau Bulu and not in a barn in Schleswig-Holstein. 'We caught them all and put them in the baskets they were going to sell us in.'

'And then we left them in the nests that Tchraee destroyed!' twittered Kupo.

'Yes. That was TerTaWa's idea,' grumbled Patah. 'I wanted to feed them to the crocodiles, but I guess the gibbon was right. Kraa would probably take revenge on Shrii for that.'

'He certainly would,' agreed Lola, landing in front of Winston's sneakers.

TerTaWa had not been the only one to lower his head when Shrii's name was mentioned. Knowing that the young griffin was still Kraa's prisoner made all his friends feel that their own freedom was a betrayal. It was the same for Ben and Barnabas too.

'Did this have to be our meeting place?' asked Patah with a disapproving glance at the Whispering Tree.

Twigleg had asked Me-Rah to dictate him an account of the way to it, and had left it and his backpack in the dish in front of the griffin statue, trusting Lola to find it there. Of course the rat had not disappointed him.

'The parrot's idea, was it?' Patah nodded to Me-Rah in annoyance. 'Did she tell you what we call this tree?'

Even TerTaWa looked at him with obvious discomfort.

'Monkey Strangler!' called Patah accusingly.

The branches, laden with blossom and birds, rustled as if the tree thought Patah's hostility was amusing.

'Hey, it's laughing!' observed Hothbrodd, delighted. 'And it says it doesn't strangle you unless you steal eggs from the nests in its branches.'

He approached the huge tree as hesitantly as a child approaching Father Christmas. Not because he was afraid of it (he was afraid of nothing but wasps, a secret that the troll carefully kept to himself). No, the Whispering Tree of Pulau Bulu made Hothbrodd so happy that his own feet would hardly obey him, and he stepped under its crown, which smelled of cinnamon and nutmeg, with bated breath. When he touched the silky, pale grey bark, a shower of blossom fell on him. The laughter with which Hothbrodd picked the pale green flowers out of his hair was so loud that all the birds above him, pecking at the golden pollen, flew up in alarm. Only when the tree whispered soothingly to its leaves did they disappear into the deep flower-cups again.

In the protection of a tree that spread so much peace and joy, it seemed to Ben almost disrespectful to be planning a rescue that couldn't take place without a fight, not to mention the theft of a sun-feather. Winston felt the same. He couldn't remember any place where he had ever felt so safe and at peace with the whole world. The poachers, the griffins, the noise and restlessness of the human world where he had been born, all seemed nothing but a bad dream from which the Whispering Tree had woken him with the rustling of its leaves. All you wanted to do under this tree was to sit between its roots and forget the world! But Barnabas knew trees almost as well as he knew fabulous beings, and he saw that the Whispering Tree of Pulau Bulu would have to withstand many battles to protect those who took refuge in and under its crown.

'My dear Me-Rah!' he said, lowering his voice so as not to offend the monkeys. 'Thank you. You have brought us to a perfect place! Here, maybe we can make a plan not only to save the Pegasus eggs, but also to set Shrii free!'

'Oh, yes,' growled Hothbrodd, running his green fingers over all the marks left by claws, teeth and machetes in the bark of the Whispering Tree. 'We're sure to think of something under this tree.'

A long scar, black as soot, showed where lightning had once struck the tree, and more than a dozen lead bullets had grown into the bark. The Whispering Tree told the troll the story of each of them, while the dragons rested on the flower petals covering the ground between its roots with a fragrant cushion. The branches above them spread so far that in spite of their own size, both dragons could easily find room under the tree. When Ben knelt between Firedrake's paws, Winston knelt between Tattoo's, whereupon Berulu looked at the dragon with unconcealed jealousy, but Winston tickled him behind the ears to reassure him as he himself leaned back against Tattoo's scales. After all, new friends shouldn't make us forget old ones.

'Unfortunately, as you all know, time is short,' Barnabas began. 'And not just because of Shrii. Twigleg has just been working it out again. We must set off for home tomorrow if the mission that brought us here is not to fail! So we only have tonight to carry out our plan!'

'Right!' twittered Kupo. 'What is the plan?'

And the discussion began. The light of thousands of glow-worms flickered over the dark water of the river. Fluorescent tree fungi bathed the jungle around them in ghostly green light, and countless eyes peering through the thickets of leaves and twigs watched the strange assembly that had gathered: animals, humans, fabulous creatures. Even for Pulau Bulu, where so many living things existed side by side, it was a unique meeting, and not only because for the first time since the island had emerged from the sea, it had two dragons visiting it. But by dint of good luck – or maybe because of the protection of the Whispering Tree – out of all the pairs of eyes observing the dragons and their friends, not one belonged to a servant of Kraa.

CHAPTER THIRTY-EIGHT

A Shortage of Space

To achieve great things two things are needed:
a plan and not quite enough time.
Leonard Bernstein

Cling-clang. The foals were growing, and their tiny hooves were now hitting the eggshells so hard that Guinevere jumped every time she heard the sound, and the geese and swans keeping the eggs warm craned their necks in alarm. But the shells would not break. They would soon turn into prisons, and in the end they would suffocate the three foals instead of protecting them.

Ànemos began avoiding the stable again, simply so as not to see how short of space his children were. By now, however, Guinevere knew the Pegasus well enough to realise that he was grateful for her company.

'Have you noticed how strong Ouranos is already?' she asked, when she found him down beside the fjord again. 'I think he likes to play the clown! Vita tells me that the swamp impets are betting their caps and boots on him to be the first to hatch. And the nisses are betting acorns on which of the foals will fly fastest!'

Nisses and impets would bet on anything. It was stupid, but perhaps doing stupid things helped to keep fear at bay.

Ànemos looked at the sky and pricked up his ears. But it was only an ordinary airplane reflected in the water of the fjord. And Guinevere was certain that the Pegasus knew how many days they still had left, even though she had hidden the calendar.

Tomorrow the last three days began. And maybe the third of those days would bring the death of the foals.

CHAPTER THIRTY-NINE

The Greatest Task for the Smallest in the Team

You know how you let yourself think that everything will be all right if you can only get to a certain place or do a certain thing. But when you get there you find it's not that simple.
Richard Adams, *Watership Down*

The thing about plans is that they don't always work out as expected.

The plan thought up by many heads under the Whispering Tree sounded, from the first, as if it could never, ever succeed. It contained so many *maybes* and *what ifs*, so many question marks about what awaited them in the griffins' tree, that all of those involved thought of it with a sense of foreboding. With two exceptions: nothing and no one gave Lola a sense of foreboding, and Tattoo . . . well, Tattoo hadn't forgotten how frightened he had been of his own anger on the beach, but all the same he could hardly wait to prove himself again. Above all because, for

the first time in his life, he would have a dragon rider. Although
the task given to him and Firedrake that night sounded far from
exciting.

'You're only our backup! You don't come to the rescue
unless it's a genuine emergency. Promise?' Barnabas Greenbloom
had repeated that so often that after a while even the tip of
Firedrake's tail would have shown his impatience, and not
only Tattoo but also the two dragon riders were secretly hoping
that in the end the two dragons would play more of a part
in the operation. Even Barnabas couldn't conceal the fact
that, to his mind, that seemed more probable than he liked
to admit. After all, what they were planning to do really was
rather crazy.

So what exactly was the plan?

For many years now, Kraa had been hunting only by day. His
great old age had made him blind at night, and Patah, Kupo and
TerTaWa all swore that he was certain to be asleep in his palace
nest when they carried out their plan before the first light of
dawn. That sounded like a good opportunity to steal one of
Kraa's sun-feathers. Particularly since the other griffins were
usually out hunting until it was day, and that too would make it
considerably easier to set Shrii free. Of course they could only
hope for Kraa to sleep so soundly that he wouldn't notice the
theft of the feather. And that the other griffins didn't come back
before Shrii was free. Hope was a crucial part of the plan. Rather
more crucial than Twigleg liked.

As well as the griffins, of course, there were a number of other
creatures in Kraa's royal tree who might present problems. The
jackal scorpions guarding Kraa's nest, the monkeys, snakes and
birds who served him and kept watch in the branches – they all
had to be distracted or rendered harmless in various ways. But

after all, the expeditionary team that set off just before midnight itself consisted of very different participants with very different qualities: macaques, humans, dragons, a brownie girl, a troll, a homunculus, a rat, a parrot, a gibbon, and last but not least a loris and a maki. That was nothing, of course, compared to the number of enemies waiting for them in the griffin tree. All the same, they were so numerous that they had decided to approach their target by six different routes, so as to pass unnoticed. Luckily they would also get help from the many sounds of the jungle: the rain that, as so often on Pulau Bulu, was falling from the sky, pouring and pattering; the night calls of the birds; the chorus of toads and cicadas . . . all that drowned out even Hothbrodd's footsteps.

Barnabas and the troll were the only ones going to the griffins' tree on foot, rather than through the branches of the trees or down from the sky. Theirs was the task that began the whole operation.

None of them had ever seen the griffins' tree from below. Even Hothbrodd seemed to shrink to Twigleg's size when its trunk came into sight among the other trees. The snakes lying in wait as guards between its roots bared their venomous fangs, but Hothbrodd simply lifted Barnabas up to his shoulders and threw any snakes who seemed particularly keen to attack into the bushes. Then he walked calmly over the others, and unimpressed by their hissing placed his green hands on the trunk of the griffins' tree. The troll caressed its bark as gently as if he were stroking an elephant's furrowed flank.

'Oh yes, you have many tales to tell!' he murmured lovingly. 'And you didn't choose the winged creatures living in you, did you? What do you say – shall we give them a bit of a fright?'

The huge tree shuddered. But Hothbrodd closed his eyes,

pressed his hands more firmly to the brown bark, and began whispering in a language that every tree in the world understood. And every diurnal troll.

TerTaWa, sitting high above them with Twigleg and Lola in the crown of a neighbouring tree, saw the effect at close quarters. The thinner branches of the tree began to bend without a sound, like fingers carefully reaching for something. That Something was the nests of the monkeys hanging in their dozens from the trunk of the tree or in its lower branches. The branches wound around them until the nests looked like the basketwork cages in which the griffins kept their prisoners. But that wasn't all. The tree began to shake. Only very slightly, so slightly that neither the monkeys nor Kraa were woken. But the snakes winding themselves sleepily around the branches over Kraa's palace nest fell out of the tree in their dozens, like dead leaves, and landed among the roots below. One of them brushed Barnabas's shoulder, but he seized it with a practised grip before it could sink its poison fangs into his neck.

Hothbrodd laughed softly, as if the griffins' tree had told him an amusing secret. Then he leaned his forehead against the bark and whispered words to it that sounded as if they were carved out of wood.

Another shudder passed through the trunk, and branches grew from the bark so that Barnabas could climb them comfortably, as if climbing a ladder.

'They're going to be sorry they shut a troll up in a cage like a bird!' growled Hothbrodd. '*Dum, ha! Meget dum!*'

'Hothbrodd!' Barnabas whispered down to him, before continuing to climb. 'Don't overdo it! We don't want the tree moving so much that it wakes Kraa!'

Hothbrodd replied with the usual grunt expressing his

displeasure, and Barnabas put up a silent prayer to all the gods who, like him, were on the side of animals and fabulous creatures, hoping that Hothbrodd would be able to curb his wish for revenge. That was a great deal to ask of a troll.

Hope . . . yes, the success of this nocturnal mission had so much to do with hope.

Barnabas was an excellent climber, after spending weeks in the crown of a redwood tree in California to study some climbing coyotes three thousand years old there. But he had to hurry, because above him TerTaWa was getting ready to put Lola and Twigleg down on Kraa's palace nest. The griffins had the branches of the nearby trees pruned by monkeys and parrots, so that no one could get near their nests. But no one could jump further than a gibbon.

When Twigleg saw the abyss that TerTaWa must cross, he felt sure that their whole lovely plan would break to pieces in front of Hothbrodd's green feet. The troll was thinking much the same as he looked up at TerTaWa. He was about to ask the tree to catch the gibbon if necessary. But TerTaWa was already in the air. He leaped over to the mighty crown of the tree so gracefully, without a sound, that the jackal scorpions on guard, as usual, outside Kraa's palace didn't even look up. High above them, however, TerTaWa was moving from branch to branch, until the gigantic nest was just below him. Then he came down to settle, as silently as a moth, on the roof with its surrounding battlements.

'There we go. Even a falling leaf makes more noise than a gibbon!' he whispered as he put Twigleg and Lola down on the nest.

Below them, the jackal scorpions were sitting on the gilded flight ramps that surrounded Kraa's palace nest like a ring of long spines. It was up to Barnabas to put those guards out of action, with a few well-aimed shots from the fountain pen filled with anaesthetic that Twigleg and Lola, luckily, had found in the abandoned hollow tree along with his backpack. But Kraa's guards still looked alarmingly wakeful.

'TerTaWa, can you keep an eye on the jackal scorpions?' whispered Twigleg.

There was no answer. The gibbon had gone. TerTaWa, Patah, Kupo . . . tonight all of them were interested in just one thing: rescuing Shrii, the griffin who had risked his life to protect them. Who could hold that against them?

So now it was only to be hoped that Kraa would sleep through the monkeys' rescue operation. Twigleg looked up at the basket where Shrii was held captive. The only guard he could spot was a sleepy macaque.

'Hey, Humpklupus! How about lending me a hand?'

Lola was already gnawing her way through the mud exterior of the palace nest. Hothbrodd had made the saw that she was holding out to Twigleg out of a seashell. All the equipment they had left were the few things that Lola and Twigleg had found in the hollow tree, but a stone was a good enough tool for the troll. He had made not just the saw, but also a few knives and shields and clubs for Ben and Winston, to protect them and the dragons from the claws and beaks of the

griffins if necessary. Then he had fitted them all out with wooden breastplates, including TerTaWa and some of the monkeys. Of course Patah had turned down the offer of one with a scornful gesture, and when Kupo had asked quietly for a knife and protection for her own narrow breast, Hothbrodd's answer had been a brusque No! The troll hadn't forgotten how covetously the loris had put her tiny hand out to his own knife in the hollow tree, but in the end he provided Kupo too with a breastplate and a knife that fitted into her little hand perfectly. By way of a thank-you, she carved a surprisingly good likeness of the troll with it.

Yes, Barnabas had been right. Bringing Hothbrodd along on this journey really had been a good idea. The solid wood that Twigleg felt under his jacket at least made his heart beat a little more slowly.

'I think that'll do, Hummelklups!' Lola took the creeper that TerTaWa had pulled out of the trees for them off her shoulder.

There was a hole in the roof of Kraa's nest – a hole just large enough for a rat and a homunculus.

'But the jackal scorpions . . .!' Twigleg peered over the cornice that surrounded Kraa's palace with gilded battlements. They were still awake! And one of the brutes was just below them. Lola, however, only shrugged her shoulders.

'Huh! Barnabas will see to them!' she said – and pressed the creeper into Twigleg's hand.

Twigleg had expected Kraa's palace to be dark at this time of night, but unfortunately that wasn't the case. The huge nest into which they let themselves down was alarmingly bright. Countless shining glow-worms lit up the ornamental frescoes that the lorises had made along the interior walls of the nest. They showed pictures of events in Kraa's long life. They told the tale of his time as treasurer to Cambyses, three times crowned king, and of battles when the griffin had flown in the vanguard of human armies. Oh yes, Kraa had dragged generals from their horses with his claws, and had eaten them before the eyes of their men. He had scraped gold off the walls of royal palaces, and screamed his name triumphantly into the hot wind blowing through the deserts that he still missed.

The griffin growled in his sleep as Twigleg and Lola made their way down the creeper, hand over hand. The pictures followed Kraa into his dreams, his tawny, gold-clad dreams. In the middle of his nest, the griffin slept on a platform that the lorises had built from the bones of his prey. It gleamed like polished marble in the light of the glow-worms, and Kraa's snake-tail wound back and forth on the smooth surface, while he thrust his claws into the necks of invisible enemies. He had dark dreams, as he had done every night since he had found himself on this island, where his feathers were damp with rain all the time, and his sister's son was born with plumage as ridiculously vivid as a parrot's. It's Tchraee's fault, Nakal whispered to him in his dream. It was Tchraee who wanted to fly on further east! Nakal was right. What a fool he had been. But he knew better now. He trusted no one. No one!

Kraa's growl sounded so angry that Twigleg, trembling, stopped moving – too long for Lola's liking, of course. She climbed over Twigleg and with a single leap landed on the platform, only a few metres away from Kraa's claws. But the griffin didn't hear her. Not even Twigleg's racing heart woke Kraa. Twigleg just wished his heart would finally get used to danger and adventures! Wasn't he giving it enough opportunities? Evidently not; it stumbled and raced and beat so loudly that Twigleg was always afraid it would give him away. Oh, please! he implored whatever god protected homunculi and human boys (Twigleg always pictured this god in a huge glass bottle), please let us get hold of this dratted feather without waking the beaked brute!

Kraa growled again. His head was resting between the mighty claws, and his wings rose and fell with every breath he took.

Lola stood still, and listened for sounds from outside.

Only the noises of the jungle came through the mud walls – the chorus of cicadas, the croaking of toads, the cry of a marbled cat pouncing on prey – and if everything was going to plan, then Patah, TerTaWa and the others had already overpowered the sleepy macaque and set Shrii free.

They had to hurry!

The rescue of Shrii could still raise the alarm before they had the feather! Or Kraa might wake as they plucked it out *before* Shrii was liberated, and . . . no, no, no! Twigleg felt thought paralysing his limbs. Lola was always saying, 'Don't think, Humpelkluss!' But easier said than done! Apart from the fact that Twigleg wasn't sure whether it was really good advice.

Lola for one wouldn't be wasting a moment on thinking while she scurried over to the sleeping griffin. Rodents. Yes, that must be it. Rodents were braver, that was all.

The sun-feathers were high up on Kraa's feathered throat. But as he was sleeping with his head between his claws, they were easier to reach. Twigleg just had to climb on Lola's shoulders, pull himself up by Kraa's plumage, then give a gentle tug and . . .

oh, this was lunacy! How come they had ever thought it was a good idea for the smallest members of the team to carry out the most important part of this suicidal mission? It was the rat's fault, of course. Twigleg could still hear Lola's voice only too clearly – his heart had turned to ice at her words. 'Right, it's a done deal. The humklupuss and I get hold of the feather. All the monkeys have to do is rescue Shrii, and as for the rest of you . . . you're too big and you make too much noise!'

A done deal! Lola was kneeling on the platform. The griffin's leonine chest was breathing behind her. In and out. It could swallow him as easily as the mist-ravens snacked on strawberries.

Oh dear. Lola was getting impatient!

As he climbed on her shoulders, the griffin's breath was like a hot wind passing over his face. But hard as he stretched out, he couldn't reach the lowest of the sun-feathers!

Okay, Twigleg. You know what to do.

No, he wanted to say. No! The world really doesn't need flying horses! But his mind was already assessing the distance between his fingers and the bright feather. The thing about courage is that in many people it shows up only when it's really needed. And Twigleg was considerably more courageous than he thought. He reached into Kraa's tawny feathers and ruffled them up. Only a little further, and he would be able to take hold of the sun-feather.

'Humklupus!' he heard Lola hissing. 'What are you doing?'

But Twigleg was already reaching out his trembling hand . . .

CHAPTER FORTY

The Other Mission

I will not be clapped in a hood,
Nor a cage, nor alight upon wrist,
Now I have learned to be proud
Hovering over the wood
In the broken mist
Or tumbling cloud.
W.B. Yeats, 'The Hawk'

In fact, it had been really easy to overpower the sleepy macaque guarding Shrii's cage. TerTaWa had undertaken that task, to keep Patah from any temptation to throttle him. While the gibbon gagged the macaque and put him in one of the empty basketwork cages, Kupo got to work setting Shrii free. When her furry face peered through the intertwined twigs, the griffin thought at first that he was simply dreaming of seeing the loris. After all, he hadn't eaten for days. But then he saw TerTaWa. And Patah. Kupo was so relieved to see Shrii unharmed that her usually nimble fingers could hardly open the bolts. When she finally succeeded, Shrii's limbs were so stiff from captivity that he could hardly force them, agonisingly slowly, out of the basket. But seeing Patah, TerTaWa, Kupo and all the others free, safe and sound made him so happy that he forgot his aching joints and nudged them affectionately in the breast with his beak. It had been terrible to stare down at Kraa's throne day and night, waiting helplessly for his own execution. But it had not been the fear of death that had troubled Shrii most during those endless hours. It had been the certainty that all those who had trusted and followed him had paid for it with their freedom or their lives.

It cost Shrii all his remaining strength to climb up to the branch from which the basketwork cage hung. All his muscles ached, and at the first attempt he could hardly manage to spread his wings. But the anxious faces of his rescuers spurred him on to try again. He must fly! It was the only possible way of escape. Even if he might meet the other griffins up in the sky. Flying. How he had longed to feel the wind in his feathers! But would his weakened wings bear him up? A griffin's body is as heavy as it is powerful.

Shrii unfolded his green wings for the second time. The joy of being free again drowned out the pain.

'Fly south!' TerTaWa told him quietly. 'Tchraee and the others are usually hunting in the northern mountains at this time of night!'

Shrii nodded. And raised his head, listening, when a furious roar rose to their ears from Kraa's palace nest.

'Fly, Shrii!' chirped Kupo.

'Alone? But what about the rest of you?' Maybe he could carry them in spite of his painful limbs. He had to try!

A hoarse screech responded to Kraa's roar. Kupo, horrified, clung to Shrii, and TerTaWa and Patah exchanged a glance. They all knew that voice. Tchraee. Of course. He often flew ahead of the others.

More screeching rang out from the distance, echoing through the night. They were coming.

'Climb on me!' Shrii called to his rescuers.

But Patah was already beckoning to the other macaques to climb quickly down the tree, away from the dreadful screams cutting through the night. Only TerTaWa and Kupo climbed on the griffin's back and ducked down between his wings. The voice of Tchraee had rekindled Shrii's anger. It gave him strength. The strength of the lion as he took off. The strength of the eagle as he soared into the air. And yes, his wings, painful as they were, carried him away. He left the cages and Kraa's palace far below him, and broke through the canopy of leaves, flying out into the wide night sky that sprinkled starlight on his wings.

Free!

His keen eyes could already see the shapes of the other griffins in the distance. But suddenly he sensed something above him. A presence that he had never felt before. Shrii looked up – and there they were. Powerful and strange, shining like the silver light of the moon.

Shrii forgot the other griffins.

He forgot that he was escaping.

He forgot Kraa and his days of captivity.

Dragons!

His mother had often told him about them. Tales of the times when dragons and griffins had flown side by side. Protectors instead of plunderers, light instead of darkness.

The dragons had also seen Shrii, but night made the green of his wings seem darker, and they took him for one of the other griffins. Tattoo bared his teeth, and even Firedrake lowered his horned head, ready to attack. But suddenly the huge wings below them showed green in the moonlight, and Winston let out a cry of joy.

'That's Shrii!' he called. 'They've done it! He's free!'

TerTaWa and Kupo waved to them from Shrii's back, and Ben was so relieved to see the young griffin flying over the treetops, uninjured, that he flung his arms around Sorrel's furry neck, although he knew that she hated to be hugged.

But there was another task yet to be carried out tonight.

'TerTaWa!' Ben called down to the gibbon. 'How about Twigleg? And Lola? Have you seen them? Do they have the feather?'

TerTaWa and Kupo exchanged a remorseful glance.

'Who are you talking about?' asked Shrii.

'We had to get you to safety!' called TerTaWa. 'We couldn't help them as well! Remember that roar? I'm afraid Kraa has eaten them.'

Ben thought he felt his heart missing a beat. He leaned so far over Firedrake's neck that Sorrel tugged him back.

'Firedrake!' he shouted to the dragon. 'We have to find Twigleg!'

'Are you out of your mind?' Sorrel shouted in astonishment.

But Ben was already regretting his words. Sorrel was right. Was he out of his mind? The dragons had to get away. The other griffins were coming. And then what would become of Twigleg?

'Sorrel is right. Forget what I just said!' he called to Firedrake. 'You two must get away! And take Shrii with you! I'll see about Twigleg. Just drop me off in the trees!'

Firedrake glanced at Tattoo.

The other griffins were still a long way off, but one of them was quickly taking shape. And he was making straight for Shrii. For a moment the sight of the two dragons made Tchraee forget who his prey was. Then, however, with a scream that woke every living creature on Pulau Bulu from sleep, he plunged down on the younger griffin.

Shrii was still slow after his captivity. Tchraee dug his claws into his breast before Schrii could raise his own claws to defend himself. But Schrii was young and strong. He shook Tchraee off, and when the older griffin attacked again, both dragons were beside Schrii. Tchraee struck out first at Tattoo, but Tattoo smoothly avoided his opponent's beak, and before the griffin could attack again, Winston hit him on the chest with the club that Hothbrodd had given him. Even Berulu forgot his fear, and menacingly showed Tchraee his tiny teeth.

The old griffin was hopelessly outclassed, but all the same he went on fighting, and the sole target of his furious attack was Shrii. The dragons did all they could to provide Shrii with cover, but Firedrake felt the same anger growing inside him that he had sensed when the poachers attacked. Thanks to Ben and Sorrel, he managed to tame it. But when Tchraee, striking out desperately with his claws, tore one of Firedrake's wings open, Tattoo lost his self-control, and while Winston was still watching Firedrake in dismay, the young dragon began breathing fire. Tchraee was enveloped in pale blue flames. They licked over the old griffin's fur and feathers – but instead of burning, Tchraee's body turned to ash-grey stone, and fell from the sky, rigid and petrified.

With uncomprehending horror, Tattoo watched as the stone body crashed through the canopy of leaves below them and disappeared. But there was no time to think about what had happened.

'The others!' cried Winston. 'They're coming!'

Four griffins swooped out of the night, racing towards them with furious screams of aggression.

'Shrii!' called Firedrake. 'You must fly for it! We'll cover your back, but we can't hold them off for long!'

The young griffin was still staring at the leaves below, and the place where Tchraee had vanished. But at the sound of Firedrake's voice he raised his head and looked at the attacking pride.

'No!' he called back to Firedrake. 'I've been hiding for too long! Let's find your friends!'

Ben had a protest on the tip of his tongue. But he knew

Firedrake too well to think that he and Tattoo would simply fly away.

'Oh, great!' cried Sorrel. 'Here we go again! Battle! Danger! Have I been missing all that? No, not a bit of it!'

Firedrake and Tattoo were already on course for the canopy of leaves. Followed by Shrii.

CHAPTER FORTY-ONE

Unheard Of

He was thinking of the time that comes to every leader
of every pack when his strength goes from him and he gets
feebler and feebler, till at last he is killed by the wolves
and a new leader comes up – to be killed in his turn.
Rudyard Kipling, *The Jungle Book*

Kraa hadn't eaten Twigleg. Not yet. But the homunculus was in a difficult situation. Very, very difficult. Nakal was holding him tightly in his slender brown fingers.

'The more closely I look at this creature, Tanunda,' he said with a subservient smile for Kraa, 'the more peculiar it seems to me. Just look at its clothes. And that pale skin, and its pointed nose. It really doesn't seem to be of this world!'

Well, that was one way of describing a homunculus!

At close quarters, Nakal smelled as overpoweringly sweet as the kind of flower that eats flies. Or as if he had drenched his long-haired coat with perfume. Twigleg wanted to hold his nose, but Nakal was holding him so tightly that he couldn't move a muscle. How could he and Lola have forgotten the proboscis monkey? They had thought of the jackal scorpions, the snakes, the other monkeys . . . but then again, who could have guessed that Kraa's adjutant slept under his master's wing?

Nakal sniffed at Twigleg's hair as if to find out what it was made of. Twigleg felt like saying he wouldn't mind knowing that himself, but Nakal's teeth were too long and sharp, and there was evil in his eyes that could easily rival the evil of his master.

Of course Lola had made her getaway. Twigleg still couldn't grasp the shameful way she had left him in the lurch. Although he had to admit that even such a bold rat as Lola couldn't have changed much about the fix he was in. And even if she did come back with help – by then he'd probably be half digested in Kraa's stomach. What a way to die! Were all homunculi doomed to end their lives in the belly of a monster? If only at least he had landed in the same belly as his brothers. Nonsense, Twigleg! If Nettlebrand had eaten him along with the others, he'd never have met Ben, and his master was far and away the best thing that had happened to him in his whole long life. Was he really never going to see him again?

Above him, the light of the glow-worms broke on Kraa's sun-feathers, as if they were flames in his tawny yellow of his desert plumage. All for nothing! They had failed! He wouldn't even be able to console himself by knowing that his death was saving the last Pegasi! 'Oh, stop it, Humklupuss!' He could just imagine Lola saying that. 'Self-pity is the most dangerous way of wasting time when you're in trouble!'

'Do you know what I think, Tanunda? I think this is the creature we sold to the poachers!' Nakal's expression was as por-tentous as if he had solved all the mysteries of the world by making this discovery. 'And if you ask me – the rat looked suspiciously familiar too! Why would the poachers have let those two go free? Right, so the rat certainly wouldn't fetch a good price. But this – ' he said, examining Twigleg from all sides as if he were a doll – 'this is surely a very saleable item!'

How Twigleg would have liked to give the monkey's enormous nose a good kicking. But then Nakal would surely bite his head off. 'And that really wouldn't be a good idea, Humklupuss!' he could hear Lola saying. 'After all, your head is the only useful part of your body!'

'It still looks to me like a jenglot!' growled Kraa, as he stared down at Twigleg with a disparaging expression. 'When I last ate one of those, half my feathers fell out!'

Hang on a moment! That information could come in useful, Twigleg told himself.

'Quite correct, O terrible, all-devouring Kraa!' he cried. Why did fear always turn his voice to a shrill squeak? 'I'm definitely a jenglot! In fact, I'm an unusually poisonous jenglot. From . . . from a distant kingdom where they're all as pale as me.'

Unfortunately that didn't seem to impress Kraa very much. He bent down to Twigleg and inspected him at close quarters. Twigleg felt that he would drown in those yellow eyes, the eyes of a bird of prey, like a beetle caught in amber. And that beak! Even Sorrel would have fitted comfortably into it. Sorrel . . . suppose Lola was bringing the dragons to his aid? You could never tell with rats; they just loved fighting. No. No, he really hoped that idea hadn't occurred to Lola. Or did he?

Kraa straightened up. 'I think I'll eat it later, Nakal!' he growled. 'Shut it up and find out where the scorpions are.'

Hmm, yes, the jackal scorpions. Not one of them had shown up when Nakal's scream had awoken Kraa. (Twigleg was still surprised that his heart hadn't stopped at once.) Obviously Barnabas had succeeded in his part of the plan.

Nakal turned with a portentous expression. Holding Twigleg, he strode to the way out of the palace nest. But he didn't get far.

'Wait, Nakal!' Kraa called after him.

Nakal smiled unpleasantly at Twigleg as he turned. 'Seems like he fancies eating you after all!' he whispered. 'I'm sure you're nice and crunchy, like shellfish.'

But Kraa had something else in mind.

'Ask the jenglot why he came back!' he growled. 'Maybe the poachers let him go so that he could spy on my treasure chamber!'

'Hear that?' Nakal shook Twigleg like a rattle. 'Is that why they sent you back, jenglot?'

'Yes! Oh yes, exactly!' stammered Twigleg. 'Those poachers . . . they want to steal all your gold, O terrible Kraa!'

'Really?'

Kraa scratched the back of his eagle's neck with one of his lion's paws – and abruptly raised his head.

The cry of a griffin rang through the night.

And a second cry followed it.

'Jackal scorpions!' screeched Nakal. His nose was quivering in his face like an over-ripe fruit. 'Where are those useless creatures?'

Kraa gave vent to a deep, a very deep growl. Coming from a beak, it sounded even more menacing than the roar from a lion's mouth. His snake-tail writhed in the air, baring its venomous fangs.

'What's going on out there, jenglot?'

That gigantic, unspeakably horrible beak came so close to Twigleg that it touched his nose!

'Nothing, nothing!' he managed to say. 'Or rather . . . no, wait, to be honest that's not true. The other griffins are in league with the poachers. They've been making plans to steal your treasure for a long time. And they . . . they want to crown Shrii king!'

What luck that he had centuries of practice in telling lies to megalomaniac monsters!

Kraa stared at the hatch on which he slept. Its outline was just visible in the middle of the platform.

'Nonsense! Tchraee would never betray me!'

'Tchraee? Tchraee is the ringleader!' cried Twigleg. He hadn't the faintest idea where his lies would lead him, but maybe the others would turn up after all and rescue him. No! No, he wanted his master to stay where he was. Safe on a dragon's back! Far away from that beak and those terrible claws!

Kraa was listening for sounds from outside again. A shudder ran through his wings, and every muscle in his lion's body was taut under the tawny coat.

The screams were getting louder.

'Treachery!' bellowed the griffin. 'Treachery everywhere!'

He spread his wings, and his beak uttered a scream of

aggression that Twigleg felt to the marrow of his bones. Even Nakal flinched in terror, so that his fingers closed even more tightly on Twigleg. Crushed by a proboscis monkey! No, even being swallowed by a griffin sounded better than that.

Kraa swung around and bent down to Twigleg. His beak looked as if it were smiling all the time – in a very cruel way.

'It's true that I lost a lot of feathers when I ate that other jenglot,' he growled, 'but as you may remember, Nakal, it also made me much stronger. And it was deliciously juicy and crunchy at the same time!'

'Unlike me! Jenglots of my kind aren't at all crunchy and juicy, O sharp-clawed Kraa!' Twigleg tried desperately to free himself from Nakal's grasp. 'We really aren't. We taste like . . . like . . .'

He hesitated. Who could say what a griffin would find tasty? Kraa opened his beak.

'Get in here and bring it down to me, Nakal!'

The proboscis monkey raised the hand holding Twigleg – and froze rigid when a sound came in from outside that made even Kraa stand as motionless as the pictures of griffins on his walls.

It was a roar that he had heard only once before in his long, long life. On a starless night hundreds of years ago.

'Do you hear that?' his father had asked him and his brothers. 'That's the voice of a dragon. If you drink its blood, it will make you immortal, and as powerful as the griffins whose statues adorn the palaces of the ancient kings.' And in reply another roar had come from the sky, as if the dragon had heard the challenge. But their father hadn't let them fly after it. At the time Kraa had wondered why. 'Maybe because he's frightened of the dragon!' his youngest brother had whispered. Kraa had pecked his brother's wings until they bled for saying that.

'What's that, Tanunda?' whispered Nakal. 'I've never heard a roar like it.'

Kraa was still standing motionless, with his feathers bristling.

A dragon.

He had always wanted to be immortal.

CHAPTER FORTY-TWO

The Challenge

There is one fairly good reason for fighting –
and that is, if the other man starts it.
T.H. White, *The Once and Future King*

Barnabas Greenbloom had known many dark hours in his life. But it was unusual for anything to weigh on his mind so heavily as knowing that his actions had brought two dragons within reach of a fearsome enemy.

He was kneeling beside one of Kraa's jackal scorpions to check that the anaesthetic was still working when Firedrake and Tattoo, with their dragon riders, broke through the branches above him.

No! Barnabas wanted to call to them. *Fly away – please!*

But then he saw Shrii, landing on the throne platform along with Firedrake. A griffin beside two dragons! That was a sight that perhaps had never been seen in the world before. For a moment it made Barnabas forget his fears – but only for a moment.

Then Kraa stepped out of his palace nest. With the proboscis monkey at his side. And the monkey had Twigleg in his grasp.

Ben cried out in horror. Sorrel was only just in time to catch hold of him before he slipped off Firedrake's back.

How Barnabas cursed himself! After all these years, how could he keep hoping that ventures like this one might be achieved without a fight? It's because you're a hopeless romantic, Barnabas, he told himself. Because you won't come to terms with the fact that in this world, violence always leads to more violence.

And then the other griffins arrived as well – except for Tchraee, who was nowhere to be seen. They settled in the branches above the throne like a flock of hungry vultures. The hatred in their eyes as they stared down at the dragons was outdone only by their revulsion at the sight of Shrii.

The young griffin returned their glance with proud defiance. He had fled, he had hidden, and he had been Kraa's prisoner. It was time for him to confront the old griffin freely and openly at last. Shrii was well aware that the confrontation could very easily end with his own death, but it would be a much better death than the one that Kraa had planned for him.

'Let me talk to him,' he whispered to Firedrake.

Tattoo was about to protest, but Firedrake nodded.

'Try it,' he whispered back. 'But don't forget, we want our friend back alive, small as he is!'

The griffins' tree was still holding Kraa's monkeys captive. They could be heard moving noisily about in the nests as Shrii walked past the empty throne and stopped at the edge of the platform.

'This is our quarrel, Kraa!' he called up to the palace nest. 'Let the jenglot go!'

'He's a homunculus!' Ben called down from Firedrake's back. 'And . . .'

The words died away on his lips. To Kraa's right, something was moving between the pillars surrounding the palace nest. Barnabas! Oh no! Ben realised at once what his adopted father was going to do. He knew him only too well.

Barnabas Greenbloom stepped out of the shadows hiding him from Kraa, and bowed to the griffin as if he were saying hello to a neighbour's cat.

'Terrible Kraa!' he called up to him. 'Accept me in exchange for the unfortunate homunculus. This honourable proboscis monkey could break all his bones simply by holding him rather too tightly. I am sure we can come to an agreement. We arrived on this island with entirely peaceful intentions. Maybe we can even negotiate between you and Shrii. But please, first let the homunculus go.'

The growl that came from Kraa sounded both amused and disapproving.

'Peaceful intentions?' he repeated. 'Peace is something for chickens and geese. Is your little brain too clouded by fear for you to remember that you are addressing a griffin? And what, by the gods of Babylon, is a homunculus? Do you by any chance mean this jenglot? I'll tell you what Kraa the Terrible is going to do with him. Eat him, and you too.'

Barnabas was careful not to utter any sound of pain when Kraa took hold of him with his right front claw. This is really no worse than back in the desert, Barnabas, he told himself as he felt the mighty claws pierce through his clothes; there was no ignoring them. Do you remember? When Nettlebrand came crawling out of the well and you had to hide underneath him? Well, maybe this time it *was* rather worse . . .

'Let them go!' shouted Ben. He was still sitting on Firedrake's back.

'Oh, this isn't good!' muttered Sorrel, putting a mushroom into her mouth to calm herself down. 'This is not good at all.'

Firedrake said nothing.

He walked slowly, very slowly, over the platform, stopped beside Shrii, and looked up at Kraa.

It was a declaration of war.

Kraa craned his neck, and stared down at the dragon, delighted.

'I hadn't finished my sentence,' he croaked. 'I was going to add: I'll eat them both unless' – and his snake-tail wound its way through the air until Barnabas thought he could feel the forked tongue on the nape of his neck – 'unless the lindworm will face me in a duel!'

'No!'

Several of them spoke at the same time: Tattoo, Sorrel, Winston, Twigleg, Barnabas . . . even the other griffins seemed far from enthusiastic about Kraa's proposition. Only Ben said nothing. The last few days had taught him a few things. After all that he and Firedrake had been through together, he had been so sure he knew what it meant to be a dragon rider. But he would never forget the disappointment in Firedrake's eyes – not just because Ben had lied to him, but because he hadn't left it to the dragon himself to decide whether or not to put himself in danger to help them save the Pegasus foals. How could he and Barnabas ever have thought they could make that decision better than Firedrake himself? Were they, after all, like most human beings in thinking themselves cleverer than all the other inhabitants of the planet, dragons included? Ben had promised himself that he would never again let Firedrake down like that. And Firedrake wanted to accept Kraa's challenge. Ben could feel the dragon's muscles tensing themselves already. Firedrake would need his dragon rider in order to control all the anger and aggression now stirring in him. Ben himself felt something dark emerging in his heart: a wish to see Firedrake's teeth buried in Kraa's neck as the dragon took revenge for all that the griffin had inflicted on them and this island. It was an intoxicating sensation – intoxicating and terrible at the same time. It even made Ben forget his anxiety for Firedrake. That's what revenge does – it drowns even love. If the challenge was accepted, both the dragon rider and the dragon would have to help one another to control that darkness.

'No?' Kraa repeated the unanimous answer that had come from so many mouths. 'You didn't say that, lindworm. But I don't hear you say Yes either. Hand me the jenglot, Nakal. I'll have him as a starter, and my main course will be the glass-eyed man.'

It was very obvious that Nakal liked that order. He hurried over to Kraa, eager to please him, bowed, and held the kicking homunculus under the griffin's beak like a ripe fig.

Firedrake gave a roar that went right to Ben's heart. It merged him with the dragon and made them one, as if they were a single living creature.

'I accept your challenge, Kraa!' cried Firedrake.

He had known what he was now feeling only once so keenly before. On the day when he had challenged Nettlebrand: a lust for battle so old and powerful that it seemed to be stealing out of a dark past and into his heart. Even the hatred that stirred in him at the sight of Kraa's cruel beak seemed older than himself. Dragon against griffin. Griffin against dragon. No, that enmity was nothing to do with him. But Firedrake saw, in Kraa's eyes, that he would kill Barnabas and Twigleg as casually as he snapped up flying squirrels and young monkeys.

'Sorrel, get on Tattoo's back!' Firedrake told her as he let the darkness in – into his sinews and muscles, into his mind, but not, he hoped, into his heart. 'You too, Ben,' he added.

Ben and Sorrel exchanged a glance. It wasn't often that they were in total agreement, but this time Ben knew he could count on the brownie girl.

'You're talking nonsense!' said Sorrel. 'We're exactly where we belong. And Tattoo has a rider of his own.'

Firedrake was about to answer. But now it was Shrii who turned to Kraa.

'What's the idea?' he called up to the old griffin as he spread his wings threateningly. 'I challenged you first. I, not the dragon, Kraa! This island is my home, and you will have to fight me for it!'

The other griffins ducked down on the branch where they were crouching, ready to pounce.

'Stay where you are!' Kraa called to them, holding the glass-eyed man in his claw like a captured mouse. 'No one here is fighting except me and the dragon! It will be like the old days. Single combat will decide it.'

'Decide what?' Tattoo came to Firedrake's side.

Kraa didn't trouble to answer him.

What a night! The arrival of the lindworms was the best thing ever to happen on this eternally damp island. A challenge worthy of him at last. It made up for all the uneventful years when the only diversion had been trading with a few ragged poachers. Although these dragons were probably young idiots like Shrii. The silver one was clearly the older of the two, but even he couldn't be more than two or three hundred years old. All the same, he was an impressive opponent. Kraa scrutinised the dragon's long, jagged tail with satisfaction, Firedrake's powerful flanks and curving horns . . . how often had he used them in battle? Most lindworms were very proud of their peaceful natures. But the one with the patterned scales was as excited as if he couldn't wait to attack. A beginner. He, Kraa, had fought a thousand duels in his life, and he had won all of them. All of them.

Kraa ran his beak over his tawny wings – so much more distinguished than Shrii's parrot plumage – and looked up at his opponent.

'Announce the conditions, Nakal!'

'Conditions?' The proboscis monkey looked at his master in surprise.

'Promise them anything you like!' Kraa whispered to him. 'Promise them the blue out of the sky. It makes no difference, because I shall win. As for my price – demand the usual. You know what I like.'

'Oh yes. May I express a wish?' Nakal tapped Twigleg's pointed nose with one finger. 'I'd like to keep the jenglot?'

'Why not?' growled Kraa. 'Maybe he really is poisonous.'

Twigleg wasn't sure whether this was good news or bad news. He was clutched so tightly in Nakal's fist that he could hardly feel his arms, but Barnabas was in a considerably worse situation. Kraa had lowered his claw and was bracing it, together with his captive, on the flight ramp where he was standing. It was a wonder that Barnabas was still breathing.

'These are the conditions of Kraa the Terrible!' cried Nakal to the challengers. 'The two prisoners will get their freedom should the dragon be victorious, and the young parrot –' he made Shrii a mocking bow – 'will be lord of this island.'

The other griffins ruffled up their feathers disapprovingly, but Nakal gave Kraa a conspiratorial wink.

'Excellent,' he growled. 'And now tell them my price!'

Nakal cleared his throat.

'If the mighty Kraa wins the duel,' he announced in such a loud voice that Twigleg wished he could put his hands over his ears, 'he will eat the glass-eyed man alive, as well as all who have supported the traitor Shrii. Then Kraa the mighty, Kraa the feathered storm, Kraa the bringer of a thousand deaths, will drink the blood of the dragon, rip out Shrii's beating heart and eat it, so that everyone on the island will know who is their king.'

It really isn't easy to breathe when a griffin's claw is squeezing your ribs. But Barnabas was choking even more with anger at himself. It seemed to him as if he had betrayed all that he had fought for and believed in during his life. Peace instead of hatred and war, protection instead of destruction, working with others rather than against them . . . all of that was lying in the dirt with him, and soon two fabulous beings would be killing each other on his account. It was no consolation that the griffin might, after all, be the loser. Even Kraa's death would be a loss to the world and the variety of creatures in it. Just as the death of every tiger was.

'Listen to me, Kraa!' gasped Barnabas, trying again to struggle out from under the claw that was pinning him down. 'Please!'

The griffin took no notice. Only his snake-tail wound its way towards Barnabas and hissed in his face.

'Good!' cried Firedrake. 'Here are my conditions.'

The green of the jungle was reflected in his silver scales. It was almost as if the dragon had become part of the island.

'I will fight you only if you agree to free the prisoners, even if I lose. Swear it! Swear by your treasure or whatever is sacred to you. After this battle, whatever its outcome, the prisoners and all who have rebelled against you may leave this island uninjured.'

Kraa scrutinised the dragon like a prey animal that he had spotted down by the roots of a tree as he flew past.

'Of course!' he growled. 'Why not? A griffin should crown his victory with magnanimity. You have my word, lindworm.'

'Liar!' cried Barnabas, as loud as he could. 'Don't believe a word he says. Firedrake! Griffins take no prisoners. And certainly they don't let anyone go. I forbid this fight! Do you hear, Firedrake? Take Ben and fly away!'

Kraa bent so low over him that Ben cried out in fear. The snake-tail fell over Barnabas's throat.

'Humans!' snarled the griffin. 'You chatter all the time like monkeys. Not surprising, considering the close relationship. I'm sure you'll go on chattering even in my belly!'

Then he opened the claw holding Barnabas on the ground.

'Get out!' he snarled. 'And let the jenglot go as well, Nakal. Then we'll see whose word can be trusted. The word of a griffin or the word of a dragon!'

Hesitantly, Barnabas stood up.

It was too good to be true.

Nakal gave Twigleg a regretful glance, but in the end he opened his fist. Barnabas felt Twigleg's heart beating like the heart of a frightened bird in his fingers as he reached for him.

'O terrible Kraa!' he stammered as he threw himself on his knees in front of the griffin. 'I will get you treasures, I will fill your palace with gold, but please let the dragons go. They are here only because of me!'

And because of three unborn Pegasus foals, Twigleg added in his thoughts. He really did hope they were worth all this.

Kraa did not condescend to answer Barnabas. He had eyes only for Firedrake.

'What do you say, lindworm? I have fulfilled your condition. What about you? Will you fight?'

Firedrake exchanged a glance with Tattoo. If the griffin killed him, what would become of Maia and his unborn children? He hardly dared to think of them for fear it would make him vulnerable. But Tattoo understood and nodded. Yes, he would look after them.

'Wait!' cried Ben. 'There's one more condition. If Firedrake wins, you give us one of your sun-feathers!'

Kraa growled with amusement again. 'I'm going to dip all my feathers in the blood of your dragon friend, little human, but yes, if he wins you will get one of my sun-feathers. Kraa's word on it!'

'I wouldn't give a button mushroom for his word,' whispered Sorrel as she tightened the belt holding her on Firedrake's back.

Ben did the same. The belts revived memories: of a golden dragon and a cave full of dragon-fire. At the time they had had to fight. There had been no alternative. But this time fighting seemed so useless. Only a feather, that was all they had wanted to ask for. Would they have set out at all if they had known how high the price would be? Ben saw the same question on Barnabas's face. He was standing high up beside Kraa's nest, and he looked desperate. No, they probably would not have come here at all. But perhaps it was better that they hadn't known how the whole story would end. Maybe some things just had to happen.

Nakal climbed on Kraa's back. A few wingbeats that brought a stormy wind into the tree, and the griffin landed on the back of his throne. He was a fearsome sight.

'Firedrake, let me fight him,' Tattoo whispered. 'There's no one waiting for me. It won't even interest the others if I don't come back. But you are their leader.'

Firedrake bent his head, so that neither Kraa nor Nakal could read his answer from his lips. 'The griffin will break his word!' he whispered to Tattoo. 'As soon as he thinks I can defeat him he will call on the other griffins to come to his aid. That's when I'll need you, so be ready for that moment. And tell Shrii.'

Kraa was watching them furtively.

'I want that feather, Sorrel,' Firedrake whispered. 'Try to pluck it out.'

Kraa leaped down to the seat of his throne, and from there to the platform.

'What are you waiting for, lindworm?' he croaked. 'Do your friends have to encourage you? Or are you getting them to tell you how to fight a griffin? Look at the pictures adorning my palace. They'll show you how a fight like that ends.'

'Oh yes? Any fool can see that your pictures tell lies, you boastful great beaked show-off!' Sorrel called back. 'I mean, do you see a brownie on the dragon's back?'

By way of answering, Nakal drew a machete out of the sheath that he wore on his belt, and swung it threateningly through the air.

'The pictures don't show our riders either!' growled Kraa. 'They show only the main point: the griffin always wins.'

Then, with a hoarse attacking cry, he beat his wings and made for the dragon.

CHAPTER FORTY-THREE

Griffin and Dragon

We all have to meet our match sometime or other.
Richard Adams, *Watership Down*

Feathers and scales. Claws and paws. Tawny yellow and silver-grey wings, Kraa's dreadful beak, Firedrake's bared teeth . . . Barnabas had seen many fights between fabulous creatures before, but this time he soon took off his glasses, with shaking fingers, because he simply couldn't bear to watch. Even sharp eyes could scarcely make out where the dragon ended and the griffin began. But the sounds, if anything, were even worse. The dragon's roar, the griffin's screech, Nakal's screams of hatred . . . Ben's voice mingled with the noise of battle, and so did Sorrel's curses as she called on all kinds of poisonous fungi . . .

Who would be victorious? Sometimes the dragon seemed to be stronger, sometimes the griffin. Barnabas couldn't have said whether he was more worried about Ben or Firedrake. Or rather, he could say: he was more worried about the boy, of course. Nothing about being a father is harder than giving your own children the freedom to do dangerous things now and then.

Of course, Ben didn't know anything about such anxieties yet. He hadn't even had time to think about the danger. He and Sorrel were at the heart of a storm. The breastplates that Hothbrodd had made them saved them more than once from the thrusts of Kraa's beak and his terrible eagle's claws. Whenever Nakal's machete glanced harmlessly off the wood, Nakal gave vent to a screech of frustration. Firedrake's scales protected him, but all the same Kraa's claws inflicted minor wounds on him. Again and again, Ben managed to warn the dragon just in time for him to avoid the griffin, or he fended Kraa off with the club that Hothbrodd had given him. But the griffin was fighting to kill. Every blow of his claws, every thrust of his beak wanted Firedrake's blood, and Ben soon began to fear that the griffin's unbridled bloodlust would make him stronger in the long run. But the less control Kraa showed, the more restraint Firedrake displayed in fighting back. With Ben's help, he avoided the griffin's attack as smoothly as if he had turned into the fire that he could breathe, although he did not use that ultimate weapon, even when Kraa's beak finally opened up a more serious wound. The griffin stared at the blood running over the dragon's injured shoulder like someone dying of thirst who sees water. Firedrake's next attack, however, made Kraa stumble, and Sorrel took her chance to reach into his tawny plumage. She had her fingers already closed around one of the sun-feathers when the griffin realised what she meant to do. Kraa almost pecked her hand off, and now it was Firedrake who lost his self-control at the sound of Sorrel's scream of pain. His attack drove Kraa back until the griffin was standing on the edge of the platform with his wings quivering, his feathers and coat wet with sweat, and his beak open as he struggled for breath.

Firedrake was also breathing heavily, but Ben felt that he still had enough strength left to go on fighting.

'Surrender, Kraa!' the dragon cried. 'Surrender, and honour your promise.'

The griffin was staring at the wound he had inflicted on Firedrake.

'Do you know what we tell our young about the origin of the dragons?' he croaked. 'It's said that they crawled out of the flesh of a dying demon like maggots. And that they were created only to make griffins immortal.'

Kraa was trembling with exhaustion as he spread his huge wings again, but he was still a very menacing sight.

'There's only one king on this island!' he screeched, striking out at Firedrake with the last of his strength. 'And you will curse the wind that brought you here, lindworm!'

Then, with a shrill scream, he gave the other griffins the order to attack.

With wings threateningly spread, Shrii leaped to Firedrake's side. Tattoo did the same. But the five griffins who had come to Pulau Bulu so long ago, and from so far away, stayed motionless on the branch where they were perching.

'You're defeated, Kraa!' called Roargh down to his leader. 'Give the lindworm what you promised him, as our honour demands.'

Kraa stretched his neck, and looked up with hatred at his fellow griffins.

'Honour?' he screeched. 'This island is mine, and I decide what its laws are!'

He fluffed up his feathers until they adorned his head like a crown, and then turned back to the dragon.

'You've defeated the eagle and the lion, lindworm! But you

forgot the one who has scales, like you!'

His snake-tail rose as the griffin swung around, and the viper dug its poison fangs into Sorrel's arm.

Firedrake bit its head off, but the venom was already working. Ben was just in time to catch Sorrel before she fell off Firedrake's back, and the dragon felt his own anger like lava in his veins. This time it was so wild and dark that Firedrake couldn't control it.

That was exactly what Kraa had hoped for. Only the silver dragon could burn away the shame of his defeat. After all, there was no more honourable end for a griffin than death by fire.

Maybe Firedrake would indeed have given Kraa what he wanted. But Tattoo beat him to it. He soared into the air and breathed fire down on Kraa. Flames licked around the griffin's coat and feathers, the ghostly grey fire that decades of petrified sleep had given Tattoo. And when it went out, Kraa and Nakal had turned into the same stone that had held Tattoo captive for so many years.

The other griffins stared at their leader in motionless dismay, looking as if Tattoo's dragon-fire had turned them to stone as well.

'Firedrake!' Barnabas called down to the dragon from Kraa's palace. 'Quick – get Sorrel to Hothbrodd!'

The dragon obeyed, without asking for an explanation. He shot down through the air, past the nests where the captured monkeys were calling for their feathered master, down and down through leaves and branches, with his heart hurting worse than the wound that Kraa had given him. It seemed as if the trunk of the griffins' tree would never end! But at last they saw Hothbrodd sitting down among its roots.

Ben was still holding Sorrel in his arms as Firedrake landed beside the startled troll. She wasn't moving. Ben couldn't even make out any heartbeat!

Hothbrodd dropped the branch that he had been carving with the knife he had made from a seashell.

'The griffin . . . his snake's tail!' That was all Ben needed to say.

The troll shaved the fur off her skin with his knife where the snake had bitten her. Then he made deep cuts in his own green thumbs and rubbed his pale, troll's blood into the snakebite.

Even though Sorrel had closed her eyes, she was muttering mushroom curses. Of course. Ben didn't know whether to laugh or cry.

'Don't worry, she'll recover!' Hothbrodd clapped him on the back so hard that he fell on his knees. Then he gave Firedrake his most confident troll smile. 'Have you lot finished up there?'

Ben looked at Firedrake in dismay.

The sun-feather! He saw Kraa's plumage before him, all of it turned to stone. No! Had it all been for nothing after all?

'Shriiii!'

Above them, the griffins were calling the name of their new king, but Firedrake had forgotten both them and the Pegasus eggs. He had eyes only for Sorrel. An eternity seemed to pass before she finally opened her eyes.

Firedrake sighed with such relief that his breath struck sparks.

'Why do I stink of fish?' murmured Sorrel, sitting up unsteadily.

'Herring!' grunted Hothbrodd. 'Troll blood smells of herring. Would you rather smell of dead brownie?'

Sorrel touched the bald patch on her arm. The pain brought back the memory of the viper's fangs, dripping poison, and Kraa's triumphant glance as they dug into her furry arm . . .

'What happened to the griffin?' she asked.

'We'll tell you later,' said Ben. 'Twigleg, Barnabas, and Lola are still up above us. We must bring them down, but you'd better stay here.'

Naturally Sorrel didn't like that at all. 'Great stinking crested newt, what the . . .'

'Ben is right. Don't you move from the spot!' Firedrake interrupted her sternly. 'And be nice to Hothbrodd!' he added before he spread his wings.

'Nice?' Sorrel called after him.

She already sounded more like herself. Troll blood was a strong antidote to poison.

CHAPTER FORTY-FOUR

Too Late?

Fear tastes quite different when
you're not just reading about it.
Cornelia Funke, *Inkheart*

They would be back too late! If they ever came back at all! By now Ouranos had grown so much that he could hardly move. Chara was kicking the shell that surrounded him in increasing panic, and even Synnefo was trying in vain to turn around in the egg, or even lift her wings. When Guinevere saw them, she found it hard to breathe, as if she were with them in the prison that their eggshells had become. Ànemos was circling in the air above the fjord and the surrounding forests all the time, in the desperate hope of seeing Hothbrodd's plane appear in the distance. But for all the inhabitants of MÍMAMEIÐR, that hope was dwindling with every hour that passed. It was so hard to believe that all was not lost. The foals, Ànemos, Ben, her father, Hothbrodd, Twigleg, Lola . . . Guinevere repeated their names as if she could protect them all like that, but she was so

- 312 -

frightened that she could hardly think straight.

Professor Spotiswode was already carrying out tests on diamonds for possible ways to open the eggs without hurting the foals after all. And Vita was frantically getting in touch with friends and members of FREEFAB all over the world to see if they could think of anything.

Two days left, said Guinevere's calendar. Forty-eight hours. But Guinevere wasn't even sure whether they had as long as that. And there was no sign of life from Ben and her father. Her mother had asked every conservationist in Indonesia to look out for them, but they seemed to have vanished without trace, like the griffins they had set out to find.

CHAPTER FORTY-FIVE

A Royal Price

Today I have so much to do: I must kill memory
once and for all. I must turn my soul to stone.
Anna Akhmatova, 'The Sentence'

When Firedrake came down on the throne platform again, Tattoo was standing beside Kraa's petrified form with his head bent. Winston and Berulu were with him, and so was Barnabas, who with the aid of several lianas had actually managed to climb from Kraa's palace down to the platform on his own. With Twigleg in his pocket. After all the experiences of the last few hours, the climb had seemed almost easy. They were all still alive, which seemed a miracle. But none of them felt anything like joy, let alone a sense of victory.

It had all been for nothing. The long journey, running all those risks . . . for nothing.

Ben picked up one of the many feathers lying on the platform. Most of them were Kraa's, but there was no sun-feather among them. The sun-feathers now turned to stone, were around Kraa's petrified neck. Telling Vita and Guinevere about their failure was going to be an ordeal. And the Pegasus ... Ben could hardly bear to think of Ànemos.

Even the fact that they had rescued Shrii couldn't really console Ben. He had only to think of the photograph of the motherless nest in his pocket, and his heart was heavy with grief and disappointment.

They were the only ones still standing by the stone figure of Kraa. All the others had followed Shrii when he and the other griffins flew up to Kraa's palace nest.

Shrii ... no, it had not all been for nothing. Pulau Bulu would be a happier island when they left it again. Who knew what would have become of Shrii, TerTaWa and all the others but for their arrival? Twigleg was telling himself the same thing as he stood between Barnabas and Ben, looking up at the sun-feathers on Kraa's stone neck.

'Maybe they'll work even now they've been turned to stone,' said Twigleg, with faint hope in his voice.

'I can't really imagine it,' murmured Ben. 'I think we'd better fly home.'

Tattoo groaned, and lowered his head so far that he almost bumped his nose on Kraa's claws.

'It's my fault! All my fault!'

But although it was obvious how disappointed Barnabas was, he shook his head vigorously. 'Nonsense! Kraa didn't make it easy for any of us to think clearly. You were only trying to protect the others.'

'Exactly. What else could you have done?' Winston stroked Tattoo's patterned scales comfortingly, while Berulu uttered a sympathetic squeak. Sometimes the maki sounded almost like a ...

... rat!

Twigleg looked around.

'Has anyone seen Lola?'

The others shook their heads.

Oh no!

'But she must be here! She got away when Nakal grabbed hold of me!' cried Twigleg. 'I thought she ran to Barnabas!'

Oh, that confounded rat! Even if Twigleg still thought poorly of the way she had abandoned him to Nakal and Kraa on his own, he was genuinely worried! Suppose the stupid rodent had let something or other eat her? After all, she wasn't half as big as she thought she was!

Lola had not let anything eat her, but she was in a fix. Rats can squeal quite loudly, and their shrill voices carry considerably further than their body size might suggest, but even a rat has trouble making herself heard above the noise of dragons and griffins locked in battle. And when the agitated chattering and squawking of monkeys and parrots is added to the racket, the prospect is hopeless!

Lola had tried shouting until her throat would produce nothing but a hoarse squeak, but no one had heard her. Of course she had left the humklupuss only to fetch help! But in doing so she had crossed the path of one of Kraa's jackal scorpions, those infuriating nuisances. Wasn't it bad enough for the brutes to have pincers? Did they have to snap at her with jackal's jaws into the bargain? The anaesthetic in Barnabas's fountain pens had already made her pursuer sleepy. But it could still have hunted rats, and Lola's life would probably have come to a sudden end there on the island of Pulau Bulu if she hadn't spotted a hole in the mud wall of Kraa's nest just in time to save herself. It was a ridiculously tight fit, since after all, she wasn't the most slender of rats, and her hideout stank of monkey and bird droppings. But the worst of it was having to crouch there while her friends could be heard fighting for their lives outside. And to make the situation even sillier, Barnabas's anaesthetic had sent the jackal scorpion to sleep just outside the hole, barring her way of escape with its horrible pincers.

When cries of jubilation suddenly rang out, and the griffins were screeching Shrii's name, Lola began shouting again. But her hoarse squeals were still not much louder than the squeak of a frightened mouse, and it seemed ages before Twigleg peered over her sleeping pursuer and looked into the hole.

'And about time too, humpelklumpus!' Lola snapped at him, while Barnabas moved the scorpion aside in what seemed to her an exaggeratedly considerate way.

'Not a word!' she said as she squeezed herself out into the open. 'I don't want to hear a word about it! I've missed it all, right? All the fun! But no, Barnabas didn't want to put anything stronger in those fountain pen cases. Huh!' She kicked the sleeping scorpion in the side with her tiny boot. 'That dose wouldn't even have knocked *me* out!'

This was too much for Twigleg.

'All the fun?' he repeated, outraged. 'I'd just have loved to change places with you, Lola Greytail! Do you think it was more fun being held in a proboscis monkey's perfumed paw, waiting to be fed to a griffin as a snack?'

'Well, of course I'd have changed places right away!' retorted Lola snippily.

Which was probably the truth. Twigleg was still trying to think up a good answer when someone cleared his throat behind them.

TerTaWa was squatting on Kraa's abandoned throne. He had pinned a jasmine flower to his jacket in honour of the day.

'Shrii asked me to take you to him.' The gibbon could hardly speak, he was smiling so broadly. 'Shrii Dragonfriend! Shrii Emeraldfeather! Shrii Conqueror of Kraa . . . I'm still working on his titles, but anyway, he wants to see you and say thank you.'

And with that he pointed invitingly at the entrance to Kraa's palace nest.

It was brimful when Ben and the others followed TerTaWa in. But the tiny birds who built the griffins' nests knew their trade. Kraa's palace easily held all the visitors. Except for Hothbrodd and Sorrel, all those who had helped to end Kraa's reign were there. When Ben followed Tattoo, he saw Patah in the crowd. The macaque was looking rather contrite after not only the gibbon but even Kupo had shown themselves braver, yet even his face, which was usually so glum, showed some happiness and relief.

Shrii was sitting on the platform where Kraa had slept, and the other five griffins were standing in front of it. They had lowered their beaked heads, but Ben wasn't sure whether that expressed defiance or submission.

Shrii had laid his snake-tail around his paws and claws, and was looking down at the other griffins watchfully. His emerald-green feathers shone as if the jungle had grown in through the sand-coloured walls. The griffin was such a magnificent sight that Ben felt his heart beating faster. And it was surely not the only heart to do so.

'Yes, you heard correctly, Roargh,' said Shrii, while Ben went over to Firedrake's side. 'Choose one of yourselves as your new king. It makes no difference to me. I shall go away. I never wanted to sit on Kraa's throne.'

Neither TerTaWa nor Shrii's other supporters seemed surprised by what he said, but Roargh let out an angry growl. He did not bother to hide the fact that he still disliked Shrii. But Hiera, the youngest she-griffin, took a hesitant step forward.

'If you will allow us,' she said, bending her neck to Shrii, 'we will come with you, Shrii Dragonfriend.'

A second griffin, Greiir, joined Hiera. 'I'll follow you too,' he said with a bow, 'if you will let me.'

Roargh stared fixedly at the two of them.

'You will both be welcome,' said Shrii, standing up. 'And don't worry, Roargh,' he added. 'We will leave you a fair share of Kraa's gold – when our visitors have been compensated for the lack of hospitality they have been shown here.'

Roargh and the other three griffins who had not joined Shrii turned around, looking at Barnabas and Ben with such a hungry expression that Firedrake raised his head watchfully.

'Oh, no, no!' said Barnabas hastily. 'We take as little interest as you in treasures, my dear Shrii. Gold has as devastating an effect on humans as on griffins. All we wanted was a sun-feather. Now, sad to say, they have been turned to stone – like Kraa himself, but we have won the friendship of a griffin, and that is such an unexpected and wonderful gift that we can leave this island feeling grateful. I am sure we will never forget it.'

Roargh examined the claws of his right forepaw as if he were imagining ripping Barnabas's head off with it.

'Nobly spoken, I'm sure, glass-eyed man!' he growled. 'Your species always has a liking for sentimental talk. I've eaten many of you just for that.'

Shrii came down from the platform and stopped so close to Roargh that their beaks were almost touching.

'I think you failed to hear why they came to this island,' he said in a soft voice – soft, yet it still expressed both derision and a threat. 'They need a sun-feather.'

Roargh returned Shrii's glance with barely concealed hostility.

'So?' he croaked as he fluffed up the feathers on his head. It looked as if a gust of wind had blown on him.

'You have three sun-feathers,' stated Shrii, and the threat was still there in his soft voice. 'Give them one of those feathers.'

Roargh's laughter reminded Ben of the barking of hyenas.

'Has your parrot plumage made you forget what a sun-feather looks like, Shrii Dragonfriend? I don't have any. Not a single one.'

His snake-tail wound its way around his hind legs, with the forked tongue darting out, and both Firedrake and Tattoo tensed their muscles in alarm.

Shrii, however, looked at TerTaWa with an enquiring expression.

Jumping on his back, the gibbon pointed to Roargh's neck. Roargh's plumage was the colour of pale yellow desert sand, but Ben couldn't see a sun-feather in it.

'He has them painted by *The Hands,*' said TerTaWa. 'Kupo has seen it. But she didn't want to tell the humans.'

Everyone looked at Kupo. You could tell how frightened she was of Roargh, but when his glance fell on her she stood up very straight, even though she was trembling all over.

'Kraa had two sun-feathers, Roargh has three,' cried Kupo. 'He knew Kraa wouldn't forgive him for that, so he hid them. It was poor Manis who usually had to paint them for him. Maybe that's why he killed her when they destroyed our nests!'

Patah stroked her tiny head consolingly when she began to sob.

Roargh cast TerTaWa an icy look. By way of an answer, the gibbon only bared his teeth maliciously.

'What are you waiting for, Roargh?' asked Shrii. 'Pluck out one of your three feathers and give it to the humans. Perhaps it will console you to think that by doing that, you are paying your dead king's battle debts.'

Ben felt Barnabas gripping his arm. Maybe the Pegasus foals were not lost after all.

'Suppose I don't pay them?' retorted Roargh. 'Will you set your dragons on me?'

Tattoo gave vent to a growl.

'You'd like that, wouldn't you?' said Shrii. 'No. I've seen all the fighting I want to for the time being. You have two passions that I don't share, Roargh: for war and for gold. Give the humans the sun-feather, and I will give you my share of Kraa's treasure.'

Roargh's eyes widened with distrust. And greed. That was a royal price to pay. No one knew better than Roargh how much gold Kraa had hoarded in his long life. All the same, Ben could see that he would rather have eaten them all, probably tearing TerTaWa and Kupo to pieces first. But Firedrake and Tattoo never took their eyes off Roargh. Curse the lindworms! They were looking at him as calmly as if they owned the world. Yet they didn't seem to have the faintest wish to rule it. Roargh imagined crunching their scales in his beak like seashells. But he remembered the stony figure of Kraa only too clearly.

'Well, why not?' he croaked. 'Give me your share and they can have the feather.'

Shrii nodded to TerTaWa.

The hatch over the treasure was secured with hundreds of knots. Kraa's lorises had tied them, and only they could undo them. But Kupo had been one of those lorises for long enough to know how.

The treasures that she and TerTaWa heaped up before Roargh's claws were of enormous value: the crowns of long-forgotten kings, silver-plated chainmail worn by Kraa in equally long-forgotten battles, golden circlets that he had used to adorn his paws like bangles . . .

One of those looked very familiar to Twigleg, and he was not the only one to have noticed it. TerTaWa reached for it before it rolled over to Roargh's beak and put it in Barnabas's hands. 'I think this is yours, Greenbloom,' he said. 'I'm sure Kraa will ask no more payment.'

As Barnabas thankfully put Bağdagül's bangle in his pocket, Roargh dug his beak into the treasures with as much relish as if he were going to warm himself on the gold.

'See that! Shrii isn't just brave, our friend is also clever,' Barnabas whispered to Ben. 'He's sowing discord among his enemies. Do you see how enviously the other griffins are staring at Roargh?'

Roargh straightened up, with his claws planted on his loot. Then he pushed his beak into the plumage around his neck, plucked out a feather and threw it at Barnabas's feet.

Barnabas bowed as if he didn't notice the hatred in the griffin's eyes.

'I will treat this feather with the utmost respect, Roargh,' he said. 'I know it was won with great courage.'

The griffin moved his head, and for the first time looked at Barnabas with a touch of interest.

'That feather grew when I killed three sand basilisks who were foolish enough to attack our nests. It was ten times ten years before the colour turned golden. Don't tell me what you want it for, or I might kill you after all!'

Yes, he might well have done that very thing.

Barnabas was careful not to pick the feather up too quickly.

'Will Shrii grow a sun-feather for today's fight?'

'Very likely,' growled Roargh. 'And I hope one day a human comes along wanting that feather. But a more warlike human than you, glass-eyes. One who will repay Shrii's treachery by drenching this island in his blood!'

Then he turned abruptly, and with his beak he beckoned several monkeys over to his gold.

Barnabas stroked the tawny down of the feather. Yellow loam came off, colouring his fingers, and the feather began to shine as if the light of the sun were nesting in it.

Ben hardly knew what to do with himself, he felt so happy. They had done it. They had actually done it!

Shrii was standing beside Firedrake and Tattoo. Barnabas went up to him and bowed so low that his glasses almost slipped off his nose.

'Noble Shrii!' he said. 'I must confess that before I came here I did not have a very high opinion of griffins. But you have taught me better!'

Shrii gracefully returned the bow.

'And I did not have a very high opinion of your species, Barnabas Greenbloom,' he replied. 'Maybe we should choose our friends not by their species but by what their hearts are like?'

'A wise rule,' Barnabas agreed. 'And I understand very well why you do not want to be a king. But may I say that you would have been a good one?'

'I'm not so sure of that!' replied Shrii. 'Do you know that our kings have to sit on their thrones without moving for hours every day? I'm afraid that after a week I'd have been as cruel as Kraa!'

Shrii did not change his mind.

*

When Ben visited the island a few years later, with Winston, Shrii was living on the other side of it with a family of very colourful sons and daughters. But Roargh and the other griffins had disappeared, and Kraa's royal tree was inhabited by a colony of gibbons who had chosen TerTaWa as their leader. The stone figure of Kraa still stood in front of his throne, now weathered by wind and rain, and the frescoes on the outside of his nest looked as if they were hundreds of years old. But *The Hands* had added a new picture to the interior. It showed two dragons with human boys on their backs, a man with glass eyes, a rat in a flying suit, and a jenglot in very strange clothes standing fearlessly on the head of the petrified Kraa.

CHAPTER FORTY-SIX

Time to Leave

Everything has to come to an end sometime.
L. Frank Baum, *The Marvellous Land of Oz*

B en was standing outside Kraa's nest with Firedrake, looking out at the jungle as it slowly filled with the light of a new day. They had said goodbye to TerTaWa and Shrii, to Me-Rah, Patah and Kupo. And they had promised to come back again.

Barnabas was already on his way to the beach with Hothbrodd. But they didn't have the sun-feather with them. Tattoo was going to take it to MÍMAMEIÐR. Even Hothbrodd's wonderful plane was slower than a dragon in flight, and if Twigleg's calculations were correct, there was hardly a day left until the foals would be too large for their eggs. Sorrel was busy feeding Tattoo moonlight-flowers so that he could fly even in daylight, and as well as Winston and Berulu, Lola was going with their party as a pilot. After all, neither Tattoo nor his two dragon riders had ever been to MÍMAMEIÐR, and Ben ... Ben would be setting off with Firedrake to the Rim of Heaven.

To his relief, Barnabas had taken his decision calmly, although he hadn't been able to hide his sadness.

'I understand. You were a dragon rider before we met,' he had said, giving Ben a hug. 'But if you feel you'd like to be with humans, don't forget that you're a Greenbloom too!'

How could he ever forget that?

Ben glanced at Firedrake. He had made the right decision – hadn't he? Twigleg, up on his shoulder, heaved an unhappy sigh. Firedrake lowered his head until he could look into Ben's eyes.

'I am honoured that you want to come with me,' he said quietly. 'You know there's nothing I wish for more. But the Rim of Heaven isn't the right home for you. Ask the homunculus if you don't believe me.'

Twigleg nodded to the dragon gratefully.

'You belong with your own kind, master!' he stammered. 'Believe me, I know what I'm talking about. You'd be very lonely in the valley of the Rim of Heaven. In spite of Firedrake!'

'True,' agreed the dragon. 'And you'll be much more useful at MÍMAMEIÐR. That's what life is all about, isn't it? Being useful. And the Greenblooms need you, just as you need them.'

But I need you too! The words were on the tip of Ben's tongue, but he didn't say them. He knew Firedrake was right. If only he wasn't so tired of doing without him.

Tattoo and Sorrel came out of Kraa's nest. Winston and Berulu were already sitting on his back, and of course Lola had tied herself into her place between his horns. There had to be the spice of a little danger, even if the crazy rat said she'd chosen that place so that the dragon could hear her better.

'I think you're going to have another rider too, Tattoo,' said Firedrake.

Winston smiled at Ben, but his smile showed that he already

understood how difficult it was for a rider to be parted from his dragon.

'Boletus and mildew fungus!' murmured Sorrel as she climbed on Firedrake's back. 'I wish I could say the same of myself. It's so much nicer in MÍMAMEIÐR.'

But Ben stood where he was, and couldn't move towards Tattoo.

'Do you have the scale safe?' Firedrake nudged him in the chest with his nose.

Ben felt for the locket. Yes. And now and then, when he wanted to be with Firedrake too much to bear, he would hold the scale. Just to send the dragon his love.

'Off you go, then. We'll see each other soon. Tattoo will bring you with him when he comes back,' said Firedrake. 'After all, you have to see our young dragons.'

Tattoo! Yes, of course. From now on there would be two dragons who could take him to the Rim of Heaven. Tattoo would be flying back!

Ben's heart felt so light – almost as light as the feather that they would be taking to MÍMAMEIÐR.

'Right!' he stammered. 'Right! Then . . . then maybe I'll fly to MÍMAMEIÐR first. Guinevere will need me to help her. I guess that three Pegasus foals will give us a lot of work! If the feather works!' he added.

'It will. I'm sure of that,' said Firedrake. 'And once the foals don't need you any more, you can come and help me teach young dragons how to fly.'

That sounded almost too good to be true.

Ben flung his arms around Firedrake's neck, while Twigleg crept into his pocket.

'Hey, dragon rider! Time for us to leave!' called Lola from the top of Tattoo's head. 'Do you want us to arrive too late, after all the trouble we've been taking?'

She was right.

Ben let go of Firedrake, and looked up at Sorrel.

'See you soon,' he said.

'And when you do I hope you'll have a few chanterelles in your backpack!' replied Sorrel. 'And some porcini. And one or two . . .'

'Ben!' shouted Lola in a high-pitched squeal. 'If you're going to hang around waiting to hear Sorrel's entire wish list of mushrooms, pretty soon there won't be any Pegasi left on this planet, that's for sure!'

Firedrake gently pushed him over towards the other dragon.

'Tattoo!' he called as Ben buckled himself on behind Winston. 'You have a dragon rider of your own now, so don't go thinking you can steal mine as well. I want him back.'

'I promise!' cried Tattoo, as Ben hauled himself up by his tail. The wings that the young dragon spread looked as if the surrounding trees had sprinkled flowers over them.

'Dragonmail for MÍMAMEIÐR!' cried Winston, while Berulu scrambled into safety under his jacket.

Tattoo took off from Kraa's throne platform, and soared into the sultry morning air.

Ben turned back to look at Firedrake until the jungle hid the griffins' tree from his eyes. It hurt. But not as badly as usual, because every one of Tattoo's wing-beats was a promise that he would soon see Firedrake again.

CHAPTER FORTY-SEVEN

At Last

To come to the end of a time of anxiety and fear!
To feel the cloud that hung over us lift and disperse –
the cloud that dulled the heart and made happiness no
more than a memory! This at least is one joy that must
have been known by almost every living creature.
Richard Adams, *Watership Down*

Guinevere was having breakfast with Vita and a few nisses when Gilbert Greytail suddenly appeared in the doorway. His whiskers were quivering, a very unusual sight in the always self-controlled rat, and Guinevere almost forgot to breathe. Gilbert had undertaken to keep an eye on the radio equipment.

'They're bringing it!' he cried. 'They're bringing the feather!'

Vita spilled coffee on her bread and marmalade, and Guinevere jumped up so quickly that two of the nisses fell off their chairs.

'But . . . but, Gilbert!' she said. 'There's no more than a day left! And the flight in itself . . .'

'Guinevere Greenbloom!' the rat interrupted her impatiently. 'I hadn't finished my message! The feather will be arriving by dragonmail!'

Guinevere and Vita exchanged a perplexed glance. 'Dragonmail? But Firedrake . . .'

'Guinevere!' exclaimed Vita. 'What are you waiting for? Go and tell Ànemos!'

Yes, of course.

Guinevere raced out of the house so fast that she ran down the fungus-folk and their straw handcart. She looked around, but the Pegasus was nowhere to be seen. Guinevere hoped he wasn't flying on patrol with the mist-ravens just now. She ran down to the fjord. Nothing! Until one of the winged pigs finally told her that he had seen Ànemos outside Slatebeard's abandoned cave.

The Pegasus was standing where the old dragon often used to lie. The ground there was still as warm as if the sun had been heating up the stone. Ànemos raised his head as Guinevere appeared at the mouth of the cave. She had run so fast that she was fighting for breath and couldn't get out a word. But she didn't have to say anything. Ànemos read her good news in her face.

For a moment he just stood there, looking at her.

Then he walked over and leaned his forehead against Guinevere's shoulder.

'Climb on, human girl!' he said, spreading his wings as he carried her out of the cave.

Guinevere felt how fast her heart was beating as he flew above the forest and the meadows with her. The good news had already spread. Dozens of fabulous beings were waiting outside the stable, but the mist-ravens made sure that none of them went into it.

Of course, the geese who were looking after the nest knew what had happened. They were cackling in such excitement when Ànemos and Guinevere entered the stable that they forgot to protest as usual when she put her hand under their feathers. She reached carefully for the first egg that her fingers found. Ouranos was a tangle of legs and wings.

'It's going to be all right!' whispered Guinevere, dropping a kiss on the egg where the foal was unhappily pressing his nose to the shell that was now too small for him. 'Everything will be all right. And soon I'll be riding you all, one after the other, and we'll fly races with your father!'

Ànemos came to stand beside her as she carefully tucked the egg under the goose feathers again. Guinevere hugged the geese, although they didn't think much of such human expressions of emotion, and she smiled at Ànemos.

'You see?' she said. 'My father is very good at keeping his promises.'

CHAPTER FORTY-EIGHT

A New Dragon in MÍMAMEIÐR

Is there not glory enough in living the days given to us?
You should know there is adventure in simply being among
those we love and the things we love, and beauty too.
Lloyd Alexander, *The Black Cauldron*

Anemos could already see Tattoo when Guinevere and Vita could make out only a dark spot in the pale blue sky. Gilbert Greytail had expected the feather to arrive in the afternoon, but Tattoo had made considerably better speed than that. The Pegasus flew to meet the dragon at once, along with the mist-ravens.

'That's not Firedrake, Mum!' said Guinevere when she saw Tattoo more clearly through the binoculars. 'It's another dragon!'

Raskervint didn't need binoculars to see Tattoo, but she looked as baffled as Guinevere. 'Do dragons come patterned these days?' she asked.

'Yes, that's new to me too,' replied Vita.

None of them would ever forget the sight they saw that morning: the Pegasus and the dragon side by side, and Ben, waving to them in excitement over the shoulder of another boy who had a small furry something in his arms. The fear that had been dammed up in Guinevere's heart over the last ten days turned to amazement and delight. Although her mother's grave face reminded her that that the hope of the griffin's feather saving the foals was still just that: a hope.

Most of the inhabitants of MÍMAMEIÐR had gathered around the Pegasus stable when Tattoo and Ànemos landed behind it.

'Guinevere!' called Ben from the strange dragon's back. 'Let me introduce you! This is Tattoo! He brought us here faster than the wind. And this,' he added, pointing to the other boy, 'is . . .'

'Winston Setiawan,' said Winston, introducing himself. He pointed to his small, furry companion. 'And this is Berulu.'

'A maki – he looks a bit like a brownie,' whispered Guinevere.

Berulu twittered something in Winston's ear.

'He's pointing out that he is *not* my pet. Okay, I'll tell them,' said Winston, climbing down from the dragon's back. 'Because brownie-makis don't like that kind of thing at all.'

'No wild animal does,' said Guinevere, smiling at Berulu. 'We know that here in MÍMAMEIÐR. Don't worry!'

She was taking great care not to stare at Tattoo. After all, she knew that no wild animal likes that either. But Tattoo himself was totally bewitched by all the fabulous creatures standing around him. He had never been so happy before. Or so proud, because he knew he had flown fast enough.

'What are you waiting for?' he asked Ben. 'Show it to them!'

Reaching into his backpack, Ben took out the bag containing

the feather that Barnabas had given him. When he took it out, it shone like a sunbeam in his hand. It was almost as long as his forearm, but the quill on which all their hopes were set was not much larger than a pencil, and Ànemos looked at it with an expression that was full of hope and doubt at the same time.

'Quick! Take the feather to Professor Spotiswode!' Vita told Ben. 'He'll dilute the marrow in the quill so that we can paint the eggs with it. And then . . .'

Vita didn't end the sentence.

Then they would see what happened.

CHAPTER FORTY-NINE

The Griffin's Feather

*Life is always a rich and steady time when you
are waiting for something to happen or to hatch.*
E.B. White, *Charlotte's Web*

The glaze that Professor Spotiswode was stirring, made from the marrow of the feather – with some egg white and a few drops of resin, as a recipe from ancient Persia specified – shone like gold, almost as brightly as the feather from which it had been taken.

Ben was just leaving the house with Twigleg to take it to the stable when Lola came running over the yard. She was coming from the direction of the runway that Hothbrodd and two other trolls had built in the meadow, in such a way that it disappeared again after take-off and landing.

'They're back!' called Lola in her shrill voice. 'The troll has just landed! By the heart of all tornadoes, he must have flown like the devil!'

'Or like Lola Greytail!' Twigleg whispered.

The news came as a great relief to Ben. It would be wonderful for them all to celebrate together if the feather worked. And if it didn't they would all need Barnabas's encouragement. He was the best of helpers in bad times as well as good.

Barnabas himself, of course, was very glad that Hothbrodd had brought them back on time, but he also had another reason to look cheerful when he and the troll came to the stable.

'Well, if it isn't Ben Greenbloom!' he said. 'I really wasn't expecting to see you here.'

And then he hugged Ben for a very long time.

Barnabas had shed a great many tears on the plane, but he and Hothbrodd kept that secret to themselves. And they didn't tell anyone that instead of coming back to MÍMAMEIÐR, Ben had almost stayed with Firedrake. Even Vita and Guinevere didn't hear about that until many years later.

Of course they all wanted to see whether the magic of the griffin's feather would really make the Pegasus eggs grow, but Hothbrodd stationed himself at the stable door, and let in only those who had been involved in either looking after the eggs, or searching for the feather. Hothbrodd himself stayed outside, officially to shoo away all the inquisitive impets and nisses who had gathered near the stable. But the troll wasn't nearly as thick-skinned as he made out, and the fear that the magic of the feather might not work after all was too much for his big troll heart. Tattoo also stayed outside with Winston and Berulu, because a dragon really did take up too much space. Raskervint didn't join the crowd for the same reason (and because she very much wanted to talk to Hothbrodd and Tattoo). Gilbert Greytail and his various informants were working on a map of Iceland, and several geese discovered that the idea of the eggs they had protected so carefully being painted with a magical substance made them too nervous to watch.

All the same, it was very crowded in the stable when everyone whom Hothbrodd had allowed in gathered around the nest.

Barnabas had given Guinevere and Ben the job of painting the eggs with the golden paste. Gilbert had let them have two of his best brushes, but it was not a good feeling to see the foals disappear more and more behind the golden glaze. Ànemos snorted so anxiously that Barnabas put an arm around his neck, and after the first few brush strokes Twigleg, finding the suspense too much for his stomach, stole out of the stable.

The others watched with bated breath as the three eggs slowly changed to gold. They really did look golden when Ben had painted the very last drops of the glaze on Synnefo's egg. They might have been made of that solid precious metal. Only the tapping of their hooves showed that the foals behind the shells were all right.

'Now they just need warmth!' said Vita. 'May I ask you, ladies . . .?'

The two geese who were down for the next shift were not enthusiastic about the sticky film that gilded their feathers, but finally, resigned to their fate, they settled on the nest.

'How quickly do you think it will work?' Ben whispered to Guinevere.

'Very quickly, I hope!' she whispered back. 'It's terrible not to be able to see the foals! They must be so frightened!'

In spite of all the spectators, it went very quiet in the stable. Terribly quiet.

Even Lola, who in the normal way was always fidgeting, stared at the nest as if she had been turned to stone.

And then . . . then one of the geese began cackling excitedly.

And the other goose joined in.

They beat their grey wings, got off the eggs and retreated from them.

The eggs were growing, as if the breath of the foals were stretching their shells.

Soon the stable was full of shouts, cackles, and whinnies of joy.

The three eggs finally left lying in the nest, which was now almost too small for them, were so large that they reminded Ben of the eggs of the legendary elephant bird, thought to have been extinct for over three hundred years.

'Good heavens!' Barnabas whispered to him. 'I think we'll have to get a few ostriches flown in to keep them warm!'

'I've already asked Inua to do that very thing,' said Vita. 'He's sending two ostrich hens who are delighted to help. They'll arrive this evening.'

The growing process had turned the eggs transparent again, and Ben and Barnabas couldn't take their eyes off the foals. After all, the sight was new to both of them. Ouranos, Chara and Synnefo moved their wings, stretched legs that were as thin as drinking straws, and seemed unable to believe just yet that they had enough space again all of a sudden.

'Suppose they go on growing?' asked Guinevere. 'We've used up half the contents of the quill!'

Twigleg, who had been brought back to the stable by the cries of joy, thought the foals were more than large enough already. In fact they were the right size for a homunculus – if he had ever ventured to ride a winged horse!

'One more treatment should be enough,' he told Guinevere, while Barnabas opened the stable door wide so that Hothbrodd and Tattoo could at least catch a glimpse of the Pegasus foals. 'It's said that Pegasus foals are not much larger than a chicken when they hatch!'

Guinevere thanked the homunculus with a smile of relief for his information. It would be wonderful to see three foals, not much larger than chickens, flying over the meadows around MÍMAMEIÐR.

'What beautiful children, my friend!' Barnabas said to Ànemos, as he wiped the condensation of deep emotion off his glasses.

Ben gently touched the egg in which Chara was pressing his nose against the shell.

'Yes,' he murmured. 'Really, really beautiful.'

He sent a silent message of thanks to Shrii and TerTaWa, to Patah and Kupo and the Whispering Tree. Even to Roargh, although he hadn't plucked out his feather entirely of his own free will. And he couldn't wait to send Firedrake and Sorrel a photo of the foals.

'What do you say?' Barnabas whispered to him, as they made way for Winston and Berulu to take their place beside the nest. 'Isn't ours the best work in the world? Even if it does land us locked up inside a cage from time to time?'

'The very best!' replied Ben. 'But now that this adventure is over,' he said, lifting Twigleg up to his shoulder, 'who are we going to rescue next?'

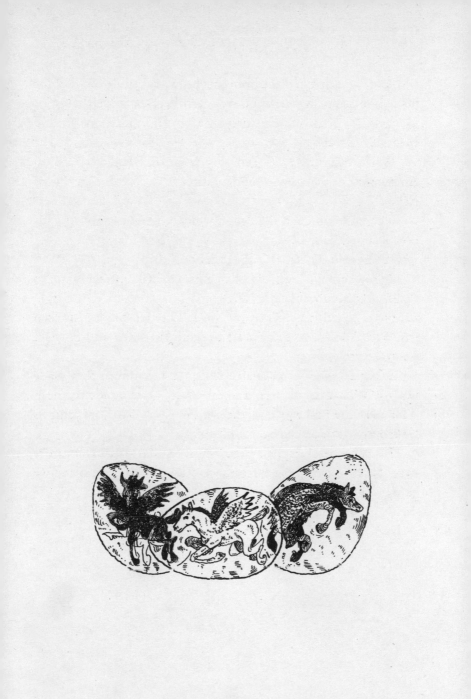

WHO'S WHO

Human Beings

David Atticsborough, FREEFAB specialist, and one of the most highly respected makers of wildlife films in the world.

Catcher, leader of the poachers looking for prey on the island of Pulau Bulu.

Inua Ellams, FREEFAB specialist in winged fabulous creatures.

Bağdagül Ender, childhood friend of Barnabas who has devoted her life to the conservation of endangered creatures in Turkey.

Barnabas Greenbloom, Ben's adopted father and co-founder of FREEFAB, an organisation for the conservation of endangered fabulous creatures.

Ben Greenbloom, aged 14, lives with his adopted family, the Greenblooms, at MÍMAMEIÐR in Norway, and helps to study and conserve the fabulous beings of this world. Ben has a very special friend, Firedrake the silver dragon, whose dragon rider he became two years ago.

Guinevere Greenbloom, Ben's adopted sister. She is mainly concerned with the water creatures of MÍMAMEIÐR. Until she meets the last Pegasus . . .

Vita Greenbloom, wife of Barnabas, mother of Guinevere and adopted mother of Ben. Co-founder of FREEFAB and expert on winged fabulous creatures.

Jane Gridall, FREEFAB expert and inventor of a sign language which has made it possible to communicate with almost every species on the planet.

Dr Phoebe Humboldt, teaches Ben and Guinevere the study of fabulous beings.

Kamaharan, a poacher, one of Catcher's team.

Jacques Maupassant, FREEFAB specialist in fantastic water creatures.

Maisie Richardson, FREEFAB expert on grass fairies and fern fairies.

Winston Setiawan, a boy who is an animal-lover, from an island near Pulau Bulu.

Professor James Spotiswode, teaches Ben and Guinevere all branches of the natural sciences, also a specialist in telepathy and robotics.

November Tan, FREEFAB expert, researching the dietary habits of fabulous beings.

Holly Undset, a talented veterinary surgeon who sometimes also has to treat nixies, impets and a Pegasus.

Non-human Beings

Ànemos, a Pegasus stallion. Even in MÍMAMEIÐR these winged horses of Greek mythology were thought to be extinct, until the Greenblooms discovered Ànemos and his companion in Greece.

Awan Petir, a black macaque who supervises the poachers and makes sure that they pay up.

Berulu, a brownie-maki and companion of Winston. Brownie-makis, also known as tarsiers, are small, nocturnal, tree-dwelling animals, with strikingly large eyes, a very mobile neck, and the long hind legs that enable them to jump long distances.

Dr Eel, a famous marine biologist and spokeswoman for all water creatures (being one of them herself).

Eight, a Great Kraken in the ocean off the Indonesian coast, and Eugene's friend. Eight is looking for another Great Kraken.

E-Mas, the Golden Gibbon. Gibbons are primates that have no tails. A striking feature is that their forelegs are considerably longer than their hind legs, so that they can move by swinging from hand to hand through the branches of trees, a form of movement unique to them in the animal kingdom.

Eugene, a four-eyed crab met by Firedrake and Tattoo on the island of Pulau Bulu. Loves shiny things and picks them up.

Gilbert Greytail, a white ship's rat from Hamburg and a brilliant cartographer. He now lives with the Greenblooms at MÍMAMEIÐR, and teaches Ben and Guinevere geography.

Hafgufa, a Great Kraken living off the Norwegian coast.

Hothbrodd, a rather grumpy but good-hearted diurnal troll (he is awake in the daytime), who carves wonderful things with his knife. Hothbrodd can talk to trees, and is an indispensable member of FREEFAB. He lives at MÍMAMEIÐR.

Kachang, one of Kraa's macaques.

Kupo, a slow loris and very talented carver. She has suffered under Kraa's rule for a long time. Lorises are a family of primates from the lemur group. They are relatively small nocturnal, tree-dwelling animals, found in Africa and Asia. The slow loris has developed a slow form of movement that is unique among primates.

Lola Greytail, a daredevil rat, Gilbert's cousin. An aviator who performs aerobatic stunts and is the best scout anyone could wish for.

Lyo-Lyok, a grey goose.

Manis, a slow loris and a carver who was killed by Kraa.

Me-Rah, a nervous chattering lory who guides Ben and Barnabas to Pulau Bulu.

Nakal, a proboscis monkey and Kraa's master of ceremonies. The most striking feature of proboscis monkeys is their large, pear-shaped noses.

Patah, macaque from Shrii's retinue.

Sorrel, a Scottish brownie and Firedrake's companion. Every dragon needs a brownie, even if the brownies can be bad-tempered at times.

Professor Sutan Buceros, a rhinoceros bird of considerable size and legendary age, who has often helped the Greenblooms in the conservation of South-East Asian fabulous creatures.

Synnefo, a Pegasus mare, companion of Ànemos.

Synnefo, Chara, Ouranos, Pegasus foals, the endangered children of Ànemos and Synnefo.

Tabuhan, macaque from Shrii's retinue.

Tallemaja, the cook at MÍMAMEIÐR, who is also a huldra.

TerTaWa, a gibbon, faithful companion of Shrii.

Twigleg, a homunculus: as described in the late Middle Ages, a homunculus is a human being artificially made by an alchemist. Twigleg and his eleven brothers were bred in a glass flask. Twigleg served Nettlebrand the Golden as his armour cleaner until he helped Firedrake and Ben to defeat him. Since then he has been Ben's devoted, if not very brave, companion. He also teaches Ben and Guinevere history and languages.

Tyra Raskervint, a female centaur, a hybrid between human and horse, as described in Greek mythology. An old friend of Vita Greenbloom.

Fabulous Beings

Dragons

Bruk, Rgyak, two young dragons who followed Firedrake from Scotland to the Rim of Heaven.

Firedrake, a silver dragon from the Scottish highlands. In the previous story, *Dragon Rider,* he and Ben defeated Nettlebrand, the dragons' worst enemy, and found a refuge in the valley of the Rim of Heaven for the last dragons in the world.

Maia, a silver she-dragon, Firedrake's companion.

Slatebeard, the oldest living dragon. Was unable to make the long journey to the Rim of Heaven, and now lives under the protection of MÍMAMEIÐR in Norway.

Shimmertail, Maia's cousin.

Tattoo, a young dragon with patterned scales who accompanies Firedrake on a long flight.

Griffins on Pulau Bulu

Chahska, one of Kraa's retinue.

Fierra, one of Kraa's retinue.

Greiir, one of Kraa's retinue.

Hiera, a she-griffin, one of Kraa's retinue.

Kraa, the cruel leader of the griffins on the island.

Reee, a she-griffin, Kraa's sister and Shrii's mother. Sad to say, she is dead when the story begins.

Roargh, one of Kraa's retinue.

Shrii, a griffin with colourful plumage who rebels against Kraa's rule.

Tchraee, Kraa's adjutant.

Fabulous Beings Related to Horses

elfin horses, tiny horses bred by grass elves.

kelpie, a supernatural water spirit in the shape of a large horse, sometimes with a fish's tail.

seaspray horses, form from the foam of the sea, and dissolve with it, only to be reborn with the next breaking wave.

water horses, a general term for many fabulous relations of horses living in lakes, rivers and seas.

wind mares, like to mate with the *cloud stallions* who live in dense clouds and seldom show themselves. They resemble veils of mist in horse form. The mating is so fast that it is usually invisible to the human eye.

Fabulous Beings Related to Birds

Arctic chattergoose, very talkative northern member of the grey goose family.

crow men, resemble crows at first sight, but they have arms as well as wings and they like to pick at human eyes.

elephant bird, extinct member of the flightless bird family.

Healing Bird of Heaven, pale blue bird resembling an albatross. It sleeps in flight, and cures many diseases if you touch its feathers.

mist-raven, a raven with grey plumage that can make itself invisible. Mist-ravens act as scouts and deliver messages in MÍMAMEIÐR.

nightingale-geese, blue-feathered geese with golden beaks. They owe their name to their wonderful song. They keep the orphaned Pegasus eggs warm in the nest.

Pelangi bird, appears only when there is a rainbow in the sky. Its feathers also shimmer in rainbow colours.

Phoenix, mythical bird that bursts into flame at the end of its life cycle and is reborn from its own ashes.

ratbird, an ancestor of Lola Greytail.

Water Creatures

fossegrim, a spirit that lives in the waterfalls of Norway and is a virtuoso performer on the fiddle. Several human violinists are said to owe their masterly playing to the teaching of a fossegrim.

Nyai Loro Kidul, Indonesian queen of the sea. Sometimes depicted as a fish, sometimes as a snake.

nymph, female water spirit with a love of dancing and music.

sea serpent, general term for many snake-like sea monsters.

Sjöra, golden-scaled water nymph only found in Swedish lakes.

water-sprite, general term for fabulous beings in human form that live under water.

Other Fabulous Beings and Mythological Creatures

climbing coyotes, a species of coyote found in the crowns of the redwood trees of north California.

cloud-hound, dog-like fabulous being with a cloud pattern on its short-haired coat that makes it invisible and able to fly. Found chiefly in Turkey and Arabia.

compass ship's rat, see *singing rat*.

coral nixies, female water spirits who live in the coral reefs off the Indonesian coast.

crystal snails, snails with bodies and shells as transparent as glass, but luckily not so breakable. They are excellent window cleaners, because they like to lick dew and rain off glass and ice. They love the damp climate of Norway.

Cyclops, one-eyed giant mentioned in Greek mythology.

Draugen, undead men from Norse mythology.

duende, Spanish imp or hob.

feathered frogs, exactly what they sound like: frogs with feathers.

fern fairies, tiny fairies that, as their name suggests, are found only under fern fronds.

figlings, fabulous creatures shaped like fresh figs, mainly found in fig trees.

firemander, a species of salamander whose bodies can be as hot as liquid wax.

fungus-folk, fabulous little creatures who, as Sorrel discovers, look like walking mushrooms of various species.

giant salamander, a salamander the size of a cow.

grass fairies, bumblebee-sized fairies that are most commonly found on meadows.

griffin, a mythical hybrid creature. It is usually shown with the body of a lion and the head of a bird of prey, with a powerful beak, pointed ears and wings.

hedgehog-men, hedgehogs that walk upright, are very cunning, wear clothes and shoes, and furnish their burrows in a very human way.

hobs, short for hobgoblins.

hobgoblins, British impets.

huldra, Scandinavian forest spirit.

impet-eater, a badger-like creature that walks on two legs and, as the name suggests, likes to eat imps.

jackal scorpions, Kraa's cruel guards, with the body of a scorpion and the head of a jackal.

jenglots, dwarfish zombies who drink blood. Found mainly in Indonesia.

leprechaun, Irish impet. Leprechauns like gold and making shoes.

Medusa, the snake-haired mother of all the Pegasi. Nothing like as terrible as she is made out to be in Greek mythology.

mustard impets, Welsh impets whose hair is the colour of mustard, and allegedly tastes like it too.

nisse, Scandinavian impet.

photomeleon, when in danger takes a photograph of its surroundings which develops and is recorded on its skin.

prickly mud-eater, fabulous creature rather like an anteater. Lives mainly in the mud on the banks of rivers and lakes.

Scylla, huge sea monster mentioned in Greek mythology.

singing rat, fabulous relation of Gilbert and Lola Greytail.

sphinx, winged hybrid between a lion and a woman. A guard and prophetess.

stone-dwarves, Scottish dwarves who played a large part in the liberation of the dragons and now live in the valley of the Rim of Heaven.

tent-lice, lice-like creatures that can unfold their seemingly tiny bodies to form big screens, or even tents, under which one can get a comfortable night's sleep.

tomte, Swedish impets who often step in to help when they are needed.

treasure-hunting snakes, build their nests from coins and jewellery. Often found in old tombs.

watobi-pigs, flying dwarf pigs found chiefly in the Congo.

wood-gnomes, humanoid fabulous beings, often with spindly arms and legs. Can be well- or ill-disposed, depending on how people behave in the forests where they live.

wool-spinner oaklings, round-bellied spiders with human heads who spin warm woollen padding for their nests, and with a little persuasion will spin for humans too.

Ordinary Animals

(who, of course, are extraordinary all the same – and probably have fabulous beings in their ancestry!)

bee-eater, a bird in the temple of Garuda.

binturong, also known as the bearcat, a beast of prey of the *Viverridae* (weasel) family.

hoopoe, a bird in the temple of Garuda.

Indian roller, a bird in the temple of Garuda.

peacock, bird with a loud screech, one of whom Ben and Barnabas meet in the temple of Garuda in India.

Places

India, the second stopover for Barnabas, Hothbrodd and Lola, and the place where they meet Firedrake and Ben. Luckily they also meet Me-Rah, the chattering lory, who turns out to be a very useful member of the team.

MÍMAMEIÐR, secret conservation station for fabulous creatures in Norway. The home of Barnabas, Vita, Ben and Guinevere Greenbloom.

Pulau Bulu, the Indonesian island where Barnabas and Ben think they may find griffins.

The Rim of Heaven, the remote Himalayan valley that is the new home of the dragons.

Turkey, where Barnabas stops off during his search for griffins to pick up something very valuable.

ACKNOWLEDGEMENTS

Richard Adams, English writer (1920-2016): from *Watership Down* (Penguin, 1974), copyright © Richard Adams 1972, reprinted by permission of David Higham Associates.

Anna Akhmatova, Russian poet (1889-1966): lines from 'The Sentence', from *The Complete Poems of Anna Akhmatova* translated by Judith Hemschemeyer and edited by Roberta Reeder (Canongate, 1998), translation copyright © 1989, 1992, 1997 by Judith Hemschemeyer, reprinted by permission of Canongate Books Ltd.

Lloyd Alexander, American writer (1924-2007): from *The Black Cauldron*, Vol 2, *The Chronicles of Prydain* (Mammoth, 1995), copyright © Lloyd Alexander 1965, reprinted by permission of The Random House Group Ltd.

Maya Angelou, American writer and civil rights activist (1928-2014): from *I Know Why the Caged Bird Sings* (Virago, 2007), copyright © Maya Angelou 1969, reprinted by permission of Little, Brown Book Group Ltd, Hachette UK.

Sir David Attenborough, English naturalist and broadcaster, reprinted by permission of David Attenborough.

J.M. Barrie, Scottish novelist and playwright (1860-1937): from *Peter and Wendy* (Hodder & Stoughton, 1911), perpetual © royalty rights Great Ormond Street Hospital for Children, reprinted by permission of Great Ormond Street Hospital Children's Charity.

L. Frank Baum, American writer (1856-1919): from *The Marvellous Land of Oz* (1904).

Savinien de Cyrano de Bergerac, French novelist and playwright (1619-1655): from *The Comical History of the States and Empires of the Worlds of the Moon and Sun*, first published in English in 1687.

Leonard Bernstein, American composer, conductor, pianist and songwriter (1918-1990): attributed quote reprinted by permission of The Leonard Bernstein Office, Inc.

Albert Camus, French philosopher and writer (1913-1960).

Christopher Columbus, Italian navigator and explorer (c1451-1506).

Confucius, Chinese philosopher (551-479 BC).

Kate DiCamillo, American writer: from *Because of Winn-Dixie* (Walker, 2014), copyright © Kate DiCamillo 2000, published by Candlewick Press, reproduced by permission of Walker Books Ltd, London SE11 5HJ.

John D. Dingell, American politician: from 'The Endangered Species Act: Legislative Perspectives on a Living Law' in *Endangered Species Update*.

Amelia Earhart, American aviator (1897-disappeared 1937).

Sylvia Earle, American marine biologist, explorer and writer:

from 'My Wish: Protect our oceans' TED Conference talk, February 2009.

Albert Einstein, German physicist (1879-1955).

Havelock Ellis, English physician and writer (1859-1939): from *The Dance of Life* (1923).

Cornelia Funke, German writer: from *Inkheart* (Chicken House, 2003), original text copyright © Dressler Verlag 2003, English translation copyright © Chicken House 2003.

Johann Wolfgang von Goethe, German writer and statesman (1749-1832): from *Wilhelm Meister's Apprenticeship and Travels*, first published in English in 1824.

Hermann Hesse, Swiss poet, novelist, and painter (1877-1962): from *Bäume: Betrachtungen und Gedichte* (Insel Verlag, 1984), copyright © Insel Verlag, Frankfurt am Main 1984, reprinted by permission of the publishers. All rights reserved by and controlled through Insel Verlag, Berlin.

Ted Hughes, English poet and writer (1930-1998): from *The Iron Man: a Children's Story in Five Nights* (Faber, 1968), copyright © The Estate of Ted Hughes 1968; lines from 'Hawk Roosting' from *Lupercal* (Faber, 1970), copyright © The Estate of Ted Hughes 1960, reprinted by permission of Faber & Faber Ltd.

Helen Keller, American writer and political activist (1880-1968).

Rudyard Kipling, English writer and poet (1865-1936): from *The Jungle Book* (Macmillan, 1894); and from 'How the Leopard Got His Spots', *Just So Stories for Little Children* (Macmillan, 1902).

John Lennon, English singer and songwriter (1940-1980) quoted in Geoffrey Giuliano: *Lennon in America 1971-1980: Based in Part on the Lost Lennon Diaries* (Robson, 2000), reprinted by permission of Robson, part of the Pavilion Books Company Ltd.

Primo Levi, Italian chemist and writer (1919-1987): from *The Periodic Table* translated by Raymond Rosenthal (Penguin Classics, 2000), copyright © Giulio Einaudi Editore s.p.a. 1975, translation copyright © Schocken Books Inc 1984, reprinted by permission of Penguin Books Ltd.

Astrid Lindgren, Swedish writer (1907-2002): from *The Brothers Lionheart* translated by Joan Tate (OUP, 2009), text copyright © Saltkråkan AB/Astrid Lindgren 1973, English translation copyright © Hachette 1975, reprinted by permission of Oxford University Press.

Robert Lynd, Irish writer (1879-1949): from *The Blue Lion and Other Essays* (Methuen & Co, 1923), reprinted by permission of Tim Wheeler for the Estate of Robert Lynd.

Michel de Montaigne, French Philosopher (1533-1592): from *Essays* (1580).

Audrey Niffenegger, American writer: from *The Time Traveler's*

Wife (Cape, 2004), copyright © Audrey Niffenegger 2004, reprinted by permission of The Random House Group Ltd.

Eugene O'Neill, American playwright (1888-1953): from *Long Day's Journey Into Night*, copyright © Eugene Gladstone O'Neill 1956, reprinted by permission of Eugene O'Neill Permissions.

Pablo Picasso, Spanish artist, poet and playwright (1881-1973).

Terry Pratchett, English writer (1948-2015): from *The Light Fantastic* (Corgi, 2012), Discworld® novel 2, copyright © Terry Pratchett 1986, reprinted by permission of The Random House Group Ltd.

Abbé Prévost (Antoine François Prévost), French writer (1697-1763): from *Manon Lescaut* (1731).

William Shakespeare, English poet and playwright (1564-1616): from *Cymbeline*, Act 3, Scene 2.

Percy Bysshe Shelley, English poet (1792-1822): lines from 'Ode to the West Wind' (1820).

Alfred, Lord Tennyson, English poet (1809-1892): lines from 'Gone', song 3 of 'The Window, or the Song of the Wrens' (1870).

Vyasa: from the Sanskrit epic poem, The Mahabharata First Book: 'Adi Parva', *The Book of Beginnings*.

E.B. White, American writer (1899-1985): from *Charlotte's*

Web (Puffin, 2012), copyright © E.B. White 1952, copyright renewed 1980 by E.B. White, reprinted by permission of Penguin Books Ltd.

T.H. White, English writer (1906-1964): from 'The Queen of Air and Darkness', part 2 of *The Once and Future King* (Harper Voyager, 2015), copyright © T.H. White 1958, reprinted by permission of David Higham Associates.

Oscar Wilde, Irish playwright and poet (1854-1900): from *An Ideal Husband* (1895).

W.B. Yeats, Irish poet (1865-1939): lines from 'The Hawk'.

We have tried to trace and contact the copyright holders of material that is still in copyright before publication, and if notified we will be pleased to correct any inadvertent errors or omissions.

THIEF LORD by CORNELIA FUNKE

Two orphaned children are on the run in Venice, hiding among the crumbling canals and misty alleyways. Befriended by a gang of street children and their mysterious leader, the Thief Lord, they shelter in a disused cinema.

On their trail are a bungling detective and a cruel aunt. But a greater threat to the boys' new-found freedom is something from a forgotten past: a beautiful magical treasure with the power to spin time itself.

'. . . a story that children will relish . . .'
THE SUNDAY TIMES

'A completely delicious read . . .'
THE OBSERVER

Paperback, ISBN 978-1-905294-21-3, £6.99 • ebook, ISBN 978-1-909489-15-8, £6.99

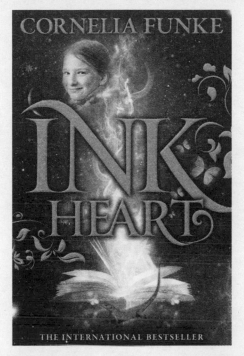

INKHEART by CORNELIA FUNKE

Meggie loves stories, but her father, Mo, hasn't read aloud to her since her mother disappeared.

When a stranger knocks at their door, Mo is forced to reveal an extraordinary secret – as he reads aloud, words come alive, and dangerous characters step out of the pages.

Suddenly, Meggie is living the kind of adventure she has only read about in books, but this one will change her life for ever.

'. . . a breathtakingly fast-moving tale.'
THE INDEPENDENT

'. . . one of the outstanding children's
novels of the year.'
THE TIMES

Paperback, ISBN 978-1-908435-11-8, £6.99 • ebook, ISBN 978-1-906427-97-9, £6.99

BEETLE BOY by M. G. LEONARD

Darkus can't believe his eyes when a huge insect drops out of the trouser leg of his horrible new neighbour. It's a giant beetle – and it seems to want to communicate.

But how can a boy be friends with a beetle? And what does a beetle have to do with the disappearance of his dad and the arrival of Lucretia Cutter, with her taste for creepy jewellery?

'A darkly funny Dahl-esque adventure.'
KATHERINE WOODFINE, AUTHOR

'A wonderful book, full to the brim
with very cool beetles!'
THE GUARDIAN

Paperback, ISBN 978-1-910002-70-4, £6.99 • ebook, ISBN 978-1-910002-98-8, £6.99

THE APPRENTICE WITCH by JAMES NICOL

Arianwyn fails her witch's assessment – instead of qualifying, she's declared an apprentice and sent to remote Lull in disgrace. Then her arch-enemy, mean girl Gimma, arrives on holiday determined to make her life a misery. But as a mysterious darkness begins to haunt her spells, Arianwyn realizes there's much more than her pride at stake . . .

'A charming tale of magic, bravery and friendship, reminiscent of Diana Wynne Jones.'
THE GUARDIAN

'The Apprentice Witch is entirely more charming, adventurous, and full of heart than a book has any right to be. Make no mistake: there's magic afoot.'
TRENTON LEE STEWART, AUTHOR

Paperback, ISBN 978-1-910655-15-3, £6.99 • ebook, ISBN 978-1-910655-62-7, £6.99